LUNAR BOUND

(SKY BROOKS WORLD: ETHAN BOOK 4)

MCKENZIE HUNTER
EMERSON KNIGHT

McKenzie Hunter

Lunar Bound

McKenzieHunter@McKenzieHunter.com

ISBN: 978-1-946457-09-7

ACKNOWLEDGMENTS

As always, I'd first like to thank McKenzie Hunter for allowing me to play in her world. She took a big chance on an unknown writer, and I am forever grateful. I would have never been able to finish Lunar Bound without the patience and honest feedback from my beta readers, Elizabeth Bracker, Stacey Mann, Sherrie Clark, Robyn Mather, Halimo Farah, and Priscilla Moxey.

Lastly, but most important, my thanks to you, the reader. Fans of McKenzie Hunter and the Sky Brooks series have been very supportive of Ethan's POV, and I couldn't feel more fortunate. Without all of you, I wouldn't be able to do what I most love to do, write. You're the best!

CHAPTER 1

I brushed a fern from my path, glancing at the forest floor for signs of the creature's passing. Steven did the same, some dozen feet to my left. Josh followed behind me, making a bored attempt at wariness. He drew the boxlike metal carrier across his body, took the handle with his other hand. Custom made and reinforced with steel bands, the carrier was designed to house a creature the size of a small dog, only much stronger.

Josh eyed the carrier with suspicion. He felt his magic would be enough to contain the creature. When it came to magic, my brother tended toward overconfidence, more so since he'd been taken and held by the witch Samuel. That was the first time in Josh's life that he'd felt truly helpless. Since then, he'd become even more obsessed with increasing his magical prowess.

"You really think the *belocka* is here?" he asked, doubtful.

"Quiet," I hissed, glaring.

He took a long stride to crunch a pinecone beneath his boot.

Steven glanced between my brother and me, but said nothing.

The creature was an elven creation, a dark, stealthy thing designed long ago to hunt and kill their enemies. The elves once prided themselves on the monsters they created. Eventually, pride turned to embarrassment. In a bid to erase their sinister history of experimentation, the Makellos, the so-called elven elite, banished their creations to the dark forest in Elysian.

A powerful curse turned the forest into a prison.

A few weeks ago, that impregnable curse had been broken. Evil, vile, dangerous creatures spilled out into the world. In their hubris, the Makellos had never planned to deal with a mass escape. Scrambling, Liam had no choice but to turn to the pack for help.

He had no idea it was the pack that had broken the curse. To say it was unintentional wasn't entirely accurate. We'd used the Clostra, one of the powerful, protected magical objects, to break a witch's curse on Sky. We'd no idea what the ramifications would be, but our need was great. As it turned out, the spell didn't remove one curse, it removed them all, everywhere.

For that, there were consequences still unfolding.

There was also opportunity.

The pack owed a debt to Liam. Weeks ago, one of his creatures had been smuggled out of Elysian and infected Kelly, the pack's nurse. She'd been an unintended victim. In our quest to save her, Liam had given us access to the dark forest, a rare courtesy. In exchange for our help now, that debt would be forgiven. More importantly, Liam had information that I needed, information that could help protect Sky.

My arm brushed against the tranquilizer pistol holstered at my hip, a custom design with a three dart clip—an expensive piece of equipment for special circumstances.

"In the last week," I whispered, "two hikers have disappeared on this trail."

The police hadn't reached the same conclusion. So far, they considered the two disappearances unrelated. The first, a college student about Steven's age, had left his car parked in a lot on the other side of the park. Thanks to Stacy, my legal assistant and expert hacker, I knew the student had texted his roommate that he'd failed his exams and was afraid to tell his parents. To get his thoughts together, he was going on a *walkabout* in the park. He'd looked up the park trails, specifically the less-traveled Northern Loop. My guess, he intended to circumnavigate the entire forest. According to my sources inside the police department, I knew the police considered the student a runaway. They were dragging their feet, expecting him to return at any moment.

The other hiker was a young mother that lived in a nearby community. According to her husband, she'd gone out on her usual morning jog, zigzagging around their neighborhood, but never returned. After the police discovered the wife had recently confronted her husband over an affair, he'd become their prime suspect in a murder investigation. They were currently looking for her body beneath the foundation of a house his company had just built on the south side of Chicago. After cracking her cloud-based browser history, Stacy found the wife had recently researched the Northern Loop of the park. She'd probably gotten bored with her usual route and wanted more time away from her husband.

Both had come to the park, took the very trail we paralleled looking for signs of their passing, or demise. So far, nothing. Josh didn't share my confidence, but it was the best lead we had.

"If the belocka was here," Josh stressed, "I doubt it stuck around. Striking here a third time would be foolish."

The secluded trail wasn't popular, but the trickle of foot traffic was regular. People often came here to be alone. It was fertile hunting ground. If the belocka was careful with its kills, it could hunt in these woods for some time before it drew too much attention.

My brother's doubts were understandable. He didn't think like a predator.

A pall settled over him, weighing on the silence between us. He'd been gloomy lately, irritable and short tempered. Cognizant of my occasionally overbearing concern, I'd not asked the obvious question: *What the hell is wrong with you?* I had some idea, but this wasn't the time for a brotherly chat. I hoped Josh shared my sensibility.

"How long have you known?" he muttered, emphasizing his disappointment with an accusatory look, like I'd just cut him to the quick. I knew I'd hurt his feelings. The Ducati Monster 1200S I'd bought him was meant to soothe his anger. What the hell says sorry more than an eighteen-thousand-dollar motorcycle? The gift had done its job, for just over a week.

I sighed, debated whether to answer.

Steven had drifted farther away, his attention fixed on a game trail.

"Claudia informed me after my grandmother's death," I admitted.

She'd handed me a death sentence.

Unanimous agreements among the supernatural factions were extremely rare. Only a true threat to us all could bring the factions together. The powerful magic of the dark elves—delivering death with a touch—had posed such a threat. The factions, the pack included, had responded with genocide—survival instinct at its cruelest.

The dark elves were supposed to be extinct. They weren't.

Unbeknownst to me, dark elf blood ran through my veins, passed down from my father's maternal lineage. He'd died when I was young, and my grandmother, the last surviving member of his family, had carried the secret to her grave. I couldn't blame her. Had her identity been discovered, all of the factions would have joined once again to kill her, to kill me.

As a child, I'd known my grandmother to be distant, cold, unaffectionate. I knew now that she lived in fear of her magic. I knew that horror firsthand. At her death, I'd inherited the dark elf magic in a fiery rush. Before I could gain a modicum of control, I'd nearly killed Sky with it.

I looked to Josh, grateful for once that we were only half brothers. We shared the same mother, but had different fathers. He'd been spared my curse.

"Claudia knew as well," he confirmed, throwing glances around the forest to hide the hurt. "Of course she did. That's quite a secret to keep. Do you blame her?"

There were layers to that question. "It wasn't her secret to tell. My grandmother tried to tell me at the end, but she'd waited too long. She'd lost too much of her mind. Once she'd died, the secret became Claudia's."

"I could've helped you deal with the magic."

"There was nothing you—"

"Don't." He glared at me, a hot warning.

He was right. When it came to magical abilities, my brother was second to none, but there were other considerations.

"You know why I didn't tell you," I growled.

"To protect me?" He rolled his eyes. "You need a new song, Ethan. That Sesame Street record is worn out."

He knew damn well that anyone harboring a dark elf would be punished, probably killed. The moment I'd told him my secret, he would've been bound to reveal me. He was bound now, but without the magic to give me away, the risk of discovery was negligible.

Ridding myself of the magic had been key.

"So you turned to Sky instead," he continued. "You put her life at risk. You're a hypocrite, Ethan."

My lips stretched into a grim line. "The Aufero was the logical choice."

The magical orb was one of several objects of power. Their origin was a mystery. Even the Mouras Encantadas that protected them—handing down the responsibility from generation to generation—had no memory of how they had come to their duty. We'd recently learned that Sky was a Moura. Her birth mother had carried the Aufero into hiding. After her murder, the object had gone missing. Somehow, it had ended up in the hands of a witch.

The orb absorbed magic.

Marcia, the leader of the regional coven, had gotten her hands on the orb, used it to punish any witch that she felt was a threat to her. She hadn't willingly parted with it.

"The orb's magic was available to Sky. I didn't have time for you to figure out how to use it."

I knew firsthand that the orb was capable of defending itself. Josh might well have injured or killed himself in the process. Now that it had absorbed my dark elf magic, the orb was more dangerous than ever. Whenever Sky tried to use the Aufero's magic, it came close to killing her.

Another problem to solve.

"Ethan—"

Josh paused. His nose wrinkled at the noxious smell delivered by the shifting breeze. I'd already caught the scent, dismissed it as a nuisance until he said, "I didn't think there were skunks out here."

There weren't.

I stopped in stride, sniffed. There was something else layered in the scent. Not a skunk at all. Steven had already noticed. I gestured to the east, signaled for silence. Josh abandoned his earlier petulance. Magic flickered around the fingers of his free hand, ready at a moment's notice. He was all business now, crouching slightly in anticipation of an attack that could come from any direction.

Steven, already ahead, continued warily. Josh fell in behind me as we tracked the scent away from the trail.

As we moved through dense brush, where anything could hide, I was reminded how little information Liam had shared about the belocka, even less than he'd shared about the other creatures we'd retrieved for him. In their rush to erase history, the elves kept no record of their former creations. All he could tell us was that the belocka was a top-tier predator. Liam had demonstrated its modest size with his hands.

"So a toy poodle," I'd commented.

He hadn't appreciated the comparison.

We knew nothing about the creature's hunting habits, how it might defend itself.

Over the next half hour, we moved slowly. Each time the scent receded, we backtracked, started over. We were getting close when Steven emerged from a copse of trees ahead, signaled for me to stop. Josh and I knelt, wary as Steven hurried toward us at a crouch. He knelt next to me, gestured to the copse.

"There's a woman on the other side, following the same trail," he whispered. "She's armed. Shotgun over shoulder, pistol on her right hip."

"Hunter?" Josh asked.

Steven nodded. It seemed Liam was hedging his bets.

Anticipating my next question, Steven added, "It's not Ann. I've never seen this one around."

Sean and Ann were the only hunters based in the area. Neither was competent. Somehow Sean had built the better reputation, though I found him slovenly, not to mention arrogant. He was also an idiot. It seemed Liam had made the same assessment, brought in someone from outside Chicago.

Steven continued. "About sixty yards on the other side of that copse is a meadow. She's tracking there. Green camo works in the trees but stands out in the tall grass."

"Wait here," I whispered. Josh grunted, but I didn't wait

around for the rest of his complaint. Crouched, I hurried to the copse, followed Steven's tracks to the other side. Peering through the trees, I saw her in the center of the meadow, staring down at the ground. Her back was to me. She wore green camouflage pants and a shirt. A black ponytail hung from the back of a matching baseball-style cap. The shotgun slung across her back looked military. The pistol at her hip was in an open holster, allowing for a quick draw.

I knew by the scent in the breeze that she was walking in the wrong direction. All I had to do was let her wander off, then muddle the tracks in the meadow, but she realized her mistake. I remained perfectly still as she turned, scanning the ground as she started back toward me. The bill of her cap hid her expression, but it was clear she had lost her trail, was backtracking to pick it back up.

I needed to talk her out of her hunt. The threat of violence might work, but I didn't want to have to look over my shoulder for the rest of the day. Money could grease that wheel. I always found cash made the threat go down easier. Sky wouldn't approve. I could see her frowning in my mind's eye. *Be nice.* I scowled.

"Don't be alarmed," I said aloud, moderating my tone to sound as unthreatening as possible.

The motion of her draw was smooth, fast. The pistol was in her hand in less than a second, pointing in my direction before I'd even revealed myself. She was good. She was also alone, or she'd have signaled her partners.

"Easy," I said. "I'm going to stand up."

She glanced to either side, then gestured with the pistol barrel for me to rise.

I did, slowly, keeping my hands up near my shoulders.

"We're here for the same reason," I declared. "I just want to talk to you, see if we can come to some sort of arrangement. I'm going to walk toward you, just far enough that we can talk face to face. There's no need for this to get complicated." I sucked in a breath and started forward.

Her shoulders tensed. I could feel her glare on me.

"You're Ethan Charleston, Beta of the Midwest Pack," she said, disappointed. She raised her pistol, aimed at my head.

I felt the surge of Josh's magic to my left, like an angry shout into the void.

"No," I shouted for his benefit, but too late. A force of magic ripped the pistol from her grip, threw it a dozen yards away. The hunter reached for her shotgun. A band of silver magic clamped around her shoulders, pushed down, pinning her arms to her sides. Another band appeared lower, binding her wrists to her hips. Her nostrils flared. She glared at me with narrowed chocolate eyes.

I recognized her then. The last time I'd seen her, those eyes had been staring over the barrel of a shotgun, not a pistol.

Shit. The situation just got complicated.

"Josh!" I growled.

He walked out of the copse of trees, triumphant. Beside him, Steven gave me a frustrated look. His fingers tapped and turned at his side, signaling, *Unexpected.* I brushed my anger aside with a sigh and turned to meet the hunter's glare.

"Tonya," I said. "Still working with McClintock?"

Her lips tightened into a thin line.

I gestured for Steven to take her shotgun. As he walked around her, she gathered herself as if to fight. All she had to work with was her hard head and her steel-tipped combat boots.

Josh warned her, "I could bind your legs and immobilize you completely."

She growled, gave each of us a look meant to kill, but relented as Steven drew the shotgun from its sheath. At my direction, he tossed the weapon into the grass several feet away.

I cautioned her, "Don't make this harder than it has to be. You're hunting the belocka."

"I have as much right to carry out my contract as you do," she snapped. "You've no right to interfere with me."

That was rich, coming from one of McClintock's followers. He'd always prided himself on what he called the hunter's code, but that was just bullshit. The old man played hard, and he played to win. Getting between him and a bounty was going to have repercussions.

"I'll give you one chance to walk away," she declared, trapped within Josh's binding spell.

He laughed at her audacity.

"Not this time." There was too much at stake. "Josh, take her somewhere she can't cause any trouble."

Tonya's gaze flicked to her guns in the grass.

"They'll be there when you find your way back here," I promised, then turned to Josh. "We need a couple hours."

He put a hand on the top of her cap and then they were gone.

"McClintock?" Steven asked.

"An old hunter I knew. We didn't part on the best of terms."

Steven nodded. His expression darkened as he said, "About Quell."

I growled instinctively. Quell was Sky's pet vampire. She had a habit of taking in strays. I couldn't stop her, nor could I convince her that he would likely kill her one day. He was one of Michaela's creations. For most of his vampiric existence, she'd allowed him to feed from the blood of the *Hidacus,* a rare imported plant capable of sustaining a vampire's bloodlust. She'd ended that arrangement after Sky forced Quell to feed from her in order to prevent a reversion. Michaela had claimed Sky's blood for herself. For him to feed from her, even to save his life, was a betrayal. Out of revenge, Michaela had destroyed Quell's plants, forcing him to feed from humans. In his inexperience with human blood, he'd had a problem keeping his food alive. For some reason, Sky thought it made sense to let Quell feed from her. For some reason, he hadn't tried to kill her.

I knew the reason. He loved her. Still, he'd try to kill Sky eventually. It was his nature.

Steven continued, his disgust plain. "Sky's acquired more Hidacus. She wants me to help build a greenhouse for the vampire in her own backyard."

I felt my jaw tighten, forced it loose. "Does Josh know?"

Steven's hesitation was slight. "Yes."

Now I understood why he'd waited to tell me until we were alone. Josh knew the danger to her, not just from Quell. Michaela was a jealous vampire, cruel. She'd already tried to kill Skylar once. If she succeeded, there'd be a war between pack and Seethe.

"Do it," I said, hating the taste of the words in my mouth. "But do what you can to talk sense into her. She'll listen to you." I couldn't understand why she trusted Steven more than me, but someone needed to get through to her.

"She listens but then she does what she wants. She thinks she's saving him," he said, bitter.

Josh blinked back into existence, alone. "Who is McClintock?"

"Nobody," I snapped, turning away from him. I sniffed the air, picked up on the belocka's scent. "We've got a target to track. Let's get it done."

A moment later, Steven found the physical trail. We continued tracking it and the scent until we found ourselves in a small green valley. The obnoxious scent was centered there. After searching some rocky debris and scanning the trees, I signaled toward the ground. We were looking for a burrow. Sifting through the tall grass proved fruitless. I began to question whether the creature had deliberately confused its scent when I noticed dark earth behind some dead brush along the valley's southern hillside. Peering through, I found an opening that extended into the hillside. The opening was bear-sized. The exposed dirt around the entrance was bone dry. It had been there a while. By the smell of it, the cave had been home to a number of creatures, but the skunk scent was currently dominant.

At the base of the entrance, there were odd lines in the dirt, as if someone had erased their tracks by raking the ground with a leafy branch.

I held still, listening—not even a heartbeat. Only silence resided within, a disappointment, but the burrow had to be cleared. If the belocka had been there, it might return. It wouldn't take much to turn the burrow into a trap.

I signaled to the others.

Josh scrutinized the size of the opening, raised an eyebrow at the cage he carried.

I gripped his shoulder, whispered in his ear. "Wait here. First sign of trouble, throw up a shield and hold it off until we reach you. Don't try to be a hero."

He licked his lips as he set the cage on the grass.

Turning to Steven, I gestured toward my eyes with two fingers. He nodded, quietly eased his backpack off his shoulder, and removed two pairs of night vision goggles. Taking mine, I slipped the band over my head, left the lenses pressing into my forehead. I waited until the breeze shifted, carrying my scent away from the opening, then eased myself into the burrow, blotting the sunlight behind me. In the dark, I drew my tranq pistol and slipped the lenses down over my eyes.

My wolf was close, ready for a fight.

Retrieving the elven creatures dead or alive paid off the pack's debt to Liam. To get the information I wanted from Liam, I needed to return all of the creatures alive. The belocka was the last on my list. I'd be damned if it was the first I had to kill.

The goggles took what light was available, enhanced it dramatically until the outline of the entrance was revealed in shades of green and black. The tunnel slanted downward several feet, opening into a wider space. I moved slowly, picking up each foot to avoid dragging them in the dirt, inching forward. Steven did the same behind me. As more and more of the opening came into view, I saw a nest of dead grass on the far wall. Next to the nest was a crumpled pile of clothes that reeked of necrotic flesh.

I rounded the opening with the tranq gun raised in both hands, ready to fire. I cleared right, allowing Steven to step in behind me, trusting he'd clear left. I felt his hand press against my back, signaling me to continue forward. The burrow was a single, open chamber. There was nowhere for the belocka to hide except within the nest.

I inched toward it, closer and closer. The grass was a thick tangle as tall as my knees and the width of a twin mattress. From within, I barely caught the faint sound of several tiny, fluttering heartbeats. I kept the pistol trained as Steven slowly drew out a long knife from his calf holster. He eased the blade into the nest to flush out anything inside.

Nothing. He changed the angle, slid the blade through the grass once more. Nothing. On the third attempt, I heard something brittle crack beneath the tip of the blade.

Steven gave me a puzzled look, then started pulling away the grass. While he dug, I turned my attention to the neighboring pile of bloody clothes. I expected to find at least one corpse, but found two. Both were broken, gnawed, consumed beyond recognition. Despite the blood and gore, the color and style of the clothes were discernible. I slipped off the goggles as I brought up my phone, flipped through pictures I'd collected of the two missing people. I recognized the woman's running shorts, at least.

Using my phone as a flashlight, I scanned the soft dirt floor for claw prints. Large tracks crisscrossed the burrow, revealing three clawed toes on the rear feet, and five on the front. From the length of stride, I knew the creature was bigger than we'd been told.

"Poodle, my ass," I growled.

"Ethan."

Steven pulled off his goggles as I turned my phone light onto the exposed contents of the nest—half a dozen eggs.

"Either this thing is asexual," he said, letting the rest of the thought trail off.

If there were more than one belocka on the loose, that was Liam's problem. We'd only agreed to retrieve the one. He was lucky we'd found the nest before the eggs hatched, assuming this was the belocka's first and only batch of eggs.

"Make sure there isn't another entrance." I drew a knife from the sheath at my hip and proceeded to destroy the eggs and the embryos inside.

After a quick walk along the walls, using his own phone as a flashlight, Steven gestured to where we'd entered. "Just the one."

Good. "We'll wait for the belocka to return, then trap it inside."

His gaze drifted from the creature's destroyed eggs to the gnawed corpses. "It's going to be pissed."

I started toward the exit, a plan forming in my head. That went to hell when I heard Josh's muffled groan outside. Fear gripped my chest. I charged up the burrow entrance, pistol in hand, my wolf snarling. Bright sky was suddenly eclipsed by a hulking beast and a roaring maw filled with shark-like teeth. Its breath reeked of dead flesh.

Steven cursed behind me.

Four folds of flesh closed around the mouth, revealing a single, wide eye just above.

Josh was on the other side of that thing, possibly dead or dying.

I fired a dart at its chest, then charged with the knife. The dart struck, ricocheted off the creature's skin. Before I could reach the beast, the folds of its lips drew back, then pushed out. A dark wad of thick spittle shot toward me. I ducked, pressed against the wall, but Steven didn't see the projectile in time to react. I heard the wet smack of spit striking his face. He stumbled back into the burrow and collapsed, tugging at the hardening substance that covered his mouth, nostrils, and one eye.

The creature charged in after me. Its massive body filled the opening. Its feet shook the earth like hammers.

I tossed the tranq gun behind me and let my wolf take over. Decades of experience and a deep affinity with my were-animal made the transformation almost instantaneous. My front claws dug into the dirt floor as I crouched, waiting for my moment. When it came, I ducked beneath the creature's snapping jaws, lunged. My teeth clamped onto the side of the creature's neck, bit down. The skin was hard, dense. I bit down harder, shook my head for leverage. I'd just reached the salty, copper taste of blood when the belocka reached up with a paw and easily knocked me off. The force of the blow knocked the wind from my lungs, stifling a howl as I tumbled down into the burrow, next to the pistol.

Steven, in coyote form, thrashed in the chamber, biting and clawing at the hardened mask wrapped around his muzzle. The transformation had broken some of the substance free, but the lack of oxygen made him frantic.

Both of our phones had fallen to the ground, still casting light into sections of the burrow, enough for the belocka to see the damage we'd done. It stood in the entryway, its powerful body blocking our escape, taking in the destroyed nest, the exposed and shattered eggs. The creature's entire body contracted as it opened its mouth and roared in rage. The sound, echoing off the burrow walls, was deafening.

The last of the hardened spit fell from Steven's jaws as he crouched on his front paws and snapped his jaws in answer.

He slowly backed toward the nest, deliberately drawing the belocka's ire. My ribs screamed in pain as I climbed back to my feet. Growling, I shifted to my right as much as I could, positioning the belocka to make a choice. Whether it went for Steven or me, one of us would have its back. I knew that was Steven's plan, but it was flawed. Given the belocka's size and the toughness of its skin, the two of us weren't enough to bring the creature down. We needed the pack. We needed Josh's magic.

He was either dead or dying just outside the burrow entrance. His only chance was for Steven or me to reach him. For that, one of us was probably going to die.

When the belocka started toward Steven, I lunged. Instead of taking its back, going for the neck, I snapped, forced it to face me. It plodded toward me, head low. The belocka hissed hot steam as I drew it back until I felt the dirt wall against my back. I was cornered, but I'd given Steven the room he needed to escape, to rescue Josh.

Instead he leapt onto the belocka, dug his teeth into the back of its neck. It roared, rose onto its hind legs as it reached up to rake Steven with its claws. Before it could, I bit into its exposed belly. The skin there was just as dense. I heard the thump of Steven landing somewhere on the other side of the creature. I dodged a swipe of the belocka's arm. Desperate to find a weak spot, I bit at the back of its heel. The tendon was defined there, the skin thin, but the creature was too fast. It spun away, casting me aside with a sweep of its arm. It was fast when it wanted to be, too fast. I bounced off the dirt wall, stunned. Something was beneath me. I recognized the shape of it.

As the belocka closed in for the kill, I changed into my human form and scooped up the tranquilizer pistol. There were two more darts in the cartridge. It probably wasn't enough, probably wouldn't save me, but it might slow the creature down, give Steven a chance to get out. Raising the pistol, I waited for that deadly mouth to open. The tissue would be the thinnest there.

The creature seemed to intuit my plan. Instead of roaring or opening its jaws to bite off my head, it rose onto its feet and drew back to rake me with its claws.

Before it could strike, a weave of flickering orange light enveloped the creature. It resisted, clawing uselessly at the magic web that tightened around it until the belocka's limbs were bound against its body. Struggling, it lost its balance and fell sideways with a pathetic whimper, revealing Josh standing in the light of the entryway. A clump of hardened spit still stuck to his jaw and his chest was heaving.

Relief washed over me. I'd feared the worst for him.

Steven, in human form, shuffled out of the shadow, clutching his side.

The spell completed, Josh drew a spark of light in his palm, revealing the entire burrow. He scrutinized me from head to toe, smirked. "Any chance to be naked, right?"

"How long will that hold?" I retrieved my phone from the dirt while Steven retrieved his.

"Not long." Josh frowned at the struggling belocka. "If you're going to tranq it, now would be a good time. I'll open a gap."

"Don't bother." I holstered the pistol, gestured toward the creature. "It's not going to be enough to put it under. I need you to transport back to the retreat, get a bigger dose from Dr. Baker. Make sure he gives you his thickest needle."

For once, he didn't give me a hard time. In a blink, he was gone. I glanced at Steven, taking in his injury. He waved off my concern, gestured to the belocka.

"I thought we were looking for something like a toy poodle with big teeth."

I scowled. "So did I." Liam had a lot to answer for.

A moment later, Josh reappeared with a change of clothes and Dr. Baker, a large syringe in his hand. As he took in the surroundings, I directed him to the creature on the floor. I tensed, prepared for the worst as Josh opened a small hole in the web at the belocka's back, closing it again as soon as Dr. Baker completed the injection. The drug took effect immediately.

He frowned down at it, shook his head. "I probably overestimated the dose," he admitted, looking to me. "It might not survive."

At the moment, I was just glad we hadn't taken casualties. Dead or alive, Liam owed me.

Taking the bundle of clothes from Josh, Steven and I dressed. Next, I called Marko. He answered immediately.

"What's up?"

"We're going to need a bigger cage, and a van. I'll text you the coordinates."

Once done, I texted Liam.

Two hours later, I drove a black van into the parking lot of the South Loop Home Depot. The cage in the back slid, causing the creature inside to thrash and roar. The sedative had worn off a few minutes ago, but Josh's web held. He'd recast it while the creature was sleeping, using enough magic to constrain the belocka until we'd delivered it. After that, it was Liam's problem.

"Take it easy on the turns," Josh growled. "You're riling it up."

I grinned back at him.

The parking lot was full of SUVs, vans, and company trucks loading and unloading large pieces of equipment and construction supplies. Transferring a single large metal crate between two vehicles wasn't going to draw anyone's attention, unless the contents of that crate rocked and growled and threw a roaring hissy fit.

Perhaps the parking lot of a Petco would've made a more practical exchange.

Their white van was already waiting, parked in the back of the lot near one of the light poles. At my approach, three van doors opened, depositing four J-Crew catalog models into the parking lot, Liam among them.

That was unexpected.

In the last two weeks we'd made a dozen such deliveries. Each time Liam had sent his minions, but never bothered to join them. Wounded pride, I'd assumed—not just from needing the pack's help. The Makellos' belief in their own superiority was a foundational principle of their existence. He'd gambled on an alliance with the witches and lost. We'd handed his ass to him just a few weeks ago, in an alley behind one of Marcia's magic shops. We'd handed her ass to her as well.

I drove past the van, parked behind it facing the opposite direction to make the transfer easier. The crate with the belocka inside weighed three hundred pounds, at least, a difficult burden made awkward by the active, angry beast inside. That wasn't our problem. We'd gotten the crate into the van. The Makellos could get it out. They were better known for their fashion sense than their physical strength.

After a moment's thought, I eased the van forward and parked in the next spot, increasing the distance between the vans.

Josh rolled his eyes, gave me a sly smile. "Have you ever met an ant pile you didn't poke?"

"Be ready for anything."

His smile faded. He glanced into the side mirror as the elves approached the back of the SUV, waiting for us to open the doors. "You think he'll renege on the deal?"

"If he's figured out it was the pack that broke the curse, yes."

Josh nodded and opened his door. I opened mine, sliding out to greet Liam. Neither of us bothered to extend a hand.

"Ethan," he said in a tone that suggested nothing could be more beneath him than addressing me.

I answered with a mirthless smile. "Liam. Haven't seen you since the battle. I almost didn't recognize you from the front."

The other elves scowled. I recognized two of them, twins who had previously guided us to the dark forest. The other woman was new to me. She had a hard but elegant look, with stylishly short-cropped hair. More aggressive than the twins, she clenched her fists, shifted her weight toward her front foot in anticipation of violence. Liam waved her off with a gesture.

There was an apparent similarity to their style of dress. "I see the spring catalog is out. Pastels are in."

Liam lifted his nose as he declared, "You only defeated us with Samuel's help," as if that explained everything.

"Any time you want to test that theory…"

Josh scowled between us. "Go ahead. Get it out of your system. I'm sure two guys bumping chests in the parking lot won't draw security, which can't possibly lead to the police showing up and asking to look inside the crate." Still scowling, he opened the back of our van and stepped back to give the Makellos access. "Do you have enough testosterone, or shall we order out?"

"The witch is right," Liam said, gesturing for his minions to transfer the crate.

The police weren't a danger. We had pack members within the force. At each transfer, I'd made sure that one of them was patrolling nearby. If our activity elicited a call, a friendly officer would be first on the scene. Josh knew that. He was being diplomatic. I'd challenged Liam—a mistake, considering our objective. Josh had given him a way out.

Liam didn't bother to assist as his Makellos gripped the

crate. Grunting, they pulled it out a few inches before the belocka began thrashing. The twins shared surprised glances. Liam raised an eyebrow. I knew then that he hadn't lied to me about the creature.

I glared down at him. "It's a little bigger than you described."

He glanced about to make sure the angry beast wasn't drawing civilian attention, then gestured for his elf to move their van closer. Once the van was repositioned, it was just a matter of pushing and pulling the crate from one to the other.

"This is the last on your list," I reminded him.

"Agreed. Your debt to me is paid."

"It is," I growled. "That wasn't the extent of our bargain."

The Makellos sighed with relief after giving the crate a final push. Once the van doors were closed and locked, Liam drew an envelope from his pocket.

When I reached out to take the envelope, he lowered it to his side, tapped it against his gray linen pants.

"The curse that bound the creatures within the preserve of the dark forest was a powerful one," he noted, "not easy to break."

Josh lied with a perfectly straight face. "There must've been a flaw that someone exploited."

"Perhaps, but our curse wasn't the only one broken. The Tre'ase are unbound, free to spread their mischief to the world. In fact, not a single curse that we know of remains intact, including Marcia's curse on your little wolf, Skylar."

Tre'ase were tricksters, probably demons, but no one knew for certain. According to one rumor, they were once human, witches who'd traded their humanity for immortality and power.

When I didn't answer Liam—preferring to look bored with the topic—his eyes narrowed. He turned to Josh, who remained unaffected.

"How that curse must have chafed at you," he said, fixing his gaze on me. "You care for her, like a master with a puppy."

I growled, "Your point?"

"When I ask myself how anyone could manage the sheer power required to unbind every curse, I can't help but consider the spells within the Clostra. Conveniently, the artifact is in your hands."

"One of the three books is in Samuel's possession," I corrected him. "Should he obtain the two under the pack's protection, he intends to destroy all magic. Instead of throwing around conspiracy theories, you should thank us."

"You have an alliance with Samuel," he said, the words bitter on his tongue.

"A temporary truce, which has expired."

"If the pack is using the Clostra—"

"I've got better things to do than listen to wild accusations."

Once more, I held out my hand. He stared down at my waiting hand, grunted, then handed me the envelope. I passed it to Josh, who checked the contents, nodded.

"We're done here."

While I drove out of the parking lot, making sure we weren't followed, Josh took a closer look at the pages from the envelope. He whistled. "Toronto, Florida, Kansas, Oregon. We're going to have our hands full."

We'd already exhausted the list of local Tre'ase that Chris had given me. Now that the Tre'ase were free, our search was going to get harder. Liam's list of addresses was based on the curse that had kept the Tre'ase bound to their homes. With the curse lifted, his list was losing value by the day. There were too many names. Some of them were going to slip through our fingers.

I only cared about one of them, the one that had created the spirit shade Maya. Eventually, that Tre'ase would die.

Maya would die with it, and she was the only thing keeping Sky alive. While still in the womb, her mother had been turned by a vampire. The mother was human, but Sky had inherited her wolf through her father. The vampire infection was a poison to Sky. The change would've killed her. To save her daughter, Sky's mother had made a bargain with Maya, welcoming the spirit shade to live within Sky once she was born.

Even if we knew how long of a life span Tre'ase lived, we didn't know the age of Maya's creator. It could be old or sick. It could be hunted. I had to live with the worry that Sky could die at any moment, and I could do nothing to save her until I found the Tre'ase and locked it away where we could keep it safe. First, we had to find it.

CHAPTER 2

*T*he drive back to the retreat felt long. Every silent mile stoked my anger at Josh. *He should've told me.* I chose to not confront him on the spot. I needed to talk to him alone, when I was calm.

The pack kept a number of homes in various locations, but the retreat was our current home, tucked away from view on three hundred acres of private wooded land. The boundaries of the property were fenced, deterring all but the most determined intruder. In a dangerous supernatural world, the retreat was our oasis.

Turning from the highway onto our private secondary road always brought a sense of calm. At the end of the narrow, winding road, the three-story brick mansion came into view. I parked the van next to Sky's Honda Civic.

Josh nodded toward Winter and Gavin's car on the other side of the garage. "Looks like the gang's all here."

"Good." My boots crunched on the gravel driveway as I led us toward the house. "We have some decisions to make."

Sky waited for us in the entryway, her arms folded over her chest. "How'd it go?" she asked, an edge to her voice. *Why didn't you take me?* was the underlying question. Behind that was a simple statement, *I don't need your protection; I can take care of myself.* She could. Her training with Winter was well advanced, and she'd developed a great deal of control when it came to magic. She'd effectively helped to capture several of Liam's escaped creatures. My instinctive need to protect her was never going to fade, but that wasn't the reason I'd left her out of the hunt; it was supposed to be a simple matter, dangerous, but not complicated. Had Liam shared the correct information about the creature, I might've chosen to leave Sky out of it as a precaution. More likely, I'd have taken her and several other pack members to give us an advantage. I'd have also come up with a workable plan to capture the creature without resorting to a nearly disastrous hand-to-claw fight. I had other reasons to leave her out of the last hunt.

Before I could answer, Josh slapped a hand onto my shoulder. "He wanted us to have some quality bro time."

I frowned at him, but Sky's irritation was soothed. Her arms unfolded, slipped down to her sides. "Did Liam give you the list?"

I brought the folded envelope from the back pocket of my jeans.

"Do you think it's accurate?"

"As accurate as can be, under the circumstances," I said, and started toward Sebastian's office. Sky fell into step beside me.

"You look like you got roughed up by a poodle," she said.

I smiled. "It was a much bigger, meaner poodle than we were informed. Nothing that won't heal."

She opened the door, went in first. Sebastian observed us from his perch on the corner of his desk. I handed him the envelope, gave him time to remove the pages and examine Liam's list of Tre'ase. I greeted Winter and Gavin with a nod. Gavin scowled back. He was sour for a were-panther, with an abrasive New York attitude. In short, he was a pain in the ass to be around, but he was strong and intelligent. That he hunted with an impenetrable single-mindedness of purpose was both asset and liability.

Winter met my gaze with unblinking hazel eyes. She was statuesque, with long straight black hair and flawless sun-kissed skin. Compared to most were-animals, she was slight of build, but looks were deceiving. She was a devil with a sword, and iron-willed. Our enemies often misjudged her, and Winter made them pay.

She was third in the pack leadership, after me. Gavin was fourth. Steven was fifth. As a blood ally, Josh didn't have a ranked leadership role, but his advice was valued. He was a powerful witch, and an asset to the pack.

Steven closed the door behind us and I gave my report of the belocka's capture.

Gavin growled. "Liam set us up."

Josh answered. "He seemed surprised when we told him how big it was. I don't think the Makellos have any idea what they've been keeping in that forest."

Sebastian considered for a moment. "Did you tell him about the eggs?"

"No," I stated.

Sky worried. "Was that its only nest? How long is the incubation period? If the belocka is asexual, there would've been more than one that escaped from the dark forest."

"Not our business," Winter said.

Josh added, "The curse that trapped the creatures probably kept them from procreating."

"Shouldn't we warn him?" Sky asked.

Winter wasn't moved. "If we'd told him in the first place, he would've used that against us, claimed our deal covered any of the creatures born after their escape. Let him pay the price of his own ignorance."

"But they'll hunt, they'll hurt other people."

Gavin nodded. "Liam's problem, not ours. The creatures

that escaped that forest should've been destroyed, not imprisoned."

"Agreed," I said, drawing a surprised look from Sky. "Liam will have to clean up his own mess. If he wants our help, he'll have to strike another bargain." I gestured to the pages in Sebastian's hands. "We needed that list to find the Tre'ase that created Maya. That's our priority." *You're my priority.*

She took that in, chewed on it. A lifetime of brutal struggle had left most of us jaded. Sky didn't share that. She'd been raised by an adoptive mother, a human. Sky'd been spared the harshness of our world. At times, the lack of hard experience was a vulnerability for her. Other times, it was an asset. Her moral compass challenged us, made us stronger, but there were times I wished I could shut it off.

"There was another problem," I said with a sigh. "A hunter on the belocka's trail."

Gavin made a disgusted sound. "More of Liam's sabotage. He hired a hunter to beat you to the creature so he could avoid paying us."

"Agreed."

Sebastian raised an eyebrow. "Sean?"

I shook my head. "A woman. I've met her before. She works with an old hunter I've encountered before. He doesn't usually cover this area. I put her off of the hunt."

Winter asked with a casual tone, "Did you kill her?"

Sky's eyes widened.

"No," I reassured her. I turned to Josh with an expectant look.

"I transported her to the Dairy Queen in Oak Lawn." He sucked in a breath, realizing he'd made some mistake. "I probably should've given her a couple bucks for a Dilly Bar."

Winter shrugged.

Sebastian asked me, "Is this going to be a problem?"

"I'm sure there'll be a discussion. I'll handle it."

He nodded, returned his attention to the list. "Now we just need to figure out where to start."

Josh said, "Logan might be able to help with—"

"No," I snapped. My brother bristled at the rebuke. Logan was a local Tre'ase, one we'd dealt with before. After we'd removed the curse that had bound him to his home in the woods, he'd wandered into the city and shown up on Sky's porch, just to let us know he could go where he pleased. Bargaining with a Tre'ase was always dangerous. We'd avoid that at all costs.

"Sky and I have some ideas how to prioritize the list," Josh offered. "We'll have to do some hopping around at first. Once we've talked to a few Tre'ase, we'll probably be able to narrow the list further."

Sebastian folded the pages, handed them to Josh. "Ethan, let O'Dowd know we'll be needing him."

O'Dowd was a private pilot we contracted with. We paid him enough that he was available at a moment's notice. Given the number of names on the list, finding Maya's creator was going to be expensive. Sky understood what we were committing to. She nodded to Sebastian, humbled and grateful, but there was no need. She was one of us. The pack spared nothing to protect our own. Even Gavin, who had once argued vociferously that we should kill Sky, hadn't questioned our obligation to her once she'd joined the pack.

Sebastian looked between Winter and Josh. "Samuel?"

She answered first. "He's like a mole, with holes everywhere. I've found ten more properties linked to him, but none of them panned out. I don't think we're going to see him again until he wants to be seen."

Witches usually operated in groups—even Josh had the pack. As a loner, Samuel was an outlier. He was on a self-assigned mission to rid the world of magic; if he had his way, every were-animal would suffer the loss of their animal, or die altogether. It was an impossible task, if not for the

Clostra. The magical artifact was one of the protected objects, a powerful spell book broken into three separate bindings. Each of the Clostra's unique spells were written across the three books, so that the spells within were only decipherable when all of the books were present together. Samuel had one of the books, the pack held the rest. He'd never give up scheming to obtain them.

As long as Samuel was in the area, we'd be looking over our shoulders.

"We should consider splitting the books," I said.

"I've already talked to Joan," Sebastian said. "She's coming to take one of the books with her."

She was Steven's adoptive mother. After Ethos had murdered the pack's leadership, its members had scattered. With our help and her natural leadership skills, Joan had brought the pack back together. She was their Alpha now. Under her guidance, the Southern Pack was stronger than ever. They were an ideal choice to protect a part of the Clostra, while keeping the books close at hand should we need them together.

The meeting was about to come to an end when Gavin declared, "Kelly is missing."

After Sebastian's rebuke of her for helping Demetrius turn Chris into a vampire, she'd returned to work, but only for a while. One day, she hadn't reported to work—no notice, no resignation. It was odd that she hadn't communicated her intentions with Dr. Baker. They were close. He treated her like a daughter. Still, she hadn't taken the rebuke well. I disagreed with her actions; Demetrius hadn't saved Chris's life, he'd killed her and brought her back to be his servant. A small smile crept onto my lips. That hadn't worked out the way he'd expected. Even in death, she was defiant. Last I'd heard, she'd skipped town to escape his control.

Right or wrong in our eyes, Kelly believed we'd drawn a line through her moral compass. We valued her. We missed her, but she wasn't a were-animal. She wasn't a member of the pack. She was a valued employee, a member of our family, but she was free to leave us in whatever way she deemed fit. She'd nearly died after being attacked by an elven sleeper. It was our job to shield Kelly from the dangers of our world. We'd failed in that regard.

If she left us, I couldn't blame her. We'd all left her in peace, hoping she'd come back eventually. There was no reason to think some ill had befallen her.

Sky looked worried.

Sebastian explained to Gavin, "We can't force her to come back."

From his sour expression I took it he didn't care any more for that answer now that he'd heard it at least half a dozen times. He and Kelly had an unusual relationship. She wasn't afraid of him, even called him kitty just to get under his skin. While the sleeper paralyzed her, he'd stayed by her side, protected her. He was trying to protect her now, though it looked a lot like an obsession.

"It doesn't make sense," he insisted. "She wouldn't leave without telling us."

"She has no enemies," I pointed out.

He snapped back, "Someone could take her to get to us."

"There's been no ransom, no demands. She has no knowledge of our operations outside of the medical bay, so she has nothing to offer."

Sebastian cautioned him, "Give her time."

Gavin's scowl nearly broke his face. He let the subject drop, though I was sure he'd raise it again.

The meeting ended. Josh and Sky paired off, started toward the library.

I called after him, my tone harsher than intended. "Josh."

He and Sky turned, gave each other puzzled looks as I took a calming breath. I gestured toward a neighboring room. "I need to talk to you for a minute."

"Later." He scowled. "We've got work to do."

"Now," I growled, then walked into the laundry room to find Marko folding clothes from the dryer. He read my expression, excused himself just before Josh walked in with a defiant swagger.

"What do you want to yell about now, Ethan?"

I walked past him to close the door, listened for a moment for Sky's breathing on the other side. Instead I heard the library door close upstairs. I turned back to my brother.

"Why are you encouraging Sky to help Quell?"

He rolled his eyes. "Steven's helping her. Did you yell at him, too?"

"Steven keeps me informed."

"Obviously."

"Do you even understand the danger to her?"

"She asked," he stated. "If I'd said no, she'd have just found someone else to do it. At least this way I can keep an eye on her. That's what you want, right—someone spying on her?" He shook his head like I was pathetic. "Brother, you have some real control issues."

My brother had a way of getting under my skin.

I took two handfuls of his Sesame Street t-shirt and pushed him back against the wall. He grinned back at me, but he was getting angry.

"You want to be her friend," I growled. "Protect her."

"Sky can take care of herself, Ethan. She's training with Winter. She's getting better at magic every day."

That was another problem. "It doesn't matter how strong she is, Josh, if she doesn't see the danger coming. She thinks Quell won't kill her because he loves her, because there's something inherently good in him. He'll kill her because he loves her, or he'll kill her because he's bored of her. It's only a matter of time. One moment, she'll let her guard down"—I pulled him enough to slam him back into the wall—"and

31

then it'll be over. And if Quell doesn't do it, Michaela will. Understand?"

His cheeks flushed as he blinked. "You know, I think I need you to shout that into my face just a few more times. Also," his gaze flicked down to my fistfuls of shirt, "you're stretching Bert and Ernie."

I felt the heat of his hand on my chest just before a magical force struck me, throwing me into the wall on the other side of the room. I had my own magic to call on. We'd played out the same fight dozens of times. I needed to get my temper under control.

Before I could break his spell, Josh released me, glowering. He held up an index finger in silent warning, then walked away.

I waited a moment, catching my breath as I forced myself to relax. It wasn't enough. I needed to get some distance from Josh. I was on my way out the door when I felt my phone vibrate. A text message from an unknown number read, "I'm calling you. I suggest you pick up. M." The call followed a second later. I walked out onto the porch before accepting the call.

"Here I thought we had us a truce," the man said. "You go your way and stay out of mine—wasn't that what we agreed to, Ethan?"

His voice was rough from decades of hard living and an innate crabbiness. "McClintock."

"Hell, yeah, it's me. Don't act so surprised. We need to have us a little parlay. Lucky for you, I'm in the area."

I scowled. "Let's cut to the chase. What's your price?"

"It ain't that simple. Meet me at the Oak Lawn Dairy Queen in an hour. You know the place, where your brother dumped my hunter."

The call ended.

Winter spoke behind me. "You want company?" Like all were-animals, she had uncanny hearing.

I glanced back at the house, decided to leave Sky with Steven.

"Bring your sword."

Next I called Marko, gave him instructions.

I didn't feel like talking on the drive into Chicago. Winter didn't seem to mind. We'd worked together long enough that she knew I'd tell her what she needed to know, when she needed to know it.

Halfway to the mall, I received a text message from Marko. "He's here, southwest corner booth. There's a woman with him, looks pissed off, so I guess she's met you already. They've got pistols on them, one at the waist each. The woman has a small caliber at her ankle. The old guy looks like he's armed to the teeth, but I can't spot anything."

I answered using voice to text. "Five minutes out. Stay inconspicuous."

"Yeah."

When I put my phone down, Winter asked, "What are the odds this is going to get fun?"

"Depends on how pissed off he is."

She nodded, thinking. "Public venue?"

It was my turn to nod.

A few minutes later, I parked my tanzanite-metallic-blue BMW M6 in the mall parking lot an hour later. She glanced around, confused. I gestured toward the Dairy Queen. She rolled her eyes and climbed out of the car, leaving her sword in the passenger seat. After I locked the car, I tossed her the keys.

"Why bring my sword?" she asked.

"I wanted you to feel comfortable for the drive over. Keep your eyes peeled. Might be more than just him and the woman."

She followed me inside, slipped into a chair next to the

door, giving herself a full view of the dining area. McClintock and Tonya were in the back corner booth, exactly where Marko had described. They were a mismatched pair, about thirty years between them. Both wore black cargo pants, with plenty of pockets to hide all sorts of tricks. McClintock wore a drab olive-green t-shirt while Tonya stuck with black. She was young, undamaged, while his rugged look was enhanced by a prominent scar that cut from the bridge of his nose across one shallow cheek. Another scar cut across the top of his left eyebrow. Tonya's long black hair—still in a ponytail—was in sharp contrast to his cropped, gray-and-black military cut.

Despite his age, McClintock stayed fit. Muscles bulged beneath his shirt.

At my approach, Tonya rose from the table and took a seat in the next booth, putting her at my back if I chose to sit. McClintock leaned back in his seat, his legs splayed beneath the table, to stare up at me with his mirthless grin.

"You going to join me or just stand there and glower?" He gestured to Tonya's vacated seat. "I know you were raised better than that."

I flicked a glance at Tonya, cleared my throat.

His grin broadened some. "See, Tonya—always cautious, as it should be." At his gesture, she reluctantly rose and took a seat at another table, where I'd be able to keep an eye on her. Once she'd settled in, I slid into the booth across from McClintock. He absently poked at his ice cream with a red plastic spoon while we measured each other.

Eventually, he got tired of waiting me out.

"You know, Ethan, I don't normally come out to these parts. Chicago's not my favorite town. I don't like the people," he admitted, giving me a pregnant look. "So when I do come here, you know it's gotta be worth my while."

"We made an arrangement with Liam to retrieve his lost creatures," I said. "He hired you to undercut our deal."

"I'm not surprised, not even a little bit. Doesn't change my situation, though. I turned down a hell of a job for this one." He shook his head as if he couldn't believe it. "Tonya said I was crazy. She might've been right, but then I saw those eggs." He nodded, his smile genuine.

He'd already found the burrow by the time I'd arrived. Tonya must've been keeping tabs on the belocka while they waited for the eggs to hatch. He'd have taken the mother then, and sold the babies before they got too difficult to handle. He might've even kept one to farm more eggs. It was a brazen plan, far-sighted, unconscionable.

"Risky," I said. "Lots of ways to get killed with that plan."

"We both know I ain't no spring chicken." He gave me a wily look. "I've been at this a long while. About time I had something to show for my troubles."

He was the oldest hunter I knew of. Most died young. If it was money he was after, we could've handled the matter by phone. He'd be paid already. I sighed, scratched an eyebrow with my thumb. "How much, McClintock?"

"You think it's that easy." He grunted. "Is that what you do as the Beta of the Midwest Pack? Do you write checks all day and make the pack's problems disappear? You want a number? I'll save you some time. We can skip the bargaining. Let's say I started with something ridiculous and you worked me down until we both agreed that an even hundred thousand was a bargain."

It was my turn to grunt. "Your mind is addled."

"You get what you pay for, Ethan. I assure you, the other option is going to be a lot less comfortable."

"If you brought me here to threaten me, you're wasting my time."

"A hundred thousand." He shook his head. "I can't go any lower. My pride won't allow it."

"You should look into that other job. Maybe it's still open."

"Oh, it is. It's just," he thought for a moment, shook his head, "some jobs stick in your craw, you know? Aw, hell, we're both soldiers. It wouldn't be the first time I'd done something I wasn't proud of."

I agreed. "It happens."

He leaned back, draped an arm over the back of the booth. "Well, I guess we're done here. Can't say I expected much else from you. You're a stubborn son of a bitch, Ethan Charleston."

"Good luck," I said, rising.

"You too." He gestured absently to the dining area behind him. "Don't forget your wolf."

Marko was seated a few tables away, hunched over a burger he'd nibbled on while pretending to read a book. I'd made a point not to look at him when I'd walked into the restaurant, but McClintock didn't need the visual cue. The Finnish wolf was tall, with a severe look.

"You all stand out," McClintock explained.

I gestured to Marko, letting him know that his cover was blown. He straightened, sighed in frustration before rising and crossing the restaurant to join Winter.

"Drive carefully on your way out of town," I warned the old hunter. "A guy like you probably draws all kinds of attention from the local authorities."

"I'll take that under advisement."

I gathered Winter and Marko and led them out the door.

"I really don't get to use my sword, do I?" she pouted, returning my keys.

After unlocking the BMW, I turned to Marko. He looked guilty as hell.

"I'm sorry, man," he started. "I don't know how he made me. I never looked at him directly, or the woman."

Winter propped an arm out the passenger window, offered, "It was probably the neck hair—just cries wolf."

He grunted approval. They made a game of taking jabs at each other.

"Find out what McClintock's driving and get Tim on him," I said.

"On it." He plodded back toward the restaurant.

We were halfway back to the retreat when Winter said, "That other job—why tell you?"

"Leverage," I guessed.

"Sounded more like a warning to me."

It did. I fished out my phone, called Artemis. She answered with the enthusiasm of someone expecting to get paid.

"Hello, Ethan. What can I do for you?"

"There's a hunter in town—"

"McClintock."

I could hear her grin on the other end of the call. Not much got by her without being noticed. "Find out what he's up to, where he's staying. He's got a job offer he's dragging his heels on. The usual price."

She answered cheerily, "Will do, chief!"

"Artemis," I said before she could hang up. "Be careful."

Her voice dropped to an enthusiastic growl. "Careful costs double."

I grunted approval and hung up.

Winter looked skeptical. "The were-fox? You don't think she'll sell you out?"

There was always a risk using someone who made their living threading the needle. Artemis had grown up an orphan on the streets, finding and selling information. Over the years, I'd cultivated a mutually beneficial working relationship with her. I'd even come to her rescue once or twice, but I'd no illusions. Security was her primary motivator. Her loyalty could be bought, but she wasn't fool enough to throw away a future of steady employment for a single paycheck.

She also knew that if she betrayed me or the pack, I'd run her out of town.

Winter continued, "If he puts a gun to her head?"

When it came to the shadows, Artemis was more skilled than any hunter I'd ever met, including Chris. "He'll never know she's there."

I spent the next few days staying clear of Josh and Sky while they worked through the list of Tre'ase. They'd already come up with a few targets. In a few days, O'Dowd would have his schedule cleared for the next two months. We'd all be spending a lot of time together, and I wanted to leave my anger behind.

Getting Sky away from Quell for an extended period of time was a bonus. She'd accelerated the construction of her greenhouse in anticipation of leaving him on his own. He'd become fixated on feeding from Sky. I didn't like it. Sebastian didn't like it. I'd no doubt that Michaela didn't like it. Quell was going to be forced to adapt. With any luck, time apart was going to solve that problem.

Once I'd had enough time away from Josh, I reached out to make sure we were fine. I didn't need the tension following me onto O'Dowd's Gulfstream jet.

Josh wasn't taking my calls. After a while, I gave up.

I had other concerns to worry about. Destroying every curse in existence had altered the supernatural world. We'd no idea what dangers we'd unleashed. There might be other, more positive ramifications.

I found Claudia in the office of her art gallery. Always elegantly dressed, she wore a pearl-colored pantsuit with a string of pearls over a pink camisole. Matching silk gloves rose nearly to her elbows. On her desk was a glass of red wine next to a stack of paperwork.

"No need to get up," I offered as I walked in.

I greeted her with a smile, kissed the air over her cheeks, before she gestured for me to join her at the small tea table. I took one of the hand-carved wooden chairs while she took the other. For a moment, we waited each other out with smiles.

"I'd like to talk to you about the *Vitae.*"

Her smile remained, but her shoulders tensed, her lips thinned, almost imperceptibly. She was a Moura. The Vitae was the protected object she was bound to protect. It was a subject she didn't like to talk about. The best secrets were the ones forgotten. I'd struggled with whether to broach the subject with her.

She waited for me to continue.

"Is it possible the curse on Josh has been lifted?"

He didn't know that he'd been cursed to die. In her time, our mother was a powerful witch. Like Josh, she'd been highly independent, which made her a threat to the Creed. When she'd cast the *rever tempore*—a forbidden spell—to save a friend, the Creed's punishment was swift and brutal.

One of her two sons would pay the price of her sin, cursed to die at the moment of his eighteenth birthday. In a cruel twist, the choice was hers. Had she failed to choose, Josh and I would've both been killed. Despite the pack's reputation for violence, we were never cruel. We killed out of necessity. The Creed killed for sport. Without allies, my mother stood alone against the Creed. As strong as she was, she couldn't challenge their combined strength. Backed into a corner, she'd made the hard choice. She'd chosen Josh. He was younger than me, giving us an extra six years to find a way to break the Creed's curse.

He was the strategic choice. From thereafter, she'd focused all of her energy on breaking that curse. With Claudia's help, they'd at least found away to keep the curse at bay. Josh was saved, but our mother had never been the same. The choice had killed something in her, something vital.

The solution was Claudia's. The power of the Vitae was to give life, but she didn't dare wield it openly. Instead, we'd melted down the metal of the small, helix-shaped artifact and combined the liquid metal with black ink. Josh had no idea that he wore the protected object as a quarter-sized tattoo just above the top of one thigh. He'd been a small child then, and had no memory of receiving the tattoo. To this day, he thought the magic that kept him alive was a simple birthmark.

Claudia was skeptical. "Have all curses been lifted?"

"So far, that seems to be the case."

"You want to remove the Vitae from him?"

"No." I stared at my palms for a moment. There was no need. "I'd like to not worry about losing him."

She smiled, reached across the table to give my hand a comforting squeeze. "You really think you'll ever stop worrying about your brother?"

I grunted, returned her smile. "It would be one less thing, at least. I was hoping you'd have some insight."

"We're in uncharted territory now."

"Sky wants me to tell him."

She hesitated, just for an instant. "You told her."

"I did," I said, frowning under her judgment.

"It's your decision, Ethan. It will hurt him."

It shouldn't. "Our mother made a logical decision," I stressed.

"You can't stop that hurt with logic. If you want my blessing, I can't give it to you, but I'll respect your choice."

He had a right to know, didn't he? Sky thought so. She'd convinced me, but I'd grown less certain. I'd promised to tell him, but I'd never said when. The timing wasn't right. The pack was facing too much uncertainty. Telling Josh now would just complicate his life when the pack needed him most.

It could wait. I felt a burden lifting from my shoulders.

"Thank you, Claudia."

I sped back to the retreat, glad to see Sky's Civic was still there, next to Josh's black Ducati.

"They're in his office," Winter informed me.

I approached the library door when I heard Sky ask in a voice meant to sound casual, "Has Ethan talked to you recently?"

I froze.

"About what?" Josh asked, disinterested.

"Nothing."

"We fight, Sky. We get over it, until Ethan starts another one."

She grunted in reply, then asked, "You have a birthmark, don't you?"

"Of course," he chuckled. "You've seen it. Do you want to see it again?"

She'd promised not to reveal my secret. Scowling, I walked into the room, unnoticed. She sat at a large, cluttered table, watching Josh pace in thought nearby. In front of her was one of the Clostra books, open, and the Aufero.

"He actually has two birthmarks," I said, announcing myself before she could do any damage. A look of surprise came over Sky, as if she'd been caught talking in the back of class. I met her gaze with a stern warning. "I don't think it's necessary for you to see them."

"Hi, Ethan," she said, reacting to my tone. "Nice to see you, too."

I glanced between her and Josh. "Did I interrupt anything?"

"Nope," he said, continuing to pace. "Just working."

"I called you several times."

He shrugged. "I must have left my phone at home."

"Really?" I picked up his phone from the table—right next

to the notebook he'd been working in—accessed his call history, and held it up for him.

His lips twisted into a defiant scowl. "You're not the boss of me."

"Josh." I started toward him. As I neared the Aufero, it came to life. A gray, opaque field snapped into existence around it. Wary of its power, I stopped in my tracks. Holding my breath, I slowly backed several steps away. After a tense moment, the orb seemed to determine I wasn't a threat. The field collapsed and the orb went back to sleep. I'd felt its wrath before. Once was enough.

Josh and Sky glanced between me and the orb, wearing their fascination.

"What?" I demanded.

He shook his head as he lifted his jacket from the back of his chair. "I need a break," he informed Sky, then walked past me without another glance.

Once he left, I cautiously took his place at the table. Keeping one eye on the orb, I sifted through my brother's notes. I could feel Skylar's intense gaze on me, building toward a question.

I sighed. "What is it, Skylar?"

"Nothing," she declared, turning her attention to the Clostra.

Her heart betrayed her. "77 BPM."

She scoffed at me. "Stop that!"

"I will when you start being completely honest with me. Don't tell me something isn't wrong, when something is."

"Really?" She stared back at me, wide-eyed. "*You* are giving me the 'you should be honest' lecture?"

I waited, refusing to take the bait.

Guilt weighed on her expression. "I don't like that you are keeping information from your brother. And I hate that I am part of it. You have to tell him." She swallowed, then added, "Or I will."

My reaction was automatic. I wasn't used to receiving ultimatums.

In a single stride I rose from my chair and was next to her, intimately close. Startled, she sucked in a sharp breath. Her heart raced. I asked in a low, steady voice. "So you'll break the promise you made to me?"

She frowned, confused. Did she not remember?

I moved closer until my lips lightly brushed hers. "You're a lot of things, Skylar, but a person who would go back on her word isn't one of them." I let that hang in the air before I backed out of her space. "I will tell him when I'm ready. I don't think it's necessary for him to know, so I will tell him when I damn well please. Let's have enough with the idle threats. I don't like it."

"I don't like keeping your secrets."

"Then forget that you know it," I suggested. I never should've shared that secret with her. This was my mess.

Her anxious gaze turned hard, determined. "You have two days, or I am going to tell him."

As angry as I was, I admired her resolve. Once roused, she was unshakeable. She didn't seem to appreciate my admiration; for a moment, I thought she'd throw a punch.

"No threats," I warned her, my tone deliberately soft. "I will take as long as I need and will tell him when I am ready." I leaned forward and kissed her lightly on the nose. "Tell Josh to stop being such a jerk."

"If I can't convince you to stop being one, what makes you think I can persuade him?"

I chuckled on my way out of the library.

CHAPTER 3

was on my way to the kitchen to heat up a steak when I received a text from my legal assistant. I'd spent the last few months negotiating a big-ticket buyout for an up-and-coming Chicago tech startup. The contract I'd drawn up was meticulous, perfect. Days away from putting signature to paper and finalizing the deal, the client was getting cold feet, making new demands. Most of my practice involved mergers, buyouts, negotiations. Occasionally I helped a little fish stand up to a big fish, but I wasn't looking to make a splash. I didn't want to walk out of a courthouse to find a dozen microphones in my face.

I texted Stacy that I was on my way to the client's office, got into my Hennessy Venom GT—my newest purchase—and put its steering system to the test speeding along the narrow, winding private road that lead to the local highway.

Formulating a strategy to tackle the problem proved elusive as other worries intruded—Sky, for one. Drawing Michaela's ire was dangerous. Sky wasn't defenseless, not the way she'd been when we'd first saved her from the Seethe. Winter trained Sky hard, and she'd committed. I'd bet on her in most fights, but Michaela was in another league. There

44

weren't many in the pack I'd expect to go up against her and come out in one piece. She was cunning, patient, and never met a grudge she wouldn't nurse for years in order to exact her revenge.

Worries rattled around in my brain until I realized I'd parked in Sky's driveway, next to Steven's car. I must've been on autopilot that last few miles, following my thoughts. Grimacing at my lack of control, I put the GT in reverse, but couldn't make myself back out of the driveway. Curiosity got the better of me. I needed to see this greenhouse with my own eyes to believe that she'd go that far to please Quell.

Climbing out of the GT, I put my palm over the hood of Steven's car. The engine was still warm. Walking around the property, I noticed David—one of Sky's nosey neighbors—on his porch with a cup of coffee held frozen halfway to his lips. Following his stare, I found Steven in Sky's backyard, a tool belt around the waist of his jeans. The muscles of his back rippled as he pulled off his t-shirt and tossed it over a nearby sawhorse.

David must've felt the pressure of my stare. He met my gaze, panicked. He jerked his coffee toward his lips and spilled it onto his shirt. Mumbling curses, he strode inside.

Steven didn't seem to notice, or didn't care.

As humans, David and his partner Trent didn't pose a direct threat to Sky, but they weren't harmless. The pack thrived in the shadows. Like all supernatural beings, we kept humanity at arm's length, integrating only whenever and to what extent was necessary to maintain our anonymity. There was always a risk of our world bleeding into theirs. Sky's neighbors felt protective of her, closely watched the comings and goings on her property. They could easily see something they shouldn't. Worse, they could become collateral damage. I'd argued both points with Sky and lost. I wasn't sure if she'd befriended David and Trent out of defiance or to maintain her link to humanity.

She'd grown up among humans, believed herself one of them. Until Demetrius's vampires had broken down her door and killed her adoptive mother, Sky'd thought she was an anomaly.

I couldn't stop her from buying her townhouse, but I'd done my due diligence investigating her neighbors. David worked as an event planner, while Trent was a PR consultant with a large Chicago firm. Neither had a criminal record and their social circle was largely comprised of their upper-middle-class clients and fellow professionals—they had no supernatural connections outside of Sky. I could manage their nosiness. If they saw too much or became too nosey, there were indirect pressures I could apply through the pack's municipal connections to encourage the men it was time to move along. That was a last-ditch option, useful to protect David and Trent as well as Sky, but I could hardly keep them safe if she was going to start a war with Michaela.

Steven turned at my approach, threw a frowning glance at the nearly finished greenhouse. All it needed was some trim and a paint job. I walked around the structure, noting the unearthly plants inside that reeked of fruit and blood. How a vampire could feed from such an abomination when human blood was so plentiful and easily obtained mystified me. The Seethe had its share of human admirers that volunteered their blood, yet Quell had fed exclusively from the plants until Michaela had destroyed them.

Sky thought he was special, a vampire that could be saved. Quell was only suppressing his evil nature. Since the loss of his own Hidacus plants, his nature was closer than ever to the surface. He'd left a trail of at least three bodies that we knew of. So far he'd controlled himself with Sky, but that wasn't going to last. Scowling, I considered destroying the plant myself.

The consequences would be severe.

"She showed it to him this morning."

That was a surprise. "Did he feed from it?"

I followed Steven's gesture to a dark ooze that covered a part of the plant where a stem had been snapped off. So much for a final plea for Sky to change her mind. Quell had fed from the plant, violating Michaela's order. I could hear Sky's argument repeating inside my skull. *"She forbade him from* having *the plant. It's* my *plant at* my *house. She doesn't get to have a say."*

It was a legal argument. Michaela wouldn't care about semantics.

"Quell loves her," Steven said, his disgust plain.

I growled, "I'm aware."

My expression hardened into a mask as I asked, "Does she love him back?"

He nodded, then hedged. "It's not the same. She plays along because she thinks his obsession with her is innocent. It's getting worse. I tried to talk some sense into her but..." His frown deepened as he glanced back toward the house. "I can't stay here. I can't watch her do this to herself anymore."

A small weight slipped off my shoulders. Steven and Sky shared a sibling-like bond that I'd never been comfortable with. I tolerated his presence in her house because he provided her an added layer of protection. Once our preparations for our trip to find Maya's creator were complete, we'd be away from Chicago for at least a month. I'd already decided Steven would stay behind. He'd have time to settle into his own place, and Quell would learn to survive—or not—on his own.

The long trip could solve multiple problems. I just needed to get Sky on the road before the situation with Michaela got out of hand.

"It's probably for the best," I said.

He nodded.

I was going to say more when a movement caught my

eye, something in the woods behind Sky's house. Steven noticed as well.

"Don't," I whispered as his head started to turn. "Jackal."

Steven's eyes widened slightly. Jackals were rare.

Most were-animals in the Chicago area belonged to the Midwest Pack. The rest we kept tabs on. Unaffiliated were-animals largely kept to themselves, but there were a few minor packs. Only two of those deserved my regular attention. The Worgen were one such pack. According to Steven, that was the name of a race of characters in a video game. Made sense considering the Worgen spent most of their energy streaming video games online. They were also accomplished hackers. We hired them on a few occasions, watched them closely the rest of the time. Most of their wolves were turned, which helped explain their awkwardness—some of it anyway. They had their own ideas about relating to their animal, and not much of an idea how to relate to the rest of the world, supernatural or otherwise.

Sebastian had invited the Worgen to join our pack. They weren't a fit, but their skills were valuable. We didn't want another faction turning them against us. Integrating them would've been a challenge, but they'd turned the offer down. Rather than take offense, Sebastian recognized that the Worgen weren't ready to give up their fraternity lifestyle— they'd created a banner that featured beer, pizza, and gummi bears. We'd give them time to grow up. Eventually, danger would find them and the Midwest Pack would be there to pick up the pieces.

If the Worgen had a jackal, I'd know about it.

The Ares Pack was of slightly greater concern. Anderson, the Alpha, was ambitious. In recent months, he'd stepped up his recruiting, which meant he had a plan. I doubted whether it was a good plan. Last count, Ares had just tipped over one hundred members, but they were also made animals—inferior. From what I'd seen, Anderson preferred sheer numbers to actual training. Their fighting skills were poor. Still, Anderson was going to force our hand eventually. Even ants could be dangerous if the host was big enough.

Ares didn't have a jackal, either.

I intended to find out how a strange were-animal found itself outside of Sky's house. Might be random, might not. For the moment, its attention was fixed on the neighbor's backyard, where David and Trent appeared to be setting up a small picnic on their patio. While David deliberately ignored Steven and me, his partner did little to hide his peeking in our direction. Distracted by Steven's bare chest, they'd yet to notice the jackal hunting them.

As long as Steven and I were within sight, it would have to be patient—assuming the neighbors were the jackal's target.

I gestured to the greenhouse, raising my voice for the jackal's benefit. "Let me know when you're done here." I added in a whisper, "I'll go around into the copse. Wait for my move."

"Will do."

He pretended to go back to work while he positioned himself for the best possible run at our unexpected visitor. As I strode away, I made a point to twirl my car keys around my index finger. The moment I rounded the house and was out of sight, I pocketed the keys and hurried around the far side of the house, crouching below the top of the fence line. Where the fence ended, I dropped into a narrow gulley, crouched until I reached the copse, then warily made my way toward the jackal's position. A light breeze rustled the brush, bringing with it the jackal's scent. My nose wrinkled. It was off somehow, not quite natural.

My ideal move was to veer deep into the copse, position myself so that Steven and I could close on the jackal between us. The presence of witnesses complicated the situation. We'd have to drive the jackal deeper into the woods and run it down. Tricky, giving the jackal an avenue of escape, but I doubted it could outrun my wolf, or Steven's coyote. If it did, we'd track it as long as necessary.

I kept close to the edge of the copse, watching the ground beneath my boots.

The dense brush prevented line of sight, but I knew by the jackal's scent it was just a dozen feet ahead. As long as the breeze was on my side and its attention was fixed on Steven and Sky's neighbors, I might be able to take it down alone—easier done in wolf form, but that was too risky. If seen, the jackal could be confused with a large dog, but my wolf was much larger.

The breeze swirled, shifted direction. Before it could deliver my scent to the jackal, I charged through the brush in front of me. In three strides I caught sight of the dark stripe on the jackal's flank as it turned and darted deeper into the woods.

I heard David ask in surprise, "What was that?"

Still hidden from sight, I shifted into my wolf, leaving my shredded clothes behind as I raced after the intruder.

Behind me, I heard Steven declare just before he crashed into the copse, "It's a wild dog. Go inside!"

For a few strides, there was just the scent to follow as I leapt over broken branches, darted under dense overgrowth, until the jackal cut across my line of sight twenty feet ahead. Behind me, I heard Steven's coyote catching up. Desperate to escape, the jackal veered toward a hiking trail. I grinned as I lowered my nose to the ground and slipped beneath the low-hanging branch of a half-fallen pine tree. On an open trail, the jackal was able to accelerate away, but speed wasn't its advantage. It should've stayed in the brush, used natural obstacles. On an open trail, Steven and I were nearly twice the jackal's speed.

By the time the jackal realized its mistake, I was snapping at its tail. It veered right, tried to dart back into the woods.

Steven cut it off, leapt, and landed in the dirt with nothing to show for his efforts. The jackal had disappeared, snatched from existence in the blink of an eye.

Magic hung in the air.

I stood next to Steven, sniffing as he climbed back to his feet. We changed back into human form at the same time, gave each other troubled looks.

"That's not possible," he said, catching his breath.

I nodded. Even rarer than a jackal was a were-animal that used magic. I did, inherited from my mother, but few knew. Were-animals that could use magic had a tendency to die young, thanks to the witches. They thought they had a monopoly on magic and were willing to kill for it.

Steven's nose wrinkled as he sniffed the air. "That animal doesn't smell right."

There was that, too. I didn't like mysteries. I liked them less when they circled around Sky.

"Ares?" he asked, doubtful.

"A loner, most likely. Probably looking for easy prey. Put out the word. If that jackal's not already on its way out of town, it will be soon, but I'd prefer to get some answers from it first."

"I'll get someone to watch Sky's house."

"She has enough on her mind to worry about," I said, surprising him. "She wasn't the target. A loner wouldn't have a reason to target her, and Anderson wouldn't start a war by attacking Sky." His first move would be to take out me or Sebastian. If he were smart enough to take out our top five ranks at once, he might have a sliver of a chance. "Still, I'll pay Anderson a visit, make sure he's not getting too big for his britches."

Steven nodded. "You want me to go with you?"

He wanted the chance to make his own feelings known, but that wasn't necessary. By walking into the Ares Pack alone, I wanted Anderson to know just how little I thought of him.

By the time we returned to the house, David and Trent had locked themselves inside their home. While Steven went inside to dress, I found my keys and phone among the shredded remains of my jeans. Half a dozen text messages from Stacy waited for me; the situation with my client was deteriorating quickly. I growled at the distraction. The pack came first, but putting Anderson in his place was more formality than necessity. He could wait until I'd cleaned up this other mess.

The heart of the problem was a power play between two board members—pack politics played out in suits, in conference rooms at the summit of a high-rise office tower. I went through the motions my job required, negotiating between the board factions, trying to keep the deal alive, but the endgame was obvious. In the end, the board would have a new Alpha. The deal, which would've benefited them all, was the sacrificial lamb.

Pointless.

I'd seen packs consume themselves with challenges. It was a flawed system, but it was the way of all packs going back to the first, when survival was a constant physical struggle. We'd evolved since then, but the old ways held; pack cohesion depended on it. Challenging an Alpha who could no longer lead was a necessity. In my time, I'd seen brothers, friends, and lovers kill and maim each other for the good of their pack. Challenging a capable Alpha strictly for the sake of personal ambition was an abomination, but it happened more frequently than we cared to admit.

Sebastian was a modern Alpha. He'd made the pack strong, brought stability, but he'd also made the pack prosperous. He didn't face frivolous challenges because I, as the pack's Beta, didn't suffer fools. A were-animal who couldn't put the pack above their personal ambition got shipped to the fringe packs. Within the Midwest Pack, I was the only were-animal strong enough to challenge Sebastian, but there was no need, not unless he became incapacitated or otherwise unable to lead. In that case, I'd have no choice but to challenge him.

With Sebastian, all challenges were to the death, no exceptions.

He was in the prime of his health and faculties, and not prone to needless risk. Challenging him wasn't something I considered likely, or desirable.

It was midnight before the house of cards finally collapsed. On the drive home I considered stopping by Sky's to check on her. I started to text her to see if she was awake, but I was exhausted. By the time I reached my own bed, I was already half asleep.

I woke up two hours later to my phone ringing. Steven.

"Yeah," I said, sitting up on the edge of the bed.

Steven's voice was level, controlled, the way it was when shit went south. "Michaela burned down the greenhouse. Sky almost killed her."

My heart raced. I was instantly alert. "Is she hurt?"

"She's bruised a bit, but nothing serious." He sounded incredulous as he said, "Michaela got the worst of it."

I switched the phone to my other ear as I fished fresh clothes from my dresser. "Is she still there?"

"She's gone. Sky is at the neighbors' house."

That was a mistake. If Michaela returned to finish the fight, she wouldn't hesitate to kill David and Trent to get to Sky, or to spite her. Eventually, Michaela would come for revenge. The only question was whether Demetrius would join her.

So much for the trip.

"I'm on my way."

I texted Tim to find out if the fire or the fight had been called in, then remembered the time. I'd have to assume a call had been made. Steven would know how to control the situation, but that didn't stop me from getting there as fast as possible.

At nearly twice the speed limit, I only had a few minutes to bury my anger. Sky had ignored my warnings and possibly started a war. I had to talk some sense into her before she went after Michaela or decided to rebuild the greenhouse. She was stubborn that way, once she'd made up her mind. If I'd learned anything in my time with Sky, yelling at her only made her dig in her heels. I needed to calm down, get my emotions under control.

Focus on the problem.

The fire department was the first challenge. They'd realize right off that the fire was arson. That meant an investigation, questions. Teenagers, I decided, an isolated random incident. Sky caught a glimpse of them running away, but nothing identifiable. Not the easiest story to sell, but without an insurance claim the fire investigators would find it difficult to challenge Sky's story. The theory of a psychotic, vengeful vampire wasn't likely to come up.

There would be police as well, as there were with any fire call, but they'd defer to the fire investigator—unless the fight was reported, a distinct possibility. The only neighbors close enough to notice were David and Trent. The investigation might quickly get out of hand unless one of the pack's detectives caught the assignment. At this time of night, that wasn't likely.

I needed to get Sky aside, explain the story before the questions started.

Turning onto her street, I noticed a dying trail of gray smoke rising from her backyard and a notable absence of fire or police. The lights were bright at Trent and David's house. Through the curtained windows I could see people moving about, as if pacing. I parked in the driveway next to Sky's car and walked into her townhouse. Steven was inside, waiting.

Before he had a chance to say anything, I asked, "How bad was it?"

"Sky did some damage." He couldn't avoid a proud smirk, despite his worry. "I think Michaela underestimated her. Sky was about to stake Michaela when I stopped her."

That was no small feat. Next time, Michaela wouldn't underestimate Sky again, and there would be a next time. Sky should've let the greenhouse burn and left it at that. Instead, she'd nearly killed Michaela, who was not the forgiving sort. Fortunately a war with the pack wasn't in Demetrius's interests, but she could be patient when it came to blood. She'd whisper in his ear for years until she steered him onto a violent path, or she'd just take her revenge and cover her tracks. Demetrius would stop her if he could, but I doubted he'd give her up or even punish her after the fact. If she was determined to start a war, she'd probably get it.

"Have you called Sebastian?" I asked.

"Not yet. I figured I'd wait for you."

"I'll talk to him. Let our people watching the Seethe know to stay awake."

The pack kept a low-key surveillance on the comings and goings of the Seethe. It wasn't round-the-clock, but frequent enough to catch any major developments on their part. We'd have to increase the surveillance until we were sure there would be no retaliation. With any luck, Michaela might take a short vacation to lick her wounds rather than show the Seethe how close she'd come to being killed by Sky.

Steven casually took a bottle of water from the fridge, retrieved his keys from the counter, then left. Glancing outside the window, I watched him give an appreciative glance at my GT before driving away.

Rather than join Sky next door, I decided to keep my interactions with the neighbors to a minimum. They'd be asking a hundred questions. I had no idea how she was answering them, but I didn't need the same questions thrown at me. Better to wait. She'd come home eventually, and I needed the time to push my anger even further down. She'd be expecting a fight. I wasn't going to give her one.

I was starting to lose my patience when I heard someone outside, whispering. Striding to the front door, I was surprised to find David fondling my GT like he'd just discovered love. Next to him, Sky's hair was drawn back into some bastardized version of a fishtail braid, as if a child had done it.

He squatted down to examine the Savini wheels on gunmetal titanium rims.

Sky gawked at him in disbelief. "I think when you ogle something like that, you should buy it dinner first."

"Sorry, it's gorgeous."

"Thank you," I said, startling them both.

David jerked upright. For a moment, he blinked at me, then glanced away rather than hold my gaze. Sky gave me a sheepish frown, anticipating a reprimand and an ensuing argument.

"Gotta go, Peaches," David declared, catching Sky by surprise as he hugged her tight. She winced from the pressure around her ribs. The triggered groan was quickly calibrated to sound amused, but her pain was obvious. She didn't want me to know that she'd probably broken a rib or two in her fight with Michaela.

I walked back into the house and waited at the kitchen counter, leaving the front door open for her. She took some time before joining me to get her dander up for a fight. I was still struggling to hold my anger and worry in check, but the unguarded surprise in her expression at my comforting smile was worth the effort. There was no point in being predictable.

She glanced back to the front door, as if she might've walked into the wrong house.

"Hi." Rising from the counter, I gently slipped a finger under her chin and examined her injuries. A small cut swelled beneath one eye and blood still smeared her lips, streaking across her pink-bruised cheeks where she'd attempted to wipe it away. Her shirtsleeve was torn near the shoulder.

Self-conscious, she stepped back from my touch, glanced into the hallway. "Where's Steven?"

"Gone. I wanted us to be alone."

Her gaze narrowed at me, waiting, but I remained silent. Sky didn't like silences; they annoyed her.

After a long minute, she blurted, "She started it."

Still smiling, I circled her once. "*Você estás magoado?*"

She hesitated, surprised. I'd been studying Portuguese for months without telling her, as a surprise. It was a language she'd only shared with her adoptive mother, who'd passed away several years ago, killed by the vampires that had tried to kidnap her.

When she didn't answer, I thought I'd spoken wrong.

"Probably a broken rib," she admitted, reluctantly raising her shirt to show me the bright red lines that wrapped around her side. One rib was slightly out of place, rising above the others beneath her skin.

Listening to the slight hesitation in her breath as she inhaled, I knew she was in pain. She handled it well. Training with Winter had given Sky plenty of experience in dealing with injury. Pain was a temporary state, to be tolerated rather than coddled. Unless silver was involved, we healed quickly.

I laid a gentle hand against her side, intended as comfort. The warmth of her fingers wrapped around mine, guided my hand over the displaced bone. A slight shiver rippled beneath my touch. Her skin was hot to the touch. At the slightest pressure, she hissed, scowled.

I asked softly, *"Você quer um pouco de gelo?" Do you want ice?*

Defiant, she pretended to not understand.

Humoring her, I repeated in English as I slowly walked around her, "Do you want me to get you some ice?"

"No."

"Do you need anything?"

"No, I'm fine."

"Good." Taking her wrist, I gently guided her to the sofa in the living room. "Let's talk."

She sat, still defiant as I chose the oversized chair across from her, leaving an ottoman between us.

"So at what point of the day did you decide that your life wasn't complicated enough and you needed to start a war between us and the vampires?"

"She destroyed my property!"

"Did she?" I heard my tone hardening. "Or did she destroy something of Quell's? You don't require a greenhouse nor do you have a use for Hidacus, do you?"

"It was something on my property for Quell," she insisted. "Michaela destroyed my property. How can you all just allow her to behave like this? She does whatever she wants with impunity and everyone just turns their heads because it's Michaela, the otherworld's psycho bitch, and she gets a pass. Well I am not going to give her a pass."

"She's also the Mistress of the North and responsible for creating the most vicious of her kind. Yes, she warrants certain consideration. But you didn't answer my question, what exactly did she do to *you?*"

I moved to the ottoman, surprising her. "Skylar, answer me," I pressed. "What did she do to *you?*"

She remained silent, glaring, but I saw through her defiance. There was no need to repeat my argument.

Shifting the conversation, I asked, "What exactly are you doing with him?"

"What do you mean?"

I held her gaze for a moment while she searched my expression. "I want a real answer, Sky."

"We're friends, nothing more, nothing less."

It wasn't entirely the truth. Their relationship was far more complicated than it should be. "If he is your friend, then you need to make better decisions to ensure that he stays alive—or whatever vampires are. You've played your hand. She knows how much you care for him. Michaela would rip off her own nose to spite her face and isn't above killing him just to get back at you."

She uttered a slight gasp at the thought, knew it was true. "Okay."

Rising, I walked to the door. "If you have another one built, you won't have to worry about Michaela destroying it. I will." I left before the yelling started.

CHAPTER 4

I woke at sunrise to a text message from Sebastian. He was already at his office at the retreat, waiting.

I took a quick shower, dressed, and skipped breakfast. On my way to the front door, I picked up the keys to my GT from the entryway table and froze. Next to the keys was a cheap black folding cell phone I didn't recognize. From the sticker on the cover, an obnoxious yellow face smiled up at me. Suppressing a growl, I remained perfectly still, listening. The angry thump of my heart echoed in my ears, but beyond the steady hum of the refrigerator and the faint ticking of a clock upstairs, the house was silent.

Whoever had infiltrated my home had left no discernible scent.

Checking the doors, I found no sign that the locks had been picked. The windows had not been forced open. After searching the entire house and finding nothing, I considered that magic had been used, but that would've left a trace.

I returned to the phone, already certain what I would find. Flipping it open, I called the only number in the address book and waited. Each unanswered ring brought me closer to hurling the phone against the far wall. When the call finally connected, I didn't wait for the voice on the other end.

"McClintock," I growled. "You've got my attention."

Through his voice I could see his smug grin. "Thought I might."

"Why the theatrics?"

"Thanks to you, I had to burn my old phone. Can't have you tracking me."

"If you have a point to make," I snapped, "make it."

"Here, now, I thought I made my point clear just yesterday." An edge crept into his voice. "Last chance. Hundred thousand buys my forgiveness for your unprofessional transgression."

"No chance."

"Ethan," he sighed decades of pent-up exasperation, "you know how I feel about you."

"You don't like me."

"I do not like you, but I've always respected you. I'd never put myself between you and a target."

"Shit happens. Get over it."

"I figured you'd be a prick about this. Had to give you a chance. Fair warning, I already took the other job."

"If you're so desperate for cash, I'll give you ten dollars to tell me how you got into my house—twenty more to tell me how you masked your scent."

"Tonya sends her regards."

He killed the call.

I stared down at the flip phone before I twisted the two halves into separate pieces. I'd missed something. No matter how pissed he was, extortion wasn't McClintock's game. He also didn't make hollow threats. Breaking into my home was his way of letting me know he was serious. There was a piece of the puzzle I didn't have. I didn't like not knowing what.

Glancing around, I'd have to do a more detailed sweep for listening devices, maybe explosives.

"I don't have time for this."

I was halfway to my Venom GT when I noticed the tires were completely flat, all four of them.

With some effort, I unclenched my jaw to growl, "Tonya."

Unlocking the garage, I was relieved to find the tires on the AMG were undamaged. A short drive later, I turned onto the retreat's private road when I answered a call from Claudia.

"Ethan, I might have a solution to your vampire problem. Can you come by the gallery today?"

"I'm going into a meeting with Sebastian. Give me an hour."

"I look forward to seeing you."

"Me too."

I parked in the garage and found Sebastian in his office. Winter, Steven, and Josh joined us. I looked to the door, expecting Gavin.

Winter explained, "He's out looking for Kelly."

"Still no word from her?" I was beginning to wonder if he was right. "Has anyone checked out her house?"

"It turns out Gavin has a key," she said with a cocked eyebrow and a droll voice. "He says nothing is out of place. Since he's stalking her, I guess we can assume he'd know."

Steven added, "She hasn't been at her dance classes." Taken aback by our surprised, suspicious looks, he quickly explained, "Gavin told me."

"There's a surprise." Winter grunted. "I'll bet he can describe her tap shoes down to the individual bits of glitter."

Sebastian interrupted, "She's entitled to her privacy." In giving Chris to Demetrius, Kelly had taken what she saw as a moral stand against the pack, against Sebastian in particular. I didn't agree with her then, or now. She'd put him in a difficult spot. He'd come down hard on her. He figured he'd pressed too hard, frightened her. I knew he blamed himself for her skipping town. Up to now, I believed she'd skipped town as well, but the questions were beginning to mount.

He gestured to me. "Steven told me about the jackal."

"Probably a wanderer," I answered. "We let him know he'd wandered into the wrong backyard. By now he's probably out of town."

Steven informed me, "Sky's neighbors said they'd seen some strange animals in the subdivision behind their house. Based on their descriptions, it sounds like our jackal and maybe a lynx."

"When?" I demanded.

"A few times over the last week."

I wondered why Sky hadn't told me, then remembered I'd walked out on her last night. If the jackal had a friend, there were probably more. If the friends shared the jackal's special ability, we might have our hands full.

"The jackal used magic," I informed Sebastian. From his lack of surprise, I knew Steven had already shared that part of the story as well, but Josh was hearing the news for the first time, and he didn't like it—like he needed another reason to resent me.

Winter said, "There must've been a witch nearby."

"We'd have smelled it."

Josh demanded, "Describe the magic to me. Don't leave out any detail, no matter how small."

"It was a transport spell." I'd seen Josh use the same magic a hundred times, but I humored him. After my description, he nodded surprised agreement.

"Samuel?" Sebastian asked Josh.

"Could be Samuel has new allies," he answered, reading my mind. "I doubt he's sitting around waiting for us to make a mistake and leave the Clostra books unprotected."

I added, "He might try to use Sky as leverage."

Samuel had already tried holding my brother hostage. That hadn't worked out well for him. He wasn't dumb enough to dip into that well twice, but he was desperate. His entire existence seemed to be wrapped in his scheme to use the books to rid the world of magic.

A rush of panic passed through me as I became acutely aware of her absence. I turned to Steven. "Where is Sky?"

Winter answered for him. "Gavin recruited her. I saw them leave earlier this morning."

I relaxed a little. Gavin was a pain in the ass, but he was one of our best fighters. He'd never wanted her in the pack, but he'd risk his life to protect her.

I said, "I'll make some calls, see if I can find where this magic-using jackal came from. Shouldn't be too hard to track down with a wide enough net."

I'd put the word out coast to coast, if necessary. Once I found the jackal's origin, I could follow his path to Chicago and figure out who he was working with.

"We have another problem," I said, meeting Sebastian's gaze. "I assume you've already heard."

Winter smiled, impressed. "Sky nearly killed that psychotic bitch."

"The Mistress of the Seethe," I clarified.

"Yup. That one." She glanced at her fingernails, sighed, "Sky must have an excellent teacher."

She took notice as Sebastian stated, "We're not fighting a war to preserve the Lost One's right to botany."

"I put Marko on the Seethe," I said. "There's been no movement there."

Winter suggested, "Michaela was probably too embarrassed to tell anyone."

I agreed, but remained quiet while Sebastian thought through the ramifications. "We've given Sky every opportunity to bring this Quell situation to some kind of resolution that she can live with."

Steven said, worried, "She thinks she's preparing him for

her absence, making him independent. From what I've seen, they're only getting closer."

Winter's nose wrinkled. "What does she see in him?"

"A pet," I growled. Turning to Sebastian, I asked, "Do you want me to kill him?" Sky would never forgive me, but I'd do it to protect her.

"What about Michaela?"

"It solves a problem for both of us. She won't like it, but she'll see it as a political act, not personal. With any luck, she'll forget about the fight with Sky and go off to create a new psychopathic plaything."

Sebastian considered carefully. Despite his cool affect, I'd been in on too many hard meetings with him not to recognize that the issued worried him. Killing Quell was practical, but we'd be robbing Sky of an important lesson, alienating her in the process. If she couldn't learn to let the vampire go, she'd find some other lame pet to protect.

"I'll talk to her," he decided. "If she doesn't heed my warning, we'll have to act."

I nodded. He was being more than fair, though I wasn't sure Sky would see it that way. I'd warned her until I was red in the face, but she trusted Sebastian more. Unlike me, he didn't yell. I wondered if she'd learned yet that the more quiet our Alpha became, the more dangerous he was. He was never more dangerous or angry than when he smiled.

"I may have another solution to Quell," I said, remembering. "Claudia."

He leaned back in his chair, surprised. He nodded.

Claudia's gallery was in the heart of Chicago. Walking in, I noticed an attractive woman admiring a recent addition, a marble statue of Icarus reaching for the sun even as his wings melted. Her ethereal beauty struck me. For a moment, I thought she was fae. Even before her scent gave her away, I caught her humanity in her honey-colored eyes. Sensing my attention, she turned, offered me a barely shy smile.

"Ethan," Claudia declared, joining us. I took her gloved hands and air-kissed over her cheeks. "How good to see you. Fiona"—she turned to the woman—"this is my godson, Ethan. Why don't you join us?"

"Of course."

Uncertain what my godmother had in mind, I followed them as Claudia led us into her office. The small table had only two seats. While Fiona and Claudia sat across from each other, I stood patiently in front of her desk, wondering just what my godmother had in mind.

"Fiona just moved here from Colorado," she informed me. "She's been coming to the gallery every day for the last month."

"I've never seen such a beautiful collection," Fiona admitted. A silence hung in the air as she waited for a response from me. I could hear her heartbeat climbing a ladder as the pressure built in her to fill that silence. "Your godmother has been very kind to entertain my questions. I didn't know much about Chicago when I arrived, but Claudia has made me feel right at home."

"The city can be a lonely place," Claudia said comfortingly, then turned to me with an innocent look. "I believe we both know someone Fiona would like to meet."

Taking in Fiona's elegant heart-shaped face, her flowing blond hair, the similarities to Sky were obvious. Claudia's time wasn't worth spending to find Quell food, and neither was mine. I stared back at her, folding my arms over my chest.

She peeled off a single glove and placed her bare hand over Fiona's. My arms unfolded, my hands absently falling to my sides. Claudia was letting me know that there was something important about this woman. She didn't use her powers lightly.

"Fiona, give us a moment, dear."

"Of course."

Fiona politely excused herself and left the office, closing the door behind her. I listened for her breath behind the door, but she'd stepped away into the gallery, honoring the request for privacy. Confused, I looked to Claudia for answers.

She explained softly, "Her mother was a witch. The youngest of five, she's inherited no abilities, but she is familiar with our world."

"What is she doing here?"

"She thought she was in a relationship with a vampire in Colorado, but it became apparent she was only property. She chose flight rather than be controlled." A look of concern blanketed her expression. "I'm afraid she has an incorrigible fascination with vampires."

"You want me to give her to Quell?"

She smiled an amused rebuke, declared, "I want you to introduce them."

If she were anyone else, I would've walked out of the room, but Claudia never did anything without a purpose. Her wisdom gave her the respect of all of the factions. Even Demetrius deferred to her. Despite my uncertainty, I knew better than to discount her. I waited respectfully as she continued.

"The Seethe's garden grows lost souls. Fiona's fascination is more intellectual. I believe it's a vampire's immortality that draws her. She won't fear him or worship him, which will appeal to Quell, and they are both intellectually inclined."

"He's still a vampire."

She observed, "He has a reverence for women that is unusual."

"He does not consider his attitude as reverence."

"Well, he wouldn't be the first to lie to himself." She thought for a moment. "I've grown rather fond of Fiona. I'd hate for something to happen to her, but I fear she's going to get herself into trouble unless we can steer her in the right direction."

"Tinder?"

She ignored the remark, waited.

"He has difficulty with control," I reminded her. I'd be walking her into a death sentence. "He's killed at least three women."

"When it comes to matches, you'll have to trust me." Claudia slipped on her glove, silently reminding me of their importance.

If she was right, Quell would have someone other than Sky to obsess over, making him less of a threat to her and the pack. Claudia's interest was obvious. If left alone on her path, Fiona would likely choose another vampire who would abuse her. In that, Claudia was right; Quell was unique. He didn't want to kill. I still believed he would eventually fall to his true nature. Apparently Claudia agreed with Sky that he might be redeemable.

She watched me closely. "Will you make the introduction?"

Claudia rarely asked anything of me. While I didn't share her confidence, I trusted her. "Of course."

"The sooner the better, I think."

I'd have a hard time getting Sky on board with the introduction. She'd ask a lot of questions. She'd be protective and try to manage the encounter, if she even agreed to the attempt. Better I made the introduction without her. Sebastian would have her full attention tonight, for a couple hours at least, while they talked over dinner. I was pretty sure she'd run straight to Quell after receiving her warning.

"How about this evening?"

"Sebastian has lost his patience, hasn't he?"

I nodded as she rose from the table.

"I suspect Fiona is ready. I'll talk to her and get back to you about the arrangements."

Fiona was quiet in the passenger seat of my AMG on the drive to Quell's farmhouse. She wore a pink flounced shirt over parchment skin and a pair of blue slacks. She half smiled to herself as she stared out at the passing soybean fields. Her heart rate was accelerated, excited and nervous, but no more than I would expect for someone being taken by a stranger to meet a blind date.

"You're not scared."

Her smile broadened. "Should I be?"

According to Claudia, Fiona knew exactly what she was getting into. Still, I found it difficult to swallow, delivering her into a vampire's arms.

"You don't have to do this."

Her eyes widened and she gave a nervous laugh. "I want to. You've met him. You know what he's like?"

I wasn't going to sell Quell. "You understand that he's a vampire." I took my eyes off the road for a moment to see the recognition in her eyes. "You understand that you're food to him?"

"Vampires are...complicated. They have friendships and romantic relationships just like humans."

I thought of Demetrius and Michaela, Chase and Gabriella. "Some people keep pigs for pets. They love them and care for them until they're ready to eat the bacon."

The humor in her smile faded. Clearing her throat, she turned away to stare out the window. I was playing out the same arguments I'd had with Sky, and getting the same results.

After a long, calming silence, I assured her, "I want to make sure that you're fully aware of the risks you are taking."

Her fingers brought her hair over one shoulder, teased

the ends. "Immortality gives them a unique perspective on life. The things we worry about—the petty annoyances and the desperate need to do something meaningful before we die—vampires don't care about that. They're not neurotic. They see the world for what it is, its beauty and its ugliness." She must've read my mind when she added, "I'm not naïve. I've seen vampires at their worst as well as their best."

Satisfied, I kept the rest of my opinions to myself, but I couldn't shake the nagging sense of responsibility for her safety.

She sat up straight, prepared herself as I turned onto Quell's driveway. I parked behind his dark-blue Subaru, then checked the tracking app on my phone to make sure Sky was still at the restaurant with Sebastian. By now, she was starting the meal with her dessert.

"If you change your mind for any reason," I assured Fiona, "I'll take you away. There's nothing he could do to stop me."

Something I said reminded her of whatever she'd left behind in Colorado. She replied with a grateful smile, but said nothing.

At a signal from me, she followed closely as I approached the front porch. The door opened before I could knock, revealing the vampire known among the Seethe as the Lost One. He stared at me hard, suspicious. Curiosity flashed across his visage when he noticed Fiona. His gaze fell back to me, waiting.

"This is Fiona. Sky wanted me to introduce you."

A lie, but using Sky's name seemed to set his doubts aside. I made note of the weakness. He glanced over my shoulder, noting suspiciously, "She's not with you."

"She meant to surprise you. At the last minute, Sebastian required her attention for pack business. Since Fiona was ready to meet you, Sky asked me to make the introduction."

His eyes searched mine, but I was a better liar than he gave me credit for.

"She'll come later on."

After a long moment, he introduced himself to Fiona with a pleasant but reserved tone.

"I'm Quell. Come in."

I sat on the edge of an ottoman. Fiona sat on the couch across from me. Quell joined her, leaving a respectful distance between them. He was uncomfortable, but curious, and the woman intrigued him.

"Fiona is a psychology professor," I said, sparking a conversation between them as they compared academic backgrounds. I didn't really enjoy the view, but at least I didn't have to participate. Still, I kept a close eye on them both, watching to make sure she was comfortable, that he wasn't losing control with her. Initially the weight of the conversation was on Fiona, but she skillfully put him at ease, drew him out. After a few minutes, Quell was holding his share of the conversation, asking and answering questions.

It was a long, tedious conversation. After the first hour, I could've left them alone, but I didn't want to miss the fireworks. Glancing at the tracking app, I noticed Sky was on the move, heading in this general direction. I smiled, waited. Soon I heard her vehicle pull to a stop on the gravel driveway.

By the time I stepped out onto the porch, she'd recognized my GT and started to back out. She stopped at the sight of me, scowling at me over the dashboard. Even without my enhanced hearing, I could make out the series of expletives she unleashed, banging on the steering wheel for emphasis. When she put an arm across the back of the passenger seat and peered out the rear window, I knew she was going to make her escape.

Before she could back away, I was beside her car, holding her door open for her. Her eyes narrowed at my extended hand. For a moment, I thought she would unleash another torrent of curses. I had a hard enough time keeping a straight face as it was. Eventually, her lips spread into a broad, mirthless smile. She took my hand and stepped out of her car.

I smiled back. "I'm so glad you are here. As if you could stay away." My fingers entwined with hers, I led her toward the house. She hesitated at first, then followed the pull of my grip.

"We asked you to stay away," I reminded her, "which undoubtedly ensured that you would be over here as soon as you could."

The excuses came quickly. "I hadn't heard from him in a couple of days. I was just checking on him."

"Of course. After all, him managing to stay safe and alive the seventy years he had prior to meeting you was clearly a coincidence. And he can't possibly take care of himself."

"I thought I heard Sky outside," I announced as we walked into the house. Quell and Fiona had moved to the middle of the couch, next to each other. She'd brushed her hair to the side, exposing her long, bare neck to him. Her attention was fixed on him, observing his every reaction as he greeted Sky with a genuine smile.

She paused, blinked as she glanced between the happy pair. A hint of jealousy passed through her expression before she suppressed it. The look she gave me could've killed a lesser man.

"This is Fiona," Quell said.

Sky greeted her coolly. "Nice to meet you."

I moved across the room, leaned against the kitchen counter for a better view. "Fiona is a professor of psychology at the community college nearby," I explained for Sky's benefit, glancing to Quell. "That was what you studied as well, am I correct?"

Judging by Sky's glare, that bit of information must've been proprietary. Claudia had her own sources.

My smile broadened at her irritation.

"Yes," Quell said, "that was what I studied, and when I returned I continued on to get my Masters."

"Returned?" Fiona asked him, surprised. "From Germany? Ethan told me that you were involved. What branch of the military?"

Sky threw a hot look at Fiona, who pretended not to notice. Sky muttered miserably, "I guess we're telling everyone about us now."

"Army, ground," Quell admitted, a long story revealed within the bounds of two simple syllables. Suddenly unable to meet Fiona's gaze, he took on a distant look as if viewing some distant battlefield.

Fiona finally caught the rebuke in Sky's glare. Fiona's smile faded as she instinctively scooted back into the couch, demonstrating her intention to hold her ground. When her smile returned, it was cautious, annoyed. She inquired of Quell as she possessively slid her hand over his, "Freud, what do you think: genius or unjustly revered idiot? There have only been a couple of times I wished I were a man and they all were during a road trip when I couldn't find a restroom. Other than that, I'm pretty happy with what I have."

The vampire laughed, a surprisingly deep rumble, before engaging in a lively debate. Claudia was right. The two were a perfect match, and they knew it. Sky didn't appreciate the pairing, but Fiona might just save Quell's life, assuming he didn't lose control and kill her.

As the conversation quickly devolved into a discussion of minutiae, I took Sky's arm and gently led her toward the door.

"Sky and I are going to leave," I announced, adding as I opened the door, "Quell, Fiona's the coach for the debate team, good luck."

I opened the door, glanced over my shoulder as Fiona mouthed a thank you. My hand on Sky's waist, I felt her turning to stay and hustled her outside. On the porch, she turned away from my touch, glowered at me. I pressed my fingers to my lips.

"We don't need an audience," I said, a barely audible whisper.

She yanked her arm from my grip and stormed toward her car. I followed, leaned against the front end as she opened the door.

"Okay." I sighed, rolled my eyes at her. "Go ahead with it. This should be entertaining."

Watching her lips twist in rage, I realized I'd underestimated the depth of her attachment to Quell.

"Go on, Sky." I stiffened. "Say your piece so I can go home, it's late."

"If it's past your bedtime, then shouldn't you be at home instead of trying to pass off one of your half-night stands to Quell? How insulting it must be for her to have you give her away like a free sample with purchase."

"I haven't been with her. If you have a problem with Fiona and her interaction with Quell, discuss it with Claudia. She's the one that considered them a good fit. She's the one that wanted me to introduce them."

Sky rolled her eyes at me. "Funny, how did she find out about it? Did you run to Mommy and tell her that I wasn't doing what you wanted me to do? Did I miss the tantrum?"

I started toward my car. "You should hope that his interest in you is redirected to her."

"You will not do anything to him, or—"

"Or what, Skylar?" I turned on her. "What exactly will you do? Yell? Not speak to me? Get into a little huff? Run off and hope none of the many people you've pissed off find you? Go ahead, tell me exactly what you plan to do!"

"Ethan," she said softly, her tone cautious or frightened. "I swear, I have this. This is *my* problem and *I* will handle it."

"But you're not handling it!" I snapped, walking up to within inches of her. "This is getting worse." I looked away, checking my temper. After several slow breaths, I said, "I can assure you I don't want to deal with this. Quell means nothing to me. I could go in there right now, kill him, and not give it a second thought. But he means something to you, so I'm trying to get this Michaela situation under control."

She bristled at the name.

I rested my hand over her hip and silently gathered myself. Snapping at her wasn't going to help. After a moment, I inched closer to her, softened my voice. "Are you jealous of Fiona?"

"So she's supposed to be my replacement? It will not change anything between Quell and me, we are friends. That will not change."

"Answer the question."

Frustration and doubt played in her eyes as she struggled to explain. After a long moment, she shook her head, but that wasn't enough.

"I need to hear you say it," I said.

"No."

Her heart betrayed the lie. My hand fell from her waist.

"Am I telling the truth?"

"You want it to be the truth," I said over my shoulder as I walked toward my car. She might even believe it.

"We're friends," she insisted, following me. "I care about him. I want to keep him safe and I want to make sure he doesn't hurt or kill anyone when he feeds. Why is that wrong?"

I stopped, turned, my gaze downcast as I battled with my disappointment. When I looked up, I saw a flash of something behind her watching from the fallow field. Resisting my instincts, I forced my body to relax while I kept the field in my peripheral vision. The jackal's long snout and dark stripe gave it away.

Sky realized something was wrong.

I whispered, "Do you see it?"

She turned her head slightly, just enough to catch a glimpse of the jackal out of the corner of her eye.

"Is it the same one?" I asked.

She gave the slightest of nods.

"How fast can you change?"

She licked her lips. "Not as fast as you can."

My attention directed at Sky, I shifted my weight, opening my stance in the process to give myself an uninhibited line toward the were-animal.

"In your car," I whispered. "Cut him off from behind, okay?"

She was bringing out her keys when I broke toward the jackal, sprinting. In three strides I'd changed midair into my wolf. Behind me I heard Sky start her car and put it into drive.

The jackal turned to flee, but too late as Sky drove into the field and cut it off. Faced with the challenge of her car or my wolf, he chose the latter.

We circled each other, lips drawn back, baring our teeth. Something about the jackal was off. Its movements lacked fluidity, like an animal new to its skin. It barked a challenge. I answered with a howl and then we charged, leaping in the air toward each other. I snapped at its throat, my teeth gnashing empty air as the jackal disappeared mid-leap. Landing on all fours, I glanced around for signs of the jackal, or a nearby ally that could explain the use of magic. Sky looked as well, standing outside her car.

The feel of magic lingered in the still air. There was a scent to it, like death, or something unnatural. From Sky's screwed expression, I knew she'd caught the scent as well.

After a moment, I changed back into my human form and walked toward her. Only when she sucked in air and tried to avert her eyes did I remember that I was naked. The hint of a smile twisted my lips as I enjoyed her discomfort, a brief reprieve from fresh worry.

From the trunk of my car, I retrieved a pair of boxer shorts. I usually kept a shirt and pants as well, but I hadn't planned on Tonya sabotaging the GT. As I slipped on the boxers, Sky informed me, "I saw the jackal at…earlier, when I was with Sebastian."

The jackal had just climbed to the top of my to-do list. It was stalking her, but why? I needed answers, fast. Magic was the only clue I had to work with.

"Go home, Sky."

She watched me as I eased in behind the steering wheel. She was safe, for now. The jackal would assume it was hunted. It would go into hiding, at least for the night. When it emerged depended on how badly it wanted Sky, and why.

"I need to see Josh," I said, then sped away before she could ask questions.

Once back on the road, I called Steven, asked him to keep an eye on her. He was the only one who could without arousing her suspicion. The last thing I needed was for Sky to hunt the jackal on her own.

CHAPTER 5

After three unanswered calls, I turned off the road to Josh's ranch house and headed for the pack's club. As the manager, he spent most of his nights there. The job was a perfect fit for his personality—too perfect. His hands-on approach to entertaining the club's patrons often led to excess. At some point, that life was going to catch up to him. I'd often wondered if my warnings only encouraged him.

A long line of hopeful entrants complained as I strode past the queue, past the bouncer. The vibration of a hard techno base beat engulfed me as I stepped through the door into a black-lit night. Early, the club was already bustling, the dance floor crowded. Thanks to Josh's touch, the club was now a premiere attraction for Chicago's social elite, from old money and CEOs to celebrities. The club provided the pack with a wealth of valuable connections, and information.

A look from me and the bartender gestured toward the back of the club. As I followed her gaze, a rowdy group cheer rose from the roped-off VIP room there. Walking around the dance floor, I saw Josh downing a shot to the delight of a small, captive audience, men and women dressed in black tuxedo t-shirts. Finished, he held up his empty glass, wrapped it in his fingers. He opened his hand again to reveal the glass had disappeared. Captivated, the audience watched closely as he reached behind a woman's ear and revealed a new glass, whiskey included—her glass. The classic magician's sleight of hand, misdirecting the audience's attention from the actual trick. In this case, the trick was actual magic. Josh had transported his original glass into my palm. With all eyes on his hand behind the woman's ear, he'd transported her glass into his hand. The woman gaped, the audience clapped, as he drank her shot.

I scowled at the unnecessary risk, his excuses already ringing in my ears.

At my approach, a delighted murmur spread among the group. It was almost casual until one of them—the drunkest—loudly declared, "The strippers are here! Woooo!"

Josh turned, grinned at me. "I think they want you to dance."

"I need to talk to you."

"Come on, Ethan," he teased, "show them your moves."

I leaned closer. "That wild animal we're looking for, it's tracking a friend of ours."

His smile faded as one of the men gasped, "A wild animal is on the loose!"

"I hope it's a sexy werewolf," said another.

Another said, "I'd rather a sexy vampire."

The group laughed, then launched into an intense and graphic debate.

Forgotten by his audience, Josh led me to his second-floor office. The door closed, the noise of the club grew instantly dim. The soundproofing did little to stem the pulsing vibration beneath our feet.

He asked, "Are you sure the jackal is after Sky?"

"It tracked her twice tonight, different locations. The last time, I nearly got my teeth into its neck before it transported away." I continued while he paced his office, chewing absently on his nails. "It's not a natural creature."

"What do you mean?"

"There's something off about it." I couldn't put my finger on it. "The magic isn't right."

He smirked behind an accusatory look. "I'd hate to challenge your knowledge about were-animals using magic."

I ignored the taunt. "I don't think it comes by its magic naturally."

"Agreed." He returned to pacing. "With Ethos dead, there aren't many who could pull off that kind of magic. Samuel, maybe, if he had help. A Tre'ase, more likely. We don't know what the ceiling is on their magic."

I growled, "Logan."

Josh paused, turned to me with a determined look. "He has motive. At least he thinks he does."

Sky had gone to him to remove Marcia's curse. Chris had been the price. I guessed he wanted her to fulfill some twisted Tre'ase fantasy. He couldn't just compel her, which meant there were at least some limitations on his magic. He'd instructed Sky to use the *servus vinculum* spell, which replicated the master-slave relationship between a vampire and its creator. Since the spell could only bond a vampire to a human, Logan couldn't use it himself, but once Sky turned Chris into a personal slave, Sky could order Chris to obey Logan, effectively making the Tre'ase her master. It was an ill deed. That Sky had agreed to the bargain had been a sign of her desperation, but Machiavellian politics didn't sit well with her. When she couldn't go through with the spell, Logan had been furious. He'd claimed she'd broken their bargain, but Sebastian had called Logan out on his bullshit. He hadn't removed the curse. Sky hadn't taken anything she'd been obliged to pay for. Still, he felt hard done by. The jackal could be part of some intricate revenge plot.

Josh continued. "We should at least talk to him."

My answer was immediate, more from habit than resolve. "No."

"If Logan isn't involved, he probably knows who is."

Involved or not, a conversation with a Tre'ase was always dangerous, more so if he had the information we wanted. The price he'd exact would be tempting, but buried in the details was always some lurking horror waiting to be unleashed the moment the bargain was sealed. Nothing Logan could offer would be worth his price, and he had a way of teasing out an unwitting agreement. Even at arm's length, he was dangerous.

"And if Logan is behind the jackal," I declared, "we'll be walking into a trap."

"He's not trapped in his house anymore. If he wants to get his hands on Sky, he doesn't need to draw us to his front door."

My arms folded over my chest as I weighed the potential rewards against the risks. I couldn't wait around for the jackal to play its hand. Logan was my best lead—my only lead. Josh wasn't ignorant of the risks involved. He'd made his own assessment.

He pressed the issue. "Logan could also narrow down your list of Tre'ase that might've created Maya."

I met his gaze, weighing his judgment. At the least, a visit to Logan could flush him out into the open if he was behind the jackal—we'd know who we were up against. At the worst, the Tre'ase would trick us into a bargain that would enslave some or all of us to him, forever.

"Agreed," I said, surprising Josh.

For a moment, he remained suspicious.

"We'll have to go in force." I sighed as I fished out my phone from my pocket. "We'll take Sky with us."

Josh bristled. "Why?"

"If he is behind the jackal, there'd be no better time to move on Sky than when we aren't there to protect her."

"And if he is behind the jackal, you're going to deliver her like a meal on wheels."

I stiffened. "If he wants to harm her under my nose, let him try. Meet me tomorrow morning at the edge of Logan's property."

"The cul-de-sac?"

I nodded. "Eight sharp. Be ready for anything."

The next morning, I parked my black Maserati GranTurismo in Sky's driveway and waited. A moment later, she emerged from the townhouse carrying a drawstring tote. She eyed the car with a sly smile. "I guess the saying is true," she said as she slid into the passenger seat, "'the difference between a man and a boy is the cost of their toys.'"

I glanced over my shoulder, backed out of the driveway. "You and I both know that this car isn't the only difference between me and a boy." Once on the road, I glanced at the tote in her lap, noting the muted orange glow of the Aufero within. "Why did you bring that?"

Surprised, she frowned at the glow that had betrayed her. "I brought it just in case."

"Josh said it was responding oddly and making it difficult for you to use the magic."

"It is, but if we are dealing with Logan, bad magic is better than no magic."

That was my brother's argument—reckless—but I didn't argue the point. She was anxious, looking for security. "Josh will be there."

Her jaw shifted slightly, and her shoulders relaxed as relief replaced some of the tension in her body. Leaving her alone with her thoughts, I focused on the road. It wasn't long before the silence between us became uncomfortable. The furtive glances started. She was building to a question, something important to her. She wasn't one to hold back long. When the question didn't materialize, I started to worry.

"Go ahead with it."

"With what?"

"Your breathing increased, you're blinking less, and your heart rate has increased, short inconsistent bursts. This always happens when you are frustrated and have something you want to talk about. Talk."

"Okay," she said, nodding. "Well, I know this guy, let's call him E, and he has this really creepy and weird skill that freaks everyone out. He counts physiological responses. He's a total freak. And it doesn't help that his mercurial ways are off-putting and he's kind of a jackass, but doesn't seem to care. If he doesn't change his ways, I think he is going to die alone. What should I do?"

"Sky," I chuckled, "ask your question."

"Have you heard from Fiona?"

I wondered when that would come up. "Yes."

"Is she okay?"

"We didn't talk long; she was still at Quell's when I spoke to her this morning." I glanced at Sky, reading her reaction.

She let the news sink in, weighed it, before answering. "Good." There was a finality in her tone, determination. Claudia might have actually found the perfect match for Quell and saved his life in the process, but Sky couldn't let him go. She was going back to him at the first opportunity. I glanced out the side window, suppressed a growl. My fingers clenched around the steering wheel. There were plenty of risks ahead of us, confronting Logan. I needed her focused. An argument now could only be a dangerous distraction.

Struggling to brush my frustration aside, I sighed and searched for anything to break the tension. Dark clouds in the sky were breaking apart, revealing clear blue. "Looks like it's not going to rain," I said, fumbling. Sky was too lost in her thoughts to notice. I turned my attention to Logan. At our last meeting, he'd taken an uncomfortable interest in me, probably due to the dark elf magic. Relieved of that curse, I hoped he'd behave himself. Brushing that concern aside, I focused on the road.

With each isolating mile, houses grew scarcer, until signs of civilization were limited to the occasional decrepit barn or shack. Despite Logan's newfound freedom, he preferred to live in seclusion. The paved road gave way to crunchy gravel as the cul-de-sac came into view. Josh's Jeep Forrester was there, parked next to Sebastian's black SUV. They watched our arrival, standing next to the barrier that declared, "Private Property." Beyond that, a twisting gravel path disappeared into a dense forest of high grass, shrubbery, and willow trees.

"Stay alert," I said as Sebastian led us onto the path that forced us into single file. If Logan meant us harm, the narrow path was perfect for an ambush. At my direction, Sky fell in behind me while Josh took up the rear. From the slight crackle in the air, I knew he kept his magic close at hand.

Silent, we followed the path into the gloomy darkness of the forest until the trail ended at the door of a small brown cottage shrouded beneath protective foliage. At our approach, the door slowly creaked open to reveal no one behind it. Was Logan being creepy or just lazy, or was this the trap? Sniffing the air, I caught the base scent of the Tre'ase, and someone else—human, female. The added scent was faint, a recent visitor or someone trying to cover her scent. Sebastian and I exchanged knowing looks before he walked through the door into Logan's kitchen. I took an extra look around, peering through the dense foliage before following.

Logan waited just inside, leaning against a counter, next to a rack of drying dishes. A smug smile spread across his lips. He'd changed since I'd last seen him, but that was one of his magical talents. Anything was better than his true visage. The horns and twisted facial features were gone, replaced by flowing chestnut hair and chiseled good looks. The off-putting lavender eyes remained. Like Josh, Logan loved his body art. Beneath his crisp button-down shirt, his torso and arms were covered, but the tattoos were more than decorative. His magic resided in them. Little of the body art was visible beyond the sleeve cuffs, but I kept an eye on them. Josh did as well.

At the sight of me, Logan's heart raced toward excitement. He pushed off from the counter, approached me slowly. I couldn't tell if he was being cautious or just savoring the moment. As he approached, his breath quickened. His pupils dilated like eclipsed moons. The tattoos on his arms shifted and rolled. So, not the dark elf magic then. Josh eyed the interaction with a silent rebuke for me. I held back an annoyed sigh, refusing to be provoked as I endured Logan's game until he reached out a tentative hand to touch me, as if he wasn't sure I was real.

"Step away," I growled, glaring down his wide-eyed wonder.

Either he missed the warning or found it exciting. His hand continued toward me until I gripped his wrist. Logan blinked at the speed of my movement, but there was no fear there.

"Now."

He scrutinized my expression like a child appreciating a feisty pet. I held his gaze, unblinking. He didn't have the common sense to look away. In a were-animal, I'd take that as a challenge. Sky watched our interaction, confused and worried, while Sebastian casually shifted his weight toward Logan, ready to strike.

After a long moment, his smile broadened and he went back to his counter. From there, he studied us once more. His gaze darkened as he took in Sky. Immediately, the glow in her tote bag caught his attention. His head tilted. His weight shifted as if to approach her.

I shook my head once, slowly.

He relented, turning his attention to Josh. Looking my brother up and down, Logan seemed to regard Josh's magical ability with amused appreciation.

"Let me see what we have here," Logan said. "The Midwest Alpha, Beta, and their witch." He frowned at Sky. "And my betrayer."

She bristled at the accusation. "I didn't betray you."

Unmoved, he turned his attention to Sebastian. "To what do I owe this pleasure?"

To the point, he stated, "I need your help."

Logan snorted. "I am sure Ethan has informed you that I am all out of favors for you. And now that I know your pack can't be trusted, I choose not to enter into any agreements you will not honor." His voice deepened as he turned a snide look to Sky. "I definitely do not care to do business with you."

"We aren't going to bitch fight about how 'wronged' you feel by Skylar's alleged betrayal," Sebastian said. "It was a foolish agreement anyway. If you knew her, there isn't any way you'd have thought for one second she was going to give you a person as a pet, so get over it."

Logan's jaw set. The tattoos peeking from beneath his cuff came to life once more, this time moving in a frenetic fashion. Beneath the magic tempest roiling around him, his glamour flickered, revealing flashes of the grotesque creature beneath. "We had an agreement and she reneged."

His magic began to gather around Sky. I tensed, prepared to charge. He was too close for me to shift, which left me vulnerable to his magic. I'd only have a second or two to get my hands around his neck. I'd have to go for the quick kill.

Logan sensed the threat. Before either of us could react, Sebastian put his anger on display.

"You want to screw Chris," he snapped, pacing, gesticulating to draw Logan's full attention, "seduce her like anyone else. Don't pull us into your sick little perversions. Please don't think for one moment that I am naïve enough to believe you only wanted her for companionship, you sick bastard. The subject is moot. I am not giving you a fucking person. And I advise you, if you plan to try seducing her, this look—get rid of it. Looking like Ethan is not going to help you get in her bed any faster than the way you probably look without your little glamour."

"You know what I want." Logan folded his arms over his chest and threw a pointed glance toward the door. "If you're not going to give it to me, there doesn't need to be any further discussion."

We didn't budge.

Logan relaxed as an idea occurred to him. He raised a finger, declared, "If not Chris, then Winter."

Sebastian's lips spread into a violent sneer. For once, Logan felt fear. His heart betrayed him, though he did his best to look bored as he leaned against the counter, sighed. His power wasn't limitless, after all. Sebastian noticed, pressed the advantage. His pacing took on a wilder tone, like he might lose control if pushed too far.

"Okay," Sebastian shouted, "let's get all this out of the way so there isn't any more of this foolishness. I am not giving you anyone, whether it be Chris or Winter. No one. Period. We can be mutually useful to each other. You seem to be enjoying your new freedom, which is only possible because of us. Do you think curses are just magically removed because you willed it? We did that. Just as easily as we removed it, we can restore it."

Logan scoffed. "Do you expect me to believe you had anything to do with the curse being removed?"

"We have the Clostra, so yes, we had everything to do with it."

That put a dent into his smugness. He covered his fear with a show of admiration, but Sebastian had found his weakness. Logan had spent a long time trapped in his home and didn't want to lose his newfound freedom. "How did you manage that?"

"We have two of them and access to the third if we need it."

A lie couched in truth. Not quite convinced, Logan's magic receded. His tattoos stilled. Sebastian responded accordingly, softening his tone and his movements. Logan would investigate our claim, find out we did in fact possess two of the books. That was likely enough. I doubted he'd hunt down Samuel to find out if we really did have an arrangement to share.

Sebastian declared, "I think we can help each other."

"What do you want?"

"Are you able to find out who created a particular spirit shade?"

"Yes."

Sebastian nodded. "Good."

Anticipating a bargain, Logan's excitement returned. Magic filled the room once more as his tattoos came back to life.

I caught a worried look from Josh.

A Tre'ase was most dangerous when a bargain was being struck.

"And if I can do this for you," Logan said carefully, "what do I get in return? Do you accept this as an obligation you must fulfill?"

"No," Sebastian stated. "If you can find it, you will remain as you are, free to roam the city, the world, without restrictions. If you don't—" He shrugged, an implied threat. A bluff built on the prior lie. He took a seat at the kitchen table, clasped his fingers behind his head, and stretched out his legs in front of him, meeting Logan's glare with a calm indifference. "So, are we going to do this?"

"Give me a week," Logan declared flatly. "I am flattered by your confidence in me, but this isn't something I do often and it requires a few days to prepare."

"You have three days. I am quite confident you can make it happen in that time frame. I trust that you will not betray us or try to leave without doing this. Am I correct in my assumptions?"

Logan rolled his eyes, admitted, "I enjoy my new life."

Sebastian grinned.

"Are we done?" the Tre'ase asked.

Taking the opportunity to further annoy Logan, Sebastian made a slow glance about the room as if deciding whether to stay awhile. After a moment, he rose with a bored sigh and walked into the cozy living room. Anger flashed across Logan's visage. Before he could interfere, I was next to him. He chose to endure the intrusion, smoldering. He'd already given the game away. The woman was here, in the house. Given the Tre'ase's intentions for Chris, we weren't going to walk away without investigating.

His body stiffened as Sebastian approached a closed door on the other side of the room.

He pressed his ear to the door, demanded of Logan, "Who's in here?"

"That isn't any of your concern."

"Of course."

Sebastian opened the door and walked inside.

Logan threw me a hostile glance, but withheld his protest. The Clostra gave us leverage. He stewed at the murmur of conversation drifting from the other room. A female voice, calm. After slight encouragement, Sebastian emerged with an attractive young woman dressed in an oversized shirt. Her gaze was distant, her manner torpid. Was she under the malaise of his spell, or was her dullness her natural affect? He couldn't bind a human with the *servus vinculum* spell, but there could be other ways.

At the sight of her, Sky sucked in a sharp breath. Josh's anger manifested in the magic gathering at his fingertips.

Logan's scowl deepened. "She's not here against her will."

Josh asked the woman, "Do you want to leave?"

She answered with a slow shake of her head. "I want to stay here, with him." She looked to Logan for confirmation—perhaps permission—but her posture was no more tense than it should be when confronted by a group of scowling strangers. Her heart rate was surprisingly calm. She wasn't lying, nor was she looking to us to find some hidden plea in her words. She was confident in her desire.

There was no accounting for taste, but she'd made up her own mind—at least until she'd seen the real Logan.

Sebastian, Josh, and I exchanged silent agreement.

Sky remained skeptical, waiting for Sebastian to take the woman's hand and lead her out of the house. When he started for the door, Sky's confidence collapsed. I nodded toward the door, directed her and Josh to follow Sebastian out. Confused and reluctant, she fell in line behind him, but the hard set of her jaw told me she wasn't ready to let the situation go. Following her out, I noticed the vein in her neck begin to throb in time with her rapidly increasing heartbeat, as if the threshold we'd crossed had been some kind of moral barrier.

Stepping off the porch, she scowled back at the house, then me. The moment she heard the door click shut behind us she turned back. My hands on her back, I gently steered her toward the path.

"She wants to be there," I whispered. "You can't take her, Sky."

"But—"

"But, nothing. The topic isn't up for discussion. You can't

make her decisions for her. She wants to be with him. Period."

"She doesn't know what he is, and I am sure that if she did, she would want to leave. I just need to talk to her."

"That is what you want to believe, but it doesn't mean it is reality. You feed a vampire regularly, something most of us find reprehensible, but it is what you choose to do."

She reacted, stunned. "Stop doing that!"

My tone deliberately soothing, I asked, "Doing what?"

"Just stop it," she growled and caught up with Josh a few feet ahead.

The journey through the woods continued in silence. I understood her desire, empathized with it, but it wasn't our place to stop the woman from making a foolish mistake. Once we reached the cars, Sky followed Josh to his Jeep. I followed, intending to pull her aside and explain why we'd left the girl with Logan when a familiar scent fouled my nostrils. Sebastian and Sky caught the scent just before the jackal emerged from a shroud of foliage a few feet away. Magic swelled around it, racing toward an explosion. I reached for Sky to pull her behind me when the jackal vomited a blast of magic from its maw.

The force of the blast hit like a wave, threatening to topple us. Josh slammed into the door of his Jeep, winced but kept his breath, an incantation on his lips. The rest of us kept our feet, barely. Before the jackal could strike again, Josh raised his hand. A shimmering wave of magic enveloped the jackal, squeezed it. He grimaced with effort as another gesture drew the were-animal toward him.

Unable to break Josh's spell, the jackal let out an angry howl. Growls and snarls surrounded us as six were-animals emerged from the woods. I recognized the snow leopard, the Beta of the Ares Pack. With him were two wolves, a puma, a coyote, and a lynx. I guessed Anderson was making his move, but where was the rest of his pack? I wondered if he was making a simultaneous move somewhere else, like the retreat. Suicide, but he wasn't the most strategically sound leader.

The leopard uttered a low, rolling growl at Sebastian as they locked gazes. In two strides, he transformed and crashed into the leopard, driving it back. Its claws flailed against Sebastian's flanks as he threw the leopard to the ground.

I placed myself in front of Josh and Sky as the rest of the Ares closed in around us. Josh was the most vulnerable, his magic largely useless against were-animals. The Ares were in for a surprise if they underestimated Sky, but she wasn't experienced in fighting multiple attackers. If the Ares focused on her, she could be overwhelmed. I shifted into my wolf, dug my claws into the ground, growled a final warning. One of the wolves feinted, tried to draw me away. Failing, it turned back. The two wolves attacked simultaneously from either side, but their timing was off. One of them should've gone low. Pivoting, I leapt to the right, catching the neck of one of the wolves in my jaw while the other wolf leapt, catching dirt for its trouble. Biting down, I twisted, letting the wolf's momentum snap its neck for me as it fell.

I dropped the deadweight, turned as the other wolf crashed into me. We rolled, snarling and snapping for each other's necks until we were back on our feet. From the corner of my eye, I saw the puma had backed Sky and Josh against the Jeep. She shielded herself with the tote bag as the puma reached out to rake her. The canvas ripped open. The glowing orb spilled out. Sky snatched it back before it hit the gravel. Wielding the orb like a rock, she struck the puma's snout. The were-animal cried out from the blow, stumbled sideways. Sky followed up by driving her boot into the puma's ribs. Snarling, it raked her across the leg, ripping through her jeans, drawing blood.

The smell of it drove the other were-animals into a frenzy.

I noticed the lynx closing in on Josh just before the surviving wolf tackled me to the ground. Its jaws snapped at my neck while my claws scraped at its belly. Sensing victory, the wolf ignored its wounds, worked to close its jaws around my throat. I turned, twisted, until I snapped at the wolf's leg. The wolf yelped. Taking advantage of the distraction, I pushed the wolf off me and scrambled to my feet, toward Josh and Sky.

The wolf barred my way, its snout low to the ground as it bared its teeth and growled. Behind it, the puma lunged at Sky. Using the orb once more, she smashed it into the side of the puma's head. The puma fell, stunned. Letting out a ferocious roar, Sky leapt onto the were-animal, straddled it. The two struggled as she scrambled for a clear shot at its head. Behind her, Josh desperately threw rocks at the lynx, buying time while the lynx waited for an easy opening.

I fixed my gaze on the wolf between us.

Before I could strike, the air filled with dark magic. The jackal's high-pitched bark drew the fight from the were-animals. The wolf backed away, as did the lynx. The puma pushed off Sky, leaving her vulnerable to a counterattack, but the puma ignored her. It scrambled to its feet and disappeared into the woods with the other were-animals.

Glancing at Sebastian, I noticed the coyote's blood-drenched flank before it limped into the woods. He shifted back into his human form, glanced down at the snow leopard's corpse at his feet.

The jackal was nowhere to be seen, but that wasn't surprising.

Josh remained alert, magic shimmering around him as he reacted to the dark magic dissipating around us. "What the hell was that?"

My gaze shifted to Sky, to her tattered shirt, the splotched blood on her jeans. A panic rushed over me until I recognized the blood was minimal. Her wounds weren't serious, but they would need tending.

Sebastian calmly retrieved a pair of pants from the backseat of his car and began to dress, while I retrieved a change of clothes from my Maserati. "The snow leopard was the Beta of the Ares Pack. Anderson will want revenge for me killing his second-in-command."

He met my gaze. Had Anderson committed his pack to the ambush, he might've overwhelmed us. Where was the rest of the Ares Pack? Why had the jackal called the attack off? Now that Sebastian and Josh had experienced the jackal's magic directly, they understood the anomaly of it.

Sebastian stated, "We need to pay Anderson a visit."

I placed the keys to my car into Sky's palm, watched the set of her jaw as she pushed the keys into the pocket of her jeans and started toward Sebastian's SUV.

"Be careful going home," I said, barring her way.

She blinked at me for a moment. For once, she didn't put up a fight. After some residual hesitation, she turned and walked to my car. She glared at me from behind the wheel as she revved the engine. A rush of panic flooded my cheeks. The GranTurismo was an expensive high-performance vehicle, more power than she was used to driving.

I said, my voice deliberately soft, "Drive carefully."

I winced at the horrendous grinding noise as she put the car into reverse and backed up a few feet before stopping. Still glaring, she grind-shifted her way through the gears looking for first. Once found, the car lurched forward. I stared aghast as she scrapped the rims against the curb on her way out of the cul de sac before finally driving away.

On the drive into the city, I made a few calls to find out if Anderson had made another move against us. He hadn't. After a few more calls, I informed Sebastian, "Gavin and Tim will meet us there. They'll bring reinforcements." After some thought, I added, "Anderson might be behind Kelly's disappearance."

Josh was surprised. "We think she's been kidnapped, now?"

I scowled. "It's worth considering. He might've taken her for intelligence." Outside of our medical facilities, she didn't have much more to offer. We'd always been careful to keep her out of the pack's inner workings, for exactly this reason.

"Sable threatened Kelly," Sebastian stated. "To hurt Gavin."

That was a surprise—more so that Gavin hadn't told me. I took in the new factors, weighing how that changed the situation. The news increased my newfound fear that Kelly might be in danger. Anderson was a fool, but he wasn't cruel. Sable was a psychopath, a trait she'd displayed well before becoming a vampire. Her obsession with Gavin made her even more unpredictable.

Sebastian continued, his eyes fixed on the road. "Sky told me at dinner. I talked to Sable, and to Demetrius. She admitted to the threat, but denied following through."

By his flat tone, I knew he wasn't convinced.

"He should've said something." As the head of security for the pack, I'd a right to know of any threats to our members, and allies like Kelly. Her safety was my responsibility as well.

"I'll address the issue."

The chip on Gavin's shoulder didn't always make him amenable to correction. I suspected Sebastian would find a way to get his point through.

The Ares Pack leased an old warehouse in the city. I knew the location because the Midwest Pack bought the property six months ago. Since I'd retained the same property management firm, Anderson didn't even notice the transfer in ownership.

We arrived to find a pair of police cars parked in front of the warehouse, lights flashing—Tim and three other officers who were pack members. Tim and Anderson appeared to be having a conversation. I counted thirty behind Anderson, facing a dozen more of mine that included Gavin, Winter, Marko, and Steven. A lot of tense, angry faces watched our SUV as Sebastian casually brought it to a halt next to the police cars. Sebastian, his jaw set, emerged from the SUV as casually as if he were out to dine. Josh and I followed.

Most of the Ares grinned at our approach like they'd just found a mouse in a trap. They held faith in their numerical advantage, but our were-animals were stronger, faster, and immensely more skilled at fighting. I knew we had enough on hand to permanently deal with the Ares, should Anderson let the situation escalate. Anderson himself looked just as confident as his pack, but looks were deceiving. The presence of the police had rattled him. That the officers were were-animals belonging to a rival faction didn't matter. If the officers were harmed, the rest of the Chicago police would come for revenge, precisely why I'd invited Tim. I intended to use every bit of leverage available to nip Anderson's ambitions in the bud. So far, he hadn't done any real damage. If the pack could be saved, it would be.

I scanned their faces, searching for a stranger. My own magical ability gave me the ability to sense the magic of others. If the jackal was among the Ares, its dark magic would be apparent. Josh was making the same survey.

Sebastian walked directly up to Anderson, who stood his ground. Shorter by nearly a foot, he stared up at the Elite. His chest puffed out and his shoulders pulled back. In contrast, Sebastian was calm, clinical. They stood like that for a long, quiet moment, staring, unblinking, Alpha to Alpha. For all his bravado, Anderson's heart pounded. If violence broke out, he knew he'd be the first to die.

When his pack stirred, impatient, Anderson signaled

them to sit tight. Looking at those chomping at the bit for the taste of blood, I wondered if he had enough control over his pack to keep them in line.

After a long, tense quiet, Sebastian finally spoke. "Your Beta is dead at my hands."

The muscles of Anderson's jaw rippled as an angry murmur passed among the Ares. Sebastian offered no excuse, no justification, no reason for Anderson to accept the offense. Either he responded with a challenge, as his pack expected, or he was weakened before them. He knew that challenging Sebastian meant a fight to the death. Anderson had to know that his chances of success were nil. Judging by the buzzing anger of the Ares, it seemed their Beta was popular. I wondered if Anderson wasn't happy to be rid of the competition, but that didn't explain their alliance with the mysterious jackal.

For a moment, I thought Anderson was going to fall victim to his mob and issue the challenge, until he visibly relaxed. His shoulders dropped. He nodded once.

"I heard. Benson stepped out on his own initiative. I'd known nothing about it until a few minutes ago. The others thought they were following my orders. They're blameless."

Sebastian turned to Josh and me. I answered with a slight shake of my head. Josh did the same. The jackal wasn't here.

Sebastian pressed the issue with Anderson, his tone unforgiving. "What is your relationship with the jackal?"

"Not one of us. A stray Benson picked up. He wasn't Ares, never would be."

Sebastian answered with a dangerous smile. "A diplomatic answer."

"I'm not lying."

"No. Your statements were carefully chosen. Tell me everything you know about this jackal."

"That's easy." Anderson gestured broadly. "I don't know anything. Didn't like him, didn't ask. I don't know where he came from, where he's going. I couldn't even tell you if he lifts his leg when he pees."

Again, he wasn't lying, but there was a lot of daylight between his statements.

Sebastian stared Anderson down a moment, just to make him uncomfortable. "I have a claim on the jackal. If Ares encounters him again, notify me at once. Don't try to apprehend him on your own. You're no match for him."

Seeing the insult strike home, I allowed myself a hint of a smile.

Sebastian continued, his smile broadening. "If I find out you've failed in your obligation, there will be consequences." When Anderson nodded, Sebastian gave his attention to the rest of the Ares for the first time. "Your ranks are growing."

Anderson shrugged. "We picked up some strays recently."

"You're creating were-animals."

"A few," he lied. "There's no rule against making."

"There is now, until I say differently."

"For everyone," Anderson asked, indignant, "or just Ares?"

Sebastian assured him, "Just Ares."

Anderson asked, emboldened, "Does the size of my pack worry the Elite?"

"In the same way I'd worry about an overflowing trash pile."

Anderson stiffened. The gallery of were-animals made some noises, just enough to be heard without consequences. Staring them down one by one, I saw the real fight had left them after they'd already seen their Alpha acquiesce to the Elite.

"You're growing beyond your ability to control your pack," Sebastian said. "Prove to me you can control your pack and I'll consider allowing you to grow further."

Sebastian cut Anderson's authority with a surgical blade.

"Keep your people in your own territory. The next time

one of your were-animals gets near Sky or any of my people, I will hold you personally responsible."

"Well, I see your point," Anderson stammered, "but this is all just some minor misunderstanding. I assure you, the Ares Pack is no threat to you."

"No. It isn't. Are you working with Samuel?"

"The witch?" he asked, genuinely taken aback. "Even if I knew where he was, I'd stay away from him. He's a fanatic. Ares has no share in his interests. If I hear anything about him," he added, "I'll be happy to let you know." He threw an anxious glance toward Tim. "I hope you'll call off your dogs."

"You have a lot of people here," Sebastian noted. "Where do you park your cars?"

Anderson frowned, confused. He pointed to the ware-house. "Some inside, the rest out back. Why?"

I gave Tim a look. He stepped forward with a smile.

"We'll be happy to take a look around," he told the two Alphas, "make sure everything is properly licensed, lights all working, etcetera—for the public good."

Anderson exclaimed, "Shit."

Sebastian nodded to Tim, gestured for the rest of the Midwest Pack to leave, then led us back to the SUV. Once inside, Sebastian looked to me.

"I'll put more eyes on Ares," I said. "I'll also put the entire pack on notice about the jackal. If he hasn't fled Chicago, we'll find him."

Sebastian nodded, then started the engine.

made the necessary calls from home. While others helped spread the word, I turned my attention to my other problem. So far, I'd let McClintock play his little games, but that was about to change. He'd made himself a proper pain in the ass and it was time for me to return the favor. First, I needed to put some obstacles in his path, slow him down. Sean made for a less-than-perfect obstacle, but steering him into the elder hunter's path would be simple. Another hunter might consider McClintock a mentor. Sean's arrogance made him hyper-competitive. Anne, the only other hunter in Chicago, was small-time, hardly a threat to him, but Sean had spent the last month spreading rumors and lies about her. He wasn't going to suffer competition, ever. With any luck, Sean might already be onto McClintock's presence.

An hour later, I drove into an affluent Chicago neighborhood popular with young professionals. Sean's camouflage-painted Ram Macho Power Wagon was parked outside a cluster of luxury townhouses. I shook my head at the gaudiness of it. Most hunters didn't like to announce their presence until they had their prey in their sights—not Sean. He might as well drive a clown car that played Little Brown Jug on an endless loop.

His townhouse was at the back of the cluster, on the other side of a courtyard. An opulent fountain gurgled as I walked past. Peaceful, except for the loud techno music blasting from Sean's home. As I approached his porch, the front curtains snapped open, revealing a young man with short-cropped dyed-blonde hair that stood on end. Sean wore a camouflage button shirt split open to reveal pale, hairless skin. Grinning, he fluffed his pot belly with both hands until he saw me coming. The joy drained out of his smile. His hands dropped to his sides. A second later, he snapped the curtains closed, as if I hadn't already met his gaze.

Not quite the reaction I expected.

The music grew louder by a couple decibels. I was about to pound on the door when a feeling came over me. Either Sean was going to pretend to not hear me, or he was using the music to cover his escape. I walked around the townhouse in time to find Sean, a duffle bag in hand, locking his back door. He'd taken the time to button his shirt, at least.

My approach startled him.

"Is there something you need, Charleston?" he stammered. "I'm a busy man."

"You remember me." I scowled. "I'm flattered."

"I never forget a grouchy face. I'm really sorry about this, but I have a strict autograph policy—between twelve and twelve thirty only. If you'll excuse me..."

I remained in his path, unobliging. His heart raced as he glanced about, as if expecting were-animals to appear from the shrubbery. I noticed his bag, the bit of white underwear poking from the closed zipper—he'd packed in a hurry. "You're running."

"From you?" He chuckled nervously. "I'm on a job. When I'm on the hunt, I've got a singular focus." He made a slow slicing gesture with the edge of his open palm as he explained, "It's just me and the target, man. Everything else just falls by the wayside."

He was doing his best to tame his racing heart, soothing it with rising bravado.

"We'll catch up some other time, yeah?" He trotted down the steps, trying to skirt me. "I'll have my secretary call you."

I gripped his arm, held it in place. Glaring, I said, "For a hunter, you're behaving like prey."

Frowning at my grip, he jerked his arm free and took a step backward. "You know, don't you?" He rubbed a thumb across his forehead where sweat had started to bead. His heart raced like a Ford engine. "It's not what you think. Being a hunter, sometimes I have to do things that I don't agree with. I wasn't really going to follow through. It's just business, yeah? Don't make it personal." He repeated like a plea for mercy, "Don't make it personal."

If I just silently stared at him, he'd spill all of his petty secrets, but he wasn't worth my time. "You think Anne hired me," I stated. "You think we're mercenaries for hire, like you?"

He stammered something unintelligible.

I continued, putting his mind to rest. "She has no relationship with the pack."

"If that's…" He smiled, genuinely relieved. "So why are you here, exactly? Never mind. Duty calls." He pointed toward his waiting Macho Wagon. "I've got some really important shit to do. You don't even know. Can we skip to the part where you tell me what you want from me? I'll name you my price, which you'll call ridiculous, and then we can go our separate ways."

"You're focused on the wrong threat."

"What do you mean?"

If he knew about McClintock, Sean did well to hide his knowledge. The key was to answer his questions with small bits of information to see if he'd slip up, tell me something he shouldn't know. "There's another hunter in the area."

Disbelieving, he demanded, "Who?"

"McClintock."

His nose wrinkled at the name. "That old coot? Last I heard he was living on some island in Georgia. There's zero chance he'd come up here and earn himself a slice of this."

Sean proudly thumped his chest.

"You didn't know?"

He scoffed. "No."

"You haven't talked to him in the last few weeks, traded messages?"

"No."

I frowned, but the disappointment was expected. McClintock wouldn't waste his time with a bumbling hunter like Sean.

He thought for a moment, decided to shake off his indignation. "Probably doing some grunt work for Demetrius, tracking down pretty girls or something lame. I've got more important work to do."

"McClintock didn't come all this way to corral the Seethe's garden."

"You think he's making dough?" Sean read my silence the way I wanted him to. His cheeks darkened. "I'll tell you, there's no respect left in the world. He and I are going to have a little chat. Nobody hunts in my backyard without paying a tithe. You know where he's crashed?"

When I didn't answer, he remembered to fish in his pockets for something hard to find. "I appreciate the information. Here, one sec." He scrunched his expression as he dug deeper, dropped a pair of pennies to the concrete as he pulled out a crumpled handful of small bills. He counted, offered them to me. "The Seaninator always pays for good intel."

I glowered at the insult.

He explained as if embarrassed, "It's only eighteen. I usually pay twenty but there's a recession coming." He pushed the bills at me. "I'll catch you on the flip side for the rest."

"If you find McClintock," I growled, "tell me where he is."

He shrugged, pocketed the bills. His eyes brightened at the prospect of earning a profit. I expected the insistence that he'd find the hunter, that he needed to be paid, half now, half when the job was complete. It was all there in his eyes, another minute of my life gone to waste. Instead, he only nodded.

"That's it?" he asked, hopeful. "That's all you wanted?"

"I'll send Anne your compliments."

Walking across the courtyard, I determined to send some business her way—nothing important, or dangerous, but enough to keep her afloat while I quietly worked to squash Sean's rumor mill.

Approaching my car, I noticed a six-inch horizontal scratch along the driver's side door, like it had been keyed. Tonya. Glancing around, I didn't expect to catch sight of her, but I needed a moment to repress my anger. She was racking up a hell of a bill. Eventually, that bill was going to be paid. Glancing through the window, I noticed a white flip phone waiting on my seat. The door was unlocked.

I snatched up the phone and called the first and only number on speed dial. The call connected immediately. On the other end I heard a ragged breath.

I growled, "Don't push me, McClintock."

The quaking voice that answered surprised me. "Ethan." Artemis. "I-I'm sorry."

I tensed, barely stopping myself from crushing the phone in my hand. I listened for any sound in the background that might give away their location, but got nothing.

"I don't know how he found me."

"Put him on."

A moment later, I heard McClintock's smug drawl. "Hello, Ethan. We should probably talk about your little friend here. She's a plucky one, clever. I'd just hate to have to hurt her, but…you know how things are."

"You're trying my patience, old man."

"As I see it, as I've previously stated it, you owe me a hundred grand. Now pardon me if I'm jumping to conclusions, but I do believe you were going to have your police friends chase me out of town without you paying."

I shook my head. "Extortion was never in your repertoire."

"There's a big picture here, you just don't see it."

"Retirement? You're not exactly buying yourself security."

"Don't you worry about me. I'll be just fine. Shall we discuss the terms and location of the drop, or should I just put your were-fox out of her misery while I have you on the phone?"

His threat was accompanied by the distinct click of a pistol being cocked. In the background, I heard Artemis gasp.

"As a philosophical matter," he said, "you know I don't make idle threats."

I forced a calm into my voice, a hint of disinterest. "She's a contractor. If she got caught, she's no good to me."

"We both know that's a lie." He chuckled. "Artemis tells me you two go way back. You like this kid. I can see why. She's talented—don't think I caught her easily. She's got heart. She's got a sob story of struggle and redemption. She hits all your buttons, Ethan. For all your ruthlessness, you just can't help picking up a stray. For the sake of expediency, let's just pretend that I cut her, she screamed, and you dropped this pretense."

My wolf rode a surge of fury to just beneath the surface of my skin. "What do you want?"

"Like I said before, a hundred thousand. Cash, obviously. I'll call you in one hour with instructions."

"I don't have that kind of money lying around."

"One hour. Come alone. If I see anyone else in the area, I'll leave and I'll scorch the earth in my wake."

He killed the call, probably before I unleashed a string of expletives. Even if I had that kind of money accessible, paying McClintock off wasn't an option, but I couldn't just abandon Artemis, either. Checking the time, I called Tim, hoping he'd come up with something about McClintock's whereabouts.

"He's like a ghost," Tim said.

I gave Stacy, my legal assistant, the phone number I'd called from the flip phone, then sped like hell to the retreat. By the time I'd parked the car in the garage, she'd traced the number.

"Sorry, boss. I couldn't get a lead. That number only made the one call, and it pinged half the cell towers in Chicago in the process. No idea how. There hasn't been a signal since, which means it's probably powered off."

I threw the phone into the Maserati, watched it bounce off the seat and crack the passenger window before clattering into the well.

Returning to the retreat, I walked through the garage looking for Josh's Jeep. It wasn't there. Neither was his Ducati. *Good. One less thing to worry about.*

I found Sebastian lifting weights with Marko in the basement gym. He read my expression, toweled off the sweat, and led me back to his office.

"McClintock's becoming a problem." I paced in front of Sebastian's desk while he leaned against it, arms folded over his chest. "He's holding one of my informants for ransom."

He raised an eyebrow, let his arms slip to his sides as he gripped the edge of his desktop. "That's not like him."

It wasn't.

"He wants a hundred grand for her." I rattled off the possibilities. "He's looking to retire, gone senile, trying to pay a debt—I can't explain it. "

A debt—or some other leverage—made the most sense. Put someone under enough pressure, they'll do all kinds of stupid to survive. Only, McClintock wasn't just anyone. Hunting wasn't a job for the weak-minded. I wondered what it would take to push him over the edge.

I continued, letting out my frustration. "I've put the word out, but so far he's kept his head down."

"Tim?"

"Will run across McClintock eventually, but I'm out of time."

"Do you think he'll hurt the hostage?"

A matter-of-fact question that deserved a brutal answer. I sighed, admitted, "He'll have to. He's committed now."

Sebastian remained silent for a long time. When he finally spoke, his tone was measured—empathetic, but resolute. "The pack doesn't pay extortion."

I stopped, rubbed the stress from my forehead as I took in a calming breath. "I need enough to convince him the payoff is real, in case he inspects the money before I make my move. I have the cash in stashes, but not enough time to gather it. I'll cover anything that's lost."

"How much?"

"Twenty thousand—some big bills wrapped around bundles of small bills."

He didn't blink, but it was a tall ask. Artemis and McClintock were my problem.

"Which informant?"

He was doing the risk-reward analysis I'd make if I was advising someone else. She was a valuable resource, but she was also a mercenary working for the highest bidder. Her merchandise was information. For all her usefulness, she could just as easily sell me out, or the pack, if the price were right. Having spent her life as an orphan on the streets, she didn't fully give her loyalty to anyone, but she'd never turn against me. When a small pack of were-animal professional thieves tried to strong-arm her into scouting their marks, I sent them packing. When she'd drawn the amorous attention of a wandering vampire, I made sure her dust was scattered across a cornfield in South Chicago. For my help, I'd never taken cash or trade. For the information she provided, I paid well and on time. For Artemis, that made me family.

His fingers tapped against oak as he held my gaze. After what seemed like an hour but was probably less, he slowly pushed off from the desk. "I'll get you what you need. Who are you taking with you?"

Hiding my relief, I answered quickly. "Marko and Winter."

"You're sure that's enough?" he asked, meaning he thought I should take more were-animals. "He'll be expecting a trap."

"I'm going to give it to him."

He considered asking for more detail, but changed his mind. "Josh?"

"McClintock took Artemis to get leverage on me. I'm not going to hand him a shot at my brother." After a nod from Sebastian, I started for the door, hesitated. Josh wasn't my only vulnerability. "I'd prefer Sky doesn't know about the exchange or the kidnapping. She'll insist on being involved."

"Agreed."

I found Steven in the game room, playing air hockey with Hannah. "Stay close to Sky tonight."

He frowned, decided not to ask why. "We're having a movie night."

"Will she be suspicious if you stay over?"

It was an odd request coming from me, considering I'd never approved of his living with her.

"I'm still packing, so she's expecting me to stay over." He

rose, picked his jacket off the back of a couch. "I'll head over there now."

"I'll let you know when it's over."

He nodded, then left.

McClintock was expecting a trap, which meant he'd take every advantage to decipher what form the trap would take. Putting myself in his position, I'd go straight to the source. Once the location of the exchange had been given, I'd want to know how many were-animals left the retreat headed in that direction. Observing the comings and goings of the pack wasn't hard. It just took a camera with a cellular signal positioned to observe where the road leaving the retreat met the local highway. Random sweeps of the area were a regular part of the security routine, but usually done once a month except in times of crisis. Winter and I made a fresh sweep of the area. It only took me five minutes to find a camera strapped to a tree branch.

I turned the camera over, noted the serial number was filed down to a plastic smear.

Marko noted the hiding spot. "Didn't hide it very well."

"No," I growled. Too easy. "Keep looking."

After twenty minutes, Winter found another camera obscured by a shroud of foliage. As expected, the serial number had been destroyed.

Winter asked, "You think there's more?"

"Probably." I scrutinized the area, then checked the time. "But we're running out of time. We'll have to assume there'll be eyes on us when we leave. I want you and Marko to head out now, split directions here. Make sure you're not followed before you meet up at the staging area. I'll text you the location of the exchange once I have it."

"Is he paranoid enough to spoof a cell tower?"

I scowled. He was. Stingray devices weren't easy to

obtain, or cheap. A crypto phone could detect the spoofing, but I didn't have one—something to look into for the future.

She offered, "I can call Matthew."

He was one of the Worgen Pack. They were savvy and paranoid enough to possess both devices.

"No time. I'll wait to contact you until I'm away from the retreat." I checked the time again. "You'd better get Marko and get going."

After prepping the ransom money and stowing it in a blue designer tote bag, I decided to wait for McClintock's call in the retreat library. With Josh gone, it would likely be empty. While the rest of the pack used the library as needed, the collection of supernatural histories, rare compendiums, and old magical texts were not commonly needed. For Josh, however, the library was an oasis. His frequent and long visits led to jokes about adding on a bedroom for him. I shouldn't have been surprised to find him seated at the large oak table, bent over one of the Clostra books. He'd probably transported in. From his sour expression, he was as disappointed to see me as I him.

I started to leave when he announced, "Something's going on."

Forcing my stress to the background, I put on a casual affect and made a show of browsing the nearest bookshelf. I pulled one out, surveyed the cover. "What makes you say that?"

The legs of his chair dug into the Persian rug as he turned it to face me, legs splayed, hands draped lazily over his lap. He frowned. "It's bad, isn't it?"

I gave him a tired look, picked up another book. "You're paranoid."

"I have to hand it to you, Ethan. I don't think anyone is better at hiding their emotions. I'll bet you're even doing that controlling-your-heart-rate thing, even though I can't hear it. Don't bother." He slowly shook his head. "I've known you for too long."

Scowling, I snapped the book shut, returned it to the shelf. My arms folded over my chest as I waited for the rest of his speech.

Josh didn't disappoint. He gave me a sideways look as he declared, "You're not going to tell me. Let me guess, you're shutting me out in order to protect me?" I didn't give him the satisfaction of a reaction, but he continued anyway. "Aren't you tired of that? I am." His ocean-blue eyes turned midnight as magic filled the room. "Just how powerful does a little brother have to get to earn your trust?"

"You're the most powerful witch in the region," I stated. "It's your judgment I don't trust."

His square jaw set before he forced a casual shrug. "Perhaps I can convince you otherwise. In fact, I'll bet I can pick the perfect book for you. How about this one?" He made a subtle sweeping gesture with an index finger, and a book from the shelf behind him launched at my head. I pivoted easily, letting it fly past me and smack into the wall behind me.

"If you're looking to fall asleep, this will do."

With another swipe, a book launched at me from the shelf to my left. I slapped it aside, had just enough time to scowl at Josh before he launched another, a fat and rare encyclopedia that catalogued everything known about the various types of fae. I caught the book at my chest, absorbed the blow.

"Or perhaps you'd like a story," he growled, "something about a real prick."

"Enough," I shouted before he could swipe again. I walked up to the table and set the encyclopedia down. "If you're trying to show me your judgment has improved..." I stopped myself from continuing, changed tack as I watched the rising anger burn his cheeks. "I should've told you about the dark elf magic."

He blinked, stunned by my admission. The blue slowly returned to his eyes as his magic dissipated from the room.

"If it had been you," I said, "would you have sought my help knowing you'd be putting me in danger?"

His lips pressed thin as he struggled with an answer he didn't like.

"I made a choice. You don't have to like it. But you're right, I do need to trust you more." *Just not now.*

He looked away, turned back to give a mistrusting look. His eyes searched mine for subterfuge. He wasn't sure if he found it, but he calmed anyway.

"So," he said expectantly, "what's going on?"

My mind raced. I had to tell him something or risk another magical tantrum, but I wasn't about to let him join me in the exchange.

"McClintock."

Josh's lips pulled back into a so-what expression. "The hunter?"

I explained the hostage situation, and my plan to get her back, giving as few details as possible.

His expression hardened, determined. He closed the Clostra. "When do we go?"

Now the delicate part. "I don't need you at the exchange."

He growled, "Ethan…"

"McClintock's just pushing my buttons. He wants to see if I've gone soft. Once he realizes he's trapped, he'll leave with his tail between his legs."

Josh wasn't convinced. "You don't think he'll put up a fight just to prove something?"

"He's not the type to waste his energy on a hopeless fight." McClintock was exactly the type. He wouldn't put his life on the line, but he'd make sure not to leave the impression that he could be pushed around. Word traveled fast in our world. McClintock couldn't afford to just lay down at the first sign of trouble.

"Still, I should go with you."

I tapped a finger on the leather-bound Clostra. "You've got more important work to do."

"Why do I think you're playing me?"

"You worry too much. If I get into trouble, you'll be the first call I make." I clapped my palm on his back with a little too much force because I knew that annoyed him. "You can transport in like the cavalry."

I started toward the exit when the door swung closed on its own. I sighed, turned back to Josh.

"What if he's hunting you? This could all be a trap to get you in a vulnerable place."

"You think there's a bounty out on me?"

He winced with a smug smile. "You kinda piss people off."

I grinned. "He takes me and Sebastian will have every pack in the country on his scent. He knows that."

"Does he? He seems pretty crazy."

"I've known McClintock a long time. I know how he thinks."

"Do you?" Josh chided me. "Because he seems to have gotten the better of you so far."

Before I could answer, I felt McClintock's burner phone vibrate in my pocket, accompanied by an ominous-sounding musical march.

Josh gestured to my phone as I fished it out. "I know you're not into pop culture references, but that's Darth Vader's march from Star Wars. He just owned you with a ringtone."

I gave him a who-gives-a-shit look as I flipped the phone open. A text message flashed with GPS coordinates, followed by a simple message, *Come alone.*

While Josh looked up the coordinates, I texted them to Winter and Marko. I'd already informed them to approach from opposite directions and park at least a half mile out from the target. The rest of the distance they'd cover by foot, using whatever cover was available.

Staring at his laptop screen, Josh declared, "I don't recognize the location."

Looking over his shoulder, I did—Artemis's house, her sanctuary. She didn't have friends or family. No one dropped by or sent her cards. The location of her home was a well-guarded secret shared with none. Having lived most of her life on the street, she valued above all else the safety her privacy afforded. I'd only found the location after a great deal of effort and a bit of luck. McClintock was sending a message—nothing was safe from him.

Josh read my anger. "You know where this is?"

"I thought he'd picked her up off the street." I pointed to the screen. "He didn't connect me to Artemis and then find that house in one day. Someone helped him."

"Chris?"

I dismissed the idea out of hand. She'd left Chicago when she'd left Demetrius.

"You said McClintock and her go way back," he pressed. "Maybe she went back to him."

"She's got the Seethe on her tail. She's not going to alienate the pack as well. Besides, if she tapped into any of her old sources, I'd know." I started for the door. "Whoever he's working with, I'll find out."

Josh called after me, "All the more reason to assume this is a trap."

I turned, read the concern in his expression. "If I need you, I'll call."

He objected, but I was already out the door.

On the drive over, I retrieved my clear Bluetooth device from the compartment between the seats. Once I was set up, I put Winter and Marko on speaker phone and gave them the general layout of Artemis's neighborhood. "Best cover is from the east. Marko, that's your approach. Winter, approach from the south. You won't have much time to set up your diversion."

She answered, "All I have to do is kick a few rocks and whistle while I walk."

"Don't be obvious. Keep your eyes peeled. Tonya knows her business. She might not be the only one out there waiting for us."

"I brought a few surprises with me." I could hear the swagger in her voice as she declared, "By the time I'm done, they'll think they chased off the entire pack."

"Too much."

"Half the pack?"

Remembering something McClintock had said to me at the Dairy Queen, I said, "Two."

She sighed, suddenly bored. "Fine."

"Marko," I said. "Hole up about fifty yards out, wait for the distraction before you close in. Once the exchange starts, move in on the garden gate. There's no other way into the yard without power tools. Whatever happens in the house, you stay on that gate. McClintock doesn't escape."

He asked almost casually, "Lethal?"

"He and I have some things to talk about, but he doesn't escape."

"Understood."

I glanced at a passing street sign. "I'll check in when I arrive."

Half an hour later, I called them back. "Positions?"

Winter answered, "Ready."

Marko said, "Yeah. In the neighbor's backyard, watching the gate from behind a stack of firewood. Looks to me like this location is perfect for a trap on both accounts."

It was, indeed.

He continued, "Whoever goes in first is going to be at a disadvantage."

I didn't answer. The odds were against finding McClintock already inside, not unless he'd already cut and hidden a way out through the hedge. He'd had plenty of time to prepare, but I figured he'd make me wait, show up late after taking a good long look around.

I parked in front of a small, rundown rambler in the suburbs. The house was in a state of disrepair because no one had lived there for years. Artemis used it as a mail drop. Her quaint, one-bedroom home was just down the street, hidden from view by a shield of dense, seven-foot-tall privacy hedges. The only way through was the back gate tucked into the green wall.

"From here on, the line stays open."

Resisting the urge to reach up and press the Bluetooth deeper into my ear—and give away that I wasn't alone—I picked up the blue tote bag from the passenger seat and climbed out of the car. Wary of an ambush, I strode toward Artemis's hidden house. Would she stay there, once this was over? In her life on the street, she'd slept with one eye open, never comfortable. Nowhere was safe. The house was the oasis she'd never had growing up. McClintock had taken that from her.

Pausing next to the hedge wall, I listened for the occupants in the house. If I could count more than one, I'd know he was already there, in my trap. Faint, cheerful music played within, obscuring any other sounds. The hedges were too dense to allow the house or yard lights on the other side to reveal them. Peering through was impossible. I glanced at the ground, looking for footprints along the hedge, but found only animal tracks, a day old by the looks of it.

Winter whispered in my ear through the Bluetooth. "Ready to get this party of two started."

I whispered back, "Thirty seconds after the dialogue starts."

Warm light spilled through the gate. From there, I had a clear line of sight to the small brick house's kitchen windows, as well as the stone path that led around both sides of the narrow yard. The gate was unlocked, slightly ajar. Scuffs of dirt appeared on the first few entry stones, veering to the left path. In places, the smear was broken, revealing the presence of at least two pairs of feet. So McClintock was already at the house, or had been recently. It appeared he'd walked through the gate, but appearances could be deceiving. I took another tour around the hedge wall, tugging and pulling, looking for a secret passage. I sniffed, smelling for fresh-cut foliage. I found neither.

Pushing on the gate, it creaked open. I made one last glance over my shoulder before walking into the narrow yard and following the path around the house to the front door. For someone intent on avoiding visitors, I noted the oddity of the bright welcome mat on the porch, the plastic green wreath on the door.

From the porch, I listened closely. Hearing nothing unusual, I tried the door. The handle clicked. The door gently swung in. Light and music spilled out. Peering in from the threshold, I found the small, cozy living room empty. Couch, recliner, and coffee table were exactly where I remembered. Shelves were stuffed with books and the odd knickknacks that Artemis considered her treasures, mementos that told a life story she'd never share. A vinyl record played eerily from a turntable in the entertainment center.

I checked the base of the threshold for a trip wire, then walked inside to the turntable. The record complained as I lifted the arm, leaving the room in welcome silence disturbed only by the hum of the refrigerator—no heartbeat, no breath, no shifting of clothes. Wary, I walked through the kitchen, noting the empty sink, the clear counters. From the short hallway off the living room, I peered into the bathroom and the single bedroom. She was tidy, but there were simple signs of her presence—nothing to indicate a struggle.

My search complete, I was alone in the house.

The sudden, obnoxious Darth Vader music blaring from the living room drew me to a white flip phone tucked into the arm-pocket of the leather recliner. Scowling, I picked it up. The phone was heavier than expected, as if carved out of a brick of lead. I flipped open the phone, answered.

"You spend a lot of money on phones, McClintock."

"When dealing with wolves, one can't be too careful."

"I have your money," I growled, glancing at the tote in my left hand. "You coming in, or are you too scared to face me?"

McClintock chuckled. "Aw, you are right where I want you, Ethan. You can leave the bag on the ottoman, the one to your left."

My gaze flicked around the room until I settled on a camera duct-taped to an upper corner of the wall across from me.

I could hear the smug smile in his voice. "Aren't you going to wave?"

"This bag isn't leaving my hand until I have Artemis."

"That is what we agreed to, but first there's the little matter of your friends waiting outside."

I stared hard at the camera, refusing to blink, to twitch, to give him anything but steadfast contempt. So far, the team could only hear my side of the conversation. Winter had started her countdown, but he'd already spotted her. Or had he found Marko? I needed to warn them without tipping him off in the process. Deliberately relaxing, I let my hand with the phone slowly slide toward the Bluetooth in my ear while my thumb tapped the volume, maxing it out.

McClintock continued, "It warms my heart to see you haven't lost your arrogance."

"Spotting my trap doesn't change the fact that I'm still the one holding the money," I shouted for my team's benefit. If they heard me, neither replied.

"That's because you're dangerous," McClintock said, "when you're on your game. That's your weakness, Ethan. From here out, you do what I say when I say and nobody gets hurt. You get your were-fox back. Everybody walks away happy, your bruised ego aside. Now put that bag on the ottoman."

Still silence from my team. At least one of them was compromised and neither of them knew it. I placed the tote with the money onto the ottoman, using the dramatic gesture to hide shifting McClintock's phone closer to the Bluetooth so that they touched.

Winter whispered in my ear, "Now."

"You're compromised," I said aloud, giving up the game.

I heard some noise from her end, followed by whistling.

I snapped, "Winter."

"I'm practically traipsing through the woods," she complained, oblivious to my warning. "Nothing is happening."

Panic rushed into my chest, pushing the air from my lungs. I pressed the Bluetooth against my ear. "Marko! You're both compromised!"

Marko whispered, "It's gotten awfully quiet in there."

Winter answered him. "You seen anyone going in or out?"

"Nothing."

McClintock said, "Time to pay the piper, Ethan. After all, you broke your word. Pick one of them, preferably your least favorite."

Blood rushing to my face, I plucked the Bluetooth from my ear and shouted directly into it, loud enough for them to hear a block away, "You're compromised! Back off! BACK OFF!"

"Eeny, meeny," McClintock sang in a bored voice. "Miny, moe."

Marko's voice came from the Bluetooth. "Something's going down now. I'm moving in."

Winter answered, "Almost there."

"Bang," McClintock said.

A blast immediately followed that sounded like a cannon firing a single shot outside. I bolted out the door, racing around the house while pressing the Bluetooth back into my ear to hear Winter, an anxious edge to her voice.

"Marko?" she called.

His answer came as a distant groan.

I ran for the neighbor's fenceless yard. Behind the wood pile in the near corner I saw Marko laid out on the ground, blood gushing from a gaping wound on the right side of his chest. Forgetting my own safety, I rushed to his side, crammed McClintock's phone into my pocket, and used both hands to put pressure on the wound. Winter was beside me a moment later, sword in hand.

"Shit," she exclaimed. "The heart?"

I shifted my hands to fix the location of the wound. "No, but close. He's loosing too much blood."

All were-animals shared the ability to heal rapidly. Marko's wound should've already started to heal enough to slow the bleeding. The blood flow showed no sign of slowing. "Silver," I growled.

"We're sitting ducks out here," she said as she reached a hand under Marko, feeling for the other side of his wound.

"McClintock's gone."

"There are exit wounds." She frowned. "Small, several of them. A frangible round."

The bullet had broken up on impact, turning into numerous silver fragments, most of which were still in Marko's body. He wasn't going to live long unless we got the silver out. We needed to get him to the retreat's medical clinic, to Dr. Baker. I doubted Marko would survive the drive.

"Call Josh," I said, pressing harder on the wound to try to staunch at least some of the blood flow.

Blood gurgled from his lips as Winter made the call.

"Hang on," I commanded. "Josh is going to transport you straight to Dr. Baker."

He struggled to speak, straining with effort to manage one word, "S-silver."

"I know."

Winter clapped a palm against her phone, tried the call again.

The panic in my chest turned to dread. "He compromised your phone. Mine too."

She started to fish for Marko's phone in his pocket.

"Forget it. We need to drive, now."

Her eyes were reptilian slits as she declared, "He's not going to make it."

"The hell he isn't. Take over the pressure."

She pressed her palms over the wound as I pushed both hands under Marko, got my feet under me, and lifted. Grunting with the effort, I managed to jog with him in my arms and Winter awkwardly maintaining pressure. When we got to the Maserati, she let go long enough to fish my keys from my pocket and unlock the car. After I laid him across the back seats, she climbed in on top of him to continue pressuring his wound. I jumped into the driver's seat, started the engine. A few seconds later, I was speeding toward the highway.

I sped through a traffic light, relying on the Maserati's steering to weave through traffic. My eyes fixed on the road, I turned on the car's computer system.

"Call Josh," I said as I raced up the highway on-ramp and into traffic.

The computer tried to connect to my phone, failed.

Winter's voice was tight as she said from the back, "I don't think he's going to make it."

Marko gasped, "Ethan."

I shouted, "Hang on!"

Accelerating, I pushed the limits of what I could safely drive. Surrounding cars became slow-seeming obstacles to weave through. My entire being was focused on the road, the cars around me, hoping none of their drivers panicked and did something stupid like swerve in front of me. At nearly a hundred miles an hour, a collision would kill us all. Part of me knew the race might be futile. If Dr. Baker wasn't at the clinic, Josh would have to bring him. I doubted Marko had that much time, if he even survived until we reached the retreat. He was tough, wouldn't give up, but at some point the blood loss wins.

I let loose a string of expletives as I was forced to slow to take the turn onto the retreat's private road, losing precious seconds in the process. "How is he doing?"

"He's passed out." She felt for his pulse. "Heartbeat fluttering."

I accelerated into the turn and began honking my horn until I brought the Maserati to a quick stop that nearly sent Winter through the windshield onto the front lawn. Instead, she crashed into the back of the seats, barked a curse as she climbed back onto Marko.

Dr. Baker and a handful of were-animals—Gavin among them—rushed out of the house to meet us, quickly assessing the situation as I climbed out of the car and pointed with bloody hands to the back.

Winter remained in the car while Dr. Baker ran to my side. I pulled the seat forward for him to climb in. I backed away, breathing hard as I watched. I didn't even notice Josh arrive until he was next to me, taking in the scene.

He demanded, "Why didn't you call me?"

I growled, "Not now."

Dr. Baker waved Gavin and the others over to help him extract Marko and carry him to the clinic.

Josh got in my face. "I told you it was a trap."

I took two fistfuls of my brother's Sesame Street shirt, smearing it with Marko's blood, and pulled Josh to within an inch of my teeth. "I said, not. Now."

I pushed him aside and started for the house.

He called after me, voice taut with anger. "Sky was attacked."

I turned, glared.

"I tried calling you," he chided me.

Striding back to him, I resisted the urge to grip his shirt again. "Is she safe?"

He nodded. "Sebastian is with her."

"What happened?"

"Some lone were-animals tried to kill her, or capture her. That's not clear yet."

Ringing started in my head as my anger boiled over, pushing the edge of blind fury. "McClintock's going to pay for this."

"It wasn't him. Apparently they confessed to being hired by Sean. The rest of the pack is out looking for him now."

"Where is she?"

"Sebastian took her to a safe house, one I didn't even know about. He texted the address to both of us. I'm heading out now to take her some supplies and put up a ward."

I glanced at the trail of blood leading through the retreat's front door, then to Josh. "You're sure they're safe."

He nodded. "Steven was there, but she fought them off on her own. Apparently she cut off one of the attacker's arms with a sword. She wasn't wounded. If she had been, I'd have taken Dr. Baker to her."

Before I could ask for more detail, McClintock's phone rang.

Josh watched as I pulled it out of my pocket. I answered the call with silence.

That damn confident drawl that flowed like molasses spoke first, "Did he make it?" When I didn't answer, he said, "Thanks for leaving the money behind. You were a little light, but I won't fault you given the circumstances."

"You wounded him and drew me out in the open, but you didn't take your shot. You really should have."

"The parameters of my mission are to bring you in alive, if I can. Dead is fine, but alive pays better."

My lips twisted into a snarl as I realized, "This was never about a ransom."

"Hell no."

"You want to come for me, do it!"

"When you're ready, Ethan."

"All I need," I said between ragged, angry breaths, "is a time and place."

"You don't get it, I'm training you, son! Like a dog. I've got a crate right here, waiting for you when you graduate from McClintock University. I took your orphan, I took your money, and I killed your friend—probably; way I see it, it's your move now. I'm waiting, Ethan."

The call ended. Furious, I hurled the phone. It bounced off the grass a few dozen yards away. Immediately, my phone began to vibrate as backed-up text messages arrived from Josh and Sebastian. Voicemail alerts appeared on the screen. Realization dawned on me. Cursing the old man's ingenuity, I strode across the yard toward McClintock's phone, watching my phone as I went. I was within a few yards when the signal on my phone dropped. I stopped, stepped back, and noticed the signal return.

Josh appeared next to me, confused.

I snatched up the flip phone, handed it to Josh.

He felt the weight of it in his palm. "Heavy."

"The phone blocked my signal. Winter's, too. If I'd left it

at the scene, I would've gotten your messages about Sky. I could've called you to bring Marko here in time to save his life."

"How?" Josh turned the phone over, examining it. "How could it receive a call and block your phone at the same time?"

I said as I walked toward the front door, "Figure it out."

The clinic was chaos. Dr. Baker had recruited Winter to help him, but she needed too much instruction. She couldn't anticipate what he needed the way Kelly could. Glancing at the monitors, I saw the thin string Marko's life was hanging from, his heartbeat barely registering. Gavin and the others were gathered around, watching in horrified anticipation.

I turned my back on the clinic and walked back to the game room where Josh examined McClintock's phone on a table. His attention focused, he didn't notice me start to pace. I turned within, finding my rage building toward explosion. I'd failed at every turn. Sean had been afraid of me because he thought I knew he'd been hired to attack Sky. As a threat, I'd dismissed him out of hand and Sky nearly paid the price. Marko paid for my underestimation of McClintock, possibly with his life. Reaching down, I picked up the end of a couch and hurled it into the wall across the room. From there, everything was blind rage as I tore the room apart. At some point, Josh tried to use a field to stop me. I broke it easily.

By the time the rage subsided, there was nothing left intact except my brother, who had slipped into the side room to avoid being hit by flying objects. Exhausted, I collapsed onto the floor among the broken remains of couches and chairs. My chest heaved as I caught my breath. Tipping my head back to open my lungs, I saw the Xbox embedded in the ceiling, controllers dangling.

Josh walked into the room but remained quiet.

"Go," I said between breaths. "Sky needs you."

She was safe with Sebastian, even safer once Josh arrived

to put up his ward. I needed to get my shit together before I could be of any use to her.

Glancing over my shoulder toward the clinic, I said, "I'll follow as soon as I can."

He opened his mouth, glanced at the carnage around me, and decided to leave. Smart choice.

CHAPTER 7

After some digging, I found my phone on the other side of a hole in the entertainment center. Sebastian's text was there with the address of the safe house he'd taken Sky to. As head of the pack's security, I knew all of the pack's safe houses. This house wasn't on the list. It was Sebastian's, something he maintained in secret even from me. While the Midwest Pack was stable and challenges were infrequent, life for any Alpha was never comfortable. Sebastian carried an Elite-sized target on his back. It was only natural that he had a secret retreat. He probably had several. I did. The secrecy wasn't personal, but practical. That he chose to burn one of his safe houses in order to protect Sky reflected his level of concern for her. The pack retreat wasn't safe for her. For the time being, we had to assume that Sean was competent. He'd pulled off the first attack. If it weren't for Sky's fighting skills, she'd be dead. Whoever was behind Sean had money and motive. We had to assume there was another team of assassins. We had to assume they'd be desperate to finish the job.

Sebastian wasn't taking any chances.

The sooner we found Sean, the sooner I could beat answers from him.

My thoughts wandered to Sky. For the time being, she'd embrace the comfort of a safe place, until the shock of the assault wore off. She wasn't one to be locked away. She'd want to be involved. I figured we had a day, maybe two, before she did something dangerous—sooner if she got bored or wanted something that wasn't part of Sebastian's emergency stock. I texted Josh to pick up a few items on the way: M&M candies, potato chips, her favorite brand of water.

Next, I replied to Sebastian, letting him know I was on my way. In my room, I retrieved a fresh change of clothes and started a shower. My blood-drenched shirt stuck to my belly—Marko's blood. The sight of it brought a fresh memory of him in my arms, blood rushing from his body. I remembered the sound of his labored breath, his slowing heart. A sick dread fell into my stomach.

I growled to myself as I yanked off my shirt. *He's not dead yet.*

For now, there was nothing I could do for Marko. He was in Dr. Baker's competent hands. Sky needed me—hours ago. I glanced at the time, tried to calculate how long it had been since the attack. *She's with Sebastian,* I reminded myself. Josh should be there soon as well. She was in a secret location, protected by one of the most powerful witches in the country and the only were-animal I knew that was stronger and more dangerous than myself. Still, nothing would stop my worry until I was at her side. No matter how capable she became of protecting herself, I would always protect her.

The path to Sky came through me.

After I showered and changed, I gave Gavin instructions to increase patrols around the retreat. He was short-handed, with plenty of ground to cover. It was going to be a long night for everyone.

An hour later, I arrived at a secure, luxury apartment building in the heart of Chicago. Were-animals tended to prefer rural areas, on or close to wooded land where our animals could run free. The only trees around here were the few dotted along the sidewalk in front of the building. In every direction as far as the eye could see was concrete jungle—an unlikely location for Sebastian, which was why he'd chosen it. No one would expect to find Sebastian or any were-animal here. Looking up at his penthouse suite, I figured this was Sebastian's number one safe house, and he'd given it up for Sky. Now that Josh, Sky, and I all knew of the location, it was useless to Sebastian. Once the current crisis was over, he'd dump the penthouse and find a new location.

Using the passcode from his text, I drove through the security gate and double-parked my Maserati in Sebastian's reserved space without caring who the other space belonged to. Josh's Jeep was nowhere in sight, but he had to be upstairs already. He'd had more than enough time to shop for the list I'd given him and get here. By now, the blood ward should be in place around the penthouse.

Since Sebastian had a private entrance, it was likely no one else had noticed the faint but bloody shoe prints that led to his private elevator. Realizing the prints matched the size and shape of Sky's shoes, I took a calming breath against the sudden rush of anxiety. *Not hers,* I reminded myself. People didn't tend to walk through puddles of their own blood. And according to Josh, she hadn't been injured in the attack. *She severed an arm. There would have been plenty of blood, easy to step into.*

The elevator required Sebastian's passcode. Once entered, I stared at another bloody print at my feet until the elevator stopped at the penthouse. When the doors slid open, I found Sebastian mopping prints from the hardwood floor.

"She's fine," he said, nodding toward the hallway behind him. "In the shower."

I could just hear the faint hum of running water from behind a closed door. My immediate need was to go to her, but I needed a moment to calm myself. It wouldn't do to show her my anxiety. It helped to focus on the apartment's security. In a penthouse, there wasn't a lot of risk of forced entry, but when dealing with the supernatural, we couldn't be too careful.

I glanced around the wide, open living room, looking for Josh. The room was bright, bare eggshell-colored walls lit by sunlight through floor-to-ceiling windows that provided an expensive view of the city. Furnishings were spartan: three plain, sturdy couches; a coffee table on a patterned rug. Except for a set of beverage coasters, the table was bare. The neighboring galley-style kitchen was expansive, well-stocked with hanging pots and pans. A coffee machine percolated on the counter.

Returning to the living room, I tapped on one of the windows—dense.

"Bulletproof?"

Sebastian nodded.

Magic was the only threat then. Josh's ward would protect against spells, including transport. Except there was no ward. I felt the distinct absence of my brother's magic in the room. Sniffing the air, I noticed his lack of scent as well.

Perhaps sensing my irritation, Sebastian filled me in on the attack on Sky.

"She did well to fend off three opponents in a surprise attack." He nodded toward the bloodstain at his feet. "She put her sword-fighting lessons to use."

He sounded surprised that she'd even listened to his instruction. As Winter often noted, Sky wasn't the easiest pupil to train. Her stubbornness was half hindrance, half asset.

"Fortunately, Steven was with her," he said as if thanking me. "He's leading the hunt for Sean, and Marcia."

At least I'd done something right tonight.

I stated the obvious. "Marcia hired Sean."

Attacking Sky wasn't a move against the pack, which meant it was personal. Michaela wouldn't deprive herself by hiring Sean. That was more Marcia's style, and she had motive. When Josh was Samuel's prisoner, Sky had traded the Aufero to Marcia in exchange for the Creed's help. After my brother's safe return, Sky had stolen back the magic orb, nearly drowning Marcia in the process.

Sebastian nodded. "She's gone to ground."

"Her bunker?"

The Creed was based out of a fortified bunker buried in the backyard of a nondescript house in the suburbs. She'd brought us there for the curse that was placed on Sky, which was meant to keep her from reclaiming the Aufero. To maintain the bunker's secret location, we'd been driven in the back of a blacked-out van along a winding route. Hubris, really. The witches had at least thought to block our phones from using GPS. They should've taken the phones instead. With them, Winter and I were able to time and log each leg and turn. Afterword, we combined our notes and traced the route to the bunker house.

Sebastian grinned. "A burning tire in the vent smoked them out in a matter of minutes."

That was the problem with bunkers—no matter how fortified or secure, people had to breathe, which meant an air shaft. The same pumps that sucked oxygen into the bunker just as easily sucked in smoke.

"Mostly servants inside," Sebastian continued, "but we caught two of the Creed. They were unaware of the attack on Sky, and Marcia's disappearance."

I wasn't surprised. The Creed had nothing to gain from Marcia's transgression. Word was rapidly spreading that we were after her. Her list of friends was dwindling by the second.

"You think Samuel will help her?"

Unlikely allies, but both had reasons to attack the retreat. Marcia wanted Sky and the Aufero. For Samuel, capturing the Clostra was akin to a religious crusade. Neither of them could hope to succeed alone, but together they would be formidable.

Sebastian considered the possibility, but didn't answer.

"Sky will need to stay here for a few days until we've located Marcia and Sean." I glanced around the room. "I'll need to upgrade your doors and windows."

"Whatever is needed."

I wasn't able to hide my irritation as I said, "Josh will have a ward up as soon as he gets here."

There was another matter to discuss before Sky finished her shower.

"The exchange was a trap," I admitted.

I knew by his stolid expression that he already knew about my failure. Of course he did. The pack's number six was lying in Dr. Baker's infirmary, near death. There was the issue of the pack's money, as well, but I knew that wasn't Sebastian's primary concern.

He frowned. "The timing of his attack is interesting."

I groaned with the realization. "Marcia hired McClintock to get me out of the way."

He waited for an explanation.

"There was a job he didn't want. When I captured the belocka from under his nose, he wanted me to pay him off to not take it." I ran my hands down my face, pulling at the stress. "I should've known. After I declined, he had no choice."

"The ransom?"

"A ruse. He took the money, probably as a target of opportunity. His primary objective was to distract me from the attack on Sky." I shook my head, gritting my teeth. "I knew better than to underestimate him." I held Sebastian's gaze, borrowing his steadfast calm. "I fucked up."

It was an invitation for him to replace me. The pack couldn't afford my mistakes—too many, too fast. I'd put lives at risk, including Sky's.

Sebastian scrutinized me, taking his time. His expression remained inscrutable as he weighed my offer. We were friends, as much as our positions allowed, but he wouldn't hesitate to put me aside if he felt I was a danger to the pack. Eventually, his shoulders relaxed. "You're my Beta and my head of security because there's no one better for the job— not even close. That doesn't make you perfect. We all fuck up eventually. So far, you've survived your mistakes. Learn from them. Get on top of this, now."

Unable to answer his confidence, I nodded once.

"Sky needs your strength," he said, "and so does the pack." He started toward the elevator. "I'm going back to the retreat."

Once the elevator closed behind him, I sent a sharp text message to Josh, then did my best to not punch a hole in Sebastian's wall. *Calm down,* I chided myself. Sky would already be on edge from the attack. She didn't need to process my anger as well. I needed her to relax, to feel protected.

Walking down the hall in search of her, I found an empty bathroom and two bedrooms, both with king-sized beds. The bedding in the master bedroom was displaced. Sky's underwear was on the floor near the closed bathroom door. From behind it, I heard the shower come to an end.

Intending to disarm her, I stretched out on the bed, propped up on an elbow. Forcing my lips into a playful smile, I waited for the door to open. My heart was pounding in my ears. My fists clenched beneath whitened knuckles. It took a pair of slow, calming breaths just to get my anger under some semblance of control.

The door opened. Sky emerged with a towel around her and nothing else. Surprised to see me, she pulled the towel tighter and went about untangling her hair with her fingers. The shape of her form beneath the towel sent a shiver through my body. Before I realized, I'd slid off the bed. My approach sent her heart pounding, echoing my attraction. Adrenalin still raced in her, looking for escape. Training was one thing, but it couldn't match the sheer thrill of fighting for life or death.

For were-animals, violence was the ultimate aphrodisiac.

Her gaze flicked toward the bedroom door as if she hoped someone would walk through it. "Where is Sebastian?"

"Gone."

"It's just us?"

Smiling down at her, I gently stroked her hair. Her heart answered, beating faster.

"Is that a problem?"

"No," she lied, glancing about the room for a distraction. "It's fine."

"Good."

Uncertain, she took a step back.

I followed, asking in Portuguese, *"Como você está?"* *How are you?*

"Fine."

"Diga-me o que aconteceu." *Tell me what happened.*

"I already told Sebastian."

"Now tell *me*. You might remember things a little clearer." I slipped an arm around her waist to comfort her, knowing that reliving the attack and what she'd done to defend herself brought up unpleasant memories. *"Por favor."* *Please.*

She tried to describe the events in Portuguese. Her struggle to find the right words was nothing compared to my struggle to translate what she was saying. She filled in enough of the story in English that I was able to follow.

"Sebastian was right," I said when she'd finished. "It was a very amateurish attempt."

"Since I haven't had a lot of people try to assassinate me, I'm going to take your word for it."

I read the desire in her body as I gently brushed strands of hair from her face. There was an electricity between us that wouldn't be denied, though she tried. Unable to help myself, I leaned down and gently pressed my lips against hers. She responded readily, her lips searching mine. My fingers entwined in her hair, I pulled her closer. She pressed against me until our hearts pounded against each other. Giving into our primal needs, we were lost within each other. But the distraction was brief. Resistance quickly built in her until she turned aside. Her lips parted from mine, but she willingly remained in my embrace.

My hands gently wrapped around her hips. I whispered into her ear, "What's the matter?"

She pulled away, stammered, "I need to get dressed."

"Okay," I said softly, letting go. "Then get dressed."

She glanced at the door, an unsubtle invitation for me to leave. I chuckled at her modesty. "I think we are past that."

Irritated, her eyes darkened with a growing resolve. Anger welled up in her. "I don't want to play your games. I am not some toy you get to play with whenever the mood strikes you. You said not to make things awkward between us, but you're the one who keeps making it that way."

I stepped back, tried to disarm her with an amused smile. "Tell me, what game am I playing with you and what type of *toy* are you?"

"The type that isn't going to deal with your BS. That night"—her gaze shifted, cheeks flushed—"when we were together, it didn't end the way, um…the way I expected. The way it should have, and you left without any explanation."

Aware for the first time that I'd caused her pain, my smile faded. "I thought I was doing the right thing."

"What's wrong with you? Are you really this narcissistic? How is seducing me and then leaving me without anything happening 'the right thing'?"

Scrutinizing her, I asked, "When was the last time you got laid?"

"What?"

"When was the last time you made love? Got laid? Screwed? Banged? Did the horizontal tango? Fucked? Use whatever euphemism you want, but the question remains: when was the last time you did it?"

She blinked, unable to admit the truth.

"Exactly," I said. "Sky, I'm not a teenager, and the idea of being a woman's first does nothing for me. I don't need the ego boost or have something to prove by doing that. Honestly, I don't want to be the star of your fond recounts of your first time. It was the right thing to do because for me it would have probably been just a one-night thing, and for you, it would have been more."

Her glare hardened as she hugged the towel close around her. "You're an ass."

"Eu sei." I nodded slowly. *I know.*

Deciding it was time to make my exit, I strode toward the door. Guilt stopped me. In these situations, I normally said whatever was necessary to get the result I desired. Honesty wasn't usually part of the equation. I felt the lack of it now—yet another way that Sky was different. Sometimes I missed not caring what she thought. The old days were safer, but they were gone. Sky was here and I couldn't just stop caring. I could walk away and let the guilt of hurting her gnaw at my gut, or I could be honest, for once. She deserved honesty.

Leaning against the door frame, I slipped my fingers into the pockets of my jeans and let out a long exhale. Unable to meet her gaze, I focused on a paint blemish above the bed.

"I've cheated on almost every woman I have ever dated. I have no interest in monogamy. When I get bored, it's over.

Tears don't bother me nor do they change my decision when I decide to leave. The list of women who I have left broken is long, and they are hurt. They even break my things, call me every combination with *fucker* or variations of *asshole*; but eventually they get over it." *Eventually they go away.* I didn't want Sky to fade away like that. I shrugged and ran a hand through my hair. "You would be added to the list, and you're different, I don't think you…I'm a real SOB, and I'm okay with it." *Not really. Not anymore.* "I'm probably not going to change."

Even if I'd wanted to change, I didn't know how.

Sky was speechless, fuming. If I'd expected her to understand on some level, or to at least appreciate my openness, I was mistaken. Not sure how to fix the situation, I changed the subject.

"Can you think of anything else about tonight's attack?"

I gave the redirection a fifty-fifty chance of survival. Sky was exhausted. She tried to control her anger because she didn't want a fight. I'd intended to calm her. Instead I'd pushed her nearly to the edge. If she chose to vent, I'd have no choice but to absorb her anger without rebuttal. She seemed about to lay into me when I felt Josh's magic envelop the penthouse like a warm blanket—the blood ward.

A moment later, I heard the elevator doors slide open and his cheerful voice filled the penthouse.

"I love this place," he called from the living room. "I brought food and everything on the list, just as you commanded, sir."

I heard the crunch and crinkle of bags set onto the counter before he brushed past me and walked into the room. His cheer deflated as he read the tension between Sky and me. Turning to me, he suggested, "You should check and make sure I got everything you wanted. The rest of the bags are on the counter."

I would've welcomed the out if I didn't know they were

going to talk about me while I was in the other room. My eyes narrowed at him as I measured his intention. He'd been in a pissy mood lately. Not sure I wanted to gift him an opportunity to cut me down, I leaned into the door frame. My arms folded across my chest.

My eyes narrowed at my brother. "I trust you."

"That's a first. You've always felt the need to check my work. Why don't you do it now?" He nodded toward the living room, winking at me in an exaggerated fashion. When I ignored him, he nudged me with a gentle magical force.

Still, I held my ground.

His eyebrows rose in warning.

I half smiled at him. *Try me.*

The magical force that struck my chest was stronger than I'd anticipated. I stumbled back a step before I planted my back heel against the floor, but he'd gotten me out of the doorway. With an impish grin more haughty than playful, Josh casually flicked his fingers at me. The door slammed shut. The lock clicked. Furious, I was about to break the door handle and barge in when I realized there was silence on the other side of the door. They expected me to barge in. They were waiting for the show. Unable to do anything else, I stood there, fuming.

After a short silence, I heard what sounded like a wet kiss, followed by Josh's voice.

"So, you've been upgraded to gold card membership, I hear. You know each time someone tries to arrange a hit on you, there's a little bump in your pack cred. My brother's at triple platinum status, I think."

Sky blurted, "Steven's moving out."

Josh gasped. "What?" I heard the creak of mattress springs bearing sudden weight, followed by, "Why?"

That's what they're going to talk about? I scowled. I'd just bared my soul to Sky, and she wanted to discuss Steven's departure? Appalled, I listened to the two of them chatter away about nonsense. After a few minutes, I gave up. I was about to walk away when I heard Josh compliment her.

"You're so sexy," he declared in a playful voice, "I don't know if I can keep my hands off you."

My fingernails dug into my palms as I clenched both fists. Glowering at the door handle, I imagined snapping it off, throwing the door open. I'd drag Josh out by his hair if necessary, but he'd fight me. I'd tell him to stop acting like an inappropriate asshole. He'd say something nasty, then the fight would start. Fights between Josh and me ended up involving a great deal of property damage. Sebastian had given me carte blanche to make changes that improved the penthouse's security. I doubted he meant for us to create Josh-and-Ethan-sized holes in his walls.

When the urge to break in anyway proved too much, I scoffed and walked away.

After putting away Josh's groceries, I paced the living room, glancing periodically between the clock on the wall and the closed, locked bedroom door. Sooner or later, their conversation would end. Sky would get tired. Josh would emerge and I'd give him an earful. An hour later, he'd yet to emerge. I pulled one of the couches into the hallway to give me an unobstructed view of Sky's door, then sat down.

Digging my phone from my pocket, I called Dr. Baker for an update on Marko.

Winter answered, a smoldering anger in her voice. "He didn't make it."

My heart stopped. I remained still, waiting.

She continued. "That bullet was special. For starters, it was silver. It also exploded into bits. Some of them made it into his heart. His body tried to heal, but Dr. Baker couldn't get all the silver out in time."

The loss crept over me, weighing me down until I'd slumped over, my head in my free hand. Ours was a dangerous existence. I lived with the constant reminder that death was always close, waiting to take me or mine, but I never got used to the loss. The pain never got easier. In the ensuing silence, the mundane sounds of Sebastian's penthouse gnawed at me—the hum of the fridge, the ticking of a clock on the wall, my brother's snoring from the master bedroom. Every annoying sound was a reminder that I was still alive, that I had a duty to those who weren't—revenge.

She said softly, "I'll make the necessary calls."

In order to hide Marko's death from the world, his body would be cremated and the ashes spread onto the retreat grounds. There would be no ceremony, no memorial. Wereanimals died violent deaths. In order to avoid the outside world's scrutiny, our lives once lost were quietly, efficiently scrubbed from existence. Our contacts in the banking industry would close Marko's accounts. His address would be changed to somewhere far away. His belongings would be removed by what appeared to be professional movers and dumped or donated in neighboring towns. Any neighbors or human friends that got curious about Marko's sudden departure would find some reassurance, carefully planted. Their minds and their mouths would be put at ease. A few days from now, they'd shrug their shoulders and move on with their lives. A month from now, the questions would cease.

I choked on the words as I said out loud, "The pack remembers."

Winter answered softly, "The pack remembers," and then ended the call.

My phone slipped from my fingers, clattering onto the floor. I considered waking Sky and Josh to share the news. I couldn't bring myself to tell her. She'd never been close to Marko, but she'd take his loss hard just the same. The pack was family. I couldn't do that to her, not now. Frowning, I resolved to keep the news from Sky until the current crisis was over. There was no way to tell Josh without alerting her, so I sat alone with my grief.

Numb, I wandered into the guest bedroom and climbed into bed. I didn't remember taking off my clothes until I felt fine Egyptian cotton sheets against my bare skin. The comfort gnawed at me. Marko was dead because I hadn't taken McClintock seriously. In a just world, the bullet would've struck me. The world was not just. It was cold and cruel and random.

At some point, I fell into an agitated slumber. When I woke, the sun was shining through the windows, blinding me. I closed the blinds, cursing under my breath. I checked the other room expecting to find Josh sleeping there. The bed remained untouched. His scent still lingered behind Sky's door, which remained locked. When the time was right, we were going to have a very long, possibly violent conversation about propriety regarding his relationship with Sky.

Exhausted, I banged on the door until I heard his sleepy voice answer.

"What?"

"Get up," I growled, then tried the door knob again. "Unlock the door."

"What time is it?"

I snapped, "Eight thirty."

There's work to do. By lunch I wanted a second ward on the penthouse. By dinner, I'd have another layer of security added to the elevator and Sebastian's private entrance. No one would get to Sky.

"Are you kidding me?" he howled. "Go away and come back in four hours."

"Get your ass up. Now."

"No. I'm tired."

I heard shifting on the mattress. Imagining the two of them on the bed together sent a new rush of anger through my body.

"Josh! I'm not playing with you, get up!"

I pounded continuously on the door. The hinges groaned,

threatened to break. When I heard the lock click, I stopped. *Finally!* I took a step back, waited until the door finally creaked open just enough to reveal a skeptical green eye.

Sky said, "We'll be out in a few minutes."

Peering through the crack, I saw my brother glaring at me from the bed, shirtless. His bare feet poked out from beneath the blanket. Before I could react, Sky shut the door and locked it. She whispered something to him, eliciting a laugh. My fists clenched as I glared at the door, waiting for them. Not wrapping my hands around my brother's neck when he emerged was going to be a problem. While I struggled for control, there was movement on the other side of the door. While I prepared myself for them to emerge, I heard the steady cascade of a shower, followed by Josh's slow rumbling snore.

My jaw dropped at his audacity. I'd reached a boiling point and didn't like my options. All I could do was barge in and give my brother the beatdown he deserved, or walk away. Hard as it was to take that first step, I turned and went into the kitchen. Busying myself in the kitchen was my only safe release. At first I banged every pot and pan I touched. Once breakfast started to come together, I was able to focus on preparing a meal for Sky. A forced calm followed.

I'd overreacted, and not just because of Marko. I'd let Josh push my buttons. He was angry at me for keeping him in the dark about the dark elf magic, but he was always looking for ways to piss me off. It was a game for him, but there was also jealousy. Did she realize his attraction for her?

I glanced down at egg yolk running between the cracks of my clenched fist, opened it to let the crushed shell fall into the sink. Washing the yolk under running water, I reminded myself, *Sky can see whoever she wants.* We didn't have a committed relationship. I'd just made that pretty clear to her. Still, I knew she wouldn't pursue Josh. Their relationship—in her eyes, at least—was probably something closer to her relationship with Steven, functional, supportive. Still, annoying. Bacon sizzled in hot grease as I turned the pieces over. I didn't understand either relationship, probably never would. I didn't understand how men and women became like girlfriends without sex becoming an issue between them.

Admittedly, I was old fashioned that way.

I wasn't used to being jealous. I was used to being on the other side of out. Now I understood how jealousy could make people crazy. For a moment, I considered apologizing.

Forget it, I growled.

While the bacon sizzled, I turned to the pancakes. I'd too many things on my mind, too many problems to solve. Sky's safety was the priority. After that, I needed to find McClintock and rescue Artemis. Then I'd take my revenge on Sean, Marcia, and anyone else involved in the attack on Sky. By the time I was done with them, the entire supernatural community would know the consequences of touching Sky.

Setting the last of the pancakes aside, I realized I'd emptied Sebastian's fridge and cupboard. In front of me was a full-spread breakfast for six. Steak, eggs, French toast, pancakes, fresh fruit.

Sky appeared in the kitchen doorway, dressed and smelling of strawberry shampoo. I met her gaze with an unhealthy sense of dread, but tried to seem normal. Pretending I hadn't just made a complete ass of myself. A half smile cracked her lips as she took in the enormity of her breakfast.

Trying to sound nonchalant, I snapped, "Did you sleep well last night?"

She ignored the harshness of my tone. "As good as could be expected." She filled a plate, picked a yogurt from the fridge, then sat at the table. "And you?"

In a blink I was at her side, about to apologize. Her calm demeanor stopped me. Despite my behavior, she wasn't angry. She seemed…entertained. Apologizing would only make me more the fool, though I still wanted to. I wanted to explain about Marko and McClintock and everything I'd been through in the last couple of days, but I couldn't.

She stared at me, expecting something.

Unable to lie, I turned and walked out of the room.

She called after me, "Nothing is going on between me and Josh."

I stopped in my tracks, felt the tension in my shoulders ease.

She walked in front of me to meet my gaze with a fiery look. "I'm not a teenager."

My frustrations came boiling to the surface. Scowling down at her, I met fire with fire. "Since you're not one, shouldn't you stop acting like one?"

Before she could answer, Josh walked into the room, still wearing just his pair of boxers and a smattering of chest hair, probably to irritate me.

Sky held my gaze for a moment as she walked around me. After helping herself to more fruit, she returned to her seat. She gave Josh's half-dressed state an amused smile, then made a point to notice my own boxers and I assumed my own lack of a shirt. "I didn't know breakfast was so formal."

I needed to get out of here, before I did or said something else stupid. "I'm going to see to improving the security here." I glared daggers at Josh. "You'll stick around to watch over her?"

Sky complained, "I swear I just reminded you that I'm not a teenager."

Josh opened his mouth to say something irritating. Finally measuring my anger, he stopped short. He gave me a puzzled look, and I knew what he was asking. I shook my head once, just enough for him to notice. Regret and grief washed over him, which he quickly brushed aside for Sky's sake.

On his way to the breakfast table, he said, "I'll get that second ward up."

"Good."

I dressed and got the hell out of there.

On my way out to my car, I heard the building door click open behind me. Josh caught up at a jog, stopped in front of me.

"Hey," he said, holding up a hand. "Hold up."

I gave him an annoyed look, but waited.

"We should talk about this jealousy thing."

If he wanted to confess, he could pick a better time. I was at the peak of my frustration with him. "Later, Josh."

I started around him until he sidled into my way. "It's always later. It's always about what you want, when you want it. You've got a real problem with jealousy. Are you going to simmer in that, or can we clear the air now and get past it?"

"I'm jealous?" I gaped at him. "Of you and Sky?"

"I don't know if it's going to turn into something or not," he claimed. "It would be a lot easier to find out if you stopped acting like a twelve-year-old."

Was he that oblivious? I took a calming breath, tried to set my anger aside to let him down easily. "Josh, I don't think this"—I gestured toward the apartment—"is what you think it is. Sky doesn't—"

"You just can't stand it, can you?" He pursed his lips in grim disappointment. "When it comes to girls, you always get what you want. You give them that smoky look, you scowl a lot and treat them like they don't matter, and they're yours until you get bored and dump them."

"You've never had a problem getting girls," I reminded him. He was always hooking up with someone from the club.

He gestured with his arms out, emphasizing what he thought obvious. "That's because you rarely hang out at the club. Trust me, when you come around, all eyes turn to the Ethan Show. Do me a favor," he said, backing toward the building, "for once, try to be happy for me instead of getting in my way."

The next two days were frustrating. Nearly the entire pack was out looking for Marcia and Sean. Tim and the other pack members in the police force committed their entire official patrols to the hunt. On the domestic front, we hired the Worgen to hack Sean's and Marcia's emails, phones, credit cards. We got nothing in return. It was as if the two had ceased to exist. With their plot exposed, I was increasingly certain the pair had fled Chicago. We put out the word to other packs in the region, offering a bounty for capturing the two alive. Sooner or later, they were going to poke their heads above ground and get caught. It was only a matter of time.

McClintock proved equally elusive. After reviewing our encounters to date, I was left convinced that there was more to his plan than simply getting me out of Marcia's way. She was involved. The timing of their efforts was too close to ignore, but he was building toward something. I would hear from him soon, unless Marcia's failure ruined his plan. Had he intended to build off of Sky's death, use that to draw me into another trap? Whatever his intention, he was a hired gun. If we caught Marcia, we could cut off his money supply. McClintock would walk away and I'd let him—for now.

That Artemis was still missing told me his plan was still in play. The old man had a code of ethics. He wouldn't hesitate to do horrible things to her to get what he wanted, but he wouldn't hurt her without benefit. If his plan was dead, he'd let her go somewhere.

There were too many variables and not enough information to anticipate his next move.

After the first day in the penthouse, Sky grew agitated. For her safety, a pack member was with her at all times and she wasn't allowed out of the building, not even for a walk. Her cardio was restricted to walking up and down the penthouse hall, wearing out the runner carpet beneath her tennis shoes. I tried to make her time there more comfortable by bringing her an entire red velvet cake from her favorite bakery. By the next morning half the cake was gone and she was back to pacing. By the third day, I thought she was going to start tearing the walls apart.

With no sign of trouble, Sebastian and I agreed it was safe enough for her to return home. The damage from the attack had been repaired. In the process, I'd had metal plating installed in her walls. All of her doors and windows were reinforced. I'd seen to the work personally. With any luck, she'd eventually feel safe there again. That would take time. People spent their lives believing a home was an impregnable sanctuary. In reality, a home was just a box with locks and windows. The most expensive mansions, the most secure estates in the world, were all vulnerable to a determined intruder.

Sky faced that realization now. Driving her to her house, every mile closer increased her anxiety. Her heart raced. I tapped my finger against the steering wheel in time with the rhythm of her racing heart, hoping to draw her attention to her agitation. If she noticed, she chose not to react. Josh rode in the back seat. For once he was quiet, his attention absorbed by something on his phone.

I glanced at Sky's fists clenching and releasing in her lap. "We can go back to the penthouse."

Relieved, she nodded once.

I looked for a place to turn around, when an audible shudder from the backseat got my attention. Through the rearview mirror, I saw my brother's solid black eyes staring blankly ahead. Sweat beaded on his forehead. His expression was taught as he hurriedly whispered a spell. His eyes closed with the effort.

"Josh."

He swallowed. "Someone's trying to break the ward at the retreat—"

My phone rang once before I answered it. Sebastian was on the other end, his voice cool as he informed me, "We're under attack."

"On our way."

I turned the Maserati around in an intersection, ignoring the angry blaring of horns that followed. I glanced to make sure Sky's seatbelt was on. Rapid acceleration pushed us into our seats as I sped toward the retreat.

Breaking a blood ward like the one Josh had put over the retreat was no simple feat. It took a great deal of magic, more than Marcia could summon on her own.

As if reading my mind, Josh declared in a strained voice, "Samuel."

Sky gripped the edge of her seat as I weaved through traffic. Only a few minutes later, I turned onto the winding road that led to the retreat, pushing the turns as hard as I dared. As the house came into view, we saw a pitched battle raging on the front lawn. Bodies and limbs littered the crimson field. Nearly three dozen of our pack were fighting hand to hand, claw to claw, with the entire Ares Pack.

I barely had time to wonder how Anderson could be so easily duped into fighting for the man who strived to strip us all of our animals, if not kill us outright.

At the edge of the battle, I veered toward a group of Ares trying to launch an attack around my pack's flank. At the last second, I turned the wheel and pulled the emergency break. The Maserati slid sideways into the Ares. Two of them leapt away in time. The other three thudded against the fiberglass frame, were thrown somewhere into the melee.

I needed just a moment to take in the battle. Sebastian, in human form, was at the epicenter, directing our defense, while Winter shielded him with her katana, cutting Ares down with a dancer's grace. Steven's coyote bared his teeth over the disemboweled body of a lynx. Blood dripped from his muzzle as a leopard closed in. Three wolves followed, sensing a kill. Gavin's panther and Dr. Baker's tiger crashed into the wolves from behind, killing two, distracting the third. It wheeled on Gavin as he tore open one of the wolves' throats. Its jaws snapped at Gavin's back leg. Steven's lunge knocked the wolf aside. His jaw clamped around the wolf's throat, snapped its neck with a quick shake of his head.

The leopard fled with Dr. Baker racing after it.

Josh declared in an anxious voice, "He's breaking the blood ward."

I kicked open the door in time to knock back a charging lynx. Stunned, it barely rose to its feet before I gripped its head, twisted sharply. Its neck snapped. Its body went limp as I dropped it to the grass.

Across the field, an Ares emerged from the general melee leading a small pack of angry wolves—Nelson, the Ares third, or was before we'd killed their Beta. He and Sebastian strode toward each other. The wolves, hungry for blood, charged ahead. Winter scattered them with a quick series of blows, nearly decapitating one of the wolves. The rest scattered beneath her katana. Ignoring the fight around them, the pair continued toward each other. A few more steps, and they charged—Nelson roaring, Sebastian calm. Coming together, Nelson swung wildly. Sebastian evaded the blow with a graceful shift of weight, countered with a targeted jab into Nelson's throat. A second blow followed, a flat palm driven up into his nose. The ensuing blood sprayed into his eyes, blinding him. He stumbled, clutching at his neck and gasping for breath. Sebastian threw Nelson to his belly. Standing over him, Sebastian wrapped massive hands around Nelson's chin and crown. A single quick gesture snapped his neck. Nelson's limp form collapsed into the bloody grass.

Sudden movement to my left caught my attention. Two

hyenas charged. I knocked one aside while the other rounded the Maserati, targeting Sky. Before I could call out a warning, she pivoted and drove a boot into the hyena's ribs. The hyena yelped in pain as it landed, stumbling. Before it fully regained its balance, it was on the counter attack. Sky met the hyena's lunge with a spinning kick, shattering its jaw with her heel as she knocked the hyena to the ground.

Worry crept through my rage. I didn't want to leave her side, and my brother was vulnerable. He could protect himself and Sky with a field, but the Ares in animal form were immune to his offensive magic. My wolf howled to be released, to wade into the battle where it was the thickest, around Sebastian. I belonged at the Alpha's side. First, I had to make sure Sky was protected. As she crouched, prepared to meet the hyena's next lunge, I turned to Josh. Before I could shout my instructions, the report of a single gunshot pierced the din of the melee.

My eyes widened at Josh, expecting to see blood. When I didn't, I turned a panicked look to Sky. Untouched, she stared across the lawn, mouth agape.

I turned back to Sebastian as another shot rang out. A spray of blood burst from his chest. The force of the bullet knocked him back a step. He seemed to stare defiantly into the woods where the shot had been fired, then collapsed into a heap.

Winter's eyes widened in horror. She tried to cut her way to him. The rest of the pack wheeled, abandoning their battles to converge on our Alpha. The Ares converged as well, the smell of victory and blood in their nostrils. I charged into the fray in a desperate bid, killing any Ares that strayed between me and Sebastian. So fixed on reaching him, I didn't see the cougar charging until it crashed into my side. I fell, the cougar landing on top of me. Fighting from my back, I barely fought off its snapping jaws while the cougar's claws raked at me.

After some work, I managed to force my arm into the cougar's mouth. When it bit down, its teeth tore through my skin. The urge to cry out from the sudden pain was almost unbearable. I needed to focus, to take advantage of the few precious seconds sacrificing my arm bought me. Poorly trained were-animals had a tendency to put their faith in their teeth. Once they had you in their bite, they'd hold on until they bled the life out of their opponent. Either the cougar didn't notice or didn't care as I twisted my captive arm, forcing the cougar's head to the side—enough to expose its temple. Its bite on my arm shifted, tearing before the cougar clamped down harder. This time I did cry out, right before I drove my free fist into the side of the cougar's head. Stunned, its grip slackened but didn't let go. I drove my fist into its skull twice more. The cougar's grip slipped. Its tongue lolled. Mad with rage, I twisted its head until it snapped, then cast the cougar aside.

Rising to my feet, I heard another shot ring out.

No!

Winter screamed.

Three shots. Three hits. If he was still alive, he couldn't take a fourth.

On my feet, I saw Sky sprinting into the woods after the sniper, a knife in her hand. She was alone, charging into the heart of the enemy. I couldn't worry about her now. The entire Midwest Pack was fighting to form a shield around Sebastian.

Driving toward him, I fought my way through what seemed an endless press of Ares.

Another shot rang out, tearing an angry, desperate scream from my throat. A wolf lunged at me. I caught its jaws in my hands, snapped them apart. Casting the wolf aside, I found a coyote crossing my path, intent on Dr. Baker, who was nearby. I drove the heel of my boot into the wolf's back, breaking its spine, then stepped over the dying were-animal. Close to Sebastian now, I found Winter positioned between his body and the sniper. Wielding her sword with a fury, she sliced and cut through a wave of attacking were-animals desperate to claim the Elite for their kill. Steven and Gavin were at Sebastian's side, shielding him from teeth and claws.

My wolf was desperate for blood. It took every ounce of control to prevent the shift. I was the only one strong enough to carry Sebastian into the house. My animal would have to stay on its leash until our Alpha was safe inside.

Before I could reach him, Josh transported to Sebastian's side. He immediately threw up a protective field around them both. Once done, he reached underneath Sebastian as if intending to carry him. A second later, the two of them transported away.

Seeing their target vanish, the Ares roared in anger. Rather than give up, they only pressed harder. For the Midwest Pack, seeing Sebastian safely removed from the battle gave them permission to unleash their rage.

Dr. Baker's tiger immediately veered toward the house. Josh would already have Sebastian in the infirmary, waiting. Every second that delayed Dr. Baker from reaching our Alpha might be his last.

Dread threatened to engulf me as I realized, *I might already be the pack's Alpha.* As long as there was a chance that Sebastian was still alive, my entire being was focused on protecting him. We needed to buy Dr. Baker time to do his work while we regrouped for a counterattack. My voice roared over the din. "Retreat!"

The word burned in my throat.

Some of the pack obeyed. Others were too lost in their lust for revenge. I had to grab Steven, throw him back toward the house. Gavin, Winter, and I fought off Ares while we collected our own, steering them back toward safety. As the Ares pressed harder, we became the rearguard, holding off the onslaught while our pack funneled through the front door of the house. Steven joined us, fighting at my side.

As we backed toward the porch, I risked a glance toward the woods for Sky. The shots had ceased, which meant she might have killed the sniper or at least chased them away. I could only hope she'd make it back to the house. As much as it sickened me not to rush to her, I was in charge of the pack —for the moment, at least. We were under siege and I couldn't abandon them.

I cursed under my breath as we slowly backed toward the front door of the retreat. Every were-animal that escaped into the house meant one less animal to fend off the Ares. Pressure around us mounted as we struggled to protect the retreat. An Ares woman in human form, a fierce expression framed with wild, jet-black hair, charged me, an axe raised above her head. Blood dripped from the blade as she brought it down toward my skull. Stepping into her stride, I drove both fists into her chest, throwing her back. She disappeared into the Ares rabble that formed an ever-tightening noose. By the time we reached the porch, there were just a few of us still outside, fighting what seemed like an endless hoard of were-animals.

I shouted, "Hold the line!"

My muscles ached as I fought back against a flurry of blows coming from multiple directions. My blows were weakening, my movements less sharp. Adrenaline faded and exhaustion was settling into all of us. Winter's katana no longer danced. She was reduced to primal, desperate swings. Gavin and Steven slowed as well. Their fur was soaked in blood.

Realization set in that we weren't all going to make it inside the house.

Leaning toward Winter, I shouted, "Get inside!"

She was the next rank in line after me. I'd no intention of leaving anyone else to die on this porch so that I could survive. *Save her first, then Steven.* Gavin was ranked higher, but didn't have the emotional ability to lead the pack. He was a loner, a fighter. While Steven weakened rapidly, Gavin still had some strength in him. It was a simple calculation—the best chance to save all of them was to hold him back until Winter and Steven were safe. When it was Gavin's turn to retreat, he would be the last. I'd order the door closed. While they barred it from within, I'd be free to spill as much Ares blood as I could before I fell.

Winter stiffened at my order. A surge of energy filled her as she pretended to not hear.

I roared at her as I smashed a fist into a hyena's snout, "Now!"

She risked a scowling glance at me, then turned and ran up the porch. Ares pressed into the space she vacated, putting me under even greater pressure.

"Steven!"

He started to draw back, then lunged at a cougar that tried to take his place. Sensing the danger, the cougar drew back and hissed as Steven's coyote tore the cougar's ear from its skull. Snarling, Steven flipped the bloody flap into the air.

Gavin used his panther's body to brush Steven back. When he did, the Ares filled that void. Gavin and I could barely keep up with the snapping jaws. Claws raked my right arm. Something cut into my left thigh as I pushed back a pair of wolves in front of me. Gavin's body pressed against me as we fought side by side, nearly surrounded. He'd no intention of retreating. Without each other, neither of us could survive the onslaught. It was now a contest between us to see who could hold up the longest.

Winter called out from behind us. "Get inside!"

Before I could order her to close the door, a whistle sounded from the Ares rear. Another whistle joined the first. The press eased as the Ares started to retreat. Whimpering with disappointment, the were-animals directly in front of us backed off. A lone coyote refused, lunging at me. At some point in any fight, exhaustion takes us all. Before I could react, Gavin leapt across my body, knocking the coyote aside. The animal struggled to rise, but Gavin didn't have the strength to finish it. He panted, watching the were-animal flee.

My chest heaved as I sucked in desperate breaths, watching the Ares quickly evaporate into the woods. Dizzy from lack of oxygen, I teetered a moment before widening my stance. I glanced around, looking for Sky, but saw nothing. My mind refused to accept that she might be dead somewhere, or dying alone in the woods. Josh could've transported to her and brought her inside.

The house door opened. I waved Gavin inside.

The fight wasn't over. They'd come for Sebastian. As far as they knew, he was alive somewhere inside the house. True or not, the Ares would come back for him soon, before we'd a chance to recover or gather reinforcements. Josh's blood ward was down. The massive house was vulnerable. Inside was a weakened pack, already contemplating the loss of their Alpha. After peering into the woods one last time for a sign of Sky, I had no choice but to go inside and hope she survived. She was stubborn. If she were alive, she'd find her way back to the house.

As I backed inside, someone closed the door in front of me and placed an iron bar across it.

CHAPTER 8

The entryway was filled with exhausted were-animals propped against the walls, collapsed onto the floor. Most were wounded, many seriously. Those able to help moved among the injured, wrapping wounds with clean towels, torn clothing—anything they could find to stem the bleeding while their natural healing ability did its work. That Dr. Baker wasn't among them meant Sebastian was still alive in the infirmary. Had Kelly remained, she would be among the wounded here, providing triage, administering first aid, spreading calm.

Fear choked the room like an invisible, smothering gas. The Midwest Pack wasn't used to defeat. Long-believed rumors of Sebastian's invincibility were shattered. Setting aside my need to check on Sebastian, I walked through the room, offering encouragement and consolation to the wounded. Gathering were-animals whose wounds were minor, I sent them to different sections of the house to guard windows and doors, anywhere the Ares could find or create an entrance. Distracted from their worry, they seemed glad for the direction.

A pack needed leadership, reassurance.

After a few minutes, fear settled into an anxious calm. I made my way to the infirmary. A crowd gathered outside the door, their nervous attention fixed on the urgent voices within.

Dr. Baker barked at someone inside, "Out of my way."

Josh emerged from the crowd as I approached, his expression grim. His complexion a ghastly white.

I asked, "How is he?"

"It's bad. I tried to help." He shook his head. "We could really use Kelly right now. If I knew where she was, I could bring her." He took my arm, pulled me aside. "They took down my blood wards like they were paper."

"Samuel and Marcia together?"

"I thought so at first." He licked his lips. "I don't think either of them could've done it that fast. This was something else. Something…powerful. I don't know what."

"Let me know when you do."

I started toward the infirmary, but Josh held his grip on my arm. "Dr. Baker is overwhelmed in there. He'll call you when he needs you."

Turning back to the infirmary, I heard Dr. Baker's voice once more. "Stop hovering and let me do my job."

Before I could make up my mind, a loud thump upstairs caught my attention. A series of thumps followed, the pounding of feet racing toward the front of the house. Gavin's shout followed them. I ran to the front of the house. At one of the main windows, I snapped the curtains open just as I heard the sound of glass shattering above me. Outside, window shards collapsed onto the grass. A trio of Ares in human form followed, landing on their feet. One of them clutched three large, ancient-seeming books to his chest. In a moment, they disappeared into the woods.

Gavin dropped into the lawn, transforming into his panther before his paws touched ground. Before he could pursue the Ares, I got his attention by pounding on my window. In mid-stride, he stopped, turned.

I motioned for him to return to the house.

Behind me, Josh raced upstairs toward the library. Gavin hissed at me, but obeyed, skulking toward the front door. I yelled for someone to unlock it, then raced after Josh. Several of the bookshelves had been wiped clean, their contents dumped onto the floor. Josh sifted through the piles, his actions becoming increasingly anxious. After a moment, he threw a random book across the library in disgust.

"Josh," I whispered. "What else did they take besides the Clostra?"

He snapped, "The *finis* book."

The book that held the Gem of Levage.

Magic rushed into the room, gathering around him. Pacing in frustration, he waved an arm at a half-empty book-shelf, sending it flying ten feet across the room to slam into another shelf. The two shelves collapsed, spilling books.

Magic gathered around him again for a fresh tantrum. In two strides I was at his side, squeezing his arm hard enough to get his attention.

I growled, "Not now."

He shrugged off my grip, giving me an extra magical shove in the process. I held his gaze for a long moment while he fumed. He took our defeat personally. The loss of the Clostra and the *finis* were salt in the wound. If Samuel were involved in the attack, the loss could very well mean the demise of all were-animals. Even if all three of the books were brought together, only Sky and her cousin, Senna, could read them—as far as we knew.

The East Coast Pack had the job of keeping an eye on Senna and her family. Reaching into my pocket for my phone, I stopped myself from calling Cole, the pack's Alpha.

He was a political scavenger, a power monger. I had to be careful what I shared with him; if he knew that Sebastian was injured, Cole wouldn't hesitate to issue a challenge. Decorum required a seven-day wait after an Alpha was injured, unless the pack was under threat, which it was. The thought of a challenge made me sick to my stomach. Still, I needed him to increase his surveillance of Senna. I sent the request by text, leaving out an explanation, then returned the phone to my pocket.

I rushed down the stairs to check on the pack. I'd reached the landing when a new uproar arose at the front door. Josh was there, peering through the looking hole. Others had rushed to the windows. A yelp from outside and Josh quickly unlocked the door, threw it open in time for Sky's wolf to charge inside. She skidded through pools of blood, nearly crashing into a wall. The door closed and barred once more, Josh quickly patted her body down, searching her fur for wounds. His obvious relief told me she was safe.

Adrenalin flooded my body. Gripping the stair rail for balance, I closed my eyes for a moment, letting the relief wash through me. I wanted to run to her, but couldn't. I'd let her run into danger alone. I'd chosen the pack over her. I'd had to, and I resented it. Up to then, I'd only ever placed my brother's life above the pack. That didn't seem to be enough anymore. For the moment, the guilt proved too much.

The noise of the house made her anxious. Human language was difficult to track in wolf form. She struggled to follow what was being said, which only increased her anxiety.

"Get Ethan in here." Dr. Baker's urgent voice rang out from the infirmary. "Get Gavin, too."

Duty took over. Striding through the entryway, I called to Sky, "You need to change."

Uncertain if she heard me, or even saw me, I pushed through the crowd outside the infirmary doors. Josh walked in behind me. Inside, I found Sebastian supine on an operating table. Two IVs were attached to his arms. Sensor cables connected him to a variety of diagnostic machines that beeped and hummed. His torn shirt hung in pieces from the table, having been torn open to reveal gaping gunshot wounds to his chest. Blood was everywhere.

Between the machines and the anxious were-animals behind me, I couldn't distinguish Sebastian's heartbeat. A nearly flat line on the monitor barely registered each feeble beat.

Winter, at Sebastian's side, turned to hide tears that she wiped away with the back of her hand.

"Winter." Josh gently wrapped an arm around her, whispered as he guided her toward the doors. "You have to move aside so he can help Sebastian."

Gavin entered the room behind me, taking in Sebastian's condition with a grim glance.

Dr. Baker met both of our gazes. "I've done what I can, but I can't stabilize him. You'll need to take on what you can."

Staring into Sebastian's gaping, gory wounds, I knew the chances of success were slim. Gavin and I could help to absorb the wounds, aiding in the healing, but we were likely not enough. Only the most powerful members of the pack could absorb another were-animal's wounds. Recently, it had taken Sebastian, me, Gavin, Sky, and Winter to save Steven, who had been on the receiving end of Demetrius's skill with a blade. Winter and Sky were no help now. They weren't strong enough to link to an Alpha.

Still, we had to try.

Taking my place next to Sebastian, I placed a palm over his stomach. Gavin, positioned on the other side of the table, placed his hand over mine. I closed my eyes, took a breath to prepare myself for the pain, then opened the link to Sebastian. Hot pain flooded my chest, threatening to overwhelm me. I gasped, leaned against the table for balance. A wet tearing sound filled my ears as I felt skin and flesh rip, exposing a gaping wound in my chest similar to Sebastian's but not quite as severe. Blood ran from the wound, soaking my shirt.

I gritted my teeth against the pain. *Too much. Too fast.*

From the void beyond my agony, I heard Gavin's cry. His hand slipped from mine, followed by a crash. Like me, he'd tried too hard, taken too much at once. I fought against the link, pushing back for a reprieve. Sebastian's shared agony receded just until I felt I could endure. After a few panting breaths, I took more—slowly this time. The only way to take what Sebastian needed to give was to slowly, steadily increase my load. I was the frog in a pot of water slowly rising to a boil.

Sweat and blood mixed in my wound. Pain and breath became one. I lost track of everything and everyone in the room until my being drifted into an agonizing black void. My heart pounded there, beating wildly.

Not enough.

I couldn't take enough to guarantee Sebastian's survival. I couldn't take more, either. I did anyway. On the verge of losing consciousness, I opened the flood gates. My wolf rose to the surface as I collapsed onto the floor, then lost consciousness.

I woke some time later to find myself lying on one of the infirmary's beds, still in wolf form. Exhaustion overwhelmed me, but the pain in my chest had lessened. The wound was still there, but had largely closed. On a neighboring table, Sebastian remained supine, his eyes closed. At a glance his wound was healing. I knew by Dr. Baker's knotted brow that he wasn't out of danger.

On another table across the room, Gavin's panther was propped up on his paws, panting. The wounds he'd taken on had healed, at least on the surface.

I heard Josh's voice next to me. "Somebody's awake."

Turning my head triggered bolts of pain radiating from my chest. Mercifully, Josh turned the wheeled table a few inches to reveal him seated next to me on a chair he'd placed there. He grinned at me, hands in his lap, his annoying tattoos displayed down the lengths of his arms.

"Do you have any idea how much magic I had to use to get you up on that table?"

My attempt at a growl became a whimper.

Josh leaned forward and squeezed my paw, the warmth of his grip comforting.

Sky's voice spoke from somewhere behind me, "Is Sebastian going to be okay?"

"I don't know." Dr. Baker slumped into his desk chair as his gaze turned to our Alpha. "They weren't regular bullets. His body was injected with silver upon impact. I think I flushed it all out, but if I didn't, then he will heal slower, respond to things as though he is wholly human. I won't know much more for a couple of hours."

From there, he went into minute detail about Sebastian's injuries, the complications involved. I didn't have to look at Sky to see her eyes glaze over. I wouldn't admit it, but I was just as lost without Kelly to translate for him. Still, the information dump was comforting, as it offered the illusion that Dr. Baker was in control.

My eyes tracked Sky as she crossed the room to Gavin. Whispering his name, she gently stroked the back of his neck. His movements were lethargic as he leaned into her and slowly pushed her away. As if that weren't clear enough, he reached out with a paw to push her, though there wasn't much behind the gesture. Her expression was confused as she turned to me. She hesitated, gave an anxious glance between Gavin and me.

Her voice cracked as she offered a feeble, "Hello," then turned toward the exit.

Longing for her soothing presence, I reached out and

snagged her shirt with a claw as she walked by. She hesitated, glancing at the contact. Exhaustion sapped my strength, but I managed to give her shirt a light tug before letting go. My eyes shut briefly from the exertion.

Buoyed by my invitation, she eased herself onto the end of the bed, the only place available to her. I could feel her gaze searching my injuries, weighing my response to her. With a great deal of effort, I inched closer and laid my head in her lap, relaxing into her warm comfort. Almost immediately, I fell asleep.

When I woke up a few hours later, Sky was in Josh's chair, lost in troubled sleep. Dr. Baker stood over Sebastian, his expression more gaunt as he glanced at the clock on the wall. Gavin and the other were-animals had left the room, as had Josh.

The wounds in my chest had fully closed. Sebastian's wounds were still healing, still exposed. He wasn't healing fast enough. I'd done what I could for him, and more. With any luck, he'd have time to heal properly. I doubted that the Ares and whoever helped them were going to allow us that much time.

I shifted as I sat up on the table's edge, the final hairs receding from my hands as I rubbed the stress from my countenance. When I looked up to Dr. Baker, his expression was grim.

"It's nearly been twenty-four hours."

I questioned him with a look.

"When I first reached him, he was still conscious. He instructed me…" Dr. Baker's lips tightened in a brief show of anger. "After twenty-four hours, I am to stop treating him."

He watched my response closely.

Josh spoke from the door as he returned. "It's getting tense out there."

I glanced at Sky, listened to her heartbeat to make sure she truly was asleep. My body ached for the same. I wanted nothing more than to wrap her in my arms, carry her upstairs, and sleep away the day with her, but that wasn't possible. What was coming was going to be hard for us both. Some aspects of pack life were still new to her. She wouldn't understand. Worse, she would hate me.

Better to let her sleep while she can.

I slid off the table, dressed. Without a word I walked out of the infirmary, Josh following close behind.

The wounded had all been treated, many hastily, but they'd had time for their bodies to heal. The house was full of them, scattered in dark corners, whispering and throwing glances at each other. Anxious stares watched me wander the halls. Focusing within, I radiated confidence, but it wasn't enough. The strength of any pack resided with its Alpha. Without strong leadership, confidence waned. Trust dissolved. Packs fractured and broke apart. I'd seen it before. When the Alpha of the Southern Pack had been killed, the pack scattered. Only a strong Alpha, Joan, was able to reconstitute the pack. In times of peace, an Alpha-less pack could take months to disintegrate. We were at war, freshly defeated with an enemy lurking outside our gates.

Without my assistance in the infirmary, Sebastian would likely be dead. By aiding him, I left the pack to consume itself with its own anxiety. Looking now into those eyes of the survivors, I knew they'd passed the point where I could bring them together as the pack's Beta. If I didn't take full control of the pack soon, my delay would be perceived as weakness.

Sebastian understood, hence his instructions to halt care after twenty-four hours. He knew that if he couldn't regain his strength quickly, a challenge would be necessary. Of course, he wouldn't just abandon his role. Sebastian was always going to be the Alpha, the Elite, until someone took it from him in a life-or-death struggle. To do anything else would destroy his legacy.

"Ethan," Josh hissed over my shoulder when we'd found

some solitude in an empty part of the house. I recognized the single, simple door in the middle of the hall, opened it. "We need to talk."

Josh followed me into a bare, unadorned room with hardwood floors that reeked of old blood. No joy came to this room. It existed for one purpose, the challenge. Josh recognized it. I sighed, expecting the next words out of his mouth to be a practice run for Sky's eventual confrontation. He surprised me.

"I talked to Sky about what happened to her." His eyes were wide, urgent. "The jackal was Ethos. Taking down my blood ward, that was Ethos."

"Ethos is dead."

"Sky found him when she went after the shooter. This was his doing. He's behind Marcia's efforts to control the Aufero as well."

I wanted to know why, waited silently to find out.

Relieved to finally have my attention, Josh continued. "He's on some kind of power trip. He thinks by getting Sebastian out of the way, you'll be grateful to him. He thinks Sky will convince you to accept Ethos as our overlord."

For a moment, I let the grotesqueness of that horror sink in—the scheme of a madman, or whatever Ethos was. We knew he was the brother of Maya—Sky's spirit shade—but little else. They were powerful, and apparently insane. To them, the rest of the supernatural world seemed like toys.

"If you challenge Sebastian, you'll be doing exactly what Ethos wants you to do."

The thought gutted me. I forgot to breathe until my lungs forced the issue. I shook my head, begrudgingly admitted, "This changes nothing."

"What do you mean, 'changes nothing'?"

"The only reason I'm even considering a challenge is because another attack will scatter the pack if our leadership isn't settled. Now we know there will indeed be another attack. Ethos won't give up. Once he realizes Sebastian is alive, Ethos will launch another attack."

My brother stalked across the room as if he couldn't bear to be near me. At the far end of the room he turned, gaping. "You're really going to give Ethos what he wants?"

A deliberate, calming breath failed to stifle my rising anger. "This pack belongs to Sebastian. I don't want it. I've never wanted it."

Josh mocked me. "You don't see yourself as an Alpha?"

"Somewhere," I admitted. "Someday, but not here. Not like this."

"So don't challenge him."

I sighed, shook my head. For all of his experience as the pack's blood ally, there were some things about pack life that Josh would never understand. Taking control of the pack was the last thing I wanted. "*If* I challenge Sebastian, it will be because he wants me to."

"And then what, Ethan?"

"This time, we kill Ethos properly."

He waved me off in disgust as he began to pace. "Explain it to the pack. They'll understand. They just need to know that you're leading them *as their Beta* while Sebastian heals."

I gestured toward the halls we'd just wandered. "You saw them."

His head cocked sideways, as if in warning. "They're frightened."

"Exactly. You've never seen what fear can do to a pack under stress. Right now, every one of them is calculating their odds of surviving the next attack."

"You don't trust them?"

"Survival is primal," I stated. "They're looking at each other, wondering who's going to stand and fight and who's going to break. Soon, that fear is going to get to someone. They will reach a breaking point and slip away. Once their absence is noticed, doubt will spread like wildfire. The rest will leave in a rush, like wild frightened animals. It's happened before. It's the same thing that happens to soldiers in battle when their commanding officer falls. I don't blame any of them for their fear."

He half turned, hands on his hips while he shook his head at his feet. He didn't want to agree, but he couldn't or wouldn't argue the point further. He stood like that, deep into his doubts for a few seconds before he looked up. He gestured to my blood-drenched shirt. "Maybe they'd have more confidence in you if you didn't look like you were about to drop dead."

The floor creaked beneath his boots as he strode across the room and out the door.

I stayed in that room for a moment, remembering past challenges, both mine and Sebastian's. My tactical mind started assessing his fights for predictors. I growled, putting that to a stop—for the moment, at least. Sebastian was the only were-animal stronger than me, but not by much. He was my friend and when it came to leadership, a mentor. We never took on the roles of teacher and student, but I learned a great deal from him. Killing him and taking over the pack would destroy me.

I walked out of the room, leaving the light on.

Stopping in the infirmary, I told Dr. Baker, "Follow his instructions," then went upstairs to shower and change. My freshly healed wounds were raw from scrubbing the thick layer of dried blood that caked my chest. The water ran cold before it ran clear down the drain. I remained there, letting the water flow off the back of my head, hoping to quit the part of my mind that planned for the challenge, the first decisions I'd make as Alpha. I hated it all. Eventually, I gave up and abandoned the shower.

Once changed into fresh clothes, I put on an air of confidence and made another tour of the halls. The pack's morale seemed to be deteriorating by the hour. On my way to the infirmary, I saw Sebastian resting in one of the recovery rooms. Winter stood at his side, willing his recovery with desperate hope. When she saw me, her gaze turned to ice.

I paused in the doorway. "Has he regained consciousness?"

"He will." Her voice was taught, deliberate. "He is recovering."

I couldn't fault her for her anger. She owed him her life.

Snakes were rare, even in Egypt. Many were-animals saw them as cursed, shunned them. When Winter first showed her ability to shift into her animal at the age of four, her human parents panicked. They found a shaman who advised them to give up their girl to a local pack. The pack did everything they could to separate her from her animal. When that failed, they planned to kill her. Winter's mother learned of the plot to murder her child. Somehow, she'd found Sebastian—he'd never told me how. This was early in his leadership, before I joined the pack. Sebastian got on a plane to Egypt and brought her to join the Midwest Pack. To save her, he'd killed the pack's Alpha and five ranked members in challenges.

He'd risked his life and saved her for no other reason than because it was the right thing to do. His greatest strength as Alpha was his genuine concern for and loyalty to even the lowest member of the pack.

Measuring her anger, I wondered if she'd challenge me after I defeated Sebastian. We'd sparred together often, knew how each other fought to the extent that any were-animal reveals in training. In the back of our minds, no matter how seemingly unlikely, there was always the risk the fight would be real someday. Only a fool revealed all of their tricks before it mattered. Winter knew she couldn't defeat me. That didn't mean she wouldn't challenge me.

I wondered just how much of my friend's blood my hands could bear to shed to preserve the pack.

"He needs a few days to regain his strength," she insisted, her point plain.

Did she think I'd challenge him as soon as he could fight just to gain an advantage?

I sighed, didn't address the issue. "Let me know when he wakes."

Not waiting for an answer, I made my way to the infirmary. As I approached the double doors, Gavin rounded a corner. Judging by his grimness, he'd been looking for me. I'd already pushed my way through the doors when he let me know what was on his mind.

"You're going to challenge him," he stated.

Sky was alone in the chair where I'd left her. The edge in Gavin's voice stirred her. I glowered at him, expressing in silent definite terms to shut the fuck up. Sky stretched. When she yawned, I noticed the thin healing line of a knife wound across her neck, courtesy of the Ares, or Ethos. For a blissful moment she was at peace. Reality settled in as her eyes focused on the empty table where Sebastian had been when she'd fallen asleep. It was clean now, sterile.

She glanced around the infirmary. "Where is Sebastian?"

"We moved him to another room."

"He's better?"

"It's been twenty-four hours, so we took him off the machines. His wishes."

While she tried to absorb the information, I handed her a set of keys from my pocket. "You have to leave. Your home has a blood ward and everything was changed early yesterday. It should be safe, but if you want to go back to the penthouse, I understand."

Behind me, Steven and Winter walked past the door. Sky noticed their hushed whispers. I couldn't meet her gaze, didn't want to try. Tension steadily filled the room as she realized what was going on. I could only await the explosion. Her face had grown a full shade darker when she finally blurted, "Ignore the fucking rules! Ignore Sebastian's requests!"

The veracity of her outburst took her by surprise. Her eyes searched mine, expecting either a rebuke or an argument. I wouldn't argue her moral compass. The ensuing silence seemed to sap the anger from her. When she spoke again, her voice was softer, pleading, "I don't want to leave."

You don't want to stay, not for this. Some part of her believed she'd be able to change my mind at the last moment if she stuck around.

"It's not about your wants, Sky," I said gently. "I am tired, don't make me force you out."

She crossed her arms as another pack member walked by, taking a good long look inside the infirmary. I knew him by the scent of his aftershave. How he could stand the smell was beyond me. I knew by his look that he was anticipating the challenge; regardless of who won, he knew a fight to the death meant a rise in rank. Every pack had their power seekers.

Sky scrutinized me for a moment, her eyes searching mine, looking for hope. Not finding what she wanted, her shoulders drooped. Her arms unfolded. Her head lowered and she uttered a somber, defeated, "Okay."

Grateful, I lifted her chin. Meeting her gaze for the first time, I bent and gently kissed her lips. Rather than risk an argument, I walked out of the infirmary. A few minutes later, I watched from the library window as her Honda drove off the property. Relieved, I returned to wandering the house, exuding a calming presence. I wouldn't challenge Sebastian until I'd no choice. Until then, I'd do everything I could to stave off the need. After organizing the pack into action teams, I sent a few into the kitchens to prepare food for everyone, with no thought of a siege. We'd empty out the fridge and the pantry, but I wanted every belly full before dark.

An hour later, with most of the pack either busy eating or carrying out their assignments, I returned to the library. Peace and quiet was hard to come by. Only a moment after I began pacing, Josh walked in. He looked haggard, like our prior discussion had taken years of his life. Seeing me, he hesitated in the doorway, considered leaving. But this was his library, his oasis. I didn't expect him to abandon it. He didn't disappoint. Out of fairness, I chose to leave him alone. We nodded to each other in passing. While he sat at the table, I strode toward the door. I had one foot across the threshold when I heard a clatter behind me.

I turned, found him sitting on the floor, his chair tipped over next to him. He was upright, his body rigid. His eyes were black. I knew before he said it aloud.

"The blood ward at Sky's is broken."

"I need you to transport me there."

When he didn't respond, I shook him.

"Josh!"

He remained distracted.

Seconds later, I was in the Maserati, speeding off the property. My only thought was to reach Sky. The front door to her house was open. The moment I brought the vehicle to a screeching stop outside her home, I threw open the door and shifted. I didn't care who saw. My claws clattered on the concrete porch. I raced inside to find Ethos with his back to me, confronting Sky. A knife in her hand, she wore the determined look of someone ready to sacrifice everything for a taste of blood. Ethos's fury filled the room as he drew on his magic.

I leapt onto his back, burying my claws into his flesh. Ethos howled, reached back to throw me off as he whirled. As he careened off the furniture, I found myself losing my grip. Against another foe, I'd abandon his back to take his leg, bring him down to the floor where he was vulnerable. Ethos was far too dangerous. I held on, shifting my weight to try and topple him. Furious, he whirled faster. The momentum caught up to me and my teeth slipped. My claws lost their grip. I tumbled to the floor. Before I returned to my feet, he was gone.

A transport spell for a being like Ethos was normally powerful enough to take with him any trace of his presence, like hair, blood. Whether he'd been in too much of a hurry or just pissed, he'd left a stain of blood soaking into Sky's carpet. Recognizing the importance, she carefully soaked up what she could with a kitchen towel. Once done, she sealed the towel and blood in a plastic garbage bag.

Quick thinking.

Josh might be able to use the blood to locate Ethos. Anyone else's blood, a sourcing spell was guaranteed to succeed. With a being of Ethos's power, nothing was certain. Thanks to Sky, we at least had a chance.

As the adrenaline faded, exhaustion crept in. I clambered onto the couch and changed to my human form. Anticipating the change, Sky pulled a throw blanket off the back of her couch, draped it over my groin. If I hadn't been so tired, I'd have laughed.

She sat next to me.

Sitting up, I deliberately let the blanket slip to the floor, enjoyed the look she gave me.

I looked her over for wounds, found none. From the looks of it, she'd held her own against Ethos. I wondered what would've happened if I hadn't arrived. Would she have killed him? She'd intended to. Offering her the best compliment that came to mind, I said, "That was a hell of a fight."

"Not really." She frowned. "I failed. I needed more time."

Entering the house, I'd seen the look in her eye as she'd confronted Ethos, the determination. "You can't blame yourself. You did what you could."

She gave me a curious look. "Did Josh tell you everything?"

"Everything, including that you went after the shooter with a knife." I rubbed the stubble on my chin as I shook my head. "So," I chuckled, "you literally took a knife to a gunfight."

She reached under the sofa and drew out a knife hidden there. With an easy gesture, she buried the blade into a displaced couch pillow on the other side of the room. "I know how to use a knife. Can't shoot the side of a house from ten feet away, but I can use a knife."

I considered her, how much she'd changed from the defenseless wolf I'd first brought to the retreat. She'd been afraid of her own shadow then. At the time, I thought she'd never survive in our world. I'd underestimated her. Sky Brooks had a talent for proving me wrong. "Something tells me Ethos didn't just come here to attack you."

"We gave each other ultimatums. His was either I allow Maya to take control or he starts killing all of my friends. Mine was I kill him unless he becomes a professional gambler in Vegas. He declined, so…"

She shrugged.

"His plan has changed then. He's focusing on Maya, not the pack."

An anxious look came over her as she nodded.

I asked softly, "Did he try to call her?"

"Fighting him was the only way to keep her from taking over," she admitted. Her gaze fixed on mine, imploring me. "You promised we'd get rid of her."

I brushed a stray curl from her eye. "We will."

She nodded, glanced down at the blood on her hands, then her shirt. "I still haven't gotten used to other people's blood on me."

You shouldn't.

As her gaze passed over the room, I noticed the distinct but fading mark of a vampire's bite. Anxiety settled back into my stomach. She'd fed Quell. That she couldn't just give him up wasn't a surprise. Glancing at an Ethos-sized dent in the drywall, I wondered if the vampire was the same threat to her that I'd believed he was. Had Sky changed enough that she could kill him, if necessary?

My fingers gently traced the line of her jaw, turning her gaze to mine. My voice was soft, gentle. "You went to see Quell first."

She tensed, turned away. For a moment, she didn't answer. "How is Sebastian?"

Deflection. She's getting good at it.

I sighed. "He's breathing on his own. Dr. Baker seems hopeful. You didn't answer my question."

When she did, her tone was reluctant. "Yes."

She expected anger. All I had was relief that she was safe.

"Okay," I said. "You should get the blood off."

I stood, offering her my hand. Reluctant at first, she accepted, allowing me to guide her to the bathroom. My gaze fixed on hers, I turned on the hot water. She raised her arms as I gently lifted off her shirt and tossed it aside. Her eyes searched mine as I unbuttoned her jeans, expecting some hidden fury or reluctance. I'd earned that much when I urged her to be with someone else. Standing this close to her, inhaling her scent, hearing the pace of her heart, I wanted it to be me. I remembered my words and her face and realized it wasn't going to be.

Setting regret aside, I helped her slip one leg out of her jeans, then the other. Still holding her gaze, I reached into the shower to check the water temperature. After an adjustment, I gathered up her clothes. Her eyes tracked me as I hesitated at the door, uncertain. Longing welled in me. I wanted to join her. Normally decisive, assertive, I found myself searching for some sign that she wanted the same. Choosing caution over desire, I walked out and left her alone.

In the hallway, I placed her clothes inside the washing machine. After finding her detergent, I twisted off the measuring lid. My hands started to quake as I tipped the container, spilling detergent over the edge of the lid and over my hand. Delayed fear rushed through me.

Ethos would've killed her.

She'd intended to kill him. I'd no doubt she would've tried, but he was more than a match for any single were-animal, myself included. The last time we'd fought him, it had taken the combined strength of the pack and the Seethe. Even then, we'd failed to kill him.

If I'd been a few seconds slower to arrive.

I imagined arriving to find Sky murdered, and the quake worsened until I clasped my hands together and squeezed, hard.

From the bathroom, I heard the shifting patterns of running water, imagined it streaming over Sky's shoulders toward the small of her back. The humid scent of strawberry body wash drifted into the hall. Longing returned, intertwining with fear until the emotions became an indistinguishable cocktail.

From the doorway, my eyes traced the lines of her curves on the other side of the nearly opaque shower door. The thought of losing her drove a desperate need to be close to her. I opened the door and prepared for rejection. Her eyes widened in surprise, then drifted down. When her eyes returned to mine, I found the shared longing that I needed. The desire and forgiveness was there. Could she possibly want me as much as I wanted her?

Steaming water streamed against her neck, over the healing bite marks, as I sidled into the shower next to her. A light shiver rippled beneath my touch as my fingers gently roved over the small wounds. Bending to her, I brushed the marks with my lips, tasted them with my tongue. Her breath quickened. With a slight turn of her head, she invited more. I obeyed, tracing with kisses along the nape of her neck, along the length of her jaw, until I reached her warm, soft lips.

As our kisses gained urgency, my hands roamed her curves, kneaded her hips. She gasped as my fingers reached the place between her thighs, sending a wild thrill through my body. Her hands gripped my hips, urged me closer until I'd pressed her against the wall. Still, we pulled at each other, trying to satisfy a shared, desperate need to become one.

Needing to satisfy the primal desire that rose in us, binding us in that heated moment, I kept her close. Blindly, I reached out to shut off the water. Guiding her out of the shower, we continued kissing and caressing, dripping a trail of water into the hallway. She leapt to wrap her legs tightly around me while I carried her to her room. Neither of us willing to let go, we landed entwined on the bed, her beneath me.

Her embraced eased as she encouraged my lips to wander. Her fingers wrapped themselves in my hair, applying a gentle downward pressure until I found her pleasure between her thighs, eliciting soft gasps and whimpers of pleasure that urged me on. The arousing sounds continued until they were just short pants. Her fingers clawed at the sheets, her hips writhing against me. I wanted her. Could I ever have considered turning her away?

Returning to her lips, my need for her became all-consuming as I nestled between her thighs, the warmth of her body beckoning me. Her hands kneaded the muscles of my lower back, encouraging me until I eased into her. She uttered a pained gasp at my entry, giving me pause. Holding her emerald gaze, I remained there as she got used to me. Warm breath passed between our lips as they lightly brushed against each other.

"Você está bem?" Are you okay?

When she finally nodded, I gently pressed deeper into her until I'd breached the barrier there. She gasped again, biting her lip against the pain. Her fingernails raked my back. Once more, I waited. When her heart slowed and I felt her body relax beneath me, I eased into my movement. Inhaling her scent, reveling in the pleasure of being one with her. Being connected to Sky. Mine. She was mine and I was hers.

Within minutes, our hips ground together in perfect unison. Shared pleasure washed over us as we continued, our gazes locked together until her eyes fluttered closed.

I whispered, *"Olhe para mim." Look at me.*

Her eyes opened, gaped into mine as we reached deeper into our pleasure. With a soft groan, she closed her eyes once more, fixing her attention on the pleasure between us. Her fingers clawed at me as she pulled me closer, deeper. A soft, throaty pleasing moan escaped my lips. Our kisses grew harder as we tried to consume each other. Our rhythm quickened, became fevered as we built toward a shared, heated ecstasy.

We remained locked in an embrace, both unwilling to yield to the other as our pleasure faded. Our hearts pounded together in near perfect unison as we caught our breath. My lips gently caressed her neck, kissed her lips. Her arms remained wrapped around me, still holding me close. We remained entwined, recovering, until her grip slackened. I eased off of her, gently easing her to her side so that I could cradle her against me. She closed her eyes, smiled, as she squirmed her body against mine. Within a moment, she was sound asleep. With her in my arms, I followed the gentle beat of her heart into a deep, blissful slumber.

CHAPTER 9

*S*ome hours later, I woke to a sunlit room. Sky's warmth remained pressed against me. Watching the slow rise and fall of her breath, I wondered if I could sustain what we had. In all of my encounters and relationships, the one constant had been my reserve. I'd never hesitated to walk away because I'd never cared enough to stay. If my partner walked away, so be it. A selfish life was simple. But I cared for Sky. Somewhere along the line, her happiness and her safety had become my obsession. If I wasn't careful, I'd push her away like the rest. Changing my ways had never been part of the equation, until her. I wondered if I'd found her too late, if being a selfish ass was too ingrained in my being.

Part of me wanted to remain there, watching her sleep, but waking at dawn was an ingrained habit. Given the brightness beaming through the windows, I'd already overslept by a couple hours. Careful not to wake Sky, I eased back from my embrace.

On my way to retrieve a fresh change of clothes from the trunk of my Maserati, I hesitated on the front porch, unusually aware of my nakedness. The neighborhood was quiet, peaceful, empty. Even if I were noticed, I hardly cared about my nudity.

Sky cares.

This was her neighborhood. She cared what her neighbors saw and how they thought of her, a consequence of maintaining relationships with them—precisely why I ignored my own neighbors. While I didn't share her concern, I respected it. Staring across the yard to my Maserati in the driveway, I considered the distance, the likelihood that someone Sky cared about might see me, the chances that the same someone might talk to other neighbors. It occurred to me that in the time I spent debating whether to act, I could've already retrieved my clothes and returned to the house. Self-consciousness gave me a headache. Finally sick of the internal debate, I grumbled my way into the house. With a bathroom towel bunched in front of my crotch, I ventured back out to the Maserati.

While I fished in the trunk, Sky's voice surprised me from the doorway. "Are you serious?"

She threw anxious glances around the neighborhood as if it was going to come alive at any moment to witness her embarrassment.

I grinned. "Good morning."

"Get in the house," she half ordered, half pleaded. "If that thing falls off, the neighbors will have you arrested."

Clothes in hand, I closed the trunk. Walking up the porch, I kissed her on the cheek. "I think I'll be okay."

"Why, because you're an attorney or because you don't think anyone will call the police on you?"

After another kiss, I said, "Both."

We showered together. Dressed, I left her in the bathroom and wandered into the living room to clean up any mess left from Sky's fight with Ethos. I'd forgotten about the Aufero. Resting on a small table in a corner of the room, it reacted to my accidental approach with an angry, pulsing glow. The warning was enough to give me pause. Even before it had absorbed my dark elf magic, the orb had shown a distaste for me. Why, I couldn't say, but the object was too powerful to simply ignore. Wary, I backed up a step. The intensity of the glow lessened some.

Glancing at the dent in Sky's wall, I wondered if the orb's magic had played a part. We knew almost nothing about the orb, other than Sky was its protector by birthright. She was getting better at wielding the orb's magic. Our ignorance of it was becoming a liability.

She appeared at my side, amused by the Aufero's hostility toward me.

I gestured to the dented wall. "You did this?"

She answered with a satisfied smile.

Raising my hands to chest level, I took a small step toward the orb, then another until the orb's protective field pushed back against my palms. My hands glided over the field, feeling its uniformity. With renewed curiosity, I asked Sky, "Tell me everything that happened yesterday with Ethos."

She repeated her story, patiently answering my frequent requests for the smallest of details. When she described a language he spoke, trying to encourage Maya from her place in the shadows, I stopped Sky.

"I know you don't know that language, but can you repeat it?"

She did, stumbling over the pronunciation. The words struck a familiar chord. I'd spent untold hours in the library poring over magical texts, sometimes to help Josh, other times for my own benefit. Searching for a spark of memory, I repeated the words over and over.

"How many languages do you know?" she asked, surprised.

"I speak four. Well…" I grinned, remembering to include Portuguese. "Five now." I turned the conversation back to

Ethos. "I knew Anderson was going to be trouble the moment I met him. I can't believe he is okay with working with Ethos."

"He was promised the position of Beta of the Midwest Pack," she reminded me. "Definitely an improvement, being the leader of two hundred to being second-in-command of thousands."

It was a toss-up whether Anderson or Cole would take the award for Most Treacherous Beta, should one of them take my place. "Whoever becomes the Alpha won't be able to turn his back for a second without having Anderson's knife stabbed into it. He will only be the Beta temporarily before he does everything to claw himself to the Alpha position." I frowned. "And the shooter? Who was it?"

"Ethos called him Derrick."

"A wolf," I remembered. "The fourth in the Ares Pack."

I growled as I drew my phone from my pocket. It was past time for me and Anderson to have a conversation about how I was going to kill him and scatter his pack.

Sky touched my hand. "Who are you calling?"

"Anderson."

She blinked at me. Her brow furrowed with concern. "I think you should wait."

I'd already waited too long. "Wait on what, Sky?"

"How will speaking with him change anything? He has an agenda, and you aren't going to coerce him to change. He sees Ethos as a means to an end, and that is where we should direct our attention."

She wanted to rehabilitate Anderson—I knew by the look in her eyes. Even if I could convince him that siding with Ethos was a mistake, he could never be trusted. Like a cancer, he needed to be removed.

"Ethos wouldn't have been able to do any of that alone," I reminded her. As powerful as he was, we were still immune to his magic when in were-animal form. Without Ares to attack the retreat, Ethos couldn't have carried out his plan to kill Sebastian and take the Clostra. "Without Anderson, how would it have ended yesterday?"

When she didn't answer, I returned my attention to finding his number.

She changed the subject. "Have you heard anything from Dr. Jeremy?"

Not the conversation I want to have right now.

I nodded, scrolling through my contacts and hoping she'd drop the subject.

"And?"

"Nothing has changed since last night."

Her frown deepened. "What happens if he survives but isn't the same?"

That was more than I wanted to contemplate. "Hopefully, he will step down."

"And if he doesn't?"

"Skylar." I sighed, held her gaze. "You know what happens if he doesn't."

"Will he accept a challenge of submission?"

"You know where Sebastian and I stand on that. It hasn't changed. If we can't handle our position and someone feels strongly enough to challenge—" I hesitated as she blinked back tears. The policy was practical. Death challenges eliminated all but the most serious. That didn't mean the practice didn't have flaws. Raw physical strength wasn't always the most useful measure of leadership. Too often, I'd seen the better were-animal die in a challenge. I'd no doubt that Sebastian was the better leader. Beyond the horror of killing my friend and mentor, the pack would never be the same without his leadership. His strength, integrity, and compassion were rare among Alphas.

"You don't have to do anything," she insisted. "It's our rules, we made them and we can break them."

Our rules were ancient, primal. Right or wrong, the survival of the pack depended on them.

"If you don't feel he is fit to lead," she continued, "do what you are supposed to do, support him. That's your job. No one has to fight. No one has to die. I won't let you do it."

"Sky—"

"No! I don't want to hear anything you have to say. Promise me you will not challenge him, no matter what. Promise."

I wanted to promise, but I couldn't. "If Sebastian isn't able to continue as Alpha," I explained, each word weighing on my conscience, "I will only challenge if he doesn't step down."

"No. No, you will not. You have to promise me you won't."

"Sky."

A tear streaked down her cheek as she jerked away from my touch. "You have to promise me, Ethan."

Seeing the desperation and fear in her eyes, an ache burned in my chest. If Sebastian died at my hands, I might lose her. My voice softened to nearly a whisper. "No. I'm not going to do that. Things are the way they are. I don't like all aspects of it, but they are our rules and nothing you say to me is going to change them. If you need to cry—go ahead, let it out. If you need to scream—do that, too, but it will not change anything."

Reaching for her once more, I gently overwhelmed her resistance, pulling her close until my forehead rested against hers. My hand on her cheek, I brushed away her tear with my thumb. "This situation is black and white. I know you want it to be a gray area, but it just isn't."

Sky gasped an angry breath and pulled away from me. Her heart was in the right place, but she wasn't being practical. Her recalcitrance was making a difficult situation nearly unbearable. Fire burned in her emerald eyes as she declared, "Is that what you want to call it to make it easier to accept? So you just plan to 'black and white' the situation? Call it what it is, you two will fight until one of you murders the other."

"You want to be a child about this," I snapped, my patience at an end. "Go ahead, Sky. A pack is only as strong as its Alpha. You've enjoyed the luxury of being part of one that most will not consider screwing with. You've never been a woman in a pack that others consider weak, because then you would understand that need for a strong pack. I don't want to kill anyone in my pack, but if they feel the need to challenge me, they see a weakness in me; and if they see it, so will others outside the pack. If you need this to feel better, then fine, get upset with me and we can fight about it all night, but after today we will not have this discussion again because it will not change anything."

A knock at the door interrupted her glower, earning a resentful glance. Another knock followed, more insistent. Peering through the peephole, I found Quell waiting on the sun-drenched porch. A growl escaped my lips, but I knew the vampire wasn't going to leave. With the ward down, he was likely to break his way in if Sky didn't respond. Surrendering to the inevitable, I opened the door.

He pushed through the opening, brushing past me to take a rigid stand between me and Sky. His gaze shifted from her to the crack in the wall, the bloodstain on the floor. Finally, his narrowed eyes settled on me, an accusation.

"What?" I demanded, daring him to challenge me.

"You failed and let her get hurt."

In less than a second, I'd closed the distance between us. Somehow Sky had gotten in the way, pushing us apart.

"You go over there," she barked at me, pointing to one side of the room, then directed Quell toward the other side. "And you over there."

Neither of us moved.

"Fine," she declared, starting for the door. "I'll leave and you two can have at it. I don't have time for this."

Anxious at her departure, Quell backed away from me, just enough to give her pause. Not fooled by her bluff, I held my ground. She'd no intention of letting the situation come to violence. Pity. Killing a vampire would go a long way to venting my frustrations. Instead of discouraging us, she simply watched. For some time, the three of us stood in angry silence, waiting on someone to reduce the tension.

Eventually, I accepted the inevitable. Addressing Quell with forced interest, I asked, "Are things with Fi going well?"

The question surprised him. After a moment, he answered with a slight nod.

"Then why the hell are you here?" I growled.

"I was worried about Sky, and rightfully so—you've proven to be inept at keeping her safe."

Before I could correct him, she answered in a rush, "Quell, I'm fine. It isn't anyone's job but mine to keep me safe."

He stepped closer to her, nostrils flaring as he took in her scent—my scent, mingled with hers. I almost bothered to hide a smirk as jealousy contorted his visage. His expression quickly hardened into disgust as he scrutinized her, then me. Sky's cheeks flushed in unnecessary embarrassment.

The threat of violence filled him. I'd warned her that Quell would eventually lose control. I took a step closer, opening my stance in preparation. My gaze fixed on his shoulders, waiting for that first twitch of action. In most creatures, the eyes betrayed an act of violence just before it happened. The lifeless black eyes of a vampire betrayed nothing.

"Quell," Sky said softly. "What's the matter?"

"I didn't want you to leave last night," he whispered, "but I couldn't stop you from doing so."

I growled in warning as he clasped her hand, but she didn't pull away.

"Fiona came by and I couldn't leave to check on you. I just needed to know you were okay. You have someone watching the house now." His gaze fixed on mine. "But where were they before, when Sky was attacked?"

"Quell." She squeezed his hand, drawing his attention. "No one attacked me," she lied for his benefit. "Don't hold anyone other than me responsible for my safety. Okay?"

He linked his fingers with hers, but I was already distracted by movement outside the kitchen window. Peering out, I saw four large wolves between the trees. "They aren't part of our pack."

I strode out the door and found Anderson with two of his pack on the front lawn. The wolves lurked among the trees. Sky appeared on the porch beside me.

"The one on the right is Derrick," she whispered. "The shooter."

The assassin. He was new to me, tall and thick, with short dark hair and menacing cognac eyes. His smirk would likely freeze on his corpse after I killed him. My wolf rushed toward the surface, called by violence. Begrudgingly, I held it at bay. Any moment the neighborhood would come to life with people hurrying to their jobs. The sight of wolves fighting on Sky's lawn would attract the wrong kind of attention.

I felt her hand on my back, cautioning me as she addressed Anderson. "This isn't the time."

His smile was condescending. "Oh sweetheart, this is the time." He turned to me. "He no longer wants you as the Alpha —your protection is gone." Anderson's teeth drew back as he started toward me. The four were-animals fell in behind, leering in anticipation of blood.

My hands clenched into fists, but I remained still. With a numerical advantage, I wanted to draw the Ares into fighting their way into the house. I'd hold our ground from just inside, forcing them to come at me through the doorway one at a time. Aside from the tactical advantage, there was less chance of drawing the attention of the neighbors.

Anderson stopped a few feet from the porch. Judging by his sneer, he was surprised I hadn't walked out to face him. "You all have grown soft, more concerned about your cars, your businesses, and the appearance of strength that you no longer have."

Sky tensed beside me, prepared to fight. Individually, none of the Ares were a match for either of us. If I couldn't draw them up the porch, she'd be forced to fight two at a time, perhaps even three as I took on the rest. For myself, I didn't mind the odds. I didn't want to see Sky injured. Anderson's bravado brought a new plan to mind.

"She's right," I said. "This isn't the time. You want to challenge me, accepted."

"Waiting, a coward's approach." He licked his lips at Sky. "And the things I plan to do to you when he's gone."

Anger lit a fire in my spine. Before I could act, I felt the dark, oppressive magic of the Aufero swirl around me as it answered her call.

"Why wait?" she snapped.

With an effortless thrust of her hands, the dark magic flowed through her. Men and wolves were thrown to the ground, an impressive display of power. They'd think twice about continuing their attack, but Sky didn't stop there. Before I could reach out, she leapt from the porch. Looming over Anderson, she gripped his throat in one hand and squeezed. Magic swirled around her as her other hand clutched at his heart.

I watched, awed as her magic seemed to suck the life from him. His heart began to fade as he struggled for breath. For a moment, I considered stopping her. Anderson had earned this death. A quick glance at the other Ares revealed they were still struggling to gather their wits. The neighborhood remained quiet, for now at least. As Anderson's heart beat slower and slower, I hissed to her, "Do it quickly."

Something about the magic she used was off, darker than the Aufero.

She brought him to the brink of death, then inexplicably relaxed her magic. He caught a pair of gasping breaths before she returned to drawing the life from him. I blinked, confused. This wasn't Sky. Even enraged, she'd never torture an enemy.

A cold, alien smile was on her lips. She enjoyed it.

Anderson's eyes bulged. He squeaked as she choked him, "Please."

She bent down until her face was inches from his. Her black eyes twitched as she searched his frightened gaze, savoring the nuances of his death. Once more, she relaxed her grip just enough to allow him a quick breath, then returned to torturing him.

This was Maya.

Her attention fixed on Anderson, she remained oblivious to the other Ares who had regained their feet. Distracted, I'd let them. Maya was a problem I didn't know how to solve, but she'd have to wait. I stepped off the porch, prepared to kill Derrick and the other man behind Anderson. They stood to either side, still awed by Sky's magic. Before I could reach them, the wolves got between us. Heads bowed, drool spilled out around bared teeth as they growled and snapped their jaws. Dropping into an aggressive stance, I picked out the largest wolf and bared my teeth. Before I could charge, Quell ran from the house at full speed. A blur, he plowed into the wolves, absorbing their attention.

Turning back to Sky, I stepped between her, Derrick, and the other man. They'd had plenty of opportunity to try and save their Alpha. Instead they watched in wide-eyed horror as Sky tortured him, terrified of the sinister magic that radiated from her. A growl from me sent them back a step. Confident they'd not intervene, I edged closer to Sky.

Her attention remained fixed on Anderson's ruddy expression as he gasped for breath. If she was aware of my presence, she didn't show it.

"Sky!" I shouted.

A ripple of recognition passed through her. She released Anderson's throat, staring at her hand as it began to tremble. Her eyes remained black, but glazed over as if she'd turned inward. As Sky and Maya battled for control, I'd no idea how to help her.

Anderson gasped as he stumbled away. The rest of the Ares followed him in desperate retreat.

"Sky!" I called to her.

She remained unmoved.

Quell brushed me aside, gripped her shoulders. Staring into her eyes, he called to her. "You must fight! If you give in, she will control you forever. You must resist!"

Sky blinked. Green swirled in her eyes as she tried to reassert herself. She glanced around the yard, uncertain where she was. When I took her hand, she jerked it free.

"Don't touch me!"

She whirled, started to stalk away. Maya was reasserting control, but I knew by her confused look that Sky was close to the surface, battling her way toward consciousness. Catching up to her, I wrapped my arm around her waist and pulled her close to me. As she struggled to free herself, I whispered into her hair, "It's okay. You're fine. You are."

After a moment, her resistance ebbed. Her body went limp in my arms, leaning into me for support. I held on tight, listening to her heart thump against my chest.

"You're okay," I whispered over and over. Her heart slowed, eventually matching my own. My relief quickly turned to fear as I realized she'd become unresponsive. She was able to stand on her own, but her eyes were glazed, her gaze unfocused.

At my side, Quell gripped her face in his palms, searched her eyes. Willing to try anything, I let him. She seemed to focus on him calling her name.

"She'll be fine for now," he said to me. "The spirit shade must be removed."

He continued, telling me nothing I didn't already know about Maya and Sky. She'd obviously confided in him. When he turned back to her, I drew my phone from a pocket. Before I could call Dr. Baker, he called me.

"Sebastian's awake," he said, relieved.

As Sky took in her surroundings, I saw her eyes had returned to normal. Relieved, I informed Dr. Baker, "On my way," and pocketed my phone.

Forcing myself between Quell and Sky, I gently took her hand. This time, she let me guide her to the Maserati. I eased her into the passenger seat, put on her belt, then drove toward the retreat. Afraid to let go, my hand gripped hers between the seats. She stared out the window, silent until I parked in the retreat driveway.

"I want her out of me," she whispered, surprising me as I removed the keys from the ignition.

The leather seat squeaked as I turned toward her, studying her closely. There were still too many questions to answer about Maya's link to Sky. I'd hoped that finding the Tre'ase who transformed Maya into a spirit shade would answer some of those questions. At the least, we'd know if Sky could survive separation from Maya. At this point, I wasn't sure Sky could survive with her, either. Any risk was better than helplessly watching the spirit shade take control.

"Okay."

"Don't just say it. Please, I want you to do something about it."

Releasing her hand, I climbed out to open her door and

help her out. Determined, she climbed out on her own. Relieved, I remained close while she lingered, gripping the top of the door for balance. After a moment, she closed it, took a cautious step toward the house. After a few steps, her confidence returned. She was exhausted, frightened, but her eyes were alert. She'd pushed Maya back, but the fight had been closer than I cared to contemplate.

Just short of the porch, she hesitated.

I sighed, worried. "What is it, Sky?"

She drew in her bottom lip, slowly shook her head, then started up the porch. "I want to see Sebastian."

Each of the recovery rooms was painted a different, single color. Sebastian was in the blue room. I hesitated at his door, worried what I would find. Now that he was awake, a decision had to be made. I opened his door to find him sitting up in bed, reading. He was shirtless, revealing barely a hint of the wound that had torn his chest open. As talented as Dr. Baker was, I knew of very few were-animals who could've survived Sebastian's injuries. Gavin and I had helped some, but not enough to explain our Alpha's recovery. He gave every impression of restored strength.

Next to me, Sky's silent relief was palpable.

My own relief quickly faded as he looked up to greet us. The muscles in his neck were taut, creating a slight stutter motion when he raised his head. There were other signs. He leaned to the right, favoring that side, which meant he was probably hiding a great deal of pain.

Our eyes met, both conveying normalcy, both sizing each other up—the predators in us never slept.

Steven watched the silent communication with deep interest from the chair beside the bed.

I forced my lips into a smile. "How do you feel?"

He shrugged and set his book aside. Slipping his legs

from under the bed sheet, he stood, not bothering to hide the effort. His physical wound had healed, but he was going to need time to recover his strength. My smile faded, the consequences of his condition settling like a cancer in my gut.

Reading my expression, he said casually, "I may need a couple of days, but I understand."

Sky glanced between us, horrified. "No."

"Sky," I said.

"No," she insisted.

Sebastian held my gaze with an almost compassionate understanding. I couldn't count the number of times we'd sparred. At the time, I'd happily contemplated his vulnerabilities, anticipating a moment such as this. But that was just an intellectual exercise. Facing Sebastian now, with violence so close to reality, the thought of challenging him gave me an ill feeling at the pit of my stomach. He was my mentor, my friend. I'd die for him, and I knew he'd die for me. Fighting each other was beyond foolish. Sky and Josh were right. If the pack needed Sebastian's blood to hold together, then it deserved to fracture. There was no better Alpha for the Midwest Pack. In time he'd make a full recovery. Until then —as always—he'd have my support. If anyone else was fool enough to challenge him, I'd make sure they never showed up for the fight.

Eventually, Sky couldn't take the silence. Assuming the worst, she started to leave.

Before she reached the door, I declared my confidence in Sebastian. "I feel very comfortable with you as my Alpha."

She gasped behind me. Steven blinked, glancing between us.

Sebastian remained still, seemingly unmoved. I'd known him long enough to notice the slight drop of stress from his shoulders, the mild tip of his chin. For a moment, he battled his relief. Eventually, he nodded once, betraying nothing. Before I could say more, Winter burst into the room. Her car hadn't been in the garage when I'd arrived. She'd probably raced to the retreat as I had, once she'd heard that Sebastian was awake. Her eyes wide with joy, she took in the sight of him standing in front of her like it was a miracle. It was. Not many were-animals could survive his wound.

His lips spread into a smirk. "Hi."

Tears welled in her eyes as she stared back at him, almost in disbelief. Her breath was quick. Her lips twitched, but she couldn't find words to express the intensity of how she felt.

His smile softened. He placed his hands on her shoulders and she uttered a small sob.

"I'd like to be alone," he said to the rest of us. Winter started to turn, and he said, "No, you stay."

Sky gestured for Steven and me to leave. Turning back to close the door, I saw Winter's tears starting to run as he embraced her.

Sky and I walked quietly for a moment in the hall. I could feel the questions bubbling up in her.

"Not now, Sky," I whispered.

Overwhelmed, I needed to do what all tough guys did to process their emotions; I changed into workout clothes and hit the gym.

Word spread fast. By the time I'd finished with the weights, gossip wafted through the gym like a wildfire. From the seat of an elliptical machine, I assessed the pack's mood—relieved, for the most part. Some concerns remained. That neither Ethos nor Ares had followed up with a second attack helped their mood. Fear was the enemy of reason. For the moment, the pack felt safe again. Sebastian and I would keep it that way.

For myself, I felt a dense, oppressive weight had been lifted from my shoulders.

My phone rang from beneath my towel on a nearby

bench. Though muffled, I recognized the tone—Stacy, my legal assistant. I'd told her I was taking a few days off, which wasn't unusual. At times, I'd take weeks off with no more than a few days' notice. My bosses accommodated my unorthodox work habits because I made them a lot of money and didn't bug them to make me a partner. Stacy wouldn't call me now unless it was important.

I got up with a sigh and retrieved my phone. "Yes?" I said, using the towel to mop sweat from my brow.

"Hey, boss. Sorry to bother you. I just wanted to make sure you were on your way to your meeting."

"I cleared my calendar for the week."

"That's what I thought," she said, confused. Her voice lowered to a conspiratorial whisper. "There's something off about this guy. I'd swear he's a vampire."

When I'd met her, she'd been an assistant to one of the lower-level attorneys at the firm. A Russian-American vampire Seethe from New York that specialized in cyber-crime and identity theft had threatened her family, forcing her to siphon money from clients' retainers. I'd discovered the theft and confronted her. She expected to go to jail. That I'd actually believed her story was a surprise. I'd put Demetrius onto the vampires—he didn't appreciate that they'd reached into Chicago without his permission—and made her my assistant. She was a hard worker and her cyber skills came in handy on occasion.

She still saw vampires around every corner.

I rubbed my fingers into my temple, wondering if I'd forgotten someone important. "What's this guy's name?"

"Mr. McClintock."

I froze.

"He's here with a Ms. Snell. They're from a law firm called Devlin, Cheatum, and Howe. Oh," she said, suddenly confused. "That's a joke, right? Is it April Fool's Day, because

I'd swear it's September. I'm sorry. I shouldn't have called you. I'll send them away."

"No," I snapped, working hard to keep my rising anger from my voice. I needed her to remain calm. If McClintock thought she was on to him…but he already knew. He'd given her his name, knowing I'd ask for it. He was taunting me. He'd gone to the one place in my life that was fully human. He'd walked right in and plopped his ass onto my cover, daring me to stop him. I took a calming breath, fought the urge to smash my phone.

"Boss? Is there a problem?"

"Where are they now?"

A nervous edge crept into her voice. "In your office. I feel like something is wrong."

"Keep them there."

She stammered, "Am I in danger?"

I rubbed my forehead with my fingers, debating what to tell her. She knew what I was, but not much else about the supernatural world. I didn't want to tell her that she'd walked a couple of killers into my office. Some people could be soothed by lies. Stacy wasn't one of them.

"They're not vampires," I said.

"Oh, good."

"But they are dangerous."

"Oh shit."

"You're in a public place, and you're not the reason they're there. I'll be there in a few minutes. Just treat them like any other clients. You'll be fine."

"Okay," she said, unconvinced.

I killed the call and made another, this one to Matthew, the Worgen. Once those arrangements were made, the urgency conveyed, I gathered Gavin, Steven, and Josh in Sebastian's room. Winter was already there when we arrived, seated next to his bed. Before closing the door, I made sure no one—Sky, in particular—was lurking to eavesdrop.

Explaining the situation left Gavin confused, but getting him up to speed wasn't an option. There wasn't enough time.

He was the first to object. "This is another attempt to draw you away before Ethos makes a second attack."

His anxiety was warranted. Sebastian wasn't strong enough to lead our defense. If an attack came, my leadership would be needed to hold the pack together. If they thought I'd fled, fear might once again take hold. Until Sebastian was stronger, the pack was fragile.

"Ethos is no longer interested in controlling the pack," I explained. "His attention has shifted to Maya."

Gavin sneered. "Dozens of were-animals died in that attack, and it was just a whim?"

Sebastian asked me, "Are you certain?"

"When Anderson came for Sky, he said my protection had been withdrawn. Regarding Maya, Ethos told Sky directly. He showed up at her house last night, tried to bargain with her for Maya."

Josh's expression darkened at the reminder that his blood wards weren't enough to stop Ethos.

Steven's eyes widened. "She faced him alone?"

"She attacked him," I said matter-of-factly.

"Wow," Winter said dryly, glancing at her nails. "I don't know whether to give Baby Spice a medal or a spanking."

I skipped through some of the details, gave them the quick version. "He fled when I arrived, probably thought I had the pack behind me."

Josh scrutinized me. "There's more you're not saying."

My gaze flicked to the clock on the wall. I didn't have time to tell them how Maya had nearly taken control of Sky. "I need to deal with this situation before it gets out of hand."

Gavin remained firm. "Anderson and Ethos could both be playing you. We have to assume he'll make another attempt on Sebastian."

"I'll go alone. If there's an attack, Josh can transport to me. He can have me back here in less than a minute."

"I have a better idea," Josh proclaimed. "I'm going with you."

I held his defiant gaze. "I go. Alone."

Gavin insisted, "It's not worth the risk. We need you here."

"He's not going to harm anyone else in my name."

"If this hunter attacks your office," Gavin said, "he'd be a fool. The building is full of cameras. The police would have his name and picture within an hour. The manhunt would be immense."

"He could still do damage there. He could even out me."

Gavin sneered. "You're being played."

"He still has Artemis," I growled. "He's looking for more leverage. If I don't go, he'll hurt someone." I turned to Sebastian. "I have to stop him."

Sebastian studied me for a long moment, seemingly oblivious to the rising tension in the room. "He expects you to come alone. It's your way, Ethan. After losing Marko, there's no chance you'd risk anyone else's life."

"Exactly." I shot a glance at Josh. "That's why I'm going alone."

"So far, McClintock has gotten the better of you."

His statement stung, but I remained respectfully silent as he continued.

"If you're going to subvert McClintock's plan, you need to defy his expectations. You need help."

My jaw clenched until I thought the bones had fused together. The weak needed help. The strong provided it. I'd spent my entire life relying on my strength. I wasn't about to swap roles now because an old hunter had temporarily gotten the best of me.

Eventually, Josh interrupted my fuming. "There's no time for debate, Ethan. I can transport you there." He showed

Gavin his phone. "If anything happens here, I'll have Ethan back before your call goes to voicemail." Back to me, he promised, "I'll stay out of sight, but if McClintock does get violent, you're going to need me."

I hated that he was right. If the old man did decide to go out in a blaze of glory, Josh's magic could save lives. Not to mention, magic would be much easier to explain away later than my wolf.

I accepted his offer with a begrudging nod. "You remember the last time you were there?"

His lips thinned as he thought, tapping his chin with his index finger. "Was that Bring-Your-Helpless-Little-Brother-to-Work Day?"

This wasn't a time for jokes. "The bathroom outside the firm, can you transport there?"

"No problem." He gestured to my jeans and t-shirt. "I'm pretty sure Wendell, Harper, and Holmes has a dress code."

Growling, I hurried upstairs, changed into a dark-grey suit with a black tie. Within minutes, I was dressed and ready. The moment Josh touched my arm, I felt his magic rush through me. My surroundings shifted. The retreat became a sterile-smelling bathroom. Expecting the men's room, I was momentarily confused by the lack of urinals.

He answered my accusatory look with a smug smile. "It's better you don't ask."

I checked each of the stalls. Fortunately, we were alone.

Josh started ahead of me toward the exit until I stopped him.

"McClintock will recognize you. Wait here. If you hear screaming"—I added before he could object—"come running."

His arms folded over his chest while he glared at me. I figured I had a few minutes before he came wandering into the firm. I had my hand on the door when I stopped.

"I'm sending Stacy to you. Get her out of here before trouble starts, somewhere safe."

"The peppy young lady that thinks I'm a vampire?"

"Exactly."

He gestured toward a wall, presumably at my firm on the other side. "I'm not leaving you alone here for—"

"She gets out of here," I commanded.

He held my gaze long enough to register his protest, then nodded.

On my way out the bathroom door, Josh loudly declared, "I'll just be here playing with the paper towels."

The large glass doors to my firm were at the end of a short hallway, the large cherrywood reception desk just beyond. Behind it, Aaron patiently took instructions from Mr. Holmes, who was showing off for two of his best clients.

Four.

I pushed through the glass doors, stopped in front of the desk to count bodies. To my right, four Japanese men with briefcases emerged from a conference room. Through the glass walls, I saw Ms. Gerard chatting with two more of the Japanese contingent.

Seven.

Near the conference room were the paralegal cubicles. The three that I could see were occupied.

Ten.

To my left was the hallway that led to four offices, including mine. All of the glass walls had blinds, only Ms. Wendell's were closed, which meant she was in an important meeting, which meant a powerful client who likely came with two assistants.

Fourteen.

Pavita Everett had the office adjoining mine. She was at her desk with a young couple in front of her. I cursed at the sight of a baby draped over the woman's shoulder, staring in my direction.

Eighteen.

Too many bodies.

The blinds behind Ms. Everett, which draped over our shared glass wall, were mostly closed on my side. I could just make out two shapes inside, seated in front of my desk. Stacy stood in the open doorway, nodding to someone—McClintock or Tonya.

Glancing around for an idea, I noticed the fire alarm on the wall halfway down the hall. Pulling it would clear the firm and the entire floor within minutes, giving me plenty of opportunity to deal with McClintock. *They'll have guns,* I reminded myself. Gunshots would be difficult to explain later.

I noticed Aaron's half-full coffee mug on the desk. Reaching over the counter, I picked up the mug and carried it toward my office. The mug was lukewarm in my hand.

Unaware of my approach, Stacy began an apology. "Again, I'm so sorry for the wait. This has been such a waste of your time. I'd be happy to follow up with your office and reschedule at your convenience."

McClintock's slow drawl answered. "My time is valuable, but I expect this meeting will be sufficiently worth the wait."

"Of course," she said. "I'll just step out and give Ethan a call to see if he's stuck in traffic."

As she turned out of the doorway, I bumped into her, deliberately slopping the coffee onto her white blouse. She gasped. Expecting to be burned, she pinched the fabric from her skin with both hands.

"Sorry," I said with little enthusiasm. I turned to find McClintock smiling at me. He'd taken the chair farthest from the door, turned it so he could see trouble coming. For a moment, outing myself no longer mattered. I imagined wrapping my hands around his throat, but set that need aside. "One moment," I said, then guided Stacy back toward the reception desk.

"Oh my God," she hissed, still struggling with the stain on her blouse.

"You're not burned. You need to leave here, now."

"Wait, that was deliberate?"

"I want you to go to the bathroom."

She hissed on her way out, "You could've just told me I had to pee."

I stopped at the end of the hall, watched her leave. Aaron gasped at her blouse, whispered to her, "He's such a jerk."

Walking back to my office, I stopped in the doorway. Tonya and McClintock smiled back at me, smug as hell. They both wore cheap suits, probably just bought off a discount rack. I noted the bulge of a pistol holster at the small of Tonya's back, another at her right ankle. If I found a small knife tucked into her dark bob, I wouldn't be surprised. McClintock did a better job of secreting his weaponry, but the human body offered only a few functional hiding places.

"There he is," he declared with a shit-eating grin, straightening his jacket as he rose. Tonya rose as well. She looked me up and down, scanning for weapons.

I smiled back, showing my teeth. Reaching behind me, I closed my door and stood there, blocking it to make sure they understood who was trapped by whom. After tightening the blinds to Latisha's office, I dropped the pretense.

"You're playing with fire, coming here."

McClintock gestured at my office, lowered his voice. "Have I finally crossed your line? Here I thought shooting one of your pals would do the trick."

My fists clenched as I focused the wrath of my glare on Tonya. "You shot him." I turned to McClintock. "And you killed him."

"So he did die." He shrugged. "Happens. I must say, your self control has definitely improved. Back in the day, someone murdered your pal, you'd be out there causing all sorts of mayhem to get your revenge, damn the costs."

Let's cut to the chase. "How much is Marcia paying you?"

He pursed his lips, grunted. "You know there's two things I never discuss, the recipe to my grand-mammy's scrumptious Lane Cake, and my clients."

"So you are working for her?"

He strolled over to my desk, ran a finger over the finished oak. "Neither confirm nor deny." With a smug look, he dropped into my chair and leaned back to put his boots on the desktop. "You have a nice office here. Nice coworkers. Is that what you call your fellow lawyers?" He looked to Tonya, who shrugged. "I can see that look in your eyes, Ethan. Your wolf is showing. I'd hate to see all these civilians get caught up in some violence. Of course, you'd expose your true self to them. That's going to get out for sure, which means a whole lot of attention is going to fall on you, the pack, and every other supernatural being out there. I might be going out on a limb, but I think that's going to really piss off the rest of the factions."

I growled, "You talk too much."

His lips spread into a grin as he declared, "That's because I ain't never heard a voice as sweet."

"Give me Artemis. If she's safe, you get to walk away."

Tonya scoffed.

"After we killed your friend, you're going to let me live?" McClintock said. "Oh, I know you too well for that."

"You're obviously here to negotiate."

Feigning confusion, he asked Tonya, "Is that what we're doing?"

Her smug smile grew smugger.

"Marcia's on the run," I said, folding my arms over my chest. "Sean is on the run. Are you prepared to hitch your fate to Ethos?"

The humor left him. "Last I heard, you all killed that thing."

"He's aligned himself with one of the smaller packs here."

"Ares," McClintock confirmed like he was putting puzzle pieces together. "The ones that just attacked your retreat."

So he hadn't been involved in the attack. I knew by his tone. When McClintock was pissed, he dropped the smug act, as he did now. I still figured Marcia was behind his contract, but she'd kept him at arm's length. Even desperate, the old man wasn't likely to bind himself to a nefarious and powerful figure like Ethos.

"This is bigger than you want to be involved in," I said. "Name your price to walk away, as long as I get Artemis safe and sound, and I never see your face again. That goes for your sidekick as well."

Tonya tensed at the label. She wanted a fight. I made note of her temper, something to make use of later.

McClintock slipped back into his devil-may-care persona. "Now what makes you think this is a negotiation?"

I let my wolf rise to just below the surface, let its need for violence fill the room. "Why else would you put yourself in a closed room with me?"

Tonya took a step back, reached toward the holster behind her back until McClintock gestured for her to stand down. Reluctant, she obeyed, but remained ready. Her drawing hand rested next to her hip, close enough to still make a quick draw. She was kidding herself. If I'd wanted to kill her, she'd be dead before her fingers touched the pistol grip.

From Pavita's office, I heard the baby cry.

I glowered at McClintock, awaiting his theatrics. He slowly pulled his boots from my desk and rose, pushing the chair back in case he needed room to maneuver. "Ethan, I'm just here to remind you who you are, what you are. I just want you to do what you were born to. I want you to hunt."

"Who?"

He raised his hands out from his sides, as if the answer were obvious. "Me." He glanced around the office. "All this, it's just wrapping paper. Your tidy desk." With a sweep of an arm, he sent the contents of the desktop clattering to the ground, triggering muffled muttering from the office next door. Next he plucked my framed law license from the wall, dropped it into the waste bin by my desk. "Your certificate of normalcy. All these people here, your assistant—they're not your coworkers. They're food. Deep down inside, you know there's just your pack and the hunt. This"—he made a gripping gesture toward his mouth and nose—"muzzle you wear, that's just someone else's leash. Take that shit off. Get mad. Show me the real Ethan."

I lowered my hands to my side. "We can take this to the parking garage across the street. The cameras there are fake. We can finish this without interruption."

"This is just a tease to get you in the mood." He strolled around the desk to stand next to Tonya. "You want me, hunt me."

I nodded, appreciating his plan. "You think the angrier you make me, the easier I'll be to defeat."

"I've owned you at every turn."

He had. It was time to turn the tables. "I'll come for you in my own time."

"Well"—he cocked his head—"time is a luxury you don't have. There's Artemis to think of. And all these lovely people here. That precious baby next door." He answered Tonya's appalled look with a resigned sigh. "Okay, we draw the line at babies, but fuck the parents. How many people do I have to hurt to properly motivate you, Ethan? You know I will not stop until I get what I want."

It took everything I had to not murder them both on the spot. "I hope Marcia paid you up front." Reaching behind me, I opened the door and stepped aside. "You have twenty-four hours to return Artemis to me unharmed."

He held my gaze for a moment, measuring me. "You have twelve hours to find me, or the girl dies and I start killing people." With a nod, he strolled out the door like I couldn't reach out and snap his neck before he could react. Tonya followed him, but without his swagger. She glanced over her shoulder as I followed them through the hall, into the lobby, outside the firm, until they disappeared behind a closed elevator door.

Josh emerged from the bathroom, alone. Noting my expectant look, he explained. "I had her show me on her phone where she lived and transported her there. She's going to need tomorrow off." He glanced toward the firm. "I checked with Sebastian. No attack. I guess McClintock wasn't trying to distract you. What did he want?"

"He wants me. That's his contract."

"Dead or alive?"

I'd no idea. "Doesn't matter."

"Why go through all this trouble? Why not just ambush you when you come to work?"

"Because he's not a fool. He wants me to lose control and walk into a trap." I turned to Josh. "That's exactly what I'm going to have to do. Wait here."

I found Stacy's cubicle. Ignoring the confused looks of the other paralegals, I retrieved her handbag, jacket, and anything else she might need over a two-week vacation. Josh waited for the elevators to close before transporting us to the living room of her apartment, only a foot from where she was standing with a shot glass of whiskey. Startled, she splashed her fresh shirt with whiskey. She gaped at the mess.

"Shit."

With a slight wave of his fingers, Josh reached out with his magic. Seconds later, any trace of the spill had disappeared.

Stacy gave him an awed look. "I want to do what you do."

Before he could brag, I placed her belongings in her arms. "You're going on vacation."

"I am?"

"Paid. I'll transfer money to your account, more than enough. Use it to get out of Illinois."

Using my phone, I made the immediate payment. We'd done enough business outside the firm that I had her bank account on my friends and family list. Her phone dinged an alert in response. Her eyes widened at the amount.

Turning to Josh, she asked, "Can you take me to the Bahamas?"

"You'll have to get there the usual way," I explained. "Go now. Buy a ticket when you get to the airport."

I called a cab for her while she packed. Once she was safely on her way, Josh returned us to the retreat. I gathered the ranking pack members once more into Sebastian's room. I gave them a quick rundown of my encounter with McClintock.

After I finished, Gavin stated the obvious. "Ethos didn't take advantage of the distraction."

"McClintock knew about the Ares attack on the retreat," I said. "But he didn't know Ethos was behind it. They are not working in collusion. There won't be another attack here, but Ethos is going to make his play for Maya, sooner or later. He knows that she's close to taking control." I met Sebastian's gaze. "I need to finish this before Ethos makes his play."

Sebastian nodded.

"We still have to find him," Winter noted. "So far, he's been pretty good at hiding."

My phone vibrated as if on cue. Glancing at the screen, I saw Matthew's name. "Tell me."

"He's a wily one," he said, glee in his voice. "We used two drones, like you requested. He used two ride share cars and a bus, but we followed him to a small warehouse in the industrial district. So far, he hasn't come out. There's an open window. I could probably squeeze a drone through."

"No," I snapped. "Did he at any point spot your drones?"

"No way. These aren't cheap little RCs, man. These babies

take crystal-clear zooms from a hundred feet. He was definitely watching his six for a tail, but he never looked up."

"Good," I said, relieved. "How long can you keep your drones in the air?"

"Other than bringing them down every hour to swap batteries, indefinitely."

"Send me the footage you have."

"I'll send you a link to the live feed as well."

Steven asked as I pocketed the phone, "You asked the Worgen for help?"

"I'm paying them for their services. I'll have an address and visual reconnaissance of McClintock's hideout in a matter of minutes. There are details to work out once I can review the footage, but I have the general plan."

Josh gaped at me. "You're just going to walk right in there all on your own, aren't you?"

"That's what McClintock expects, so yes. To defeat him, I will need"—the word twisted my tongue—"assistance."

Winter's eyes widened in mild surprise. "Three syllables to avoid one? Impressive."

"There's another matter," I said. I described how close Maya had come to taking Sky over during Anderson's attack. "Ethos tried to draw her out as well. He was nearly successful."

"She's getting stronger," Josh said, absently chewing on his nails while he thought. "We need to find the Tre'ase that created Maya, fast."

Gavin calmly noted, "Even if we could devote all of our resources to the search, it could take months."

Sky didn't have months. She might not have days. I needed to get McClintock out of the way, then Marcia.

Josh declared, "There has to be some spell or ritual to weaken her. I might find something useful in the library."

"We've been through those books a dozen times," I snapped. "If there was a solution there, we'd have found it."

"You have a better idea?" he snapped back. "I'd like to hear it."

Sebastian intervened. "Do it, until we have another option to pursue. Josh, I also need you to figure out how much control Maya has over Sky."

He nodded. "I have an idea."

"How?" I asked, suspecting his reply.

"Sky wants me to help her learn how to control the Aufero. I'll be able to push her. While I'm testing her abilities, I'll be able to see what it takes to draw Maya out."

"No." I scowled. When it came to power, Josh was careless. "The orb is too dangerous for her."

Since Sky had used the field to absorb my dark elf magic, the orb's power had darkened. Its field suffocated anyone inside its protection. One mistake might trigger Maya to take control, permanently.

"I can manage it," he insisted.

"You'll push too far."

"I'll push just enough to get a glimpse of her. I know you don't trust me, Ethan, but magic is my realm. I know what I'm doing."

Josh's confidence gave me none of the same, but we needed the information. He'd never consciously hurt Sky. Without another option, I had to trust him. He took my scowl as permission, or a dare.

"What about Ethos?" Winter asked. "We barely defeated him last time and we had the Seethe on our side."

Sebastian brought his fingertips together to form a pyramid in front of him. He considered quietly for a moment. "We'll need allies, but not Demetrius. Ethos hasn't threatened the Seethe. Demetrius has nothing to gain by helping us."

The vampire would probably relish a fight between the pack and Ethos, each side weakening the other.

I said, "The elves have nothing to gain by helping us."

"There is one option," Sebastian said. "With the rest of the Clostra in Ethos's hands, Samuel might be motivated to help us retrieve them."

Winter scoffed, "If we could find him."

He turned to me. "Claudia might be able to help."

My godmother was considered a neutral, respected by all of the factions. If anyone could broker a meeting, it was her. I'd never asked her to help us hunt him down, but the situation had changed. We needed to bargain now. Claudia's reputation was a guarantee to Samuel that intentions to negotiate weren't a ploy.

"I'll ask."

CHAPTER 10

*C*laudia wasn't surprised by the call. Whether she could get word to him or not, she wouldn't say, but she had my confidence. Whether Samuel would choose to meet with us was another question. At the end of our call, I received another text from Matthew with links to their surveillance video.

The livestream was a split screen showing the front and back view of a square, two-story, concrete warehouse. A quick public records search of the address revealed the building's history. Last in use three years ago, it had been a tool and die plant until the company went under. Since then, the building's fate was locked into a court battle between the owners. Blueprints revealed a simple floor plan. Most of the building was an open work area with a high ceiling. Pairs of columns ran up the middle from the entrance. At the south end of the first floor was a row of offices. Above that, another row of offices was the entirety of the second floor. Entrances were limited—a door at the front and back, and stairs to the roof. There were plenty of accessible windows on the first floor.

Watching the livestream, there was no indication that the

building was occupied, but they were there. According to Matthew, no one had entered or emerged from the building after McClintock and Tonya went inside. I set that laptop aside with the stream running. Using my backup laptop, I clicked Matthew's link to the footage that started with the hunters leaving my law firm's building. I played the footage twice, once watching only McClintock, then only Tonya, scrutinizing for any sign that they might've spotted Matthew's drones. That they hadn't didn't ease the worry in my stomach. McClintock was clever. If I wasn't careful, I'd find myself once again on the wrong side of his plans.

Too easy. He wanted to be tracked. I shook my head. Up until now, he'd been impossible to find. *Two cars and a bus—cautious, or just enough to look like he was making an effort?*

Referring again to the blueprints, I began to put a plan together. It started with me walking through the front door.

"I don't like this plan," Winter stated.

I met her gaze from across the cramped van cabin as Matthew drove us toward McClintock's warehouse. The van walls were crammed with shelves containing a variety of electronic equipment, including monitors and computers, most of which wasn't necessary for our purpose. From what I knew, the Worgen used the van as a mobile hacking platform. How that worked was on a list of questions I hadn't gotten around to asking. Crammed between the equipment were jump seats. Winter and Josh scowled at me from across the van, while Gavin and Steven watched my reaction from a bench seat to my left.

The van rattled as it drove over a speed bump, irritating everyone.

Josh declared, "I'm with her."

Gavin scowled agreement. Steven was somber, determined, but his eyes showed his concern.

I asked her, "You have an alternative?"

"Well," she said, her thoughtfulness exaggerated. "He's expecting you to just walk in there like you're Clint Eastwood. I suggest not doing that."

"We should overwhelm them," Gavin stated. "Attack simultaneously from multiple directions."

Steven remained silent, watching.

"McClintock expects me to trade my safety for Artemis, but he'll be on alert. Once I've met his expectations, he'll drop his guard."

Winter frowned. "You mean, once you put yourself on a platter. Did you bring the rice pilaf, because I forgot?"

Steven spoke for the first time. "He could just shoot you outright. We know he has silver bullets. The smart play for him is to kill you on sight, kill his hostage, and get paid."

He won't kill me without making a speech. I'm not the only one who is predictable. "After all this foreplay, he'll want to put on a show." Despite my confidence, I had to plan for the worst. "Should anything go wrong, make sure Artemis survives. Then kill them all."

The van veered off the road and came to a stop. Brushing a curtain aside from the window next to me, I saw we were in an industrial park. Being the weekend, this area at least seemed quiet.

Matthew looked back from the driver's seat, gestured out the window. "It's around that tan building there."

"Surveillance?" I asked.

He tapped a wireless com in his ear. "No change."

Turning the other way, he opened his door and slipped out of the van. By the time I opened the sliding door, he was there. As we emerged from the van, he handed me a delicate, clear wireless device and gestured to my ear. The others received a device as well. While we installed the devices, he retrieved a small wireless microphone and duct tape from a compartment. Knowing what he had in mind, I opened my shirt.

"We'll be able to hear everything," he explained, "but I'll be the only one you can hear."

"Once Artemis is in the van," I addressed the others, "make your move. Not before."

Winter glanced around at the quiet. "You don't think it's strange that he hasn't posted a scout or a patrol?"

"It's a trap," I stated. "Let's get this started."

Winter retrieved her katana from the van, then disappeared between two buildings. Gavin followed her, while Steven crossed the road and disappeared into a parking lot full of white vans. Thanks to the drones, Matthew had mapped out the best locations for observing the warehouse without being detected. He taped the microphone to my chest while I watched Josh wiggle and stretch his fingers, like an artist warming up.

Once I'd replaced my shirt and made sure the microphone wasn't obvious beneath, I started toward the warehouse around the corner.

"Good luck," Matthew said.

After acknowledging him, I gave Josh a sarcastic smile. "Thanks."

"I'll give you ten minutes," he declared, "and then I'm coming in."

I closed the distance between us, towering over him. "You come in after Artemis leaves, not a second sooner."

"What if he doesn't let her go? What if he decides to kill you both?"

"Then I'll kill McClintock," I growled, pressing my chest into Josh's. "Don't do anything until the violence starts."

Josh rolled his eyes as he held his ground. "That's a horrible idea." He gestured toward the warehouse. "He's prepared for you to attack him. We need to strike first, in force. Hell, I could just walk in there with you, put a field around Artemis, and take them down on my own."

"Josh," I snapped. "This is not a time for your impulsivity. We do this my way. If you go in there too soon, you'll probably get Artemis killed. I have to count on you to follow the plan. If you can't do that, then leave."

He made a disgusted smacking sound with his lips as he glanced to Matthew, who kept himself busy linking a monitor in the van to the drones.

I pressed closer to Josh, obliging him to take an annoyed step back. "Can I count on you?"

"Fine," he grumbled, holding up his hands. "Just give me a safe word."

I stepped back from him, surprised. "What?"

"Why am I not surprised you've never used a safe word?" he said with a lopsided grin. "It's a word or a short phrase. You say it and we come running. That's my compromise."

Matthew chimed in. "That's actually a good idea. I suggest 'pineapple.'"

Josh and I both gave him a puzzled look. I needed something I could speak aloud that wouldn't seem out of place, something McClintock would expect from me.

"Fuck you," I said, then walked away.

The warehouse was just as it appeared on the surveillance footage, aged concrete. Rotting wooden boards covered the front door and the ground-floor windows. The second-floor windows were murky, some broken—the barrel of a sniper rifle would be difficult to spot there. I glanced up to the roof, looking for the same. I was a sitting duck for a silver bullet to the skull. Lingering doubts came to the forefront as I walked the hundred feet of open ground toward the door. Had I misread McClintock?

Easier to shoot me once I'm inside. Use a silencer and the microphone might not even pick up the shot, though it would pick up the sound of my body collapsing to the floor.

The drones would pick up a sniper, I reminded myself, not entirely convinced. Matthew would tell me if they spotted danger. I resisted the urge to tap the device in my ear, or glance up to the sky to locate the drones.

Reaching the door, I found it was slightly ajar. After a calming breath, I opened it the rest of the way. Rusted hinges creaked. Sunlight flooding in from behind me faded quickly, revealing just a few feet of the debris-littered hallway. Beyond, a few beams of sunlight from the second floor windows revealed hints of the warehouse's better days—silhouettes of neglected machinery, tipped over chairs and shelves. On the other side of the warehouse were the two floors of offices.

The door clattered shut behind me, triggering a scurry of feet up ahead. Something metallic clattered against the concrete floor, followed by silence. Listening, I could just make out the sound of heartbeats—two or three, I couldn't be sure, the sounds were so entwined.

Mustering my confidence, I set my doubts aside and strode into the hallway, making no attempt to disguise my arrival. On the contrary, I wanted to be noticed. Several feet into the open warehouse, I stopped and called out, "Artemis."

A muffled whimper answered from somewhere nearby, about forty-five degrees to my right, followed by the brief rattle of a thin chain. Remembering the blueprints, I had some idea of where she was, though I couldn't know her immediate surroundings. I waited, giving my eyes time to adjust to the available light. I picked out two heartbeats from the direction of Artemis, one anxious, the other excited. Ahead of me, the third heartbeat was calm—McClintock, about ten feet away.

I remained still in the protracted silence. Finally, I announced, "I can do this all day."

From ahead, a click of a switch. Against the suddenly blinding light that surrounded me, I draped an arm over my eyes. Through quick, pained glances, I saw floodlights on four surrounding pillars—the light from each converged on me. Looking down, I saw a red 'x' painted on the concrete beneath my shoes.

Exactly where he wanted me.

As my eyes adjusted, I saw a frightened Artemis standing near one of the pillars, darkness beyond. Her mouth was taped. Silver cuffs bound her hands in front of her, leaving a ring of raw, burned skin. Other burn marks, harder to explain, dotted the exposed skin of her arms and legs. Next to her, gripping her arm just above the elbow, Tonya gloated. In her free hand dangled a military-grade stun baton.

With Artemis so close and able to run, I reconsidered attacking first. My mind raced through the tactical calculations when four figures—two men, two women—stepped out of the dark to surround me, armed with knives and pipes.

How could I miss four sets of breath, four beating hearts?

I noted the pale skin, the lifeless eyes, the retro-modern clothing style. Vampires, probably from out of town. They didn't have the look of the Seethe, and I doubted Demetrius would allow his vampires to draw him into a war with the pack. They had a cooped-up look, like they'd waited too long to raise hell. They'd probably been hiding out here for weeks to avoid notice, which explained how Matthew's drones had missed their presence. Four vampires I could handle, depending on how involved McClintock and his sidekick became. My gaze flicked around the warehouse, wondering if there were more vampires lurking in the shadows. They could be in the neighboring buildings as well. Josh, Winter, and the others could be surrounded and not know it.

Aware of the microphone against my chest, I needed to warn Matthew without drawing McClintock's suspicion.

An obnoxiously slow clapping sound started in front of

me, reverberating. A moment later, he walked out of the shadows, clapping his hands together with lazy enthusiasm. He was decked out for battle, with several knives strapped to his body. A sawed-off shotgun was holstered at his right thigh.

"My, my, the Big Dog himself." He grinned as he held his arms open wide, gesturing to our surroundings. "You found me. See what you can accomplish when you put your nose to the ground?"

Matthew's voice whispered in my ear. "Four—make that five—vamps just came out to the rooftop."

"Vampires?" I scoffed to McClintock, loud enough for the microphone to pick up. "Just these four, or do they have help?"

"Copy that."

Unaware of the conversation in my ear, McClintock shrugged. "You work with what's available. Obviously I had to hire from outside the area."

A scuffle broke out on the other side of my earpiece, loud enough to make me flinch. To cover for the gesture, I shifted my weight, shot quick glances at the vamps surrounding me. The ear-splitting sound ended abruptly, followed by Josh's anxious voice.

"You have vamps inside?" he asked in a rush. "Ethan, I'm coming in."

Not yet, dammit. My gaze flicked toward Artemis. *Not until I get her out.* McClintock came prepared, but that didn't mean he'd break his word. "You should've brought more," I told him. For Josh's benefit, I added, "Four, I can handle easily."

He cursed in my ear. I wasn't sure how long I could keep him from barging in.

The old man's gloat faded while he scrutinized me. Something like a mild regret crept into his voice. "You know, Ethan, there's a small part of me that hoped you wouldn't take the bait. The rest of me figures you brought this on yourself."

"You have a choice."

"You made my choice for me when you undercut my belocka hunt. That made you fair game."

Josh whispered, "Gavin, Winter, and Steven are repositioning. They'll have to deal with the vamps on the roof first. When you say the words, I'm coming straight in. And in five minutes, I'm coming in anyway."

I gestured toward Artemis. "Let her go."

"First things first."

He drew out a set of handcuffs from the pocket of his camouflage pants, tossed them at my feet. The vile scent of silver caused my nose to wrinkle. I'd expected the demand, but the vampires complicated the situation. At six to one, I couldn't start a fight and expect to get Artemis out alive.

Tonya pressed the baton against Artemis's hip, her finger hovering over the button on the pommel. Artemis's resultant whimper brought a vile smile to Tonya's lips.

Fuck you, I thought, but it wasn't time—not quite yet. Tonya was going to sing a different tune when I turned that baton on her.

Begrudgingly, I reached down and snatched the handcuffs from the dirty concrete. Pain shot through my hands as the silver seared the skin of my fingers, my palm. Contempt froze on my visage as I absorbed the pain, refusing to give the old man satisfaction. Only the sweat beading on my forehead betrayed me. Scowling, my gaze fixed on his, I cuffed one wrist, then the other. He stared back at me, his satisfaction tempered.

"Your turn," I stated.

He remained still, considering.

I growled, baring my teeth. "McClintock. You were always an asshole, but I've never known you to break your word."

Josh said in my ear, "Ethan, she hasn't come out yet. Is something wrong? The mic is only picking you up, but it keeps cutting out. I think it has a short."

The vampires shifted, positioning to attack from all fronts. No matter which way I turned to fight, two of them would be at my back. I'd need to break out beyond the pillars and get a wall to my back to keep from getting overwhelmed —that didn't bode well for Artemis. In animal form, we'd both have a better chance, but the handcuffs prevented both of us from shifting.

McClintock said in a voice that sounded perilously close to regret, "Therein lies the rub." He gestured to the grinning vampires. "My associates here have discovered the virtues of collective bargaining. I'm sure you know their kind finds were-animal blood intoxicating. I promised them yours, but"—he glanced at Artemis—"I guess that just isn't going to be enough."

He wasn't happy about giving in to the vamps. As complicated as it was, he had a code. There was still a chance I could talk some sense into him, perhaps even drive a wedge between him and his vamp mercenaries. Before I could try, Artemis smashed her clasped, cuffed fists into Tonya's nose. The vamps converged on me from four directions, forcing me into quick action.

Charging the vamp in front of me, I extended my arms, clotheslining his neck with the cuff chain. Continuing my momentum, I drove him down onto his back and rolled. I came to my feet, expecting to find McClintock a foot in front of me, but he'd disappeared. Pivoting back to the oncoming vamps, I'd at least maneuvered them all in front of me.

Opening my mouth, I formed the words that would bring Josh and his magic. Movement caught the corner of my eye just before Tonya jammed her baton into my back and lit me up. Every nerve in my body screamed. Stumbling away from the agony, I ducked beneath the first vamp's charge, then rose to flip him over my head. While he crashed behind me, I turned in time to sweep a knife aside with the cuff chain, then drove a boot into the attacker's ribs.

"Fu—"

Tonya appeared in front of me, grinned as she jabbed the baton into my gut. I doubled over from the pain, backpedalling as she pinned me to a pillar. One of the vamps appeared beside her, decided to get clever. While she continued lighting my nerves on fire, the vamp swung a metal pipe down at my head. Roaring against the agony, I reached up and caught the pipe before it struck. The vamp let out a horrified scream as electricity flooded through the connection. My own pain eased some, enough for me to slap the baton aside, breaking contact.

The vamp's pipe clattered to the floor as he collapsed.

Tonya struck again, striking the pillar when I spun away.

Backing away from her, I tried to catch my breath. Somewhere behind me, I heard Artemis's growl.

"Ethan!" Josh shouted in my ear. "What's going on?"

Before I could answer him, another vamp leapt onto my back. His arms cinched around my throat, squeezed. Josh's panicked voice was cut off in mid-shout as the device fell from my ear, dislodged by the struggle. My muscles were weak from the shocks, made weaker still by the lack of oxygen as I gasped for wisps of breath. Unable to pry loose the vamp's grip, I peddled backward and slammed him into a pillar. His grip slackened and I sucked in a gasping breath. Before I could slam him again, Tonya jabbed her baton into my chest. I gritted my teeth against the pain while the vamp on my back screamed in my ear. Every muscle in his body clenched, causing his arms to cinch even tighter around my throat. Pain ravaged me. I tried to rally, to knock the baton away, but the accumulation of shocks had done their damage. Deprived of oxygen, I could barely lift my arms. My nerves burned. Consciousness ebbed. All I could do was hope Tonya was sadistic enough to release me so that she could shock me again. Given the evil grin on her face as she watched me die, I didn't hold out much hope. She had the wild look in her eyes of a killer elated by the moment of victory.

Like Maya.

My vision faded. Pain grew distant. As my eyes started to close, I saw the shocked look on Tonya's face as she noticed the bloody end of a long knife jutting from her chest. She gaped at the wound. The baton fell from her grip, bringing the pain in my body to a merciful end. I gasped for breath as the vamp slipped from my back to the floor.

Blood trickled down the blade as Tonya gripped it with her bare hands, then collapsed, revealing Artemis behind her. Wild fury burned in her eyes.

Nodding, I reached down to the vamp on the floor and snapped his neck. As I rose, she moved closer. My chest was still heaving, muscles still recovering. I didn't have much strength left, but I could still fight. Our backs to each other, we faced off against the three remaining vamps that surrounded us. Two held pipes, the other held a long knife like the one in Artemis's hand.

Instead of attacking, the vamps held their ground. McClintock walked out of the shadows to stand over Tonya. He stared down, the muscles of his jaw rippling as her blood pooled at his feet. After a moment, he looked up at me with a cold, deadly stare.

"That is the last good thing you will ever destroy."

My chest ached as my lungs continued sucking in desperate breaths. "Fuck. You."

I expected the windows to shatter, the doors to fly open. When nothing happened, I reached for the mic at my chest, suddenly aware of the pain there. Glancing down at the blackened area of shirt where Tonya had shocked me, I realized the mic was fried. The duct tape had melted against my chest. Eventually Josh would lose his patience and the cavalry would arrive, but I guessed I'd done a good job of convincing him not to.

The irony that he'd picked now to finally listen to me brought a wry smile to my lips.

To survive, I had to fight and win, or at least survive long enough to outlast my brother's newfound patience.

Between breaths, I whispered to Artemis. "I hope you know what you're doing."

"Are you kidding?" she hissed. "A life on the street taught me more than how to hustle."

She held the knife properly, positioned her feet optimally. Artemis often surprised me, but I doubted she'd ever top this moment.

McClintock gestured angrily for the vamps to attack. "Finish them both, but remember—I need his head to be recognizable."

Two of the vamps charged me, the first leading with his knife.

Inexperienced.

Waiting for the blade, I pivoted, catching it between my cuffed hands. The sharp blade scraped silver, lodged in the chain. Rotating my hands, I trapped the blade.

"That's why you don't lead with the knife," I growled.

He should've let the blade go, reverted to his natural weapons—fists and fangs. Like a fool, his attention remained fixed on jerking the blade free. In a quick motion, I turned into him, smashed an elbow into his jaw to stun him. Another vamp came at me with a pipe, swinging at my skull. Jerking my hands, I pulled the knife-vamp into the pipe's arc. The side of his head caved in from the blow, showering me in a spray of blood and bone shards. As the knife-vamp collapsed, I took the knife from his grip. While pipe-vamp gawked at her dead companion, I drove the knife into her throat, then slashed it out, almost completely severing her head from her body. Arterial spray drenched me as she collapsed.

Behind me, Artemis dodged the other vamp's pipe, following up with a kick to the chest that knocked the vamp to the ground. While the vamp clambered back to its feet, she scanned the floor for something sharp. She didn't notice McClintock walk up behind her, raising a sawed-off shotgun to her head.

I'd come too damn far to lose her now.

I flipped the knife in my hand to grip the blade and flicked it toward McClintock. He howled as the knife embedded itself deep into his side. Stumbling, he dropped the shotgun to grasp at the pommel. Artemis gave me a wide-eyed look, then snatched up the shotgun. As her vamp picked up its pipe to take another swing at her, Artemis fired the shotgun into the vamp's face.

While the vamp collapsed, she coolly checked the shotgun to verify she'd fired both barrels, then tossed it aside.

Turning back to McClintock, I found him leaning over the remnant of an old desk. The knife in his side had been replaced by a now-crimson piece of dirty fabric that he pressed into the wound. Blood streaked his jawline. He panted on the desk, his skin pale.

A cough broke through his chuckle and he spit blood. "I should've cuffed your ankles, too."

"You lost, old man."

"Always plan for contingencies." Gathering his voice, he shouted, "Here!"

A door slammed somewhere up on the observation floor, followed by footsteps. Remembering the rooftop vamps, I pulled a light from one of the pillars and whipped it around. Their whoops and hollers echoed off the walls, making them difficult to locate. I heard a loud crash to my right as one of them landed on the main floor. When I aimed the light in that direction, I found nothing but the same debris that was everywhere. Two more vamps landed to my left, and another deeper in the warehouse. When I whipped the light around, I caught just a hint of movement in the other direction.

Artemis and I sidled toward each other, prepared for anything.

A fourth vamp landed a dozen feet in front of us and waited for my light to find her. She was tall, Nordic-looking, wearing a black turtleneck sweater beneath a leather trench coat. In both hands, she gripped a heavy, double-bladed battle axe.

Placing the light on the floor, I turned it toward us and pushed it toward the pillar I'd removed it from. Reaching behind me, I guided Artemis toward the 'x' on the floor, where we'd have the most light.

"I should probably tell you," she whispered to me as the vampire advanced, "I was mostly working on fury."

"You fought well."

The other four vampires emerged from the shadows, surrounding us. Each of them was dressed similar to the Nordic vamp that must be their leader. Three men were armed with European-style swords—flat, broad blades with a double edge. The fourth vamp was a slim, almost elfin, woman with a silver-tipped spear. Together, they made the first round of McClintock's mercenaries look like street vamps.

I asked Artemis over my shoulder, "Are you still furious?"

"Honestly," she said, a slight quake to her voice, "they might be a little out of my league."

My body was still wrecked from the baton. Our hands remained cuffed by silver. Without my wolf, our chances were slim. Whatever had happened to the others, I had to assume the worst. Josh and the others weren't coming. Hopefully he'd escaped. The vamps stopped just inside the light, grinning like their victory was preordained. It probably was.

McClintock shuffled into the light next to the Nordic

vamp, still clutching the bloody, drenched fabric to his wound.

I said between breaths, "You should've started with them."

"I didn't think you'd actually come alone."

I blinked, surprised. "What?"

Magic flooded into the room like an angry summer storm, quickly building in intensity. The vamps glanced around, their confidence shaken. A moment later, every window in the building simultaneously burst inward, showering us all in glass. While the vamps flinched, Josh appeared between Artemis and me. Before I could blink, he had a shimmering protective field around us. Glass fell on it like rain, triggering a shower of gold and blue sparks. The vamps followed, furious. Their weapons glanced uselessly off the field, but they seemed intent on beating it until it collapsed.

Behind them, McClintock screamed at me in red-faced rage. "No!"

Beyond the pillars, I saw movement in the shadows, at least two figures moving in opposite directions. Josh hadn't come alone. Gavin's panther leapt out of the darkness and onto one of the sword-vamps, his jaws clamping down on the vamp's neck. The vamp screamed as Gavin pulled it down into the shadows. Steven struck the spear-vamp from behind, driving a wooden stake through her back, piercing her heart. Reversion started even while he withdrew the stake.

Realizing their danger, the other three vamps turned their backs to us to fight. One of the sword-vamps fell instantly, her head cleanly severed by Winter's katana.

Josh dropped his shield. His eyes were midnight as he raised his hands. When he snapped his fists closed, magic engulfed both vamps, binding their arms to their sides. Axe and sword clattered to the floor as they struggled uselessly to break free. Gavin walked back into the light, his muzzle bloody. He paced angrily while Steven staked the helpless axe-vamp. Winter took the head from the final vamp and Josh released the binding.

Only McClintock remained, his face gaunt. With his wound, he wasn't going anywhere. He'd picked up one of the long knives, twisted the pommel in his hand while he debated how he wanted to die. He watched intently while Winter and Steven efficiently sent the surviving but otherwise incapacitated vamps into reversion. Eventually, he dropped the blade. Pain twisted his expression with each step as he walked to Tonya's body and fell to his knees. With a tenderness I'd never before seen in him, he scooped up her body and held it to him.

Maybe his grief was genuine. Maybe he thought I'd spare him for pity's sake. He was mistaken. He'd killed one friend, tried to kill another, and tried to kill me. Picking up the axe, I tested its balance in my hand. Winter offered me her katana. Her snake was there in her eyes. She'd taken Marko's death as personally as I had. In offering me her sword, she was offering her own claim for revenge. Grateful, I accepted, letting the axe fall to the concrete.

At my approach, the old man eyed the katana blade as if measuring the death it offered. He recognized a clean death when he saw it. In the end, we all hoped for that. With a sigh, he accepted his fate. I waited while he removed the fabric from his side, bunched it up to make a pillow for Tonya's head. After gently setting her to rest, he closed his eyes. He straightened his neck.

"Any last words?" I growled.

He swallowed. "I'd like to—"

The blade of the katana swept cleanly through flesh, muscle, and bone, emerging from the other side of McClintock's neck without a hint of resistance. His eyes went wide just before his head tipped and fell from his torso. His body followed, spraying pulses of arterial blood across the floor.

I watched as each spurt of blood lessened, until there was

nothing left but a drizzle. I'd expected relief, but found none. Despite our differences, I'd always respected the old man. We'd never gotten along, but we'd never been enemies until Marcia forced us into opposition.

Turning back to Winter, I wrapped the end of my shirt over the blade just above the guard. Drawing the blade through, I wiped it of blood. Offering it back to Winter, I tipped the end of the blade over my other arm, and gave her the pommel. The snake was gone from her eyes as she graciously accepted.

Facing Josh, I showed him the handcuffs. A flick of his fingers and the cuffs snapped apart in several pieces, leaving black rings of skin. He did the same for Artemis.

"Dr. Baker will check you out," I told her.

She shook her head. "I just want to go home."

Josh volunteered. "I'll get her there. I'll clean up the evidence here and then meet you back at the retreat."

I gave his shoulder a squeeze, then followed Gavin's panther out of the warehouse.

CHAPTER 11

*C*ourtesy of Tonya and her super-charged baton, my body was wrecked by pain. Every nerve in my body was inflamed. How I made it home, I didn't remember. I woke some time in the night, in wolf form in my bed. Embracing my animal sped the healing. By morning, the pain was already receding. I took the next day to recover, giving most of that time to my wolf. Sky called me twice, but I didn't want her to see me in this condition. She had enough to worry about. So far, she knew nothing about McClintock and Artemis. I planned to keep her in the dark, at least until Maya and Ethos were dealt with. By the second morning, I felt close to normal—weakened and aching, but I could at least hide my discomfort.

Seeing Sky helped. We spent the afternoon together at the retreat. She wouldn't admit it, but I knew she wanted to stay near Sebastian while he recovered. Our wolves hunted and chased each other across the grounds until I thought she was exhausted. Her head drooped, panting, so I led her back to the house. We were on the front lawn when she revealed her deception. While I noticed Josh's Jeep pull into the garage, she nipped my back leg—nearly tripping me—then bolted, daring me to pursue. My brother watched as we chased each other on the lawn. An odd look came over him before he walked into the house. I remembered our conversation outside Sebastian's penthouse, the accusations he'd made.

Sky nipped at my face, drawing me from my reverie. We continued chasing each other until our exhaustion was real.

In human form, we retrieved our clothes from the back of the house and went looking for lunch. We found Josh in the kitchen, pouring a mug of coffee. His gaze shifted between us, scrutinizing as Sky sat at the table and I retrieved some leftover steaks from the fridge.

She glanced at his oversized Sesame Street Big Bird mug. "Research?"

He nodded, adding cream. "Maya. I'm hoping there's something I've overlooked. There has to be a way to repress her."

She was quick to volunteer. "I'll join you."

On his way out, he smiled, held up his mug. "Bring coffee. It's going to be a long day."

A shared shower led to a nap. Two hours later, we found Josh in the library, several magical texts before him. Sky walked in first, eliciting a smile that faded some when I followed. He pushed two texts across the table to us as we sat across from him. The next few hours were unsurprisingly fruitless. I'd little hope of finding anything new about Maya or spirit shades, but the effort needed to be made until another avenue could be found.

Sky and I tried to relieve the boredom with intimate looks. We shared pages of text and talked in half sentences. Josh wasn't amused. His irritated glances grew increasingly suspicious. I was the focal point of his ire. Unable to acknowledge his jealousy without creating a scene, I chose to ignore it. Eventually, we'd talk about the accusations he'd made, but he'd have to come to terms with my relationship with Sky, better now than later.

The more fruitless our search seemed, the more obvious it became that we needed a new direction. Fed up, I pushed my book forward and leaned back in my chair, arms folded over my chest. "I think getting rid of Ethos is what we need to focus on rather than getting rid of Maya. She was fine until a couple of months ago. It's likely his resurfacing has awakened something in her." We'd witnessed his effect on her more than once. "Get rid of him and things may go back to the way they were."

Sky wasn't convinced. "And if they don't?"

"Then we worry about it then. Ethos is the immediate threat, and Claudia hasn't been able to meet with Samuel. For all we know Ethos has all three books." We'd need to start over, which meant more coffee. I gestured to the books on the table as I rose. "Find out how we can draw Ethos out of hiding."

I found Winter on her way out of the kitchen, two mugs of coffee in her hands. I didn't need to watch her leave to know one of those mugs was for Sebastian. The pot empty, I changed the filter and started a fresh batch. To kill time, I went for a walk through the house, measuring the pack's mood. The pack was recovering, thanks in large part to the calm emanating from the Blue Room.

At the top of the basement stairs, I was surprised to find Josh and Sky on their way down. When they practiced magic, he preferred the padded walls of the training room. My fists clenched in irritation.

He said he was going to test her, I reminded myself. *Hell of a time for that.*

I'd agreed to the test, though I regretted that now.

Resisting the urge to follow, I strode back to the kitchen. A few minutes of watching coffee percolate only increased my agitation. *Josh knows what he's doing* became my false mantra. My trust in him was tempered by his obsession with powerful magic, which made him reckless. It was in his nature to push. If he pushed Maya too far…

Halfway down the stairs, I felt the eager calm of his magic spilling out of the training room.

"Now use it," he urged.

I peered through the doorway just as Sky manifested a lilac-covered field around them. They stood near the far wall, a few feet apart, facing each other. She grinned at her creation. A moment later, she collapsed the field and used his magic to raise a towel from a nearby bench. Josh chuckled as the towel danced across the room, followed by the keys to his Jeep.

Testing her limits, she flicked her fingers to send a strong wave of magic toward him. His eyes widened in surprise as he fell back a step. She pushed again, harder. He strained not to fall back more than another step. His effort only emboldened her. Her next gesture sent him flying backward into the padded wall. She gasped as his head bounced off the cushion.

He grimaced, pinned. "It's still a head. Padding or not, it doesn't like to be slammed against things."

Relieved, she released him with a wave of her hand. She relished her display of power, but there was no hint of Maya's magic.

Josh winced as he rubbed the back of his head. "Make a field."

The field appeared, but weaker than before. Sky's previous satisfaction melted at the shimmering boundaries. Her ability to utilize borrowed magic had greatly improved, but remained limited. The more powerful the magic she used, the faster it dissipated.

Watching her closely, Josh retrieved the Aufero from beneath a towel. "Hold it."

As the glowing orb neared, her breath became ragged.

This is the test.

I tensed, ready to intervene if Maya made an appearance.

Sky closed her eyes as he took her hand, entwining their fingers.

"Again," he said.

I felt the flow of his magic toward her even as she drew magic from the Aufero. Dark and light, the two forces intertwined around her. A new field encircled them—powerful but dark as the Aufero's magic proved dominant. Within that darkness, I saw a spark of fear in Josh's eyes as he began to struggle for breath. I'd warned him the orb was dangerous.

"Skylar," he managed, leaning toward her until their lips nearly touched. "You need to change it."

Her lips pursed as she fought for control. I took a step into the room, prepared to use my own magic to break the field, when its color began to change. The harsh orange-and-brown glow faded as Sky converted the orb's dark magic to light, until the magic was indistinguishable from Josh's and left behind an odor like fresh linen, jasmine, and a metallic spice. His chest heaved as he took in a gasping breath. He released her hand but remained close, their lips still almost touching as they basked in shared relief within the lilac confines of her field.

"See?" he whispered. "I knew you could do it."

She nodded, exhilarated. When she opened her eyes, she noticed me in the doorway. The field collapsed. He followed her gaze.

"I got this, Ethan." He scowled. "You can go."

She started to back away from him until he slipped a hand around her waist. "No," he whispered, an angry tone meant to be reassuring. "We need to finish."

"It's okay with me if he stays," she explained, confused.

"He's a distraction."

"For who," I demanded, "you or Sky?"

He glowered. "Both."

Glancing at the Aufero in his hand, I noted the orb was

more translucent now. Sky had done more than change the magic emanating from it, she'd changed the orb itself, and without Maya's help. Sky had passed Josh's test. Maya remained dangerous. She had to be dealt with, but Sky remained in firm control.

My relief was tempered by the way he flirted with her, daring me to be jealous. There was something darker to his flirtation than how he'd been with her at the penthouse. He'd started to get a clue about us. He was toying with me now, taking his revenge for perceived past transgressions. Confronting him now, in front of Sky, wasn't what I wanted.

With some effort, I turned and walked up the stairs to the library. Waiting for them there, I paced in front of the windows. *You're jealous,* he'd said, while accusing me of a history of taking women's interest from him. That I was jealous of him left me incensed. Seeking to disprove the rest of his accusation, I retraced my memory of the women I'd met through him at the club. To my distaste, an uneasy pattern started to unfold. Preferring anger over regret, I glanced at the clock. An hour had passed since I'd left them. I wondered where the hell they were. I knew by the ripples of magic spreading through the house that they were still in the basement, practicing.

That's for my benefit.

Refusing to give him the satisfaction, I stayed away. At least, for the first four hours. As the fifth hour neared, I'd had enough. I was on my way down the stairs to bring their lessons to an end when they emerged from the training room. I paused, held my brother's harsh gaze. Our eyes remained fixed on each other as he passed me on the stairs, waiting until the last moment to break contact.

Sky watched, confused, until he disappeared.

"What's going on?" she asked.

"Nothing." The issue was between my brother and me.

With some effort, I brushed my anger at him aside. "Are you hungry?"

Her eyes brightened. "Famished."

Taking her hand, I led her up the stairs. "Your choice. Anywhere."

"You're going to regret that," she said with a rueful smile.

She ate hungrily while I stared at our shared plate, appalled.

"Red velvet cake is not a meal," I said. "It's dessert."

"So I've heard." Another piece went into her mouth before she gestured to my fork with her own. "You said you like to have new experiences."

I chuckled, but my thoughts drifted to Josh. I'd thought my interest in Sky had been plain. Perhaps not, or was he just pursuing her as a means to piss me off, my brother's favorite pastime?

"Not that I mind the PDA," Sky said, drawing me from my reverie to realize I'd taken her hand in mind. "But you've been pretty handsy since we left the retreat."

I frowned. "That's not the case."

"You led me to the Maserati with your hand on my back. And then you held my hand all the way here. If you're going to handcuff us together next, we're going to have to have a long talk about our future."

Reflexively, I pulled my hand away. "I've got a lot on my mind."

"Uh huh," she said, unconvinced. After another bite, she pushed the plate away.

"You're not finished."

She eyed the remainder with a sad expression. "Turns out, you can have too much of a good thing."

I nodded. After paying the check, I took her home.

Walking through the door, she lifted the collar of her shirt to smell it. "Oh boy," she said, turning into the hall. "I need a shower." When I followed her into the bathroom, she gently pushed me back. "Whoa. Showering is not a group project."

Surprised and not sure how to take the rejection, I left her alone. While she showered and changed, I did my best to shake a building anxiety I didn't want to recognize. The orb proved a reasonable distraction. I admired its color, impressed at Sky's skill. So far, the change she'd effected held. Josh and Sky had spent a great deal of time together over the last year, training. He was knowledgeable, an excellent trainer, but he couldn't teach her everything.

By the time she emerged from the bathroom, I'd resolved to teach her myself. She blinked at me from the hallway as I moved her coffee table to the far wall of the living room.

"What's happening?"

"You should practice."

Her mouth stood agape for a moment. "I just did. For almost five hours. I'm beat."

I took her hand, led her to the center of the room. "As with fighting, there's no better time to train than when you're tired. It's one thing to use magic when you're alert and fresh. You need to be just as sharp when you're exhausted and stressed."

I drew her close to me. "Start with a field."

After an uncertain moment, she drew on the Aufero's magic to generate the field around us. With the orb's magic changed, suffocation was no longer a problem.

"Good. While you maintain the field, manipulate some objects in the room."

She concentrated. With a simple gesture, a glass vase rose from an end table. My hand gently caressed her back while she sent the vase into a continuous orbit around us. My hand slipped around her waist. She pulled away slightly, gave me a playful look as she raised a decorative pillow from the couch.

As she pinned the pillow to a wall, I bent to her neck and kissed her, licking her pulse.

She laughed and squirmed. "Will you stop?"

I kissed her lips, slipped my fingers beneath her shirt. "You have to be able to perform with distractions."

"If this is the distraction they employ, then I'm pretty sure things are just going to get weird fast."

"Drop the field."

Drawing my fingers over the back of her hand, I eased back from her. She watched, curious as I used my own magic to split her field and slip out of it. She'd always wanted to know about my magic, what I could do. Teasing her now only aroused her amused suspicion.

She took a deep breath, slowly let it out. The field dissipated. I caught the vase as it fell, while the pillow plopped to the floor. Beside us, the Aufero continued its rhythmic pulse.

Once the field was gone, I moved closer to her. "Very good."

"Very good?" she balked. "Did you see that? I just made magic my bitch."

"That you did." I pulled her against me, kissing her.

Her body melted into mine, then suddenly tensed. She backed away, confused and irritated. "What is going on between us?"

I smiled. "It was just a kiss, Sky."

Her eyes searched mine as I entwined our fingers. I pressed closer, following her until her back was against the wall. Her lips reached for mine. We clawed at each other's clothes as our carnal passions took over. My need for her burned. After a long, passionate kiss, she stopped. Her eyes searched mine once more, but there was a fire in there, a desire and a need.

"No, it's not just a kiss," she breathed. "What happens next?"

Our hearts pounded against each other. Our bodies vibrated with carnal craving.

"Whatever you want to happen," I promised.

She looked away, thinking. I was losing her.

"What happens when you get tired of me?"

Staring into her eyes, I saw my reputation staring back at me. I'd faced such questions before. They'd never fazed me. With Sky, I felt like she'd reached deep inside of me and called out what she'd found. I was a rogue, but I didn't want to be that for her. Thrown off, I reverted to my old tactic of redirection.

"What happens when *I* get tired of *you*?" I gave her a rogue's smile. "How about when *you* get tired of *me*?"

Not fooled, her eyes darkened. "Don't play games with me. Answer the question."

"It's not very hard." I sighed. *The truth, this time.* "We move on."

What happened next was up to her. Her skin burned hot beneath my fingers as they lazily traced down her arm until I clasped her hand. The wild drumming of her heart pounded in my ear as she made up her mind.

I asked softly, "Where is this coming from?"

"I just don't want to be a throwaway," she admitted. "Someone you quickly lose interest in."

I brushed my lips against her cheek, then kissed her. "How could I lose interest in you?"

I couldn't imagine Sky could ever stop surprising me, or pushing me to be a better were-animal.

She turned until our lips almost met. Brushing her lips against mine, I heard the decision in her heart just before she kissed me back.

I woke to her stirring next to me in bed.

"What is it, Sky?" I asked before turning to observe her.

There was a liveliness to her eyes. Her pupils danced with thoughts. I wondered if she'd slept a wink since we'd gone to bed.

Gauging my reaction, she opted to lie. "Nothing."

"Seventy-seven heart rate and your respiration is twelve. You want to try again?"

"No," she said, then changed course. "I just want to know why you are such a freak."

I sat up, chuckling. "What's wrong?"

She hesitated only for a moment. "Why did Logan react to you the way he did?"

"Who knows why Logan does any of the things he does? I'm not going to waste time trying to figure it out."

"You just walked out of the protective field as though it wasn't there," she said, an accusation.

I'd shown off for her. The price to pay was questions I preferred to not answer. "Sky, you were using magic all day, it was a weak field. Anyone could have broken it. But it will get better with practice."

Her eyes narrowed in irritation. "Okay."

It was anything but.

As a distraction, I leaned in to kiss her, but her lips remained stubbornly sealed.

"I keep thinking about what Logan said about the Faeries. What if Maya was one? That would explain so much. It would definitely explain why they resorted to infanticide to get rid of her. If she is, how horrible were the Faeries that people would resort to such things?"

"If my research is correct"—I ran a hand through my hair, sighed—"I think the best choice was to kill them before they could reach their full potential."

"No," she scolded me, "that is never an option."

"Sky, the Faeries were not good people. And because of how powerful they were, they couldn't be destroyed, so what other options did they have?"

Judging by her indignant expression, I knew I was in for a lecture. Remembering a book I'd had in my car for some time, I slipped out of the sheets and started toward the door.

"Where are you going?"

"I need to get something out of my car."

"You're going out there like that?" She gestured to my penis. "Clothes, please."

Frowning, I pried open the curtains. It was dark out. Glancing at the clock on the nightstand, I confirmed it was early. "I doubt there's anyone outside. I'm used to my home."

"Well, I have neighbors, and I doubt they want to see your naked ass and junk while having their morning coffee."

I surrendered with a sigh, slipped on my underwear as a compromise, then retrieved the book. Aware of the nightmares it contained, I dropped it into her lap. She eagerly settled the book between her knees and began to read while I climbed back into bed.

Faeries were a cruel and godlike species, so dangerous that the other supernatural factions banded together to annihilate them. The cost of doing so, counted in souls, was in the thousands. In an attempt to survive, they turned to humans for procreation. The resultant progeny were much weaker. We called them fae. It was possible that Ethos and Maya were Faeries. Their powers—what we'd seen— matched: shapeshifting, necro-magic similar to the dark elves', the ability to manipulate and transfer magic as Sky did.

She hemmed, hawed, and gasped as she read. When she finished—if she could—she probably wouldn't sleep. I didn't. After she'd read enough horror, she asked, "How long have you had this information?"

"Not long."

"And you didn't tell me about it? You can't continue keeping information like this and then just springing it on me."

Faeries weren't the kind of thing to bring up in casual conversation. I'd only told her now because she asked, and because she might be right about Maya, at least.

She continued reading, increasingly appalled with every page turn. When her phone rang on the nightstand, I recognized the ringtone she'd assigned to David. Startled at first, she answered with a cheerful familiarity that told me how often they talked.

Cheerfulness became concern. "David—"

She dropped the phone on the bed and leapt up, dressing quickly.

Anxious, I followed her lead. "What is it?"

"Something's wrong."

On her way outside, she picked up a hunter's knife and the Aufero.

David answered the door before we could knock.

Sky asked, "What's the matter?"

He turned aside to reveal a blood-splattered sheet on the other side of the room, draped over a hunched figure. As we entered, he gingerly pulled back the sheet to reveal a half-naked man. He was sickly looking, lost within himself. Tufts of animal hair punctured through his skin. He was some kind of shifter, caught in mid-transformation. But he didn't smell like a were-animal.

Sky knelt in front of him. "Are you okay? Who are you? What happened?"

He tried to answer, but couldn't.

"Don't try to talk," she assured him. "I'm going to help you."

She gave me an anxious look, hoping I had an answer. I didn't.

David dropped into a nearby chair, watching Sky with the relief of a runner who had just passed the baton.

"Where's Trent?" I asked, glancing around the room.

He and Sky looked surprised that I knew Trent's name.

Admittedly, I'd never shown an interest in David or his partner. That didn't mean I didn't know everything about them.

"I had to give him something," David explained. "When the guy started growing hair, he freaked out. He's sleeping right now."

Sky explained to the injured man before she drew out her knife, "I need to take off the rest of your clothes, okay?" After gently cutting away the remnants, she placed a palm on his skin. She tried to force his change. The gesture surprised me, showed a fresh confidence. Her relationship with her wolf was always growing. As she concentrated, her heart rate slowed to a steady, calm beat.

The man squirmed beneath her touch. He gave her a desperate look, as if it was salvation she offered. Sweat beaded and ran down his face, but he still couldn't change.

I brought out my phone and dialed a conference call with Josh and Dr. Baker. For this mystery, I'd need them both. After I'd explained the situation, I knelt next to Sky and placed my hand over hers, adding my authority to her command. The animal within the man responded immediately. His back arched. He groaned at the snap and crackle of his bones breaking and resetting.

The transition seemed alien to his body, which was what made it so terrible. Were-animals who weren't born to the shift suffered greatly. Many didn't survive their first change. That's why we rarely made new were-animals. The risks were too great.

I wasn't sure if it was the sight or the sounds of the change that caused David to cup a hand over his mouth and gag.

While I continued commanding the change, Sky retrieved vodka from the kitchen. David drank directly from the bottle, only stopping to breathe. After a couple rounds, he lowered the bottle to his lap, dragged the back of a hand across his mouth, and sighed.

The stranger's hips and legs had almost fully changed. His upper body stubbornly resisted, but I'd seen worse. He was terrified. When the shift had first started, I wondered if he'd even known the change was coming.

Sky guided David to a spot on the couch. He was starting to calm when he noticed the stranger's lower half. David's eyes bulged as he gulped down more of the vodka. Between drinks, he gasped, "You didn't look like that when you changed."

"It gets better each time," she explained. "He's different and I don't know what his deal is, but when I know something, I'll tell you, okay?"

He nodded. "Oh kitten, I hate that my cupcake has to go through that every month."

The stranger's jaw cracked and snapped as his snout extended.

David gulped at his booze, then hurried down the hall and into the bathroom. The door slammed shut behind him.

By the time the stranger completed his transformation, we were all exhausted. He was barely alive, his breath ragged and his heartbeat not much more than a flutter. At least in his animal state, he had a chance to survive. With him stretched out beside me, I sat with my back against the wall.

I sensed Sebastian's approach, surprised that he'd come. Sky sensed him as well, opening the door for him. He walked in, showing no lasting signs of his wound. Dr. Baker, Josh, and Winter followed just as David emerged from the bathroom. The bottle was missing from his grip, but I knew by his breath and his staggered walk that he'd left it empty in the bathroom waste bin. Seeing his house full of people only slightly fazed him. He'd seen all of us with Sky, though not together.

His drunken gaze fixed on Winter and he stumbled toward her.

"Oh, the dark swan," he slurred, licked his lips. "How

beautiful you truly are in person. I've only seen you from a distance."

Her eyes flashed an amber warning at him, showing serpentine slits. A sober man would've cowered. David only pursed his lips in delighted awe. Were I not so exhausted, I'd have laughed at Winter's flabbergasted reaction.

Sky took his arm and gently guided him into the kitchen, where she poured him a glass of water. "It's not always like that," she whispered.

Sebastian knelt next to the wolf, ran a massive hand through its fur. He sensed and smelled the same oddness that I did. Neither of us had answers. Nodding, he rose and walked into the kitchen. In his place, Dr. Baker knelt to examine the strange wolf with a medical eye.

Next to Sky, Sebastian gestured to David. "Is he okay to question?"

I assumed the answer was "no," given the way his heart lurched at the question.

"I'm fine," he lied with a surprisingly steady voice.

Fear had a way of sobering a person.

"Can you tell me what happened?"

David swallowed. "I was getting ready for work." He took a gulp of water and I heard the plop of the glass on the counter. "I heard a light knocking. He looked injured so I opened the door. I was about to call the police when I got a look at his legs, that's when I called Skylar."

"Did he say anything?"

"Just partial words, 'kil'l'... kela' maybe. I couldn't make out any of it."

That got my attention—Josh's and Winter's as well.

Sebastian's voice remained unfazed, revealing nothing as he asked what we were all thinking. "Could it have been Kelly?"

"Maybe."

"Thank you."

He returned to the living room with Sky in tow, rifled through the were-animal's discarded clothes until he found a thin, laminated card. He frowned at it. I rose to look over his shoulder. Winter and Josh had the same idea. It was Kelly's driver's license.

Sebastian swore under his breath. "She didn't leave, she was taken."

A noise distracted us as the wolf went into convulsions, his claws scraping the wooden floor.

Dr. Baker called out in an urgent, professional voice, "I need help."

Within seconds the convulsions abruptly ceased and the wolf lay motionless. Dr. Baker checked him and then started CPR. When he glanced at his bag, Winter took over the CPR. He retrieved a medicine bottle and a syringe bag. After drawing a dose, he inserted the needle through the stranger's chest, directly into the heart, and delivered a shot of adrenaline.

A procedure of last resort to restart the heart.

The wolf remained perfectly still, life draining from his body, until a few seconds later, he was gone. Dr. Baker's frown deepened like a fresh wound. He ran a hand through his silver hair, then looked up at Sebastian with a sorrowful expression.

"I want to take him back to the retreat to study him."

Sebastian nodded.

David returned to the living room, aghast at the sight of the dead wolf.

Dr. Baker seemed old, worn out, as he rose to his feet. "Let's get him out of here."

I moved to lift the body, but Sebastian intervened. Taking it in his arms, he directed the rest of us to follow him through the garage. The sun had risen, I realized. Most likely, anyone seeing the wolf in Sebastian's arms would think he was carrying a large dog, but our presence at the house would stand out. There would be questions, followed by rumors.

After carefully placing the wolf in the back of Sebastian's SUV, I returned with him to the house. David was on the couch, weeping and utterly lost.

Sebastian took Sky aside.

"He won't say anything," she promised.

"I know. But I still need to talk to him."

"About what?"

He stared down at her with narrowed eyes. This wasn't a time for questions.

Sky read the tension in his shoulders, rushed to explain. "He's scared and you're kind of"—her eyes roved over his intimidating frame—"intense, and I think he's been through enough."

He considered for a long moment. "Give him my number and have him call me. He needs to call me, Skylar, okay?" Walking out, he added over his shoulder, "I will see you tomorrow at five for training."

Training?

"P.M., right?" she asked, hopeful.

He laughed.

Josh caught my eye, nodded toward the door. I made sure Sky was okay, then followed him to his Jeep.

"It's time to try and trace Ethos's blood," he said. "I'd hoped to practice a bit first, but there's too much weird shit going on."

"You think Ethos is behind the strange were-animal?"

"It's a safe assumption."

I considered for a moment, asked, "Makellos?"

I already knew the answer, but wanted Josh's confirmation. The magic around the wolf hadn't smelled or felt like Makellos magic. Josh agreed. To be thorough, I decided to give Liam a call. He'd no idea about the strange were-animal, and I believed him.

At his house, the tracking spell failed to reveal anything about Ethos's whereabouts. He'd used up half of the blood Sky had soaked up from her floor, which gave us one more shot.

He ran a hand through his naturally tussled hair. "Sky's help might make the difference."

I scowled, but he was right. I was less concerned about the Aufero now that she'd changed it. Having her involved with a spell that involved Ethos was another matter. Looking at the remnant of blood, I knew we had to try.

We returned to Sky's. Steven was there, checking the doors and windows.

"She went back over," he said, nodding toward the neighbors' house.

Seeing her phone on the kitchen counter, I brought it with me to David's.

He answered the door, which was a good sign. He'd sobered some, but his gaze seemed even more frightened and concerned and...interested, like he wanted to sit us down and ask questions but wasn't sure if I'd kill him for it.

Trent sat on the couch, a glass of wine in his hand, looking bewildered but excited. Questions were on his lips as well.

I glanced at Sky, wondering what she'd told them.

David stepped aside and we walked in. Once he'd closed the door, he took a seat next to his partner. The two together eyed Josh with keen interest. He answered their attention with a flirtatious smile.

Sky blinked at her phone when I offered it to her. "How did you get my phone?"

Her breath reeked of fermented grapes.

"You left it at your house."

Her hands went to her hips. "Okay, just for fun, do you want to tell me how you got in my house?"

I watched her temper rise to a quick boil before placing

the phone in her hand. "Steven let me in." Glancing around the room, I noticed several empty wine bottles on the table, accompanied by empty glasses. Grinning at Sky, I leaned in to whisper into her ear, "How many have you had?"

From the couch, David held up a hand, fingers splayed. In case I couldn't count, he mouthed, "five," then lifted a bowl-sized goblet. He mouthed, "Of these."

Sky noticed Josh for the first time. She stepped back from me, suddenly self-conscious. "Why are you here? Is something wrong?"

"I tried to find Ethos using the blood you collected, and I couldn't."

David stammered a little as he asked, "Did you find out anything about the man?"

"Dr. Jeremy is still working on it. The man's blood work is different than ours. He's definitely not one of ours," Ethan said.

Sky asked casually, "Is this Liam's and the elves' handiwork?"

My attention flicked to her. Had she drunk so much that she'd lost her mind? It was one thing for David and Trent to know that were-animals were real. They didn't need to know about elves or anything else supernatural. Glancing between her indifference and the neighbors' unsurprised curiosity, I gathered that she'd done a lot of talking while Josh and I were gone.

That was a mistake. The more they knew, the more dangerous their world became. Sky hadn't learned that lesson, yet. I wondered just how much she'd told them. Anger rose in me. David and Trent were likable, decent people who gossiped far too much. As far as I knew, they'd never talked about Sky's wolf. That didn't give them the right to probe me with questions they'd no business asking.

Putting on a polite smile, I stepped close enough to wrap my hand around her waist. She tried to back away from me once more, but I'd slipped a thumb through a loop in her jeans, using it to hold her close.

I answered David as casually as I could, not wanting to give more animus to the question.

"He says they didn't have anything to do with it." I added as a subtle warning, "But we spoke to him on the phone, so I had no way of knowing if he was telling the truth. Everyone has physiological changes when they lie. Most of us can detect them."

David's mouth snapped shut, but the sudden racing of his heart told me the message had been received.

"I don't do it," Sky lied to comfort them, undermining me in the process. "Not intentionally. Sometimes if it's really noticeable, I can, but I wouldn't do that to you all."

Josh didn't seem to have a problem with David and Trent's newfound knowledge. "I didn't detect their elven magic on the were-animal. There's something else weird about it and I can't quite put my finger on it."

"We should go," I stated.

Sky considered defiance, decided against it this time. On our way out, Trent rose to his feet, a look of awed excitement on his face.

"Can we see some magic?" he pleaded, his gaze fixed squarely on Josh.

Sky read my reaction. "We really have to go. Maybe another time."

He wouldn't take no for an answer, like a kid expecting us to prove all his childhood fantasies were real. I finally gave him a glimpse of the wolf in my eyes. He finally shut up. We were almost out the door when Josh turned back to Trent. Josh couldn't resist an audience. With a twirl of his fingers, a glass rose from the table. A bottle of wine followed. Following his gestures, the bottle tipped and poured its remaining wine into the glass. As he lowered his hands, bottle and glass slowly settled back onto the table.

Trent and David were agape.

Sky asked on our way to her house, "What do we do now?"

Josh answered, grinning, "You're going to help me track Ethos."

She smiled, exhilarated by the idea.

I sniffed the alcohol in her blood. "You'll need to be sober before we try the magic. Changing will burn some of it."

I pulled her living room curtains closed and pushed furniture out toward the walls while she changed in and out of her wolf form several times to burn off the alcohol. It was a trick I'd learned in law school.

Josh draped a towel over his shoulder, the one we'd used to soak up Ethos's blood.

While I leaned against a wall to watch, Josh and Sky faced each other in the middle of the room. He moved closer to her, to an unnecessarily intimate range. If I'd any doubts what he was up to, I lost them in the mischievous smile he gave me. Our silent exchange made Sky uncomfortable as she glanced between the two of us, looking as if she'd rather try the spell alone.

I suppressed a growl. *Going too far, Josh.*

Getting down to business, Sky raised a shimmering field around them using his magic.

"I hear you've mastered using the Aufero," he said.

"Well, if master means no one died, Maya didn't take over, and the house was still standing after I used it, then yes, I am the grand master."

He laughed, pressing closer until their bodies brushed against each other. "Then you'll take the lead and I'll help. You have access to dark magic. I think if we are tracking Ethos, you are going to be stronger."

He explained what she needed to do, giving her confidence and me an irritated gut. Once she was ready, he laid out the bloodstained towel on the floor between them. Next to it, Sky placed the Aufero, then began her invocation. The orb responded, taking on a glow that grew more intense as she progressed. Magic filled the room like a fall breeze. I'd witnessed tracking spells a number of times. How the location manifested depended upon the caster and the target. Josh's spell normally manifested the location on a 3D map. He was as surprised as I was when blood streamed from the towel to form a series of numbers on the carpet—GPS coordinates. I snatched a shopping list from the fridge. Just below where Sky had written "a butt ton of yogurt," I copied the coordinates. The numbers faded as I noted the last digit. A small amount of Ethos's blood remained on the towel.

Sky asked, "How long will it take to get the pack together?"

"We need to scout it first," I said, "see what we're facing."

I tapped the coordinates into my phone, then led Josh and Sky to my AMG.

The drive was quiet as we each prepared for what we would find. With any luck, we'd survey the location and confirm Ethos's presence without drawing attention. If our luck failed, we'd have a fight on our hands with the most powerful supernatural being I'd ever encountered. Sky appeared confident, but Josh understood the risk. Waves of powerful magic pulsed and swirled in the cab, emanating from him in the backseat. Glancing at him through the rearview mirror, I noticed his eyes were darker than normal —not yet black, but he was preparing his strongest magic. He'd faced defeat at the hands of Ethos before. This time, he'd no intention of being caught unprepared.

As we drove out of the suburbs into increasingly rural land, I began to wonder if the coordinates were correct. Following the GPS led us to a dead end at the edge of a dense, black forest. The location indicator on my phone continued flashing some ways into that darkness, but there was no sign of an access road.

Manipulating my phone, it seemed the entire forest area had disappeared from my map. This wasn't by chance. Josh and I exchanged anxious glances. I tried driving around looking for an access road into the forest. When that failed, I went back to the dead end.

Sky shook her head. "This can't be right."

"Of course it is. You don't discover this by accident. It's a perfect place."

Out of the AMG, we searched the edge of the forest until I found a rough, winding pathway. Following it, the dark woods seemed to engulf us as the trail steadily narrowed. Even the air grew thick as the presence of Ethos's foul magic became apparent. A faint, familiar scent caught my attention. Pausing to sniff, I recognized the scent as Samuel's. Worried what that meant, I grew more cautious but continued on. Eventually the path delivered us to a small house camouflaged by a tight canopy of trees and foliage.

Samuel's scent led into the house. We could've left, called for the pack. So far, it seemed we'd reached the house without being noticed. Catching Samuel and Ethos by surprise gave us an advantage I couldn't just throw away.

I caught Josh's attention, gestured toward the door. When he nodded, I signaled for Sky to hold back. She silently agreed. I quickly stripped off my clothes and changed into my wolf. As I approached the house, I felt a powerful blast of Josh's magic pass over my shoulder. The door burst into splinters. I raced inside to find Samuel sprawled out face down on the floor, unconscious. Fine white debris littered his back and the nearby floor, courtesy of several Samuel-sized holes in the plaster walls.

Otherwise, the house seemed empty. Ethos was gone, but there'd clearly been a fight. I sniffed blood that stained the floor near Samuel's body, confirming the blood was his.

Glancing around at the sparse furnishings of the one-room house, it wasn't hard to tell that Samuel had been living here for some time. We'd found his hiding place. So had Ethos, just as Josh had cast his tracking spell. Most likely, Ethos had come looking for the rest of the Clostra. If he'd found it, we were all at his mercy.

From Josh's anxious expression, I knew he'd puzzled out the same thing I had.

Sky appeared in the doorway, rushed to Samuel's side. Kneeling over him, she checked his pulse. I could hear the faint beat as he struggled at the edge of death. While she tried to revive him, I shifted back into my human form and dressed. Josh and I set about searching.

Josh stated the obvious. "The Clostra isn't here."

He chewed his nails, contemplating the ramifications. We had to assume Ethos had all three books, but could he read them? As far as we knew, there were only two people who could read the Clostra. Sky was one of them.

"I need your phone," I informed Josh. Using it, I called Cole, the Alpha of the East Coast Pack. After giving him a quick description of the situation, I asked him to check in on Sky's cousin, Senna. Finished, I returned the phone to Josh and started toward the door.

"Ethan," she said from Samuel's side. "Will you help me with him?"

I scowled. "Help you do what?"

"Get him to the car. He's just deadweight and you're stronger than I am."

"No." Samuel's sole purpose in life was to use the Clostra to rid the world of magic, likely killing all were-animals in the process. He was an enemy. The pack was safer with him dead. "We're leaving him."

Josh followed me out the door. I knew by the grunts from inside, the sound of heels scraping across hard wood, that she wasn't giving up. She emerged from the house with him, awkwardly carrying the larger man in her arms. Her lips pursed with the effort. Determination burned in her eyes. If she wanted to carry him, that was on her. Struggling behind us on the path, I listened to her ragged breath, to her grunts as she tried shifting his weight. I expected her to give up at any moment, but that wasn't who she was. Once Sky had the bit between her teeth, she'd never quit.

A quarter of the way to the car, I'd had enough. Rounding on her, I demanded, "Are you serious with this?"

She glowered. "I'm not leaving him unconscious in the middle of nowhere so he can die."

My jaw clenched with anger as I strode toward her. "If he had all three books, you know exactly what he would do to us. Or have you forgotten his goals? He doesn't want magic to exist. He doesn't want us to exist."

"Sebastian once choked me," she countered. "Winter was president, vice president, and co-founder of the 'let's kill Sky club,' and you've told me you didn't like me and have threatened me on multiple occasions. People change, things change. You don't dislike me now—"

"Don't be so sure about that part," I muttered as I lifted Samuel from her and slung him over my shoulder.

Walking behind me, she complained, "You're jostling him too much. Be care—"

"That's enough, Skylar."

I rounded on her, showing my anger. She blinked back in surprise and I continued toward the car. All the way, I could feel her fuming behind me. Once I'd propped him into the backseat of the AMG, I retrieved my phone from the glove box and informed Dr. Baker that we'd meet him at the retreat.

Samuel looked like he'd been on the run. His dirty-blond hair was long, ragged. His khaki military cargo pants were filthy and worn, like they hadn't been washed in a week. Blood stained his matching shirt, some of it old. The dried blood beneath his broken nose was more recent, courtesy of

Ethos, as were the deep cuts on his arms that probably needed stitches.

Part of me hoped he'd die on the way to the retreat, but he didn't oblige. We were still a half hour away when he woke up. Confused by his surroundings at first, his gaze finally settled on me. If he thought to fight, he quickly abandoned the idea.

His exhaustion was evident as he declared, "I don't have the book anymore."

Sky answered for me. "We know. Do you remember what happened?"

"Three of your kind"—he said with disdain—"and a witch ambushed me."

"That wasn't a witch. It was Ethos."

"That's not possible," he insisted. "Not at all. I watched him die."

"Let me guess, someone stabbed him in the neck or something equally as fatal."

"I shot him," Samuel insisted. "I shot him after he killed my best friend."

"How long ago was this?"

"Five years ago."

Sky raised an eyebrow to me. I knew what she was thinking. Faeries were hard to kill. This was twice we knew of that Ethos had seemed dead, only to rise again. She already seemed convinced that he was a Faerie. There was a decent chance she was right.

Pursuing her theory, she asked Samuel, "What do you know about Faeries?"

The question surprised him. "They are extinct. There are rumors that a few remain as spirit shades, but I believe those are just tales that keep people wishful of the opportunity to be a host and have omnipotent power."

"Then why did you try to kill Ethos?"

"He killed my friend. Like most foolish level fives, he

wanted more power, more strength, and the name Ethos was passed around like an urban legend. He would let you borrow his magic. Magic so strong you would be close to a level one. But Ethos's magic is different. The rumors of him being a demon-witch hybrid must be true. My friend called me, and when he changed his mind after making a blood contract with him, Ethos killed him. I was too late."

Noting the city looming ahead, he began to squirm. He gestured to an approaching gas station.

"Let me out here."

I gave him a hard look through the rearview mirror as I drove past the station.

He stiffened. "Am I your hostage?"

"You're alive," I growled, preferring we'd left him behind.

Sky gestured to the slashes on his arms. "You need medical attention."

"I'm fine." He shifted in the seat, grimaced at a pain in his leg. "Let me out."

Josh and I exchanged looks. Keeping Samuel against his will was going to be more trouble than it was worth. He was lucky we'd taken him this far. I eased the AMG to the side of the road, in sight of a gas station up ahead. If he wanted out, he could damn well walk on his injured leg.

"Feel free to walk," I said.

Noting the distance, he stubbornly opened the door and climbed out. He winced as he walked, favoring the one leg.

Josh leaned out the window. "We want the Clostra back just as much as you do. Our agendas may be different but we have a common goal, to possess the Clostra. I am a lot more comfortable with you having it than Ethos."

Samuel paused, limped back a step to regard Josh. After a moment, he turned his attention to me. "You could have stopped this. When magic is involved, people will always fight for more of it, to subjugate and control. It was in your control to stop this, so whatever happens, know that you could have stopped it."

I made my contempt plain. He was a crazed zealot. His view of magic was childlike, simplified to rationalize his bullshit. In his eyes, we were cursed, captives to our animal. He seemed to believe we'd somehow be saved by his spell, but the language of the Clostra was far from clear. "Laying the beast to rest" could just as easily mean death.

A look of shame passed over Sky's expression. "Yeah, I get that," she said, glancing at her palms. "I wouldn't change a thing. I don't claim to know what is best for other people. You are welcome to your belief that *all* magic in *all* people is bad, but you don't have the right to take it from others. And as altruistic as you believe your motives are, they aren't. You want to kill an entire group of people for your belief. How are you any better than the people and the magic you claim to hate?"

He remained quiet for a moment, unmoved. "Your blissful naïveté may be appealing to others, but I find it very dangerous. I find *you* very dangerous. The vampire is nothing more than an abomination, and you and your kind are a vile mockery of magic. Animals that present themselves as human are just as abhorrent as the dead presenting themselves to the world as men."

Anger swelled in her.

"Sky," I said.

He wasn't worth a confrontation.

Ignoring me, she climbed out to face him, her eyes inches from his own. "I could have left you back there and you could have died. I didn't. Yet as we stand here trying to help, your response is to tell me I am abhorrent and vile. Can you remind me, who's the real monster between the two of us? This fantasy world of lollipops, rainbows, and all babies dressed up like an Anne Geddes photo is just that—a fantasy. I get it, you want to believe that the people who live in this world are assholes because of the magic. Maybe that's the reason you are using magic to justify you being one, too. 'Like alcohol, the magic made me do it.' You forget that there are vampires who have friends and loved ones who aren't vampires. You kill them and you kill someone those people loved. How are you better?"

He remained silently unmoved.

She sighed, her anger fading. "The people who are evil with magic will be evil without it. They will just find other ways to achieve their goals. I'm not as naïve as you choose to believe I am. I know I'm not going to change your mind, but you are strong and we may need you. However you feel about magic, if Ethos and Marcia get their way, you will be a servant to one of them, and I don't think you will like that."

He ran a hand through his hair as he looked around. "I shouldn't have insulted you. I can't go back to my place. When I've found a new place, I will contact Sebastian. I will help you with this, but Skylar, my views still stand."

"We can find a place for you to stay for a while, if you need it."

I glanced to Josh, saw the anger welling in him. I'd be damned if I was going to spend pack resources helping the man who once held my brother hostage.

"No," Samuel said, catching my glare. "I'm fine."

He turned and limped toward the turnoff. Sky watched him go, shaking her head.

Measuring the distance at a glance, I figured he'd probably get to a phone in a couple hours, unless he passed out from the pain. Either way, I was fine.

"We aren't going to keep taking in your strays," I warned as she got back into the car. "Stop trying to save the world. It's not your job…"

She rolled her eyes, infuriating me.

"Do you understand?"

Her attention fixed on something outside the car, ignoring me.

"Sky."

Forced to reply, she answered in a cloying tone. "O-kay."

I shook my head and pulled back onto the road.

CHAPTER 12

The rest of the ride was silent. I dropped off Josh, then Sky. She left without a word, slamming the AMG door behind her.

I was getting into bed when Dr. Baker called me. He'd finished his tests on the deceased were-animal. The results only led to more questions. Too tired to contemplate, I went to sleep.

Sometime later, I woke to Josh calling me. The clock on my nightstand read two-thirty in the morning.

"Sky just called me and said there's a dead body in her house."

Fear raced through my body. I stiffened, suddenly alert. "Is she safe?"

"Yes. I'm heading there now."

I growled, climbing out of the bed. "I'll meet you there."

That she'd called him and not me stung, but the dead body was a bigger concern. I doubted the body was one of Sean's goons—he wouldn't dare raise his head above ground for a long time to come, never if he was smart. Racing the AMG between cars on the highway, the identity of the mystery body occupied my mind. Reminding myself that Sky was safe did little to ease my anxiety.

Josh and I arrived at the same time. Each of us looked to the other for answers, then walked to the door. Sky answered. If she was surprised by my presence, she didn't show it. Looking beyond her, I noticed a pool of blood congealing in the entryway. Fiona lay in a lifeless heap, like a doll casually discarded. A third scent lingered inside.

I stated, surprised, "Michaela was here."

A defiant look came over Sky as she folded her arms over her chest. "I staked her."

She threw a glance at Fiona's body, as if the reason wasn't obvious. Sky's demeanor was stiff, defensive, as if she expected me to admonish her. Staking Michaela, the Mistress of the Northern Seethe, was definitely a problem. I didn't need to hear the story to know that Michaela had come to confront Sky about Quell, leaving Fiona's corpse as a warning. That the confrontation had happened here, in Sky's home, made it difficult for anyone to lay the blame at her feet.

Demetrius wouldn't get involved, but this wasn't over with Michaela. The pressure of yet another reason to fear for Sky's safety weighed on me.

I nodded, but kept my thoughts to myself while Josh went about his business. His magic enveloped Fiona. A moment later, she disappeared. He did the same with her blood. Once finished, he addressed Sky.

"Are you okay?"

She shrugged, but the struggle was plain in her expression: sorrow and anger mixed with pride, a complex cocktail that left her uncertain how to feel. "I'll be fine," she promised. "I just need to get some sleep."

He squeezed her shoulder, gave her an empathetic look, then left. Alone together, I waited through a long silence until she started to fidget. Crossing to the couch, I sat, patted a cushion beside me. "Let's talk."

Her eyes narrowed.

"Please."

After a moment, her suspicion subsided. Before she could sit, I gently guided her into my lap.

"I just want to talk, okay?"

She curled into my lap, her head cradled into my neck.

"Tell me what happened."

"She'd already killed Fiona," Sky said in a distant voice that people often used when describing something traumatic. "She brought her here to make a point. She blames Quell for taking me from her, then blames me for taking Quell from her. She demanded that I somehow make Quell hers again, then she tried to kill me. So I killed her, almost. If she hadn't asked me to save her, I would've let her die. I'd have been glad to watch her die. That wasn't Maya," she added in a rush. "That was all me. Watching her die while she begged… that was something else. I couldn't do that."

I nodded, relieved. I'd been the first to push Sky to harden herself in the face of a dangerous world, but I'd never wanted her to become a stone-cold killer.

"Are you in love with Quell?"

When she hesitated, I braced myself for a difficult answer. She shifted in my lap to meet my gaze, searching. Finding nothing, she tried to kiss me. I'd taught her that, using physical affection as a distraction. She learned fast. I almost smiled.

"I need an answer, Sky."

"No, I don't think I'm in love with him." A vague answer, but not a lie. "But I hate Michaela and it is because of Quell. I hate the way she treats him. She was cruel to him for no other reason than she could be. She wants him to be a monster like her."

He was a monster. He'd been a monster since the moment

he'd first woken as a vampire. It took a great deal of control to not point that out.

Once more, she curled up in my lap. For a long moment, we listened to the beating of each other's hearts.

"Skylar, things are a mess."

She nodded, the wavy curls of her hair brushing against my neck.

"Has Dr. Jeremy found out anything about the were-animal?"

"Yeah." I sighed, tightening my arms around her. Her body tensed in anticipation as she searched my eyes. "There was a synthetic virus in his system, similar to the one that's found in us."

"Someone's trying to make were-animals?"

"Seems that way, but Dr. Baker thinks that whoever is responsible doesn't want them to change, just take on the other characteristics of were-animals. That's why his change was so difficult and he didn't survive it."

If Kelly hadn't already been infected by the virus, she probably didn't have long to wait. Whether Ethos was responsible was an open debate. After Dr. Baker's news, I had my doubts. Creating a synthetic virus required a great deal of time. Ethos could probably accomplish something similar with magic. After all, we still didn't know the limits of his powers. But if not Ethos, then who? The pack was surrounded by threats.

Sky said, "We have to find Kelly."

"Gavin's on it." He hunted with tunnel vision. Now that he knew Kelly had been taken, that she was in danger, he would not stop or waver for a moment until he'd found her. There was a fight with Ethos on the horizon. His panther would be missed. "He won't be any good to us now."

With the Clostra in Ethos's possession, our chances of survival were slim.

Sky waited for more information, but I had nothing else to explain.

"Let's go to bed," she whispered.

Rising, I carried her to the bedroom.

The next afternoon, Sky and I were at lunch when Josh called. He'd come up with a way to summon Ethos. His plan was questionable, but worth a try. He'd need help. Specifically, he needed London, his friend and occasional lover. As a level one witch, he was more powerful than her, but her skill set reached into some areas Josh's didn't. They'd been students together, until he'd decided to train on his own. I wondered sometimes if he'd regretted that choice. I knew little about her, but he trusted London implicitly, which was good enough for me.

Her help was not guaranteed. The last time they'd met, we'd asked her to help source blood that turned out to be Ethos's. Afterward, she'd made it clear she wanted nothing more to do with Josh or the pack. Since she wouldn't take his calls, or mine, we'd no choice but to show up at her door.

Josh met us at Sky's and we drove together to London's house.

The closer we got, his excitement faded into anxiousness at their impending reunion. Sky was on edge as well, anxiously anticipating another encounter with Ethos if the spell succeeded. In her bag, she held the bag with Ethos's blood. It was a rare commodity, one she wasn't keen to waste. As she alternated between stress and confidence, I tapped out the varying rhythm of her heartbeat against the steering wheel, my way of drawing her attention to her anxiety. For me, it was an amusing game. For her, it was annoying.

Eventually, she scowled. "Stop that."

I grinned, continuing.

Rolling her eyes, she turned to Josh. "Why do you think this is a good idea?"

"Samuel made me think about it. If we are able to *call* Ethos like his friend was, then we have the advantage."

"How is that going to help us get the Clostra back? You think he's just carrying them around in a satchel or something?"

"Getting them back is secondary," he insisted. "Ethos is the primary threat."

I agreed.

"We've found the Clostra before," he continued. "We can do it again."

She remained skeptical.

London's townhouse was located in a neighborhood popular with young professionals, who were out in force, walking their dogs and drinking coffee. I parked next to her VW Beetle in the driveway. When Josh didn't get out of the car, Sky and I turned in the front seats to look at him.

I wasn't used to seeing my brother's confidence shaken. He stared at London's door with a forlorn look, fully expecting to be excoriated. When he glanced at me, I nodded toward the door as encouragement.

He said in an accusatory tone, "She's not speaking to me because we involved her that last time."

I could take that blame.

"We don't have a lot of options," I said in a soothing voice. "You said we need to do it right the first time or Ethos will get suspicious. If you aren't confident in your ability to do it, we have to get someone who can. Okay?"

He nodded slowly, building his resolve.

"She'll be fine," I promised. "It'll be fine."

After a fortifying breath, he let out a resigned sigh and climbed out of the car. Sky brought the sealed bag with Ethos's blood and we followed him to London's door. When he hesitated, I stepped in front of the peephole and knocked.

After a faint shuffling from the other side, she didn't answer. I knocked harder. She could turn us down, but I wasn't going to leave until she'd heard us out. I was about to knock again when I noticed the slight shift in the window curtains, saw her peek out between them.

"London," I said.

She quickly snapped the curtains shut.

A long moment later, I heard the reluctant release of two locks. The door opened. London was a small, slight woman with a rainbow-colored pixie cut. She wore faded jeans and a loose shirt that hinted at some of her many tattoos, an obsession she shared with Josh. Behind her stern expression, I saw a hint of excitement at seeing him. For his part, he was entirely at her mercy. Like me, my brother had a reputation when it came to women. With his looks and his charm, he found their attentions easy to obtain. They came and went and he never seemed to care, yet here he was, ready to prostrate himself. I didn't mind seeing my brother humbled. It was a good look for him, on occasion.

London got straight to the point. "What do you want me involved in this time that will likely get me killed?"

Since she didn't invite us in, I walked past her into the entryway. "We just need you to show Josh how to do a spell."

He walked in behind me, hoping I'd continue to take the brunt of her hostility. His eyes widened as she walked right past me to confront him. Scrutinizing him, her hard edge softened.

"What's wrong?" she asked with genuine concern in her voice, then gestured to the sofa. "Have a seat."

Josh's shoulders drooped in relief.

Sky sat in a chair. I joined her, sitting on the arm while Josh sat next to London on the couch. Second-guessing himself, he shifted toward the end, putting some space between them. She looked to him expectantly and he told her everything. We'd already agreed that London's participation required full knowledge of what we were asking her to do, and why. While the pack had a reputation for ruthlessness, we never put someone into a dangerous position without giving them full awareness of what they were getting into.

He told her about the Aufero, that Sky was a Moura. He told her that I was a dark elf. Everything.

She was intrigued, to say the least. "A Moura and a dark elf sitting in my living room. *Hmm*, you all really know how to make life interesting. What do you want me to do?"

"Pala was a servant of Ethos," Josh said. London winced at the name, but he continued. "How did she contact him?"

Pala had borrowed Ethos's dark magic, and died for it.

"She called him." London added something in Latin. She was surprised when Josh didn't recognize it. She acknowledged his confusion with a wry smile. "It's a very old spell and although it isn't against our rules..."

Her words trailed off, her meaning plain.

"If you do this spell," Sky asked, "how do you call him specifically? Without blood or a direct link to him, how do you know he will respond?"

"For lack of a better way of explaining, it is like putting an ad on Craigslist and then you wait."

"And just wait for some random power to show up?"

She nodded. "That's how Pala became indentured to him. It was too late for me to stop her when I found out."

"What if he doesn't show up?"

"That's the risk of doing this. You open your home, and you need to be versed on the powers that show. Because if you aren't, you have no idea what you are getting yourself into."

"Have Tre'ase answered?"

I looked to Sky, impressed by the question I hadn't thought to ask.

"I am sure they have. I only know about the spell," London clarified. "I've never done it."

Sky remained skeptical of our plan, but we were out of options.

"I have some of his blood," she admitted.

London's eyes widened. "How old?"

"Five days."

She frowned. "We can try to source it, but it's old, and may not be as strong."

"We've done that already." Sky told the story about finding Samuel, including that Ethos now possessed all three spell books of the Clostra.

For a moment, London forgot to breathe. Horrified, she glanced at the door. Whether she wanted us to leave or was considering running, I wasn't sure. After a moment, she glanced down at her hand as she pulled on her fingers.

"You need to find him."

Josh asked, "You'll help?"

She answered softly, "Yes."

Sky and I were reduced to observers while they worked together. She explained the spell to him only once, using a shorthand Josh knew intimately. While they prepared, she retrieved a computer and keyboard from another room, set them onto an ottoman. I'd heard of some witches incorporating technology, but never seen it in practice. Their magic combined seamlessly, complementing each other. Watching them, I understood just how special my brother's connection to London was. I'd risked that for him once before, though unintentionally. I'd never put him in that position again.

The spell seemed more like a flawless performance than a feat of magic. Reaching the end, Josh's part was played. He stepped aside while London's fingers danced lightly across the keyboard, which I recognized as the focal point of their spell. Flecks of light darted through the room just before a pastel map appeared on the opposite wall. Josh glanced between her and the display with open-mouthed awe. She winked at him and continued. The map flickered as addresses appeared in different places, and then suddenly disappeared. Simultaneously, her computer went blank.

When her computer wouldn't restart, London cursed. "He's not a master of dark magic for nothing."

Josh stood next to her. "Let me try."

Reversing roles, Josh took the lead as they tried the spell again. London smiled as the familiar rush of his magic filled the room, whipping around like a budding storm. Where her magic was subtle, colorful, his magic was raw power. As the wind converged into a funnel in the center of the room, a map formed within. A house appeared, followed by a blurred address. As I strained to read it, the map flickered and then disappeared. Josh's eyes darkened as he brought the map back, fought to maintain it while drawing out more details. Sweat beaded on his forehead from the strain. It was London's turn to be awed. But before the address became readable, the map collapsed and disappeared for good.

The wind receded as Josh withdrew his magic. He shook his head while catching his breath.

Approaching my brother, I discreetly placed my hands against his, whispered, "Try again."

He gave me a suspicious look, then tried. As with Sky, he knew I had more magic available to me than I'd admitted to. Allowing my magic to flow with his, mine became dominant. The lights went out and a chill flooded the room. My lungs strained as oxygen became hard to come by. Focusing together, a new map formed with a spiral of light. Straining, we fought for details to emerge, but Ethos resisted. The map held for a few seconds, but not long enough for the location to become clear. It blinked out of existence and I let go of Josh's hands. The cold quickly receded as oxygen returned. Sky and London sucked in breaths in the dark, as we did.

. . .

A half hour later, London and Josh cuddled on the couch. His hand rested on her thigh with a practiced intimacy. He looked more at ease with himself than I'd seen him in a long time, which pleased me. In London's presence, he'd completely abandoned our jealousy game.

"He doesn't want to be found again," she explained.

Sky asked, "Should we try summoning him?"

"There will be an even larger chance that he might not answer. He's probably suspicious. But"—she looked down into her palms—"if I do it, I think he will answer."

Sky blinked. "Why?"

"I wasn't that different from Pala," she said, choosing her words. "Everyone always wants to be stronger, have more power, have access to magic that is forbidden. I considered borrowing from him, but when I met him, something didn't seem right. Pala didn't seem like the same person since she had gotten involved with him, and something was so off about him."

"You're sure it was him?" I asked.

"Weird blond hair, odd purplish eyes?"

Sky nodded. "That's him."

"Yeah, then we met." She glanced around her home. "I need more space. A lot more. I know a place but it's a bit of a drive."

I drew my phone from my pocket and called Sebastian.

Two hours later, Josh and London stood in a fallow field outside the city. A few feet away, I stood with Sebastian, Sky, and Winter. Winter had come for war, a katana drawn in one hand and a pistol holstered on each hip. She also carried a sheathed knife on her belt, just in case.

Behind us, twenty were-animals waited to carry out their revenge.

Josh and London poured a brownish substance that

reeked of sulfur and metal, drawing a circle. Once complete, they clasped hands and read the spell together from her phone. An unnatural calm settled onto the field, stifling any sound—a false promise of peace that suddenly erupted into raw power. The force of Ethos's arrival sent me, Sky, and Sebastian staggering back a few steps.

Somehow Winter held her ground.

Standing within the circle, Ethos fixed a wicked smile on London. Before her or Josh could react, his hand lashed out at her neck. She gasped for breath, her feet kicking, as he lifted her from the ground. He grinned up at her as she tried to wrench herself free.

"This little witch stole from me."

The *capsa*. London had given us the device that weakened Ethos by stealing some of his magic as he tried to retrieve it from his minions. Using the *capsa*, we'd stolen enough of his magic to make him vulnerable, then we'd killed him.

I should've expected he'd want revenge on her. I saw the recognition in Josh's face as he also realized we'd put her deeper into harm's way than intended. We'd brought London to perform the spell, not to fight Ethos. Once summoned, she was supposed to transport away.

Her lips moved desperately quick as she invoked a spell. Flame burst on the arm that held her. Despite the rising stench of his own burning flesh, Ethos didn't seem to feel pain. A quick invocation of his own and a small gust of ill wind smothered the flames.

She clawed uselessly at his arms as she fought for breath. Her eyes bulged, lips darkened.

His grin broadened.

With a sharp gesture, Josh sent a wall of force crashing into Ethos. Instead of breaking his grip on her and knocking him on his ass, it bounced harmlessly off a protective field that materialized at the last moment.

London's struggle slowed. Her grip on his arms grew noticeably weak.

Josh's eyes went black as he uttered another incantation. Ethos's field shattered, became a teal force wielded by Josh. Desperate to protect her, he turned that force into a field that encompassed him and London, repelling Ethos in the process. Thrown backward, he lost his grip on London. Pressing, Josh strode toward him, thrashing him again and again with a magical force.

With Ethos distracted, Sebastian and I changed into our wolves and circled around in opposite directions.

Sparks rose from Josh's fingers as he made a circular gesture. A magical band formed over Ethos's torso, tightening around him. Enraged, he dropped his human facade, revealing the charcoal demon-looking beast with fiery orange eyes that he was. His forked tail stabbed out at Josh, who deflected it with magic.

Sebastian and I closed in, snouts low, baring teeth.

Sensing danger, his black maw opened, emitting a screeching sound that ripped at our ears. Shrill and unnatural, it continued. I recoiled, a sharp pain shooting through my skull. The sound was worse for those in human form. Josh grimaced, clutching one of his ears while he struggled to keep up his attack. After a few seconds, he was forced to cover both ears.

The band around Ethos bulged, then shattered.

His tail lashed out once more, plunging into my brother's abdomen. Josh stumbled forward as the tail yanked free. I watched in horror as blood gushed from the wound. Gaping down at it, his hands clutched uselessly at the hole in his gut as he tried to apply pressure. Blood ran through his fingers as he collapsed to his knees.

Before I could react, Ethos lashed out again, this time at London. She must've sensed the attack coming. The fork just nicked her arm as she moved away.

The severity of Josh's wound sent me into rage. He wouldn't last long without medical help. *Kill Ethos* became the only thought in my mind. I charged, veering away just as his tail flicked in my direction. It lashed my side, sent me tumbling into the ground. Taking advantage of the distraction, Sebastian leapt onto Ethos's back. He bucked violently, trying to escape Sebastian's claws. His tail flicked like a whip, plunged into Sebastian's side. He continued fighting until he lost his grip and Ethos sent Sebastian tumbling in the grass.

My horror deepened as he turned on Sky, tail poised to strike. I shouldn't have let her come. I shouldn't have brought Josh. The battle was going to hell and Ethos was trying to kill the people I loved. I struggled to my feet, ignoring the sharp pain in my side.

Run, Sky!

As if she heard me, she did. She turned and ran, trying to change in stride. In wolf form, his magic couldn't harm her. Sensing victory, Ethos chased after her. If he reached her before she could change, he could transport her somewhere else, potentially miles away. We'd never find her before he could transfer Maya, or help her gain control of Sky.

On a good day, her transition could take a few minutes. With Ethos closing the distance fast, she didn't have a chance.

Frantic to save her, to save Josh, I chased after them. Sebastian ran at my side. The rest of the pack animals followed, howling for blood.

A few feet from her, Ethos's tail lashed out, cinched around her waist, then jerked her back into his grasp. Compressed against his chest, she grimaced as she reached down to her ankle sheath, drew a knife, and drove it into his tail.

Ethos screamed in agony, releasing her.

She dropped to the grass. Crouched, she started to back away.

Enraged, his tail flicked out at her one more time. Sky flipped backward, narrowly escaping the fork of the tail, but she landed poorly, lost her balance. The tail whipped around her ankle and yanked her to the ground.

As Sebastian and I were about to lunge, he threw back a hand toward us. A wave of dark magic rippled through the grass and crashed into us, knocking all of us to the ground.

The magic forced a few of us to shift, myself included.

As Ethos dragged Sky to him, she tried to reach the knife still embedded in his tail, grunting with the effort. With an easy flick, he cast her into a heap next to London. Pulling his tail close, he plucked the knife free with black, webbed fingers. He stared at it in disgust before casting it aside, then began an incantation.

I struggled to regain my feet, as did Sebastian and the rest of the pack. Ethos's magic seemed to permeate my muscles, challenging me for control. To my right, Josh lay motionless, bleeding. I'd no idea if he was still alive. Before me, Ethos had Sky in his control. Any moment he'd complete his spell and transfer Maya to London from Sky, killing her in the process.

Drawing my own magic, I clenched a fist and slammed it into the ground at my feet. The spell that bound me crumbled. A circle of dark-blue magic spread out from the impact, liberating the rest of the pack. I jumped back to my feet and charged, shifting in stride. Once more, Sebastian's wolf was at my side. Blood matted his fur.

London tried to crawl away until Ethos stomped a dense foot on her leg, crushing her leg. Her cry was agonizing.

Gavin's panther raced past us, crashed into Ethos's legs, knocking him to the ground. His form flickered as he tried to transport away. A blast of Josh's magic engulfed Ethos, disrupting his escape. Glancing over my shoulder, I was relieved to see Josh—alive—upright, his arm extended. His ghostly pale face was screwed in concentration as he and

Ethos engaged in a battle of magical will. They both strained, resisting each other.

Sebastian and I were almost on top of him. *Just a few more feet!*

Seeing the danger, Ethos opened his maw and let out a fresh shriek that broke Josh's concentration.

I leapt, claws extended, teeth bared. By the time I landed on my paws, he'd disappeared. I howled in frustration, but quickly came back to my senses.

Josh, ignoring his wound, somehow stumbled to London's side. Her body was rigid, breath ragged. The pain of her crushed leg left her panting.

"Broken," she muttered through her daze. "It's broken."

He took her hand, whispered something to calm her.

Gavin, Sebastian, and I shifted back to our human forms. I raced to my brother's side and knelt next to him. He'd lost a lot of blood. If he didn't get help soon, he would bleed out. I tried to lift him, but he pushed me away, refusing to leave London's side. I gestured to Steven, who knelt next to London.

"I'm going to lift you," he informed her in a calming voice. "You need to support your thigh to minimize the pain. Put your hands here and here," he demonstrated. "We're going to get you to Dr. Jeremy. You're going to be okay."

Her heart rate slowed with his confidence. She nodded.

"Can you transport?" I asked Josh, trying to mask my anxiety.

He shook his head.

Preparing to lift him, I warned, "This is going to hurt. On three. Ready? One."

He groaned as I lifted him. A sharp pain shot through my wounded side. I ignored it, balanced my brother's weight, and carried him as fast as I could walk to one of the SUVs at the edge of the field. Glancing over my shoulder, I saw

Steven at Sky's side. Relief washed through me as I confirmed that she hadn't been wounded.

Sebastian drove while I remained at Josh's side, gripping his hand while Gavin put pressure on the wound. When he began to drift off to sleep, I patted his cheeks until he brushed my hand away, annoyed.

"Stay awake."

"You're so controlling," he said, groggy. "London?"

"She's in the other car. She's right behind us."

That put him somewhat at ease. Seeing he was about to fade, I said in a rush to keep his attention, "You were right."

"Now I know...I'm dreaming."

"I stole your dates at the club. You should yell at me." I squeezed his hand. "You're pissed, Josh. Remember?"

"Oh, yeah. I nearly forgot. You're a-a selfish bastard."

"Yeah," I admitted. "It's my thing."

"So." He licked his lips, showing blood on his teeth. "You and Sky, huh?"

"Yeah."

"Just tell me one...thing."

I patted his hand. "Okay."

"Were you two...together...before the penthouse?"

"Yeah."

"Oh." He sighed. "That's embarrassing." He tried to laugh but the pain in his gut prevented him. "If you hurt her, I'll... send you to the place I send all the dead bodies."

"Okay," I laughed. "Deal."

"And." He half raised an index finger for emphasis. "You'll help me get the little redhead girl that lives across the street."

Gavin gave me a puzzled scowl. I cocked my head at Josh, not sure if he was joking. The van rocked slightly as we turned onto the private road that led to the retreat.

"Josh," I said. "I think that's Charlie Brown."

He chuckled. "Oh, yeah."

. . .

In the pack's infirmary, Dr. Baker gave Josh something to keep him awake. It also made him a pain in the ass. While Dr. Baker worked to stem his bleeding and start Josh on fluids, he demanded that Dr. Baker abandon Josh's live-saving treatment to tend to London's crushed leg. Even when Dr. Baker began her treatment, Josh was barking out suggestions.

"Josh," I growled, "you have to hold still."

He snarled something about fucking myself to hell.

So much for our brotherly camaraderie from the SUV.

"Josh! Calm down."

Launching into a rant, he expanded on all the ways I could fuck myself. I let him go on, nodding encouragement along the way. While he was focused on me, Dr. Baker did his best for London's leg. Only after her bones had been set and a cast placed around her leg did Josh finally calm down enough for Dr. Baker to finish attending his wound. Once the stitches were complete and Josh was quiet, I slipped out of the infirmary to take a much-needed break.

Sky found me there, leaning against a wall.

From the infirmary, we heard a testy Dr. Baker exclaim, "Would you let me do my job?"

Sky gave me a sheepish look. "Josh?"

"Of course, because apparently being a witch is equivalent to holding a medical license."

The corner of her mouth bent into a slight smirk.

"I'll be staying with you for a while," I said as she started toward the doors. Her smile faded. Reluctance quickly became relieved resignation.

"Should I stay here?" she asked.

I tensed. There wasn't anywhere safe against Ethos now. He had broken Josh's blood wards with ease. With his transport spell, he could turn up anywhere, anytime. Eventually, he would come for her. I'd have to keep her glued to my side until we could find a way to kill him. Even so, I wasn't sure I could stop Ethos alone. Even with the pack's best, we'd barely managed to chase him away.

Sky's brow furrowed as she read my concern. Cursing myself, I wrapped my arms around her and gently kissed her forehead. We remained close, taking comfort from our shared embrace until she broke the silence.

"Your skills with magic seem to be improving." She pulled back enough to search my gaze. Whatever she found there, she latched onto. "Do I know everything about you, Ethan?"

I grinned, doing my best to seem natural. "Of course not. That could take forever."

"Not about that. About magic. I feel like there is more."

"You know everything that is needed to be known." I started toward the clinic. She gripped my arm, guiding me back from the door.

"I need to check on Josh," I complained.

"Don't hide things from me, because I always find out."

Not everything. "Of course you do," I said, amused. "I need to go check on Josh."

"I know." She smiled. "But don't be *you* when you go in there."

"Who exactly should I be?"

"Someone who can be reasoned with. A person who believes that others' opinions have merit and his way isn't the only way."

I stared back at her, confused.

She sighed, gave up on subtlety. "Don't fight with your brother, please."

Inside the clinic, I found Josh sitting up in a bed, running his fingers over the numerous stitches on his stomach. Tattoos covered his arms, chest, and back. Surprisingly, his stomach was clear of them. His intense gaze fixed on London in a neighboring bed. Steven sat in a chair next to her, gently encouraging her as she tried to raise her casted leg without using her hands. Her mood was foul, understandably so.

"How are you?" I asked her.

She stopped to glare at me. "I want to go home."

Josh slid off his bed onto his feet, winced. He clutched at his stitching as he hobbled toward her. I wanted to stop him, force him back to his bed, but thought better of it.

She tensed at his approach, refused to even look at him.

He pleaded, "London."

The room filled with magic that had to be hers, but it was different than what I'd felt at her house. Her magic, like her, brimmed with anger and fear. With a twitch of her finger, she brushed Josh backward several feet. He grabbed at a counter to keep from stumbling.

"I want to go home," she insisted, fixing a determined stare on me. "Now."

She jumped off the bed in an attempt to be imposing, but was too weak. Steven caught her before she fell to the floor. Frustrated, she sobbed into her shirt.

Unable to help her, Josh was crushed. The feeling was familiar. I empathized with him.

"Just let her go home," Steven said. "Can't Jeremy check on her there?"

I looked to Josh. Guilt weighed heavily on his sullen mood. I knew that watching someone else comfort her had to cut him to the quick. He looked to me and I knew he wanted me to order her to stay. Ethos wanted her to host Maya, but his first concern was getting control of Sky. For the moment, London was safest away from us.

"Of course," I said.

She needed crutches. The pack didn't keep them around because were-animals heeled too quickly to make use of them. Sky and Steven helped her to one of the pack's SUVs while Josh shuffled uselessly behind, wincing at each step. Once London was securely in the vehicle, the others joined her and they drove off.

. . .

The next twenty-four hours were tense. Josh restored the blood ward around Sky's house, but it was just a glorified alarm. If Ethos wanted in, he'd break it easily. We were both convinced it was only a matter of time before he showed up, more likely sooner than later. We didn't share our fears with Sky. Worrying her wouldn't help, so we lied. While convincing her that Ethos wasn't likely to show up anytime soon, one of us was always at her side.

I stayed with Sky. At night I curled up in wolf form at the end of her bed. Josh took the guest room. He seemed to have abandoned his earlier jealousy. I could thank London for that. His mood had lifted since taking London home. They'd eventually talked out what had happened in the field with Ethos, how she had ended up there. She'd made her choice, but that did nothing for Josh's guilt. I appreciated his newfound desire to take responsibility. We were all relieved that her leg would heal. Thanks to Dr. Baker, there would be no major side effects.

Expecting Ethos, Josh and I had worked out our plan. Josh's job was to transport Sky to safety, then bring rein-forcements. My role was to keep Ethos busy until Sky and Josh were safe—probably a suicide mission, but I let Josh believe I could hold out long enough for help to arrive.

At lunch the next day, I reminded Sky that she had a training session with Sebastian at six o'clock.

Her expression contorted in disbelief. "Seriously?"

I smiled. "Sebastian never cancels a training session."

Just before six, we arrived at the retreat gym to find him waiting. Several swords were laid out on a table. I watched from the stairs.

I knew firsthand that he was an unrelenting teacher. For four hours, he put Sky through her paces, punishing and then correcting every mistake. She learned on a bell curve. The going was rough at first. Eventually, she caught on. I watched as Sebastian swiped her leg for the seventh time, then she surprised him. She landed on her butt with her sword arm extended, ready to defend. Fending off his attacks, she rose to her knee, then to her feet. After a quick parry, she drove her pommel into his solar plexus, followed with the other fist to Sebastian's knee. He fell with her towering over him, the point of her blade at his throat.

He grinned, as did I.

She found her success suspicious. "Did you let me win?"

"It was a good sequence. It would have worked with anyone." Coming to his feet, he placed the sword aside. "See you tomorrow, same time."

"I slayed you. How about eight?"

He chuckled as he walked passed me up the stairs. "You defended yourself well. Six o'clock, Skylar."

She grinned at me, proud. "I kind of kicked Sebastian's ass."

Aroused, I took her in my arms, brushed my lips against her cheek. "You did very well."

My lips brushed hers. My hands roved to her hips as I walked her back against a cushioned wall. Our kisses were hard, eager, as I tugged off her shirt and tossed it aside. Hungry for her, my lips traced the curve of her neck, embraced the softness of her breasts. Her aroused heart pounded in my ears. My lips tasted the firmness of her stomach while I pulled off her jeans. Eager for more, I rose, lifting her. Her legs wrapped around my hips.

"Ethan," she whispered, suddenly reminded of where we were. "Someone can—"

My lips covered hers, kissing her hard as I plunged into her. The grip of her legs tightened around me, pulling me in as I thrust. Our carnal desires became a single, primal need. Our ragged breaths became indistinguishable as our passions consumed us until we reached our pleasure together. We clung to each other as the moment subsided, kissed each other. Unwilling to leave her embrace, my hands gripped her thighs, keeping her legs secured around me.

I pressed my forehead to her, inhaled her scent.

Catching her breath, she whispered, "Should I be freaked out that kicking Sebastian's ass turns you on? Because I need to tell you this is all kinds of strange. And a little twisted."

I kissed her. "Winter has trained you well."

She kissed me back.

That evening, in human form, I fell asleep next to Sky. Some time in the night, I snapped awake to the jarring vibration of Josh's blood ward shattering.

Sky and I reached the living room to find Josh drawing magic to him. Before I could speak, the front door burst into splinters. A wolf charged through, leapt onto him. Distracted, his magic disappeared. He landed on his back, the snarling wolf on his chest.

I stepped in front of Sky. Before I could reach Josh, a wave of dark magic rushed into the room and threw us against the wall, pinning us there. Josh remained still beneath the wolf, its bared teeth inches from his throat.

A smug Ethos in human form strolled over the debris of the front door. His violet eyes flashed as Sky and I struggled to free ourselves, a futile gesture. His magic was too strong. In the face of it, my own magic paled.

Without even acknowledging us, he strode into Sky's room and emerged with the glowing Aufero in his hand. It tried to erect a protective field. Ethos dismissed it with a casual gesture. I felt the orb's magic rush to Sky, responding to her call. She turned it back on Ethos, slamming him first against the wall, then the floor. Furious, Ethos slammed his hands onto the floor. A circle of fire erupted around Sky, the flames threatening her.

"That's for you," he declared.

Fear overwhelmed Sky as the flames closed in around her. In her panic, she forgot about the Aufero. While she was distracted, Ethos muttered a quick incantation over the orb. A black fog enveloped me, sucking the oxygen from my lungs. I gasped, struggling for breath in a vacuum.

Ethos released me from the wall. My oxygen-deprived limbs couldn't do more than break my fall as I collapsed to the floor. The struggle to breathe became all consuming. Fear raced through me as I realized there was nothing I could do to break through the fog. The panicked pounding of my heart drummed in my skull, but quickly faded. My mouth hung open, fighting for even a molecule of oxygen. The void left no crumbs. My vision went black. The last faint beat of my heart carried me into darkness.

Nothingness became a gasping breath. My lungs screamed. Pain pulsed through my skull, along with a dark buzzing I'd hoped never to feel again. The sound of Ethos's voice nearby sent my fragile heart racing.

"He will be as he should have been."

Darkness returned, but at least I was alive.

I woke to a dark vibration that hummed in my body like a ringing in my ear—the dark elf magic. Sky had used the Aufero to remove that magic. Fucking Ethos had given it back to me.

Sky's voice spoke near me. "Ethan?"

My eyelids fluttered open, revealing the infirmary. Familiar faces crowded me: Sebastian, Winter, Dr. Baker,

Steven, Gavin. Josh sat in a chair next to the bed while Sky stood nearby. They were both watching me. She started forward to touch me.

"Don't," I snapped.

She recoiled.

I'd almost killed her once with the dark elf death magic, just by touching her. I'd learned to control it before, but could I control it now? I was afraid to find out.

Josh's brow furrowed. "Are you okay?"

He asked several more times before I snapped back, "I'm fine."

Dr. Baker cleared his throat. "Perhaps we should leave him be."

Sky remained while the others left. Josh, reluctant, was the last to leave. When Sky tried to touch me again, I growled, rolled off the bed onto my feet and into a corner of the room.

"You were able to control it before."

"I know," I said, wondering if I'd kill anyone before I learned to control it again. "It'll take time."

She extended her hand to me, whispered, "Come with me."

I blanked at her hand, read the confidence in her expression. Slowly, her confidence in me became contagious, enough for me to reach out and touch her hand—tentative, at first. The warmth of her fingers brushed the buzzing from my mind, for a moment.

I didn't kill her.

Relieved, I took her hand. Stepping closer, I lightly kissed her lips.

She led me out of the house and into the backyard. Watching me, she stripped off her clothes and stood naked, waiting for me to do the same.

I grinned. "Not so modest, are you?"

"Yeah." She glanced around. "It is still odd standing outside naked for the world to see all my lady parts."

Anticipating the relief of my wolf, I stripped, shifted, then darted into the woods. Sky followed, but slowly fell behind. My wolf was twice the size of hers. Realizing I'd lost her, I turned back and found her in a small patch of grass beneath a pine tree. After an affectionate nudge with my nose, I brushed my face against her neck. Then I licked her. Her head snapped around and I narrowly avoided her playful nip. When I tried again, she bared her teeth. I grinned.

Deciding to rest, I dropped down into the grass and laid my snout on my paws. The dark elf magic didn't affect my wolf. In animal form, I felt like myself. With Sky near me, I was in no hurry to return to the house. Eventually, I'd have to shift and deal with the situation at hand. Ethos hadn't taken Sky, to my relief. But he had the Aufero, which gave him all of the protected objects except the Vitae. Claudia was the Vitae's Moura. Ethos would be coming for her and Josh, next.

I brushed those thoughts aside as Sky nestled into the grass next to me.

Marcia emerged from hiding to call a conclave, inviting every sect of the otherworld. No explanation was given. We all knew it had to do with me. Ethos was playing his game, using Marcia as his pawn. I was a dark elf again, and she knew it. The conclave was a trap. It was also an opportunity.

Sebastian drove, with me, Josh, Winter, and Sky in the back of the SUV. Gavin and Steven followed close behind in a second vehicle.

"Why are we going?" Sky demanded. "There isn't anything forcing us to go. Just because Marcia calls some kind of conclave doesn't mean we have to accept."

"Skylar," Sebastian said. "We need to go. If it goes well, we have an opportunity to end the covenant. If we don't go, it would be an insult and slight to all involved and make us look guilty."

"We are guilty!" She gestured to me. "We violated it. So why the hell are we going?"

Her frustration peaked as we pulled into the driveway of a single-story stone building isolated on a grassy plain. The few windows were blacked out.

"You don't have to go," she insisted to me. "*We* don't have to go."

I sighed, sagging in my seat. "What do you think will happen if we don't, Sky?"

She didn't have an answer, which only frustrated her further.

The steel front door opened on our approach. Bernard greeted us wearing tortoiseshell-framed glasses and an impeccable gray suit. I wasn't sure what capacity he held. He served the Creed but was mindful of his own interests, which made him a vulnerability. Claudia had something on him once. He'd reluctantly come to the retreat at her behest to advise us regarding Kelly's illness. I made a mental note to look into his life, for future leverage.

"This way," he said, barely masking his disdain. He pushed the glasses up onto his nose, then led us into a narrow hallway. At the second door, he stopped. Two large men emerged from another door behind him in a show of support.

One of the men addressed Sebastian. "We will need your weapons."

"We don't have any."

"Do you mind if we check?"

Sebastian responded with a mirthless smile. If we were going to defy Marcia's call, we wouldn't have bothered to show up. She was provoking us, hoping for a reaction. He nodded, his steady gaze fixed on the guard patting him down. It was a momentary insult. The guards weren't satisfied with the handful of knives they confiscated from Sky. They'd expected more.

Backing out of our way, they remained wary, the bulk of their attention fixed on Sebastian and me.

We were directed through a door that led to a large open room. Runes were scrolled across the wall, a spell that inhibited us from changing to our animals—another insult, but nothing new. A long wooden table extended across the far end of the chamber. From the center seat, Marcia fixed an anxious gaze on Josh, staring out from deep-set eyes. Her thin lips were pressed into a hard, flat line.

Mason was at the table, though his position as leader of the elves was doomed. The election was two months away. Gideon's success, as the only challenger, was certain, which was why he and Abigail, his sister, sat to Marcia's right. Unofficially, the fraternal twins would share power. In an androgynous way, they were nearly identical, like shop mannequins. Of the two, she was the more ambitious, having already poisoned her twin to drive his political ambition.

The pack and the twins had formed a secret alliance to guarantee Gideon's rise to the leadership of the elves. Now that he was on the cusp of victory, they might find the conclave an opportunity to be rid of us.

To Marcia's left sat Demetrius and Michaela. She regarded the entire affair with an air of boredom, but I caught the vengeful look in her eyes when they settled on Sky. Demetrius smiled, enjoying his opportunity to judge us.

Next to them sat Liam, king of the *Makellos*. In a show of arrogance and self-importance, he had two of his personal guard seated behind him.

Bernard barred Josh from entering the chamber. At his gesture, a guard carrying iridium manacles approached Josh.

His eyes narrowed as Bernard declared, "You will have to wear these."

Josh fixed a defiant gaze on Marcia. In response, she raised her own bound hands—a curious touch. Scowling, he extended his arms to accept the burden.

A voice behind me addressed Sky. "You'll need to wear cuffs as well."

I turned to find another guard holding out cuffs to Sky. She glared back at him, uncooperative.

Marcia's voice echoed through the chamber. "We will ask only once."

Sky rolled her eyes as she extended her arms, held them stiff while the guard cuffed her.

Once her bindings were established, Sebastian broke the ensuing silence. "Should we get started with this witch hunt?"

"We are still waiting for the fae," Marcia declared. "They must not be excluded in this matter."

The door opened behind us. Turning, I was more than a little surprised to see Claudia walk in. She wore her ocher-colored suit with high beige heels that clicked against the floor. She was her usual, calm grace. The narrowed slant of Marcia's eyes exposed her surprise to see my godmother approach the table as if she belonged there.

"I apologize for my tardiness," Claudia declared, "but I wasn't going to miss out on a sale of one of my favorite artist's work for this contrived nonsense."

Demetrius rose, pulled out the seat for her. It was a disconcerting show of respect.

Marcia watched with irritation as Claudia settled into her seat. "I am not sure why you are here, you were not invited."

With a mild sigh, she handed Demetrius a delicate envelope from her purse. He passed it to Marcia.

The witch made a show of unfolding the enclosed letter. Her stern gaze flicked over the contents. "You are not a fae," she declared. "I am not sure why they would send you as their representative."

"I have no home, therefore I belong to all and none. The fae have welcomed me as their own. It was your request that all sects be represented. They chose me to do that. You have no business questioning anything further than that. The fae are being represented." Glancing around the table, Claudia declared, "It appears all are represented, shall we continue?"

Marcia wasn't finished. "There is no way your presence here is appropriate. You are biased and won't be able to accept all evidence against the men you have a maternal relationship with."

"You have no business here, either. You will not be able to take the same evidence and assess it without bias because you have already labeled them as your enemy. If I have no business here, then neither do you. If you would like, we can waste more time and hold it to a vote. But the vote will be for us both. Either we both leave or we both stay. If I am to recuse myself, then so should you."

Marcia sucked in an angry breath, held it as she assessed the attitudes of the other figures at the table. Her lips bent into an acerbic frown as she set the letter aside. Her heavy chair scraped against the floor.

"We all agreed that due to the nature and the danger that the dark elves posed to us, regretfully they had to be contained."

The representatives nodded, including Claudia. I doubted that her presence had been requested by the fae. She'd cashed in some favor, or perhaps offered a new mark, to put herself in this room. How the situation would play out, I wasn't sure, but I owed her my gratitude.

Marcia continued. "The covenant wasn't entered into lightly, but it was something we all agreed to uphold for our safety and of those not in this world. It was necessary to prevent exposure, but unfortunately Sebastian and his pack feel that they are exempt from any of our rules and reneged on the very covenant he agreed to." She surveyed the room, rallying support. "Even if we choose not to protect ourselves, shouldn't we protect each other from being exposed?"

Demetrius leaned back in his chair, unimpressed. He was no friend to the pack, but any support he offered Marcia might well come back to haunt him. I guessed I could thank Michaela for that; she had a habit of creating beautiful, psychotic vampires that caused a number of problems for the other factions.

Next to him, she looked up from examining her black-painted nails. Her mouth bent into a miscreant smile as she read the room, paying particular attention to Josh. Noticing, he glared back at her, to her obvious delight. He returned his attention to Marcia as she rounded the table to pace in front of it.

Her tone grave, she continued, throwing us baleful looks. "Am I the only one concerned with what Sebastian is doing? He has a witch whom he has formed an alliance with that supersedes our control. He is strong and I assure you has the potential to be dangerous. He no longer follows our rules but adheres to theirs. His final slight against us is Ethan"—she gestured to me—"the descendant of a dark elf, one who recently died. One that they kept hidden, and now—"

Claudia interrupted, her tone harsh. "Is there a point you plan to get to, or will we be treated to more of your show? I can do without the community theater. Get on with it."

Marcia remained still, but her anger was palpable. The room stirred from it. As if sensing the effect she was having, she settled herself with a quick breath. When she spoke again, her voice was calmer, but her irritation remained obvious.

"Marcia," Claudia pressed, "if you have a point, will you please make it?"

"Of course you will take this lightly. After all, you consider them perfect, entitled, and impervious to our rules."

"No, not at all. But I see this for what it is, a witch hunt. Lay your torch and spear down and let's focus on what is real. Don't make this seem more detrimental than it is. Has Ethan hurt anyone?"

Perhaps she should be more specific.

"As a dark elf," Claudia clarified. "Do you know of anyone who has been injured or killed by him?"

"Well, of course not. You and I both know that they are quite capable of covering it up if it were to occur."

"Then if that is the case, why are we here? Your argument is that they broke the covenant and are at risk of exposing us. If they are in fact covering it up adequately, why are we here?"

Marcia's control finally slipped. "Because they are dangerous, rule-less monsters incapable of being civil," she insisted. "Do you know why there isn't any evidence? They removed it from him!"

"Wait," Demetrius said. "If they are capable of removing such things, I must agree with Claudia on this, why are we concerned?"

Sebastian and I were both taken aback. It was one thing for Demetrius to take a position that happened to help us, but he was actively defending us. Was this Claudia, as well?

"Honestly, Marcia," Demetrius continued, "this is a waste of time. They keep to themselves, and whether it is out of their delusion of self-importance or they know their kind are the only ones that can tolerate them, either way, it is no concern to me. If Ethan is a danger, it will only be to them. Let them have at it. If he kills them...so? And if they can control it—then even better for them. This brings forth another issue, how are they doing it? If they can do it, I am confident they should be given the responsibility to do so.

Perhaps it will keep them busy enough to stay out of others' affairs."

A satisfied smile briefly appeared on Marcia's lips. I saw what was coming. Had Demetrius fallen into a trap, or helped set one for us? She addressed Sebastian as she returned to her chair. "Why don't you tell them why you are, or rather were, able to control Ethan's ability."

He answered with a controlled voice, projecting calm confidence, but the muscles in his neck were cords. "Recently we came into possession of the Aufero. Before it was being hidden, unused. Our research had shown that we could use it to stop more containment. Marcia, you of all people know I share your desire to maintain our anonymity to the humans. But we don't share the same belief about killing Ethan. As you so assiduously pointed out, I had it under control."

A diplomatic answer, and an impressive one. He'd deftly left out that Sky was a Moura, able to wield the orb's power. We didn't want the attention that knowledge would bring to her, but it would establish her right to retain the Aufero. For that reason, Marcia didn't mention it, either. Swallowing that knowledge raised her ire. Her heart quickened.

"Yes." She glowered. "Recently the pack has acquired a lot of things, including your little special wolf. She is quite the peculiar thing, isn't she? A wolf, with the *terait* and the ability to perform magic." She looked around the room. "You all know this, right? She is wrong, very wrong. From her recent arrival on the scene and the outbreak of chaos that soon followed."

That got everyone's attention. All but Claudia slid to the front of their chairs, their attention fixating on Sky.

"I know you all see her as a little oddity," Marcia continued. "The pack's problem. But Demetrius, were you not going to use her in a ritual to remove the curse that binds your people? It wasn't able to be used on any other were-animal but her. Is anyone curious as to why? Is that bothersome to anyone?"

Was this her trap? Had Sky been her intended target?

"Those of you who can sense magic, the variations and changes, have you noticed the change? Tre'ase, once controlled by the curses that limit their ability to wreak havoc on this world and restricted only to interact with those who seek them out, are no longer under such restrictions. Am I the only one who has noticed? Perhaps Liam can elaborate on the changes he's experienced over the past few months."

Michaela leaned her elbows on the table, formed a high platter with her hands as she regarded Sky. "Are you saying that we need to be concerned about Skylar? She seems harmless enough, but I could be wrong."

Realization was dawning on everyone. They'd all experienced the changes wrought when we removed the curse on Sky. For the first time, they were figuring out that someone had been responsible for the change. They weren't happy.

Abigail leaned close to her brother, whispered into his ear.

He nodded, addressed the table. "It seems as though we have gotten off the topic here. You brought us here to discuss a covenant that had been broken by Sebastian; now we somehow have moved on to his new little acquisition."

Sky tensed.

"Let's discuss Ethan." Gideon turned to me. "How long have you been like this?"

I'd no reason to lie, yet. "Initially seven days, then we found a way to get rid of the ability. Unfortunately, it has returned."

How we got rid of the ability was a can of worms I preferred to not open.

Mason spoke for the first time, drawing an eye roll from Abigail. "That's not really answering the question, and since your life is on the line here, it will be to your advantage to give us more."

Gideon gave Mason a dismissive look, but couldn't prevent him from exercising his authority, temporary though it was.

Before he could continue, Marcia interjected, "We would like to know how you purged yourself of the ability. After all, we had tried for years, the elves have tried and the fae as well. Yet, the were-animals with access to a mediocre witch were able to."

She threw Josh a smug look, baiting him. Marcia was in control now, steering us toward disaster. She wanted me to admit that we'd used the orb to remove the dark elf magic, which would reveal that we could manipulate the orb's power—news that could turn the other factions against us. The only counter was to tell the truth—all of it. There were risks there as well.

While the room impatiently waited for my answer, I turned to Sebastian. He gave me his approval with the slightest of nods.

With some effort, I put on a casual smile. "Skylar, our new acquisition, as you put it, is a Moura Encantada. Most of you know what they are—if you don't, she is responsible for guarding a protected object. She is the protector of the Aufero, which she had in her possession until yesterday. It was stolen from us and the spell reversed by Ethos. Before she had it in her possession, it was in Marcia's. It is odd that she used it to punish the witches but not once decided to use it to help the elves from having to kill their own. That was our intention. We were fortunate to be able to practice on me, to perfect it. The reason Skylar didn't have it in her possession before was because it was being hidden by dark magic. Now, I guess we should all consider how it was hidden by dark magic, by a witch."

My smile widened as all eyes turned to Marcia. Her face flushed. Her narrowed gaze fixed on me.

Sebastian added, "If you all can't see this, Marcia's motives aren't as pure as she would like us to believe. Last year, Demetrius's Seethe and my pack were attacked by Ethos. His sole purpose was to control us, and the rest of you were expected to fall in line as a result of it. Now let's think about what has occurred recently. Marcia had the Aufero, with the potential of removing the magic that makes dark elves lethal to us—she didn't. Instead, she kept it hidden with the use of dark magic. Ethos has taken the Aufero from us and restored Ethan to the way he was, and now, we are here. My pack and I are depicted as having this Machiavellian plan. I ask you, who is the one whose behavior seems unscrupulous?"

Marcia snapped, "My actions aren't in question here, it is their pack's, and I hope you aren't swayed. It would have been a bigger disservice to give false hope."

Abigail said, "But you didn't even do that, did you? You didn't give an ounce of hope. Instead you kept this information to yourself."

Marcia stared past Abigail to Gideon, who didn't appreciate the slight on his sister.

"My sister asked a question," he stated. "And when she does, you treat it as though it is coming from me or Mason."

I thought Mason was going to choke on that declaration. He seemed about to rebuke Gideon, but thought better of it.

All eyes were on Marcia.

"I follow the rules. Adherence to the covenant has always been of utmost importance, not falsehoods and the hope of something that may never manifest. You all are being swept up in the little smoke screen that Sebastian and his group of rule breakers are putting before you. I am not the one who needs to be discussed, they are. We have a dark elf living among us, one who will not and cannot be controlled. What do we do? Do you trust Sebastian to handle the matter? Perhaps he will handle him in the same manner as he handles his new little acquisition."

Sebastian straightened. "That's doubtful, but maybe we should stop considering how I will treat Skylar and consider what you are willing to do to get your hands on the Aufero again. After all, you went as far as to have someone try to kill her, just so you could get it back. But was it motivated by your desire to make sure we no longer needed to contain the dark elves or your desire to have more control over the witches?"

Marcia's heart thumped in her chest. Her breath quickened.

After consulting his sister, Gideon said, "I guess in this situation, we must consider him the responsibility of the elves, and if it was controlled before, I believe in good faith that Sebastian will handle it again."

Sebastian nodded his approval.

Liam disagreed. "I have very little confidence in Sebastian or his ability to control the situation. Gideon, you are now showing exactly the essential differences in how you will rule, as a fool."

He deflected the insult with a confident smile. After all, he had it on good authority that once he took power, circumstances would arise to trigger a civil war among the elves—Sebastian and Abigail would make certain. Liam and the *Makellos* didn't stand a chance.

"This has gone on long enough," Sebastian declared. "Frankly I am bored. You brought us here for a reason, Marcia, and I assume it was to vote on what will be done about this situation."

Sky gave him a surprised look. I wondered if she thought we would howl and threaten to kill everyone to get our way. Strength was good, but sometimes power was politics.

Bernard and his guards approached, prepared to escort us from the room for the vote.

"We aren't going anywhere," Sebastian declared. "Any decision I make, I stand behind it. I will not do it behind someone's back. If I decide you are going to die at my hands, I have no problem telling you to your face. I expect the same from you."

Liam shot to his feet, leaning over his hands on the table. "I will not be threatened by the likes of you."

"It's not a threat. Simply, you are asking them to kill Ethan because of what he is. Yes, we have a covenant that I supported only because the dark elven magic wasn't controlled, and it couldn't be helped. And if this was the case here, I would have supported it as well. But it isn't. It was controlled; Ethan hasn't killed anyone accidentally. So you want him killed, we have every right to know who wants it."

Demetrius casually remarked, "Everyone wants Ethan dead. The question remains should he die because of what he is? Stay, I have no problem with either of you knowing my vote or how I feel."

"You all are welcome to stay," Gideon declared. "I don't care, either. Understand that it is a collective decision. Any retaliation against any of us based on this decision is a retaliation on all of us and it will be treated as such."

Sebastian nodded understanding—hardly a promise.

Marcia said, "I think the covenant should be enforced."

"I disagree," Gideon responded.

She rolled her eyes before looking to Claudia. "Do we need to ask?"

"It would be nice if you did, but you know the answer."

Two to one.

"I support Marcia," Liam announced with an arrogant flourish, as if reciting Shakespeare. "By allowing Sebastian to circumvent this, you are condoning his rogue behavior. At some point we must stand against this man who feels that the only rules he must abide by are the ones he chooses. When chaos ensues as a result of this, I want those who do not side with us to know you are to blame."

Demetrius smiled at me, savoring the tension as he wielded power over my fate. Sky glanced back at the door as if she expected us to make a run for it.

"I think Ethan should die," he decided, "and I am very happy to be the one to do it. But it will not be this way. Sebastian is a son of a bitch and his pack of animals are an annoyance at best, but one thing I am confident of is his commitment to not exposing us and his silly beliefs and rules. If he didn't think it was within his control, he would do whatever he could to make it so. He found a way to do it before and I am sure will again."

Three to one. I win. I remained stoic, enjoying the rage that built inside of Marcia.

Her cheeks were radishes. After an internal struggle, she regained her composure, plastered a cosmetic smile on her lips. "The decision has been made. It should be respected, but those who advocated for the demise of the covenant, understand that is essentially what you have done. Now we need to hold someone accountable for controlling the situation. I think it should be the elves, the Seethe, the fae, and the Midwest Pack. I've washed my hands of this situation."

Demetrius scoffed. "I am not accepting that responsibility."

She asked in a rush, "Then you are changing your vote?"

He frowned, cornered. He took a full minute debating if the trouble was worth my life. Only when he looked to Claudia did he utter a resigned sigh. "Fine, as long as they know I don't plan an active role in this because I can't express how much I *don't* care."

Sebastian, Gideon, and Claudia agreed without reservation. Liam regarded nearly everyone on either side of the table with the contempt only a Makellos could express. Only Marcia and Claudia escaped his disdain.

"Are we done here?" Sebastian asked.

Marcia hissed, "Yes."

On our way to the door, she called my brother's name in a low, commanding voice. "Stay, we need to talk."

He gave her no more than a contemptuous glance as he offered his manacled wrists to Bernard. Once the cuffs were removed, he started again for the door.

She slammed her hands on the table, the sound ripping through the room like a thunderclap.

"Josh! We need to talk now!"

Turning back to her, he fished a small medallion from his pocket and tossed it onto the floor without a second glance, indicating the end of his association with the Creed. "There is nothing more for us to say, I am done."

I followed him out the door, the heat of Marcia's anger at my back.

Stepping outside the house, I felt the dark magic nearby. Ethos. The door slammed closed behind us. The dead bolt clicked home.

Marcia has a backup plan. Now I understood why he didn't take Sky from her house—she needed to play her part in Marcia's little treachery. Now that that was done, he'd come to collect Maya.

A signal from Sebastian and we converged on Sky, forming a square. The cleared area around the house reflected moonlight, giving us some vision. Beyond the clearing, Ethos lurked just inside the dark woods, his location betrayed by the vast stink of his magic.

Josh whispered, "He's here."

Sky took a defensive stance, worked to control her heartbeat, as did the rest of us. Fortunately, Ethos wanted her alive, or he'd probably have killed us all the moment we'd stepped out onto the porch.

Sebastian lead us toward the SUVs. Just a few feet away from them, nearly a hundred figures emerged from the woods, animals and humans—the Ares Pack. Anderson, in human form, loomed behind them as they converged toward us.

I edged closer to Sky.

Halfway across the clearing, a burly man broke into a run, charging toward Sebastian. In stride, he transformed into a cougar just before knocking Sebastian back into an SUV. Sebastian pushed the cougar back. When it lunged again, he struck it in the throat. The beast dropped to the ground, gasping for breath. A second later, it was dead, its neck snapped.

Sebastian changed into his wolf just as a coyote charged him. The two collided. Nearly half the size of Sebastian's wolf, the impact flung the coyote several feet away into the shadows.

When a hyena clamped its jaws onto Steven's arm, Sky drove her knife between its ribs. As the animal fell away, she kicked its wound. It snarled and snapped at her arm. It managed to tear off part of her sleeve, grazing her in the process. The smell of blood drove the hyena into a frenzy. It lunged. Sky pivoted away from the charge, positioning herself to stab the hyena as it passed. Gavin's panther intervened, knocking the hyena to the ground where his claws raked open the hyena's gut.

Josh, separated from us, shielded himself with a field. A lynx stood on its hind legs, clawing uselessly at the field while a dingo thrashed the field with its body. They were no match for his magic. He couldn't fight with it against the were-animals in animal form, but they'd never be able to bring his field down.

Sky started for the coyote, her knife in hand. I tried to

follow, but a cougar had other plans. He leapt at my face, exposing his belly in the process. My punch sent the animal sprawling. I called out to Sky. Oblivious, she was within inches of the coyote. I started toward her.

A wave of vile magic crashed across the clearing, scattering the Ares and knocking us to the ground. Josh's field shattered. The blow stunned me. Blinking up at the stars from my back, urgency came back to me in a rush. I climbed back to my feet, looked for Sky. I spotted her and Josh on their backs a few feet apart. They were both still stunned, along with the rest of our pack and the Ares. Only Sebastian had gotten to his feet. I started toward Sky when Ethos appeared out of thin air, crouching beside her.

I screamed, "Sky!" and ran toward Ethos.

He touched her arm and transported the two of them away.

Rage overcame me. As others came to their feet, taking in the new situation, I knew only that I needed to get to Sky. Seething, I glowered at the Ares as they began to gather themselves. Sebastian's wolf appeared on my left, Gavin's panther and Steven's coyote on my right. Winter, Katana in hand, pulled a groggy Josh behind us. I'd no idea where Sky was, or how I would find her. I only knew that I'd have to kill them all to get to her. My wolf rushed to the surface, howling for blood.

Happy to oblige, I shifted in stride. The others charged at my side.

The next few minutes were a blur of blood, fur, and flesh. Bites, slashes meant nothing to my wolf. I was violence incarnate, tearing, shredding, and killing my way through the clearing. My jaws crushed bones and ripped open throats. I fought to the point of exhaustion and beyond. *Sky* was the only thought in my head. With my pack, we killed until the remaining Ares broke and ran. Before I could charge after them, Sebastian in human form got in my way. He held his arms out to his sides.

"Ethan!"

I hesitated, panting. My fur dripped with blood. I started around him. Sebastian wrapped his arms around my neck and took me to the ground. I twisted, snarling at him, but instinctively I couldn't bite. I tried to throw him off, but he commanded the change. A second later, I was in human form, cursing him. He climbed onto my chest, pushed me down with a forearm across my chest.

"Ethan! We have to find Sky!"

I hesitated. My chest heaved as I tried to catch my breath.

"Sky," he insisted. "We'll deal with the rest of the Ares later."

All I cared about was reaching Sky. The field around us was littered with bodies. The SUVs were waiting. I nodded. Sebastian eased off of me and I climbed to my feet. Josh was nearby, watching me with a horrified expression.

"How do we find her?" I pleaded to him between breaths.

He showed me the piece of her shirtsleeve that one of the Ares had torn off. It was spotted with her blood.

Sebastian asked, "Is it enough?"

Josh nodded.

"Call Samuel," I told him as we started for the SUVs. "Tell him he can have whatever the fuck he wants. We need him. Now."

CHAPTER 14

*I*n route to a nearby safe house where Josh could source Sky's blood, he called Samuel. The conversation was brief. Samuel owed Sky, and he knew it.

How much time do we have to rescue her?

Sky would put up a fight. That would buy us some time, at least. Josh couldn't say how long it might take to transfer Maya; an hour, a minute—the clock was ticking. According to him, the willingness of the new host—

A fresh dread came over me. I looked to Josh, frightened for him.

"Call London."

His eyes widened in panic. When she answered her phone, we were both relieved.

Josh explained to Gavin after he pocketed his phone. "Ethos could transfer her to any human he picked up off the street, but without an inherent ability to use magic, Maya would be powerless. At the field, he was going to transfer Maya to London." He turned to me. "She's on her way out of town now. He doesn't have her blood so he'll have a hard time finding her on the move. He'll have to keep Sky alive until he can find an appropriate host."

Our relief was short-lived as Winter asked, "Why take her now if he doesn't have a host ready? It's not like Sky was going anywhere."

The dread returned.

"I don't understand." Steven frowned. "Couldn't they just grab any competent witch? Why Sky?"

Josh answered. "Maya needs a powerful witch to operate through. Sky can only borrow magic, but she's a Moura. Through her, Maya could access the spells in the Clostra. That's why Ethos has been trying so hard to help Maya gain control instead of just transferring her to someone else. The Clostra contains the most powerful spells ever conceived. If he could find anyone else who could read the books—"

Senna. Sky's cousin shared her abilities.

He paused, realization dawning. Before he turned to me, I was on my phone with Cole, the Alpha of the East Coast Pack. The safety of Senna and her family were under his care.

"I'll check and call you back," Cole said.

I growled, "Make it fast."

Tension hung in the air until he called me a few minutes later. His voice was clinical.

"The girl has been taken. The attacker transported in, or my people would've noticed. There were some injuries to the family, some serious but nothing critical. Tell Sebastian—"

I killed the call, resisted the urge to smash my phone. From the tension in Sebastian's jawline, I knew they were going to have an uncomfortable conversation about this later. For now, I needed to focus on the problem at hand.

Sky was running out of time. How much she had was up for debate.

We arrived at the secluded rambler to find Samuel seated on the porch, the flaps of his trench coat draping the steps beneath him. He rose to meet us as we approached the house. Before he could negotiate, Sebastian cut to the chase.

"If we retrieve the Clostra," he stated, "you'll have one of the books."

Samuel eyed him and us with suspicion. "I take the book immediately. At no time is the pack to possess all three books together."

"Agreed. No one should have access to the spells within. I'm comfortable with you possessing one of the books."

He considered asking for something else.

"Ethos has Senna," I snapped.

Fear flickered in his eyes. "He's going to transfer Maya to Senna."

It wasn't a question. I nodded anyway.

He turned to Josh with a newfound sense of urgency. "You have blood to source?"

Josh showed him. Together they went inside. While they worked the spell, I paced outside, wondering what I'd do if we couldn't reach Sky in time to save her. Over the years I'd lost more friends and pack family than I cared to count. I'd witnessed death in all of its brutality. I didn't want that for her. For the first time, there was nothing I could do to protect her. Nothing could stop Ethos from taking her. I was just a few feet away, reduced to a helpless bystander. What he might do to her now terrified me.

Magic flashed within the house.

I continued pacing, squeezing my fists, pulling at my hair. Only the lack of an enemy to kill kept me in control. Once we reached where Sky was held, nothing would stop me from reaching her, from making her captors pay.

When Josh and the others emerged from the house with an address, I had my doubts. London and Josh had taken a lot longer to source Ethos, and failed.

"You're certain?" I pressed Josh.

We'd probably only get one chance.

He nodded, confident. "Samuel made the difference."

He was more powerful than London. I grimaced as I

climbed into an SUV with the others. I didn't want to place Sky's fate in anyone else's hands, but there was no other way to find her. Once inside, I slammed the door and counted the minutes.

According to my phone GPS, the address was a simple, stone blockhouse in a secluded, sparse neighborhood surrounded by woods. The nearest neighbor was a farmhouse a mile away. We took two SUVs. I sat tense in the passenger seat while Sebastian drove, with Samuel and Josh sitting behind us. The others followed in the second vehicle.

A few minutes later, the winding road brought the house and surrounding field into sight. A gruesome scene carried out on the grass. Three wolves, heads down, backed toward the stone house dragging a supine figure through the dewy grass.

Sky.

I opened the door, prepared to jump.

"Wait," Sebastian said, slowing the SUV dramatically.

I changed in mid-leap. Gravel bit into my paws as I landed on the road. Ignoring the pain, I raced toward the wolves. As I got closer, I confirmed the figure was Sky. Relief rushed through me as I saw her try to raise her head, but she was badly injured. Blood ran from deep wounds on her side and abdomen. Her face had been slashed up to an eye.

Rage consumed me.

Closing in, I recognized Anderson as the middle wolf pulling Sky toward the house.

They were too confident in their prey.

The nearest wolf yelped as my jaws clamped on its hind leg. Bones crunched between my teeth. I flipped the wolf onto its back and leapt on top of it. Pushing through a scrabble of claws, I buried my teeth in the wolf's chest and thrashed, rending skin and flesh. Gore filled my mouth as I reached bone and tasted the marrow inside. Ribs snapped. The wolf howled in pain.

Anderson and the other wolf released Sky to challenge me from either flank. Attacking one would make me easy prey for the other. Fixing my gaze on Anderson, I was prepared to make that sacrifice to taste his blood. Gavin's panther intervened, emerging from the shadows to pounce on the other wolf. While they scrambled for each others throats, I stalked Anderson.

His snout low and growling, he sidled toward Sky. I cut him off, snarling.

From the corner of my eye, I saw Samuel reach her. Bursts of magic from just outside the stone house lit the field. I could hear voices there, could make out the growls of Sebastian's wolf.

My gaze remained fixed on Anderson as we circled each other, teeth bared, measuring each other's weaknesses. I lunged, a feint to draw him out. He sidled quickly and snapped at my snout. His jaws missed as I reared back, following with a lunge of my own. He escaped the worst, but I caught the flap of his ear between my teeth, savored the blood as I tore it from his skull.

Enraged, he dropped down onto his front paws, preparing for another lunge.

Staring him down, a vision of Sky's wounds flooded my mind.

He'd just launched at me when I bowled over him. As I knocked him onto his back, he buried his teeth in my shoulder. Amid the violent scrabbling, I clamped my jaws around his snout. Blood and gristle choked my throat as I chewed my way toward his panicked eyes. As my claws raked deep gashes into his chest, his cries only fueled my primal rage.

For a moment, there was just blood and bone and teeth. Only after his body went limp did I cast it aside. His heart still beat, but he wasn't going anywhere—none of the wolves were. Gavin had left his wolf alive—barely—to join the attack at the house. Marcia and two of her witches had barricaded themselves inside the house. The other witch lay dead in front of the door. Gavin, Steven, and Sebastian—all in animal form—waited along with Winter as Josh and Samuel combined their magic to breach the front corner of the house. A storm of magic crashed into the structure, sending stone fragments raining down on us.

There was no sign of Ethos.

Glancing back, I saw a depressed area in the grass where Sky had been. Panic set in. Samuel had taken her, I tried to console myself. But the only way to guarantee her safety was to kill her kidnappers, all of them. Racing past the others, I charged into the house before the shrapnel settled. At the far wall, Marcia's eyes widened as I bounded toward her. Terrified, she gripped the arm of the witch at her side. As I leapt, they transported away. Howling in frustration, my momentum sent me crashing into the wall. Scrambling to my feet, I found the remaining witch frantically gathering objects from a table. I recognized the Aufero as one. The books of the Clostra were there as well, along with the other stolen objects.

Nearby, Senna lay prone on the floor, unconscious. I smelled drugs in her blood, but her sedated heart still beat.

Sky's scent was everywhere.

The Aufero in hand, the witch hesitated as he noticed Sebastian's wolf entering the house. Before the witch could transport, I leapt onto his back, snapped my jaws around his neck. The delicate bones of his throat crushed easily. Fueled by his screams, I thrashed until I'd brought him down and ripped out his throat, then went back for more until I felt the last feeble beat of his heart.

While Josh and Samuel gathered the Clostra and the other objects from where they'd spilled onto the floor, I raced past Gavin's panther to where I'd left Anderson and his wolves crippled and dying in the clearing.

As I stalked them, my snout low, I picked up the scent of Sky's blood mixed with theirs in the grass. Revenge burned in my heart, drowning out the rest of the world.

The wolf Gavin had nearly killed lay still, his life ebbing with the flow of its blood. Leaving him alone for the moment, I followed Anderson's whimpers to find him limping and stumbling through the grass toward the woods. One eye was gone and his tongue lolled from a mangled snout. I growled as I approached, letting him know that death was near. He flopped, whimpering, and showed his belly. I'd no intention of mercy.

When there was nothing left of him to kill, I found the third wolf hiding in the grass. Its leg was broken and jagged ribs jutted out from a gory wound on its chest. Having heard the sounds of what I'd done to his Alpha, the wolf at least tried to fight. I left his entrails strewn out in the grass.

Sebastian, Gavin, Winter, and Steven—all in human form —stood nearby, watching as I strode toward the last remaining wolf. All but Sebastian wore their horror in their expressions. Blood dripped from my fur that was draped with bits of bone and tissue. The last wolf was only a few heartbeats from death, but my revenge remained hot. Ignoring the judgment of my pack, I pounced.

"We have Sky," someone kept repeating, the words barely reaching through the violence. "She's with Jeremy." The same voice called my name over and over. Only when I'd finally sated my fury did I realize it was Sebastian trying to calm me.

The remains of the last wolf were a puddle of gore beneath my claws.

Weighted by blood, I plopped onto the grass, panting. While the others walked away from the horror in front of them, Sebastian held my gaze.

"We have to go," he said. "Sky needs you. Josh and Samuel took her and Senna to the retreat."

My limbs too exhausted to rise, I changed into my human form. Still, it took an act of will to get to my feet. Gavin and Winter took one SUV, while Sebastian drove me and Steven in the other. Glancing over my shoulder periodically, I more than once caught Steven scrutinizing me as if we'd never met—perhaps it was the blood pooling beneath me on the leather seat.

I was too tired to care. Anderson and his wolves had gotten what they deserved. So would the rest of the Ares, once I knew Sky was safe.

I asked in a strained voice, "Ethos?"

Sebastian answered, his eyes on the road. "Escaped."

For now.

The ride to the retreat was long and understandably silent.

As we crossed the yard to the retreat house, Sebastian said softly, "Clean yourself."

Glancing down at my bloodstained feet, I knew the morning would reveal a path of bloody footprints. While the others went inside, I hosed myself down on the lawn until the water ran clear off my skin. Winter waited for me with a fresh change of my clothes in her hands. Her expression was somewhere between awe and fear.

Inside the entryway, at least a dozen were-animals waited, watching. I knew by their looks that word had spread. Good. Now they knew what I expected from them when we went after the Ares. Steven, Josh, and Gavin waited outside the infirmary doors, their worry plain. Ignoring them, I pushed through the swinging double doors.

I was met by the hum and whir of Dr. Baker's machines that were connected to Sky. Her wolf laid unconscious on a table. In addition to the wounds on her flank and belly, another gaped on her back. Dr. Baker's intense concentration was fixed on one injured eye where the slashes across her face were still raw. I gasped at the sight.

Sebastian appeared next to me. "She could lose the eye," he whispered. "The next few minutes are critical."

Let Dr. Baker work, he meant. My heart ached to go to her, but Sebastian was right. I remained at the back of the infirmary while he worked, unable to leave. I noticed Samuel for the first time, supine on a table. His hand and leg were bandaged. There was a thin cut across his cheek. His head rolled to one side to watch Dr. Baker's efforts. His worry was plain. I wanted to thank him for his help, but couldn't. Instead we watched together in silence while Dr. Baker did what he could.

Hours seemed to have passed when Dr. Baker informed Sebastian, "She needs to change."

Sebastian and I exchanged looks. He and I were both dominant. Under normal circumstances, either of us could force a change. The severity of her wounds complicated the process. We'd need to work together. He pushed open the doors and brought Steven inside. After explaining what we were going to attempt, Steven pulled a chair up to the head of Sky's table.

We'd need to wake her first.

I watched, anxious as he bent to her ear, whispered her name. Her eyes opened to slits among the swelling. She raised her head slightly, tried to look around, but she was dazed. After a moment, she seemed to recognize she was safe.

Steven gently stroked her fur. "You've been out for a while."

She tried to change, growled when it was apparent she couldn't.

Sebastian ran his hands along her side to calm her. His

voice was gentle, a sign of just how severe her injuries were. "Skylar, sweetie. Lay here and take gentle breaths, okay?" He looked to me. "We need to change her back into human form."

"I tried," Steven said. "She's stuck."

"You have to be more dominant to force a change. It's not an insult against you; I think we keep underestimating her dominance."

I went to her side, bent my knee to whisper in her ear. "We are going to force a change. It will hurt and there really isn't anything we can do right now to ease it, okay? I'm sorry."

I eased my hand against her backside while Sebastian laid his over her front legs. Together we closed our eyes and concentrated. Slowly, painfully, her body responded. Ligaments and bones cracked as her body elongated. Somewhere between wolf and human, her cries became screams. Finally human, she lay shivering. Her eyes were nearly swollen shut. Her breath was shallow, wheezing, but she was conscious. With a delicate, trembling touch, she traced the open wound in her belly and cringed. Her neck bent slightly and her eyes fluttered as she tried to see the wound.

Somehow, I found the calm she needed, though my grip on it was tenuous. I took her hand and squeezed it gently, letting the calm flow through me.

I whispered, "Close your eyes, Skylar."

She tried to rise, cringed from the pain, and collapsed.

"Don't," Dr. Baker pleaded to her.

A moment later, he gave her an injection to sedate her. Within seconds, she was mercifully asleep.

Unable to help her, I felt my rage returning, demanding blood. For a brief time, I held it at bay to be with her.

"Ethan," Dr. Baker whispered, his tone urgent but compassionate, "I need to tend to her wounds."

"Her eye?" The question caught in my throat.

"She will survive," he answered carefully. "Her eye is questionable. There may be a great deal of scarring as well. The next twenty-four hours will tell."

Sebastian squeezed my shoulder. "Ethan, we need to let him work on Sky."

After a final, gentle squeeze of her hand, I rose and pushed through the double doors, slamming them outward into the wall. Josh and Steven waited in the hall, along with Gavin and Winter.

I growled as I strode past them. "Let's finish this."

They remained still, eyes tracking me as Sebastian caught my arm.

"Ethan," he said, "where are you going?"

I rounded on him, letting the fury rise closer to the surface where my wolf was waiting for revenge. "None of this would've happened without Anderson's involvement. We should've never let them exist in the first place."

Sebastian's jaw set, but he let the rebuke pass. We shared the fault for allowing Anderson's pack to become dangerous, but I was looking to put blame anywhere I could.

"Anderson is dead," he stated.

Not enough. "Not all of them."

"Not all of the Ares participated in the attack outside the conclave."

"Does it matter?"

"Yes. The Ares Pack will be disbanded along with all of the other independent packs."

I yelled, jabbing a finger toward the infirmary where Dr. Baker was trying to save Sky's eye, "After what they did to her, you're just going to let them go free?"

I turned and strode toward the entryway as Sebastian followed. Other were-animals were gathering, drawn by my shouting. Josh transported to the door, barring my way. His eyes were wide with concern as he held up a palm, urging me to stop.

"Ethan," he pleaded, "take a moment to think about this. You're out of control."

I brushed him aside. Before I could take another step, Sebastian yanked my arm, forcing me around. Amber shone in his dark-brown eyes, his wolf rising.

"What are you going to do?" he demanded.

"I'm going to hunt," I sneered. "I'm going to kill every Ares I can get my hands on."

I turned back toward the door. Sebastian slammed into me. Air fled my lungs as he drove me into a nearby wall. Drywall crumbled at my feet as he pinned me there, his arm like an iron bar against my chest.

His voice was steady, commanding. "You need to calm down."

Blood rushed to my face, fueled by a rising rage I couldn't control. I pushed back, but Sebastian was stronger. When that failed, I tried slipping out of his grip. His glare was as unyielding as his arm. He leaned close to me. I could feel the heat of his breath as he repeatedly yelled my name to get my attention.

"Ethan!"

My wolf drowned him out, howling from just beneath my skin. Only his command prevented me from changing. My useless struggle against his hold devolved into primal grunts and growls. There were limits to what he could accept from me. I slipped beyond the rules of pack hierarchy, my resistance growing more violent.

Then I was free. He relented, or so it seemed. His movement was a blur. Within seconds, I found myself on my knees, his arm cinched tight around my neck in a choke hold. Unable to pry loose his arm, I struggled to breathe. My cheeks burned. My head buzzed. The full of his weight pressed down onto the back of my neck until I fell forward onto my face and lost consciousness.

. . .

I woke to a raging headache, the stink of iron and concrete filling my nostrils. My eyes opened to find iron bars between me and the ceiling. Groaning, I rolled onto my side to find Josh outside the cage, leaning forward on the edge of a chair, wearing a concerned look. One of his hands was bandaged. Had he been injured fighting Marcia, or fighting me? The rest of the small room was bare. The cage occupied most of it. I was in the basement of the retreat, in a secure room we used for were-animals that lost control.

"This is the third time you've come to," he said. "The other times you lost your shit again. You threw yourself at the bars until you passed out from stupidity."

I didn't recall.

I growled, rising to my feet. Josh straightened as I reached for the door. His magic filled the room as I tried to open it. Locked.

In a threatening tone, I ordered him, "Let me out."

He glowered. Before he could answer, I heard the click of a door opening at the top of the stairs. A moment later, Sebastian walked down, followed by Winter and Steven. He stopped outside the cage, coldly scrutinizing me.

I gripped the bars between us. "Are they dead?"

"That's not going to happen."

Like the start of a bonfire, the rage started in my gut once more, building.

"Keep fighting if you have to," Sebastian said, his disappointment plain. "But there's work to do. I need the Beta of the Midwest Pack, not a bloodthirsty animal."

My hands clenched around the bars, squeezed.

"Dr. Baker is going to bring Sky out of sedation later today. She'll need you. If your selfish need for revenge is more important to you, you can remain here. I'm sure she'll understand."

Like an arctic breeze, his words snuffed the fire out of my

anger, left me cold. Staring down at the concrete, I pressed my forehead against the bars.

Sebastian continued. "Anderson is dead, along with the entire Ares leadership. Most of those who fought us are dead or on the run. Their pack will be disbanded. The others will be allowed to live as long as they leave the area and never return."

I swallowed my pride, nodded.

"The other independent packs will be given the choice to join us or be disbanded. This needs to be done now, before Ethos can exploit them."

I let out a deep sigh before lifting my head to meet his iron gaze. "I'll pay a visit to the Worgen and the others. I think I'll stay clear of the Ares, if that's okay with you."

He considered for a moment before unlocking the cage. As the door swung open, he stepped aside. "We're leaving in twenty minutes."

Walking out, my muscles ached and groaned as if I'd just run several marathons. I stunk, too. "I'll get cleaned up and meet you outside."

I checked on Sky first, peering into the infirmary through the windows in the doors. If she woke up, I didn't want her to see me like this. Nearly her entire body was wrapped in bandages. Dr. Baker saw me, came out to give me an update.

"Her eye is healing," he said, to my relief.

"The bandages? Her wounds should be healed."

"The scarring. I've used nearly all of my hellfire."

He referred to the cream he'd invented for just such a purpose. Whatever he created it from, it burned like hell, but it hadn't failed yet. The extent of Sky's scars would put it to the test.

Horrified, I asked, "Will she be disfigured?"

"We'll know tomorrow."

His sad eyes lacked confidence. Scarring didn't matter to me, but it would matter to Sky if the scarring were severe.

All I could do was hope for her. I hated that. Once again, I wasn't able to help her.

After I'd showered and dressed, I was on my way downstairs when I noticed dark-green eyes peering at me through a cracked door. For a moment, I thought it was Sky. Realizing she'd been noticed, Senna shut the door. The click of a bolt lock followed.

I rapped a knuckle against her door.

She snapped, "Go away!"

"You're not a prisoner."

"So I'm free to leave," she said, disbelieving.

I smiled, remembering a similar conversation with Sky when I'd first brought her to the retreat.

"Ethos will come for you. Until we've dealt with him, you're safe here."

The door cracked open. Green eyes narrowed at me. "My family can protect me better than you can."

I sighed. "No, they can't. For the time being, you're our guest. You're free to roam the house, but not the grounds. No one will harm you here."

Her scowl deepened. "So I've been told."

She slammed the door shut.

Winter rode with me to visit the Worgen. She remained quiet, but I felt her penetrating gaze on me more than once. Of all the independent packs, we had the closest relationship to the Worgen. Rather than disband, they saw the advantages of joining the Midwest Pack. Integrating them was going to be a challenge, given their odd personalities and habits, but the skills they brought were invaluable.

Hours passed as we visited every one of the smaller packs on our list. Some joined. The rest were given a day to settle their affairs and move on.

. . .

We arrived at the retreat to find Sebastian and the others had already returned. Walking into the house, I noted the pack's mood had lightened. Eager to visit Sky, I reported to Sebastian first. I gave him the breakdown of who joined, who fled. Arrangements were made to accommodate the newcomers.

When we'd finished, he informed me, "She's awake."

I hurried to the infirmary. Before I reached the doors, I could hear her voice inside cursing up a storm. Most of the words she used were either made up or misused combinations. I paused at the windows to peer inside. The exclamations were caused by Dr. Baker, applying a fresh layer of hellfire to her backside that seemed remarkably free of scars. It seemed the hellfire was doing its job.

His hands dipped into the cream jar, drew out a glob, and spread it onto her skin. Sky hissed before shouting.

"Crap-snacks, pickle-fudge, banana-monkey turds!"

I grinned, relieved to see her back to normal.

Crap-snacks?

Laughing, I pushed through the doors. "Some of the things you yelled out aren't even curses. Are we making up languages now?"

"Let me put it on you," she said, "and see if you like it."

I dipped my fingers into the jar and spread the cream over my forearm. The pain was excruciating. My body tensed. My jaw clenched as I watched perfectly healthy skin bubble and dissolve, exposing a tender layer of fresh skin beneath. When it was over, I held back a sigh of relief under Sky's intense scrutiny. After a moment, I admitted, "It does hurt."

"Really? My screaming wasn't a good enough warning? You had to see for yourself?"

"You'll be fine."

Dr. Baker crossed the room to his desk and began shuffling papers, giving us some privacy. I kissed her lightly, then pressed my cheek against hers. My lips brushed her warm skin. "How are you?"

"I feel better than I look," she muttered. She pulled back slightly to meet my gaze. "We should remove the magic again."

"I plan to, but I want Josh to do it."

Removing the magic with the Aufero was risky. I didn't want to put Sky through that again, and I knew Josh wouldn't be put off this time. A hint of protest flashed in her eyes, but quickly subsided.

After a glance in Dr. Baker's direction, she whispered, "Do you plan on telling Josh about the Vitae?"

I tensed. Given everything else that had happened, I didn't see a reason to revisit the issue now. I couldn't say no to her, either; she'd only fight harder.

"We'll see."

"I stand by what I said. Either you tell him or—"

I pressed a finger against her lips. "You know how I feel about threats."

She bit down, drawing blood. I scowled at her as I sucked at the wound to stop the bleeding.

She grinned. "You know how I feel about people doing that to me. I understand why some things need to be kept secret, but there shouldn't be any between Josh and you."

"I'll think about it," I insisted, backing out of the room.

My lips spread into a relieved smile as I walked down the hallway. The smile slowly faded as I felt a tremor begin in my right hand. I clenched my fist to ward it off. The tremor only got worse. Raw emotion started to bubble to the surface. *Post-traumatic stress,* I told myself. The knowledge didn't help. Now that Sky was safe and herself, the barriers I'd erected to mask my fears were starting to crumble. Somehow, I held my shit together until I reached my room.

Sitting on the edge of my bed, I stared at my shaking hand, willing it to stop. I fought a while longer, stemming the tide with logic. *A natural psychological reaction to a stressful situation. It'll pass.* That seemed to work for a time, then the quaking spread up my arm. Fear and relief intermingled in my chest. Tears streaked down my cheeks until I wiped them away, willed them back. That I could stop, at least. The shaking lasted for ten or fifteen minutes, then slowly waned. Once it ceased, I laid back on my bed, staring up at the ceiling until I fell asleep.

I woke a short time later to Gavin knocking on my door.

"What?" I snapped.

"Sebastian wants to see us in his office."

I scowled. Bad timing, but expected. Too much was going on for me to hide out in my room.

"I'll meet you there."

The wood floor outside my door creaked as Gavin walked away. After a few calming breaths, I followed.

He waited for us, seated on the edge of his desk. Once I closed the door, he handed me a printout of a local map. Three locations were marked—Kelly's house, David's house, and a third location I didn't recognize. Sebastian explained as I handed the map to Gavin.

"We assumed that Kelly was being kept in a home some-where. According to Dr. Baker, the were-animal we found was infected by a man-made virus. We're probably looking for a lab." He gestured to the map for Gavin's benefit. "Sky saw a building in the area that could be a lab. We need to step up our search, expand it to include commercial buildings. I want you to concentrate on the area around Sky's and David's houses. There's a good chance that Kelly sent the were-animal for help. She would've sent him to the nearest pack member."

I added, "And he ended up at David's door, probably looking for Sky's."

He nodded.

"It's still a big search," I said. "It'll take time."

Gavin snapped, "Then let's get started."

Sebastian ignored the breach in etiquette. "Joan is going to send some of her people to help."

Gavin's scowl only deepened. His mind was already on the hunt.

Sebastian turned to me. "Chris is one of the best at finding people."

"She is. She ran away from Demetrius for a reason. I'm not sure she wants to be found, but I'll reach out."

I was in one of our communal offices, calling anyone I knew of that could potentially get a message to Chris, when Josh and Samuel found me. Their excitement was palpable.

Josh explained in a breathy rush, "We know why Ethos was collecting the protected objects. We always thought the purpose of each object was separate from the others, but that's not true. All of the objects are connected to the Clostra. It turns out almost none of the spells can be used without a specific object. The symbols next to each spell, the ones we couldn't figure out—those symbols represent which object is needed for that spell to work."

I blinked at him. "How did you figure—"

"Senna told Sky. She thought she knew." He gestured the way he'd come. "She's in the library now."

CHAPTER 15

*S*amuel and Josh sat side by side like eager schoolchildren on the far side of the table. Senna sat across from them, the three books of the Clostra open in front of her. Their eyes followed her every move as she browsed the pages, shifting from one book to the next. Standing behind her, my gaze was fixed on Samuel. He was on our side against Ethos, but his goals hadn't changed. He still wanted to remove magic from the world, killing every were-animal in the process. From the moment we'd returned to the retreat, one of the books had remained in his possession, as Sebastian had promised. He'd only agreed to allow Senna to examine all of the books together because we agreed to share her knowledge. He couldn't read the text or steal a spell without Senna's help, but I still didn't trust him completely.

Senna had softened regarding the pack since I'd last seen her peeking out from her door. Sky's influence, I assumed.

Sky appeared in the doorway, surprised to find the rest of us in the room.

Josh used a foot to push out a chair for her. "Have a seat."

As she sat, Senna turned the book she was skimming for

Sky to examine. "See this?" Senna tapped at something on the page. "This symbol here. I know this means the Gem of Levage." She opened the third book, tapped at that page. "This one is the Fatifer."

Together, they searched through the books while Josh, Samuel, and I shared a tense impatience.

Senna frowned at something on a page. "Some of them are freaking scary."

Samuel, his patience finally snapping, leaned over her shoulder. "Which ones?" The moment he looked directly at the pages, they went blank.

Senna gave him a teasing smile. "It doesn't like you."

He smiled back at her, an awkward gesture from a typically grim man. He sat back in his chair, measuring the girl with a surprisingly gentle look. "Too bad."

She winked, drawing attention from her flushed cheeks. "You seem okay to me."

Sky gaped between them.

Josh cleared his throat, not bothering to mask his irritation. "Will you continue?"

Senna pried her gaze from Samuel and returned to searching the pages. "This one is dangerous for anyone who has magic. And you need three objects to do it. It's like summoning someone, but once you call, they can't decline. With a summons or calling, they don't have to answer. With this spell, they have to. If I wanted to use this against you, I could. That's messed up."

Josh and I came to a simultaneous conclusion. Not only did we have the means to summon Ethos, we had the means to summon the Tre'ase that had created Sky—without Logan's assistance. Sky quickly caught on as well. I could hear her heart racing with excitement. To do so, we'd need to maintain access to all three books. Our arrangement with Samuel was already becoming inconvenient.

Sky asked, "What objects do we need?"

"Gem of Levage, Aufero, Fatifer, and blood."

I scowled. "We used the last of his blood."

"There's still some stain on the carpet, but I have more." She grinned, proud. "I have the knife I stabbed his tail with, and the shirt his blood sprayed onto."

I smiled back, impressed. We still didn't have the Tre'ase's blood, but we'd deal with that later. While the rest of us pondered the consequences of using the spell, Senna took the opportunity to make a tentative request.

"Can I go home to see my mom?"

Josh's eyes fell to his hands.

I rounded the table to meet her gaze, fixing on her until I was confident I had her attention. She was desperate, willing to do anything to go home. I just needed to put her on a leash, first. "The East Coast Pack will be around a lot until this is handled. If you send them away, try to lose them…or pull any of the crap you pulled before…"

I let the threat trail off, aware she'd understood the message.

Sebastian joined us and took a seat at the table. Sky caught him up to speed with what we'd learned. The decision was made to attempt the summons right away, while Ethos was still licking his wounds. We didn't dare give him time to gather new allies. The challenge would be Maya. She would make her attempt to gain control. Sky would have to fight that battle alone.

I didn't like it, but there was nothing I could do. There was one thing that needed to be done, first.

A short time later, alone in the library, Josh began the spell to transfer my dark elf magic into the Aufero. Sky had performed the spell before, turning her living room into a destructive cyclone in the process. Glancing around at the stacked shelves in the library, I wondered that Josh would put them at risk.

The storm never came. Within minutes, I felt the irritating hum of magic flow out of my body and into the Aufero, changing its bright orange glow to a dull, sickly gray.

When Josh stopped the incantation and looked at me, I blinked back at him.

"That's it?" I asked.

He shrugged and began gathering up the materials he'd used for the spell.

I gestured around the library. "Shouldn't shit be flying and breaking apart?"

He gave me a knowing look. "That's why you should've come to me the first time."

All the arguments about protecting him from the burden of knowing I was a dark elf came flooding back to me, all valid. But I bit them back, nodded. "You're right. I should have."

He smiled, declared, "Twice in one day. I can get used to that."

I started toward the door, hiding my own smile. "I wouldn't if I were you."

With just a few hours until the summoning, I went to check on Sky, who would bear the brunt of our plan.

Sky stood in the clearing behind the retreat, her palm draped over the pommel of a sword sheathed at her side. Around her, a circle was defined by a mixture of tannin, salt, and ground iron. Before her, the protected objects were laid out in a line; from right to left, the Fatifer, the Gem of Levage, and the Aufero.

I placed my hand on her shoulder, felt my brother's magic coursing through her. She was the only one of us able to cast the spell, which put her at the center of Ethos's wrath. But the Aufero's magic was too unpredictable to count on for her protection. Josh had loaned her as much of his magic as possible. In the process, he'd weakened himself, but the tradeoff was worth the risk. He would still be useful to us, but his role in the fight would be minimal. Given he was still recovering from his wound, I was glad to have him farther from danger.

Sky's heart pounded in her chest.

In a voice only she could hear, I asked, "Are you ready for this?"

She sucked in a calming breath, then nodded.

I stepped a few feet out of the circle and changed into my wolf, joining Sebastian's. Several other were-animals mingled behind us, waiting. Beside me, Winter drew her katana. A wakizashi—a twelve-inch tempered steel dagger—was sheathed at her right hip. Smaller knives were sheathed at her ankles and the small of her back.

Josh and Samuel stood much farther back to provide support when needed.

Sky checked the noise-reducing buds in her ears that would minimize the shrill sound Ethos had previously used against us. Josh, Samuel, and the others in human form all wore the same. Anxious, Sky once more squeezed the sword pommel. Sebastian's training had brought out her gift with the weapon. He'd every confidence in her ability to wield it, and so did I.

Our eyes met, a long silent communication.

After a moment, she sucked in a final deep breath and began the incantation memorized from the Clostra. Magic immediately flooded the clearing, vibrating against my fur like a static charge. I saw the hairs on Sky's arms stand straight up. Her voice rose to a crescendo as she reached the climax of the spell.

Silence followed.

I glanced around the clearing, looking for a sign of

Ethos's response. Had she made a mistake with the incantation? Sky was about to try again when orange, red, and blue lights burst into flickering life around her. A powerful force of magic followed, slamming into and then engulfing her. Within its grasp, she struggled for breath.

A demonic-looking being with oily black skin and a long forked tail manifested before her.

Ethos.

His black maw opened wide, emitting a shrill, ear-splitting sound. Sky winced, but the earbuds mostly did their job. She drew her sword when his tail whipped out and slammed against her chest. She stumbled back a step, but remained in the circle.

Ethos strode toward her, chanting in that ancient, guttural language of his. Only three words I understood —"Maya, wake up."

A dense fog of magic formed around Sky, seemingly rising from within. Her body froze as her internal battle with Maya began.

I took steps toward them until Sebastian blocked me with his body. A growl rumbled from his chest. I growled back, but remained where I was.

The fog grew darker, obscured more of her. I was about to charge Ethos—fuck the consequences—when the fog burst like a blast into his chest. The force threw him back several feet, and he landed hard on his back. As Sky strode toward him, sword raised, his hands slapped angrily at the ground, igniting a circle of tall flames around him that kept her at bay.

Sky's lips moved quickly, calling a gust of wind. The flames flickered, but remained. I felt Samuel's magic behind me, followed by a stronger gust of wind that reduced the flames to a small flickering fire.

Before the wind receded, Sky lunged with her sword. Ethos turned, trying to avoid the blow. The blade sliced cleanly through his arm. He let out a shrill cry as the limb fell into the grass, but there was an agony to it. Before Sky could strike again, a black ball of magic launched from his remaining hand. When it burst against her chest, the magic spread around her like a dark hand, binding her arms to her side. While her magic sparked and hissed, trying to break the binding, he advanced on her with a murderous fire in his eyes.

We broke the circle, charging at Ethos. His tail lashed out to pierce Sky just as Steven leapt. He caught it in his mouth, bit into the thick leather and held on. A putrid scent emerged from the wound, fouling the air. I leapt, snarling. Ethos's remaining arm struck my side, sent me sprawling into the grass. Sebastian attacked from the other flank, climbing onto Ethos's back. Before he could sink his teeth deep into that black flesh, he was cast aside, but our distraction succeeded. While we circled him, drawing his attention, Sky broke the bindings around her. Her loud grunt echoed across the clearing as she swung the sword clean through his neck.

His head tumbled into the grass. The body stumbled, fell to its knees but remained upright. I watched in consternation as the head turned, its eyes fixing on its detached form. Decapitation was supposed to be certain death for any supernatural creature. Yet we watched in horror as the two pieces of Ethos sought each other. The body reached out, blind, while the head inched forward like a worm.

The others gasped, muttered their fear. I could only watch in dark fascination.

Winter hissed behind me, "Can anything kill him?"

The answer came to me, something I'd come across in Josh's magical texts in the pack library. There were spells there he didn't recognize because they didn't suit his magic, but they suited mine. Approaching the body, I laid a hand against the scales and whispered an incantation.

The body fell in a clatter and began to crack and shrivel

in something like a vampire's reversion. After a moment, the now-dead form collapsed into dust. Ignoring the questioning stares of the others, I moved on to Ethos's head. Standing over it, I paused to stare into the eyes. Fire glared back at me. His maw was open, making a clicking sound as he tried to scream. My hand resting on the top of his head, I muttered the incantation once more. With great satisfaction, I watched the fire die in those eyes. A moment later, he was dust.

Aware of Sky's searching stare, I ignored it while I gathered up the Fatifer and the Gem of Levage. There would be questions I didn't want to answer. The Aufero wouldn't let me near, warding against my touch with a protective field.

It yielded to Sky's hand. She hissed next to me, "What the hell was that? What you did. I thought Josh used the Aufero to fix you—to fix things."

"He did."

I shrugged as if the gesture explained everything.

I started to walk away from her, but turned back with an imploring look. "Sky, don't make this into something it isn't. It was just a spell. If I hadn't done it, probably Samuel or Josh would have."

Watching her struggle against a rising tide of questions brought a faint smile to my lips. "Everything there is to know about me, you already know."

Her eyes narrowed. "You swear?"

"Everything there is to know about me," I repeated, sincere, "you already know."

With the two objects in my hands, I turned and walked toward the house.

CHAPTER 16

Whatever Ethos was, a Faerie, a demon, or a human deformed by dark magic—he was dead. That was cause to celebrate. Josh planned a weekend party at the club. Until then, there was much to plan. Maya remained a problem, though without Ethos's help her threat was significantly reduced. Sky had proven that she could control the spirit shade, for now. She still wanted the spirit shade out, but we'd yet to determine how and if Sky could live without it.

More urgent to me, there was a Tre'ase out there that held Sky's life in its hands. The Clostra gave us the means to summon that Tre'ase, but without its blood, the spell was useless. With no other alternative, we'd no choice but to turn to Logan for help. With any luck, his price would be reasonable, but he was a Tre'ase. Their bargains were anything but.

That evening, most of the pack gathered at the club. By the time I arrived, most of them were well into their drinks. They were spread throughout the club, many on the dance floor. Josh had booked an up-and-coming rapper who was putting on a good show for the crowd.

It was good to see Winter with a date. Since Abigail had betrayed her, Winter had seemed reluctant. I met them at the bar. Like all of Winter's dates, Esmine was gorgeous, a curvy redhead in a form-fitting black dress. I knew by the way Winter introduced her that Esmine was likely to be around for a while. Despite Winter's practiced indifference, she was a romantic at heart.

Leaving them to the dance floor, I looked around for Sky. Not finding her, I settled into one of the reserved tables at the back that gave me the best view of the dance floor. It wasn't long before an attractive brunette tried to flirt her way onto the seat next to me.

I let her down politely. "I'm with someone."

Some time later, Sky arrived. I sipped my Scotch, watched as she took in her surroundings. Before she reached the bar, Josh had walked onto the stage to perform with the band. I watched her rising anxiety for him with some amusement. My brother was a talented ham. She'd yet to hear him sing, but he was more than capable of holding his own. Her cheeks turned pink as the two performers slid into a practiced, well-performed duet.

Esmine surprised me, taking the seat next to me. Glancing out at the dance floor, I noticed Steven had taken her place with Winter. Tracing my look, she laughed.

"She's like the Energizer Bunny, she just keeps going and going. Where does she get the energy?"

Her animal.

I smiled. Human, Esmine had no idea about were-animals.

Sitting next to me, she struck up an easy conversation. After a moment, I felt someone's intense stare. Sky glared at me from the bar. Her gaze flicked to Esmine before she strode toward the exit.

I made my excuses and followed, catching up to Sky outside, near her car.

"Sky, where are you going?"

She frowned, more sad than angry. "Home."

She'd yet to meet Esmine. I couldn't blame her for coming to the wrong conclusion. For a moment, I tried. I didn't exactly deserve her trust. Irritation and regret intermingled until I couldn't sort the two.

"Why?" I asked.

Her hair fell across her eyes as she sagged against the car door. Frustration boiled into anger. "Because I don't want to spend the evening watching you try to get laid."

With a gentle touch, I brushed the strands of hair from her eyes. The hurt behind her anger cut me. I struggled with my own disappointment until I could summon a heartfelt apology. "I'm sorry."

She scoffed. "Sorry for what?"

I glanced aside, gathering myself. In life, I faced everything head on. An apology shouldn't be this hard. "My past. I'm sorry that it makes you jealous and insecure. I don't want you to feel that way. You don't have anything to worry about with us. We're good."

Her arms folded over her chest as she settled into her newfound power. "What do you mean?"

I chuckled, then kissed her. My tongue lightly caressed her lips before I pulled back. Backing toward the bar, I said, "I'm going back in, I really hope you join me."

"It's too loud in there," she complained, "and we have more to discuss."

"We've discussed it enough." I smirked. "This conversation is over, Sky. I'll see you when you decide to come in, okay? I'll order you a French martini, you seem to like those."

I turned and went back inside, leaving her to make up her mind. At the bar, I picked up her martini and another Scotch for me. When I returned to my table, Winter had joined Esmine. We chatted for a moment before Esmine sparked at the song change. She took Winter's hand, guiding her toward the dance floor. They passed a bewildered and somewhat humbled Sky on the way. She acknowledged the two, then slid into the seat next to me.

Avoiding my gaze, she sipped at her martini. "You could have told me."

"You could have asked." I grinned. "It's a moot point now, but a better question is, why do you smell like Demetrius?"

She flinched as if caught, then shrugged off the question. "I don't want to talk about it."

"But we will."

After a moment, she abandoned her reservation. "Michaela was forcing Quell to leave Chicago. It's my fault. I wanted to make things right for him."

Quell, again. She just couldn't let him go. I chewed on that for a moment, letting the irritation settle. "What was Demetrius's price?"

Sky's expression turned sour. "Chris. He wants me to bring her back to him."

I nodded, stared at my Scotch as I turned the glass on the table. "And what did you say to him?"

"I declined," she stated, offended by the question. "Why would I agree to something like that?"

"It's funny, when it comes to Quell, you don't seem to have a lot of boundaries and logic seems to be absent from your decisions."

The uncomfortable silence between us lasted well into our second round of drinks. I chewed on what to say, whether to let the matter sit.

"I want Quell gone, too," I admitted, remorseless. "I don't like what he does to you and everything you are willing to do to keep him safe."

She gave me an appraising look, not entirely displeased. Before she could respond, Josh plopped into the seat next to her with two shots in hand. He knocked the first one back, chased it with the second.

I frowned at the empty glasses. "That's six."

He offered me a miscreant grin. "You're counting my drinks now? You've taken big brothering to a new level, you control freak."

"I don't care how many drinks you have while you are *working*. We are going to see Logan tomorrow and I don't need you hung over."

A slight shiver passed through Sky at the reminder.

"I'll be fine." Josh took a sip of her drink, then leaned into her until his lips brushed her ear. "I will find a way to get her out and keep you." He grinned at me for a moment, then led her to the dance floor.

I spent the rest of the evening watching them dance and talk and throw conspiratorial glances in my direction. At least they'd returned to their normal, sibling-like relationship. The rivalry between Josh and me had come to an end.

I glanced at my Scotch, checked the time, and pushed the drink aside. I'd need to be sharp for the morning.

As usual, Logan's door swung open just before we knocked. The scent of mint, cinnamon, and oak greeted us as we walked inside. The smell was stronger than normal, perhaps to cover the faint smell of blood in the air.

He greeted us with a deviant twinkle in his eyes. As usual, his attention fixed on me. His eyes narrowed and the tattoos on his arms spun excitedly. He stepped closer, hand rising as if to touch me. I held out an arm to stop him. I'd had enough of his shit.

Logan hesitated, his hand twitching in anticipation. "May I?"

"No."

His breath quickened with excitement as he took another step closer. His eyes took on a strange glow as he examined me. He whispered, "Remarkable."

I growled, "Get away from me."

Sebastian intervened, stepping between us. "We need to talk to you."

Reluctant, Logan turned his attention to Sebastian. "Of course you do or you would not be here. You want me to find the Tre'ase that created Maya. Am I correct?"

Sebastian nodded. Apparently, that wasn't good enough. He turned to me for confirmation. Something was off. He was confident, like someone with an ace up his sleeve.

I sighed, my irritation plain. "Yes."

Sky walked deeper into the house, her attention fixed on the closed room where we'd previously discovered a young woman hiding. Looking around, there was no sign of her. I didn't pick up her scent in the air.

"It's empty," Logan told her. "And if it weren't, I'm sure you'd just meddle again. It has to be rather exhausting to not only deal with your own problems—and from my understanding there are many—but with those of others."

His gaze flicked to me, eliciting a smirk.

Sky wasn't impressed. "Sorry if we find your kinks disturbing."

"No need to be judgmental," he scolded gently while his gaze remained annoyingly fixed on me. "Some might think your little liaison with Quell—it is Quell? The Lost One?—is worthy of judgment, too."

Sky jumped ahead of Sebastian, asking, "Can you help us find Maya's creator?"

"Of course." He gestured to his table. "Have a seat."

She didn't move. "Is Maya a Faerie?"

Josh, Sebastian, and I exchanged glances. Our plans for the conversation had just taken an unexpected turn.

Logan considered whether to answer. "Half. Her mother was a witch, but the combination didn't decrease her strength significantly."

The answer surprised Sky. "What about Ravyn, Emmalesse, Leonel?" she said, listing the most infamous of the Faeries. She'd picked up the names from the book I'd given her. "Are they still alive?"

Logan's gaze returned to me with a curious look. "Alive is relative."

"Are they spirit shades?"

"Emmalesse is dead; it was quite violent from the rumors."

Sky asked, "What about the others?"

"Leonel is a spirit shade. Ravyn is still alive, but his whereabouts are unknown."

"Does Leonel have a host?"

Logan took a step closer to me, his fingers twitching. "I think I've answered too many of your questions without requesting anything in return. Would you like me to answer the others?"

His tattoos came alive once more, swirling toward his fingertips as he extended a hand toward hers. Magic flooded the room. I turned to Sky, hoping she sensed the danger. A wrong word now could seal a bargain she'd no intention of making. Once sealed, there was no appeal from the consequences.

She wanted answers, needed them, but caution got the better of her. She backed away from his touch. "What are you asking from me?"

Logan chortled, gestured again to his table.

Sky looked to me. With some reservation, I nodded. She sat while he gathered and placed on the table a small bowl, a knife, a powder, and resins. Satisfied with the items, he crossed to a small box on the other side of the room, returned with a peculiar candle that reeked of blood and honey.

Josh's eyes widened. "How did you find one?"

"When I said I needed days to get what I needed, this is why. Would you like it when I'm done?"

He answered quickly, "Yes."

"It's the strongest thing you can use to source someone without using their blood. And it can enhance any spell."

Sky eyed the knife with suspicion. "If you don't need blood, why do you have a knife?"

"It's for me."

Logan poured the resin and powder into the bowl and then lit the candle before closing his hand around the knife. He seemed to savor the pain as he drew the blade across his palm. With his uncut hand, he grasped Sky's. The invocation was quick, followed by a few droplets of his blood dripped into the bowl. A foul odor arose. Colors sparked to life over the bowl, became a face—Logan's face—looking back at her.

Sebastian roared, furious, "We do not have time for your games!"

The outburst amused Logan. "*Tsk. Tsk.* We will have none of that." He rose to his cabinet, removed a cylindrical jar. Floating within was a fist-sized heart, still beating. His grin widened. "Meet Kalese, Maya's creator."

I was at his throat in an instant, pinning him to the wall. "What kind of games are you playing?"

Logan continued to grin even as he struggled for breath. "I...die...Skylar...too."

Disgusted, I had no choice but to release him. Logan collapsed to the ground. He sucked in a few breaths before returning to his feet.

"As long as I am alive," he said in a strained voice, "so is the heart."

Regaining his composure, he directed his miscreant smile

to Sebastian first, then to me. "As long as I'm alive," he repeated, "so is the heart. It's probably more important than ever to keep me alive. Now, let's get down to business. You all have something I *want* and something I *need*. Let's make a deal."